"Are you wanting some tea?" Kylie asked.

"Wouldn't take more than a minute to get the kettle going."

At Michael's answering silence, she turned to face him. Just looking at him, feeling the odd, intense current that seemed to envelop them both, sent a shiver through her.

"What I'm wanting has nothing to do with food," he said in a voice so quiet and low that she had to strain to hear it over the pounding of her heart. "What I'm wanting is to come to you and undo each of the buttons on your shirt till I find what waits for me beneath. Then I'm wanting to put my mouth against your skin and learn the feel of you till I know you so well that you're part of me."

She didn't look away from his green eyes. Mesmerized, she couldn't have if she wanted to.

"But since all that would surely call for an apology, I'll be leaving now." As he walked out the door, he called back over his shoulder, "Though if you like, you can consider it your engraved announcement for our next time together."

The Last Bride in Ballymuir

DORIEN KELLY

POCKET STAR BOOKS

New York   London   Toronto   Sydney   Singapore

This book is a work of fiction. Names, characters, places and incidents are products of the author's imagination or are used fictitiously. Any resemblance to actual events or locales or persons, living or dead, is entirely coincidental.

An *Original* Publication of POCKET BOOKS

A Pocket Star Book published by
POCKET BOOKS, a division of Simon & Schuster, Inc.
1230 Avenue of the Americas, New York, NY 10020

Copyright © 2003 by Dorien Kelly

ISBN: 0-7434-6458-3

First Pocket Books printing March 2003

10 9 8 7 6 5 4 3 2 1

POCKET STAR BOOKS and colophon are registered trademarks of Simon & Schuster, Inc.

For information regarding special discounts for bulk purchases, please contact Simon & Schuster Special Sales at 1-800-456-6798 or business@simonandschuster.com

Front cover illustration by John Vairo, Jr.;
Photo credit: Johner/Photonica

Printed in the U.S.A.

To Tom, forever.

the Last Bride in Ballymuir

Chapter One

Your feet will take you to where your heart is.
—IRISH PROVERB

As he looked about his sister's house, it occurred to Michael Kilbride that he had traded up one prison for another. With its painted silks, shiny trinkets, and mysterious mixed fragrance of incense and spice, this place was intensely female. It held no point of reference for a man who'd just spent fourteen years in the enforced company of other men.

"You'll be having the upstairs room," his sister Vi said as she flung off a bright blue woolen cloak she'd worn to protect herself from the nip of an Irish winter. "There's a full bath, too. You should be comfortable enough, but I'd have an eye to the ceiling height. This house wasn't built for a man of your size."

"It wasn't built for a man at all," he muttered and shifted uneasily from foot to foot. He knew he sounded ungrateful, and half felt that way, too.

"True enough," she answered with a shrug. "This is mine, and mine alone. But you're welcome here till you can get back on your feet." She paused and frowned, a crease showing between green eyes that were mirrors of his own. "And I'm sorry for the way Mam and Da are acting."

He reached down and fingered a jewel-bright throw that curled along the back of a couch. "Don't apologize for them. It doesn't matter."

She gave him an impatient look, his Vi, who'd never been a Violet, even when a child. "It does, and I will make apologies for them. But no excuses. They're too wrapped up in their comforts to think what you might be feeling."

Truth be told, he wasn't feeling anything much but hungover. He longed for a bed with sheets any color but grayish-white. He longed for the ability to sleep past five-thirty in the morning. And he found the intimacy of this talk more than he could stomach.

Michael snatched up the duffel bag that contained his belongings. "Upstairs, you say." As he made his way up the narrow wooden steps, he heard Vi call from below.

"I'm only having mercy because of your miserable head. And mine, too. But you won't be getting out of other conversations this easily!"

Michael allowed himself a victorious smirk as he rounded the sharp bend in the stairs to his hideaway.

Then he smacked his head straight into the low-hung plaster ceiling. At his snarled obscenity, Vi's laughter drifted up.

"It's no less than you deserve," she admonished.

To Michael's way of thinking, it was just another inexact measure of blind justice.

Having negotiated the last treacherous curve of stair, he ducked till he reached the center of the room with its sloped ceiling, then surveyed his surroundings. He didn't need much, and virtually anything would have seemed luxurious to him. But as always, Vi had seen to his comfort. The bedroom was bold and cheerful, and a bathroom little bigger than a closet took up the far end of the space.

A bed large enough for two, he noted, though that would never be an issue—even if he weren't in his sister's home. In his scant four days of freedom, he'd already discovered that he attracted exactly the hard and bitter type of woman he didn't want. No great surprise there.

Michael dropped his nylon duffel in the center of the bed. The quilt, a noisy affair with concentric spirals of bronze and gold, hardly moved under the bag's negligible weight. All his worldly goods . . . One change of clothes, ten punts fifty, plus the U2 tee shirt he'd won in a dice game last night. If he'd drunk less and played more, today's state of affairs might seem less bleak. Then again, perhaps not.

He sat on the edge of the bed—so soft that he wagered he'd end up sleeping on the floor—and slipped off his shoes and socks. Standing again, he tugged off his gray sweatshirt and unzipped jeans so starchy and new that it pained him to look at them. Underwear followed. He padded to the shower, turned it on, and stood under its needle-sharp spray until hot had run to cold. A small luxury, but an appreciated one, to be sure.

When Michael returned downstairs, showered and clean-shaven but not precisely repentant for the prior evening's excesses, his sister gave him an appraising look, then shoved a mug into his hands. "I've made a tea of anise and caraway, one of Nan's old recipes. What the shower and time haven't purged from last night's binge, this should."

Purged. Michael eyed the mug suspiciously. "Think not."

"You've drunk worse," Vi pointed out. "Last night, for instance."

That comment was enough to eke out his first smile of the day. "You're hardly free of sin yourself, little sister."

Scowling, Vi busied herself wrapping her wild red hair into a loose knot atop her head. "Just trying to keep you company, that was all. Now drink. I need your head clear. We've serious matters to discuss."

Michael set the mug on the low table in front of the fireplace. "Then you'll be wanting me alive, too."

It wasn't so much that he didn't believe in their grandmother's skills, or Vi's for that matter. His pretended disbelief was as much a part of the ritual as drinking the tea itself. He sprawled onto the couch and awaited his sister's countermove. When none came he knew that it was serious business indeed.

Vi settled into an overstuffed chair at an angle from him. "Dublin was a needed thing. I knew I couldn't bring you back here without a chance to get some of the anger out of your system. We played and drank hard. But now we're home. My home. And while we're two hundred miles south and west of Temple Bar, it isn't only the distance separating us. People in Ballymuir are more conservative than Dubliners. More so than those in Vatican City, too," she added with a flash of a smile. "You'll be noticed here, Michael. Even if I say nothing at all about your past—and I plan to say nothing—rumors will fly. I'm asking you to have care, not to do anything to make it worse on yourself."

So now we come to the truth of it, he thought. "Or on you?"

Vi sat taller. "I can hold my own."

A warrior, his sister. "As can I," he replied. "And the people in town, I want nothing from them. I'll give them no trouble, either."

Vi scrutinized him for a moment, then nodded her head in a business-like fashion. "Well then, we won't be needing to have this discussion again." She stood and walked to a desk. Drawing open a drawer, she said, "I've been keeping something for you since Nan died."

Michael smiled. "Then it can't be another one of her 'recipes' or it would have gone bad long ago."

Vi handed him a slender envelope. "I suppose it is a recipe of sorts." He opened it to find a bank statement in his sister's name. "The money was left to me, but I've just been holding it for you. Nan didn't want to upset Mam and Da by leaving it to you directly."

Vi gave a nod toward the paper clenched in Michael's hand. "She wanted this to go where it was needed. It's not a fortune, but it should give you a start."

Michael focused on the statement's bottom line and swallowed hard at the zeros lined up soldier straight; it beat the shit out of ten punts fifty. "I can't be taking this."

"You can't argue with a dead woman, either."

He stood far too fast for his aching head, closed in on Vi, and shoved the statement back at her.

"Then I'm left with her living emissary." Vi and Nan were almost one and the same in his mind—different faces of the same woman. What was Nan's was meant to be Vi's. "Take it."

She balled the paper in one fist and grabbed his shirt with the other. "You're stubborn enough, but I've never thought you a stupid man. Now, I'm not a believer in violence of any kind, but I'm thinking of making an exception here. The money is yours, as it was meant to be. If Nan hadn't seen to you, I'd be doing it myself. You'll take what she left you and be thankful for it."

Michael plucked the paper from her fist and ripped it into pieces. With each tug of the paper, Vi's eyes grew narrower and more dangerous. As the shreds fluttered to the floor, she pushed away from him with a sound of disgust. "Fine show, but point-less. The money is yours."

He needed out. Michael grabbed his jacket from a

peg near the door. Turning his back on his sister, he shoved his arms through the jacket sleeves, then wrenched open the door.

"Take a walk, then," Vi said. "I'll be here waiting when you get back. And so will the money."

Michael slammed the door. He walked away from Vi's house, perched on that gray line between country and town, then down an arrow of a road leading to the rolling green fields beyond. For an hour and more, one foot followed the other, nothing but time and endless sky in front of him. Past a roadside shrine to the Virgin—a tick of a smile at that sign of home—then around a bend till the road narrowed from the respectable track it had been to what his nan would have called a *bothareen*. And still he walked. Because he could.

It was wrong to take Vi's money; it pained him enough to be staying in her house and eating her food. Still, Michael didn't delude himself about the possibility of finding work. True, things were far better than they'd been fourteen years ago. But he was thirty-two, never been to university and—though with no accuracy—had been branded a terrorist by most. They'd not be calling at his door. If he had one.

A light mist began to drift from the sky: too gentle for rain, a true soft day. And still Michael walked. The path became steeper as it led into the foothills. His shoes, a half-size too large and stiff with newness, rubbed at his heels. The sting kept him conscious of the progress he made, the freedom he owned.

But what was freedom without goals and plans? He paused, feeling an ugly sort of amusement at his own thoughts. Freedom was more than he'd had in a bloody lifetime. And as for goals, he'd become rather good at doing nothing at all.

As he readied to walk and leave his empty dreams behind, a motion caught his eye. In a far field, a girl lifted a rock and carried it to a low, meandering fence made of the rock's kin. Instead of walking, Michael found himself watching. Then, drawn to her, he traveled up a muddy track and perched himself on yet another stone fence—easy to come by in County Kerry.

She was still a distance off, and Michael found it hard to judge her age. That she wore a fawn-colored sweater with sleeves too long and a hem that dipped and sagged to her knees didn't help in the guessing. She was slender, though, and tall for her youth. But it was the grace of her movement in such a dull task that riveted him. Measured grace, something he'd never considered. Now he did.

Michael stepped even closer and sat again. The girl had to see him, but gave no sign of it. A sweep of brown hair, long and straight as a silk banner, shielded her face from him. One rock to the next she cleared the field with no tools but her hands. And he sensed that she enjoyed herself, too.

Michael went to a break in the fence. She stilled, then with one long-fingered hand pushed back her hair. The movement of her arm drew the oversized sweater tighter to her, silhouetting breasts that were no child's.

She turned to face him. Innocence: wide-set eyes of the palest blue he'd ever seen, a broad mouth that somehow appeared vulnerable in her oval of a face. His heart staggered at the sight of that purity—plain to the point of beauty.

Wariness shadowed her features. He held himself unmoving, unthreatening, under her gaze. In the time it took him to realize that he was also holding his breath, her caution faded, and that innocent mouth curved into one devil of a smile.

"You might as well come help," she said. "Standing there gaping like that, you make me wonder who's the bigger fool, me for taking on this job, or you for watching as though there's something to see."

Without thought, without intent, he walked to her. Thank God she was no child. No child at all. Reaching out her right hand, she said, "My name's Kylie—Kylie O'Shea."

He took her hand in his, and though she was tall enough and clearly strong for her size, never had Michael felt so hulking and clumsy. "Kilbride, Michael Kilbride." Out of practice for even the most rudimentary of social exchanges, his words sounded rusty.

He found himself staring down at their joined hands. Not knowing how long he'd stood there grabbing on like he had no intention of letting go, Michael dropped her hand and backed up a step.

She gave him a curious glance. "So you're staying down the road and came out for a walk? Well, your help's welcome, Michael Kilbride."

Looking at a field made of roughly equal amounts of rock and sheep droppings, he asked, "What are you doing?"

"Getting ready for spring, of course."

The absolute, irrational optimism of that statement set him back on his heels. "It's February," he said, and immediately felt like an idiot for pointing out the obvious.

"It is, and I've not many free days left between now and planting time."

Michael was the product of cities, buses, and sprawl. Still, even he could see that there was no sense in putting anything other than more sheep manure in this plot of earth.

"Planting?" he echoed skeptically.

"Planting," she affirmed. "Now either help or be on your way. It slows me down, knowing you're watching like that."

Because he had no way to take, and because he didn't want to leave the company of Kylie O'Shea, he bent over, picked up the smallest rock he could, and carried it to the growing wall.

He glanced back at her. Her brows arched in amused challenge. "Surely a man of your size can do better than that."

He surprised himself by laughing. He could do better, and did. The sight of her was worth the price of admission. After a while, Michael fell into the rhythm of the task. Time slipped by, measured by the sight of the low clouds drifting across the sky and by the solid sound of rock hitting rock. A sense of contentment came over him. They worked in near silence, something he found far more comfortable than trying to scrape together words. Watching her was enough.

He was truly surprised that he hadn't ground his knuckles raw and flattened a few toes the way he followed her every move instead of his work. Her gaze touched him more than once, too. He sensed it with a primal awareness that made him feel almost like a barbarian. He found himself wanting her. In the ancient days—those before any law other than that of strength taking weakness—he'd have had her.

But he was a modern man, Michael thought, while lifting and heaving yet another rock to the wall. She didn't know him. He didn't know her. And the ritual of meeting and dating was as foreign to him as the wanting. Even before the years away, chatting up the girls hadn't come naturally. And this one, with her smile and confidence, she'd have heard it all before, anyway.

Though the field still held far more rock than the low line of fence they'd created, after an hour or so, Kylie O'Shea stood, hands propped on narrow hips, and looked around, appearing satisfied.

"Enough," she said.

Feeling a mix of regret and relief, Michael glanced toward the road. "I'll be on my way."

The set of her mouth grew stubborn. "Not without a meal, you won't. I'm not much in the kitchen, but it's a hard thing to foul up vegetable soup. It's been simmering since morning." She gestured toward a small, whitewashed cottage further up the hillside. "Join me, won't you?"

At his nodded assent, she led the way up the path. He followed without thinking, a trait that had bought him trouble time and again, Michael knew. But Kylie O'Shea was no temptress. And he was no longer a callow eighteen. Looking at the slender, capable woman in front of him, he was glad for both facts.

It was the boldest thing she'd ever done, asking a stranger into her house. And boldness, she remembered, had a way of crossing over into stupidity.

"Make yourself at home," Kylie said, scrubbing her hands at the kitchen sink. She glanced over her shoulder at him. "The facilities are behind the door on your left, if you'd like to wash up."

"Thank you," he said in a deep voice that had her ducking her head closer to the sink to hide the blush she felt sliding across her features. In the minutes that he was in the other room, Kylie hurriedly dug in her purse for a brush and ran it through her hair, wondering how she looked, wondering why after all these years vanity chose now to show itself.

Her appearance had never bothered her before. In fact, she was thankful she wasn't the sort to draw attention. Brown wren Kylie, safe from the predators of the world. She scrubbed her face, washed her hands again, then told herself to calm down. By the time he returned, she stood placidly at the stove.

He nodded a greeting, then turned his back to her and gazed out the window. Even now he seemed wary and uncomfortable in her presence. Still, she felt a startling sort of instinctual trust. For her to have these feelings about any man was a battle of will against brutal experience.

To trust a stranger? This was a miracle, no less. In return, she wanted to put him at ease, but had no idea how to go about it.

Kylie gave the pot of soup one last stir. It seemed a bit stubborn at the bottom. She leaned closer to the soup and sniffed suspiciously. She prayed she hadn't scorched it, though scorched soup seemed a proper mate to the rather too crusty bread she'd baked that morning.

He still stood at the window.

"Are you wondering what it is I do up here?" she asked, putting a smile in her voice.

He turned, and her pulse danced and skittered. Beautiful he was, in an entirely male way. His black hair was shorter than many men wore it these days, but did nothing to detract from his appearance. Little could. All dark and big with green eyes that seemed to see into the corners of her mind, the man was a medieval maiden's fantasy landed in the wrong world. If he hadn't seemed even more uncomfortable than she, Kylie would have found him intimidating.

"You're no farmer," he said.

Kylie gave an apologetic sigh as she ladled out the soup. "Nor a chef, either." Putting a bowl at the place she'd set for him, she said, "I'm a primary teacher at Gaelscoil Pearse—one of the local All-Irish schools. *An bhfuil Gaeilge agat?*"

A smile, almost too brief to be seen, passed across his face. "I speak a word or two, but none that I'll be trotting out for an expert like you. And now you're teaching it to the young? It's a grand thing you're doing."

She felt her face color at the compliment; she received them so painfully seldom. Kylie smiled her thanks. "Milk? It's fresh this morning." At his "please," she busied herself pulling two clean glasses from the shelf and the milk from her small refrigerator.

The milk, at least, would be right. The bread was another issue. On her pay, store bought was an impossibility; home-baked, on the other hand, was a punishment. She sawed frantically at the loaf, wishing not for the first time that she'd had a mother long enough to teach her these basic things. With luck, Michael Kilbride would have a forgiving nature because he'd have much to forgive after this meal.

They sat together at her plain wooden table—scarcely big enough for one. Between swallows of overcooked soup and nibbles of bread drier than the Sahara, Kylie struggled to maintain her end of a weak conversation.

"So are you visiting the O'Hallorans or Mrs. Flaherty?" she asked, referring to the only neighbors within walking distance.

After washing down bread with a healthy swallow of milk, he said, "No, I'm staying with my sister, Vi."

Kylie immediately made the connection, and was relieved to have at least found a topic to settle on. "Vi Kilbride, the artist? She's fabulous!"

He looked amused at her enthusiasm. "Lately I've been thinking of her more as Vi Kilbride the harpy. And even when she's not set on making my life miserable, I see her as a little sister, not an artist. But you know her work, then?"

"I do, though I can't afford it. I didn't know she lived close by."

"Down the road in Ballymuir."

She set down her spoon and gave up any pretense of eating. "That's easily six miles off!"

"Is it?" He took another spoonful of the soup. Kylie thought he did a creditable job of hiding a wince. It didn't seem right to be torturing her guest like this.

"Yes, and don't be eating that on my account. It seems to have burnt while we were out working."

He was polite enough to look surprised. "So the smoked flavor wasn't intended?"

She laughed. "Not exactly."

"It was the best meal I've had in some time, Kylie O'Shea."

She liked the way her name slipped from his lips, and liked his kindness, too. "If this is the best, where have you been dining—on a desert island?"

He gave a slight shrug. "Something like that." Glancing out the window he said, "It's time for me to be home."

"You're walking." She pushed back from the table and stood. "Let me run you back to town. It's the least I can do after making you haul rocks, then trying to poison you for your effort."

He stood. "I like the walking."

She wasn't ready to let go, to slip back into the careful, colorless discipline of her life. It wasn't every day—or any other day at all—that brought a man like Michael Kilbride to her door. She'd take these moments and keep them to brighten the lonely times. "I'll drive . . . I insist."

He gazed down at her, his raised brows seeming to point out the absurdity of her words. She'd sooner be able to stop the rain from falling than this man from doing what he wished.

"Then I accept," he said.

Time passed all too quickly as she tidied the kitchen, then led Michael out to her relic of a car. Evening had begun to approach. Kylie smiled as she noted the sky's whisper of indigo meeting the orange of the setting sun.

As she drove the miles toward town, she wondered about a man who would walk this far on a day chilly enough to be best spent by a fire. She glanced over at him and felt the heat of his green gaze—hungry, yet hesitant. She knew those feelings well. Especially the hesitancy.

Hoping to defuse the strange sort of tension that seemed to be filling the car, Kylie resorted to chat about sports—the sort of things she thought a man might take to. Not Michael Kilbride. Though his answers were polite enough, he paid little attention. In fact, the unspoken conversation rang louder than the spoken. He watched her as he had earlier, and though Kylie was scared witless, she welcomed his gaze.

When he pointed out his sister's house, urgency joined the tension. Kylie struggled for a half-veiled hint that she'd like to see him again. Unable to come up with one, she pulled to the side of the road. She reached out her hand to shake his. "It's been a pleasure, Michael Kilbride."

He grasped her hand, but instead of shaking it, pulled her forward. Kylie could feel her eyes widen as he neared. Before she could even form the thought to object, his mouth settled hot and hungry over hers. She was a woman who'd been kissed neither well nor often, yet she could recognize passion beginning to dance beneath her skin. Kylie shivered. Wanting to know more, but half-fearing the power of what she might learn, she settled her hand on his shoulder, her fingers gripping the coarse fabric of his jacket.

He drew her closer, and she felt her mouth open to him. The sweep of his tongue was an intimacy so different from those long-ago clumsy, teenage kisses that were all she had to compare to this moment. As she learned the taste of him, the beat of his heart, she began to lose her sense of self, something she generally clung to as tightly as her dignity. The realization shocked her.

At her indrawn breath, Michael let her go. Kylie fell back against her seat. When she looked at him, she would have been hard-pressed to say who was more startled by the kiss—Michael or herself.

Kylie scrambled for words, but Michael Kilbride left the car without saying anything at all. After he was gone, a breathy "wow" was all she could manage.

She was in well over her head. What better time to learn to swim?

Chapter Two

If you hit my dog, you hit myself.

—IRISH PROVERB

ichael had no sooner shut the door than Vi closed in on him. "It's past six. Where have you been?"

Feeling as churlish as a teenager late home with Mam hovering over him, he snarled, "Out."

"You leave walking and come back in a woman's car. Interesting, that."

"I don't believe it. You were watching me out the window!" He advanced on his meddling sister, but stumbled on a fat little dog that seemed to have materialized from nowhere. Glaring down at the homely thing, which was more or less a stumpy second cousin to a Jack Russell terrier, he added, "And what the hell is this?"

"*This* is Roger, the only male I've yet to meet with sense enough to take care of himself." Vi reached down and scratched the dog behind the ears. The animal heaved a blissful sigh and sidled closer to his owner. "He stayed with friends while I was gathering you home. He's a fair dog, Rog is. Stay out of his chair by the fire and you'll get along well enough."

"More than I can say for us. I won't be spied on!"

She stood toe to toe with him. "You think that I was spying on you?" One finger jabbing toward the front of the room, she said, "I just happened to glance out that window when I heard the car. Can you blame me for looking twice with the show you were putting on? Make friends fast, do you?"

"She's not a friend." At Vi's astonished laugh he added, "Exactly."

"And I'd say she wasn't behaving like an enemy—exactly. Who was the little thing? I was thanking God I didn't see auburn hair or I'd think that bit of trash Evie Nolan had latched onto you."

He put aside the interesting concept of being "latched onto" for later consideration. "Her name's Kylie O'Shea. Do you know of her?"

Vi smiled. "Around here, you know a little of everyone. Whether what you know has anything to do with the truth, that's another matter." Pulling a stool away from the counter that divided kitchen from living room, she sat. "But Kylie O'Shea? She's Black Johnny O'Shea's only child, that I know for sure."

"Black Johnny O'Shea." Michael grinned at the antiquated image the name conjured. "And what does he do, rob Bus Eireann every time it rolls through town?"

Instead of laughing, Vi took the question seriously. "Well, I wasn't here when Black Johnny was about, but I've heard he was a grand schemer, and a grand thief, too. He's in prison now—a safe place for him, considering what his name means around here."

She'd intended no jab with those words. But as a man whose name held meaning itself, Michael felt the blow. All the more reason to avoid Kylie O'Shea. He doubted that she held a soft spot in her heart for ex-convicts, any more than his own family did. He mumbled some indecipherable response.

Vi tapped a long finger to her lower lip as if contemplating a matter of great import. "That Kylie, I've heard she's as proper as a nun. And if there's a committee to be formed or a charity in need of a hand, she's in the thick of it. Imagine, there she was kissing you for God and all the world to see when she's not known you for more than a few hours. I don't like this, Michael, not at all."

Prepared to launch into an abject apology for soiling the reputation of Kylie O'Shea, Michael stammered to a stop when Vi went on. "There's something afoot with that girl," she said with a stern frown. "You'd best be staying away from her."

She knocked him wordless with that. He neither wanted nor deserved his sister's protection. And while Vi had never been exactly the delicate flower for which she was named, he didn't recall her being this intractable, either. Michael wasn't certain what to say.

Vi stood and walked to the peg rack by the front

door. She pulled down a ridiculous looking orange-and-green braided leash and snapped it to Roger's collar.

"Be a love, and take Rog for a walk. He needs his fresh air. I'll have soup on the table by the time you get back."

Soup. Jesus, Mary, and Joseph, what was it with women and their soup? He'd sell the family relics—if they had any other than Mam—for even a tough cut of mutton.

Vi shoved the loop end of the leash into his hand. "Off with you." She shooed them out the door and shut it smartly behind them.

Michael scowled down at the little creature on the other end of the tether. It regarded him with a zen-like calm. "Come on, then," he muttered. "This must be my day for making a bloody fool of myself."

Roger looked especially pleased at that thought. After sniffing the air, the dog trotted down the side-walk and veered toward town center.

Resigned to his fate, Michael followed behind. He kept his head down and pretended invisibility, no simple task at his size. But it was far easier to be concerned about walking this joke of a dog than to be thinking about what had happened with Kylie O'Shea.

It was just a kiss; he knew that. From what he'd read in newspapers and witnessed firsthand in the Dublin pubs, his act was no great sin. And there was no shame in wanting a bit of fun after too many years filled with loneliness and wanting. But much as he wanted her to be, Kylie was no bit of fun.

"A few laughs, that's all," he muttered, then realized that he looked exactly like one of those crazy bastards three steps short of a jig who spent the day talking to his dog. At that, Roger stopped and stared up at him.

"I'm not looking for an answer from you," Michael said.

Female laughter echoed from a shop doorway. "And he'll not be giving you one."

She stepped out onto the walk. There was no mistaking this one for a child. The young woman was short with lush curves that were enticing enough now, but sooner or later would thicken to those of a cantilevered matron. Clearly not Kylie's fate, Michael thought, then pushed her from his mind.

"I've seen the dog before, but you—you're new." She eyed him much the same way Michael would a tenderloin roasted to perfection. "A friend of Vi Kilbride, are you?"

"Her brother."

The woman smiled, and with a practiced flirtatious move brushed long auburn hair over her shoulders. Trouble and a blatant promise shone in her dark eyes. "Better yet." She stepped closer. "My name's Evie Nolan."

His first impulse was to laugh at the coincidence of meeting Evie on the heels of Vi's words. Then he recalled the dozens of incidents from childhood on when Vi saw or knew things before their time. A safety net or noose, Vi was, depending on what one did with her bits of sight.

Looking at the female in front of him, though,

Michael thought it would be no hard thing at all to be "latched onto" by Evie Nolan. Then Vi's image superimposed itself over Evie's sharp features. Decidedly no hard thing, Evie Nolan, but no wise thing, either. He didn't offer his name, but she didn't slow a beat.

"I was just closing up my da's shop and about to head down to O'Connor's Pub. Been there yet?"

"No, but I don't think they'd be welcoming me with this in tow," he said gesturing at Roger.

"You could tie him to the lamppost," she said, dismissing the dog with a bored glance.

Somehow, Michael knew he'd be safer in tying Evie to a lamppost than he would Vi's precious child. "Maybe I'll join you another time."

Evie pared the general down to the specific with a skill he couldn't help but admire. "Monday night, then. Eight o'clock . . . And if you're lookin' to have fun, leave the dog *and* your sister at home."

She moved closer and for one wild moment he imagined her doing to him what he'd done to Kylie. Had he not been so tall, Evie Nolan just might have been up to the challenge. As it was, she brushed one dagger-tipped nail against the front of his jacket. "Will I be having your name before Monday?"

He hesitated, feeling as though he was giving up something he shouldn't. "Michael."

She looked him up and down. "For the Big Fellow, Michael Collins, I'd wager."

With his size and build, he'd heard the comment countless times before, and hated it. Collins, patriot and hero to some, spy and murderer to others. And to him, a burden. "I was named for my father."

The words must have sounded even harsher than he'd intended. A flash of surprise and anger passed across the girl's face. She stepped away warily. "Well, Michael named for his father, Monday night, then." She brushed past him and made her way down the narrow walk.

He watched her round bottom sway back and forth to a hot beat. "We'll see," he said more to himself than her.

Roger gave a low growl and tugged at his leash. Michael imagined that if he loosed him, the dog would sink his teeth straight into Evie Nolan's swinging promise of sex.

"Latched onto, all right," he said with a laugh, then followed Rog round the corner and, after several blocks' zigzagging detour, back home again.

"You're all walked out, then," Vi commented as he swung shut the door, then freed Roger from his leash.

"Eighty years on the road and I'd not be walked out," he said, hanging his jacket. During his years caged, more nights than not he'd dreamt of walking in a straight line bending over the horizon and on to forever. Past this ruined life altogether, and starting again. Starting clean and simple.

Vi was silent a while, seeing to the evening's meal. When the table was set, she said, "I can't imagine it . . . knowing I must be in the same place so long. I think it would kill me—especially when I'd done nothing to warrant being there."

To his way of thinking, sheer stupidity qualified as something, though he loved Vi for her unswerving loyalty. Michael's smile was grim. "Well, the anger's enough to keep you going a while."

In all her visits, all her letters, and all of his to her, they'd skirted the "whys" and "hows" of his existence. The life and the emotions were ugly, now best swept under the rug. Not the most courageous of acts, but one that better suited his skills at self-preservation.

Vi waved him to his place at the table. The aroma of the soup was regrettably reminiscent of his earlier meal. Michael slowly brought the spoon to his mouth, carefully tasted, then grabbed for the glass of water in front of him. A conspiracy, it was!

He glared at his sister. "Did no one teach you to cook?"

"Of course they did. I got distracted, that's all. I had the grandest idea for a new painting and had to get it down before it flew off."

He grinned. "The painting?"

"No, the idea, you ninny," she said, brandishing her soup spoon like a weapon.

"So I'm suffering for *your* art. And here I thought that was the artist's job."

"Do you suppose you could be doing any better?"

"No."

"Then don't complain." She nibbled at the bread, then asked, "So what'll it be, Michael? You've enough money for a new start wherever you want to go."

"I'd tell you not to ruin the meal, but it's far too late for that." He leaned back in his chair. "No more talk of money or the future, Vi. I've spent fourteen years doing what others commanded. I've no idea what I want to do for myself, and no idea what I *can* do. I need time. Time to think about it, and time to just *be*. Can't you understand?"

She sighed. "I can, it's just I can't bear not seeing progress made."

"I'm out. That's progress, I'd say."

"No, that's justice. You shouldn't have been in there at all. You're no terrorist and never were."

"Among my padmates, paramilitary was the preferred term," he dryly corrected. He'd been released as part of the Good Friday Accord, and even a whisper of association with the ongoing Troubles would land him back in a cell.

"Call them what you will," his sister said, unwilling to be swayed from her point. "Progress is when you can pick up and move on."

No arguing that. The soup best left uneaten, Michael grabbed some bread, then slid his chair back from the table. "Have you anything to read?"

Vi pointed to shelves built into the wall next to the fireplace. "You'll find Roddy Doyle and Joe O'Connor, as well as some poetry and a few of the classics."

He nodded. Making his way to the bookshelf, he said, "I'll be seeing you in the morning, then."

"Mass is at nine," Vi said in a tone that was more order than point of information. His thoughts must have been clear on his face because she continued in the same major-general tone. "It's one morning a week I'm asking of you. And I might point out that you stand the chance of gaining something from your effort, too."

He raised one brow. "We still have politics to argue over. Care to give it a go?"

Vi sat back and smiled. "We haven't changed at all. I'm still trying to bully you and you're still swatting me down."

"And you need it, sweet Violet," he said with a broad wink, then laughed at her answering growl. No, some things hadn't changed at all.

By half past five the following morning, Michael was willing to concede that some less pleasant aspects of his life remained the same, too. He'd not slept till past three. And even Roddy Doyle's incomparable stories hadn't been enough to keep his mind away from Kylie. To Kylie it went and to Kylie it stayed.

To have felt his mouth against a woman's for the first time in over a dozen years was surely an event grand enough to rob him of sleep. It was more than that, though. It was the rightness of her taste, the softness of her lips. It was the fleeting thoughts he'd had when their mouths met. Thoughts of days to come.

Michael gazed at himself in the tiny square of mirror above the bathroom sink. While he shaved away a day's growth of blue-black beard, he pondered the fact that a man who looked so—well, to be truthful—dangerous could be so damned inexperienced. A fine irony there, and one he'd bought and paid for with his own rash acts. Perhaps these feelings for Kylie O'Shea could be reduced to just that—rash acts and inexperience.

After sluicing off the last of the shaving cream and toweling dry his face, Michael scowled at his reflection. He summed up his life in two words: "Bloody fool."

Downstairs by six, he took pleasure out of settling into Roger's chair, then reading some more. An hour or so later, Vi, eyes still half-shut and red hair wild as any Medusa's, staggered from bedroom to kitchen.

"Kettle's still warm," he told her and tried to look apologetic as she jumped nearly to the low-beamed ceiling.

Clutching closed a wild crimson silk robe that made him wonder whether his sister had spent time in a seraglio, Vi asked, "What are you doing up and about so early?"

"I've been trained better than your dog. I expect it'll take me some time to unlearn it all."

Vi said nothing in return, not that much could be said. She clattered about in the kitchen for a while, then settled at a small desk not far from where he sat. "I'm phoning Mam— promised her I would. I need to catch her early. She's still singing in the choir, did you know?"

He didn't. Michael rose. "I'll be—"

"No, stay. Talk to her, too, Michael. She's worried about you. She truly is."

"She has an odd way of showing it."

Vi lifted the phone and began to dial. "Talk to her."

"Can't." As he trudged up the stairs to his room, Michael tried to recall the last time his mother and he had truly communicated. Not the bits and business of being in the same family, but real talk. Before his brothers were born, for certain. From the day they arrived, Pat and Danny had usurped what little time his mother had ever found for him. And now she used them like shields. "You'd best not come to Kilkenny," she had said when he'd called with news of his impending release. "It would be unsettling for the boys."

He doubted "the boys"—now seventeen—gave a dead rat's ass whether he came to town. Hell, they scarcely knew him; he'd been gone since they were three years old. His mother would be the one unsettled, her placid life of charity work, luncheons, and friends blown to hell. And his father, he'd do as he always had—work late, then come home to read the newspaper and avoid direct conversation with his family.

Home . . . He thought again of Kylie O'Shea and her rocks and wretched cooking, and knew he was indeed a bloody fool for doing it. He deserved no home and would have none.

Michael glanced at the clock on the bedside table. An hour till church. Perhaps a sermon filled with dire warnings of devil and death would brighten his day. God knew stranger things had happened.

Chapter Three

A little always tastes good.
—IRISH PROVERB

Each Sunday morning when she slipped through the plain doors of St. Brendan's Church, Kylie carried a guilty little secret with her: she liked going to Mass not only for what she got out of it, but for being seen. Her father hadn't been much of a churchgoer. Perhaps he stayed home out of fear of a lightning bolt striking straight to his heart, but more likely because sitting still for an hour and more was inconceivable to Johnny O'Shea. As was the concept of a Higher Authority.

Kylie was not her father; she believed. Each Sunday was a reaffirmation of the way she tried to live her life—*tried* being the operative word. Last night, for instance, she'd had far too many uncomfortable and inappropriate thoughts about Michael Kilbride. And today, as she settled early in a pew, she fought not to crane her neck like a spectator at the Ballymuir Races.

How she wanted him to be there. Coming in with Vi, as he would, there'd be no missing him. Between her height and her flame-red hair, Vi stood no more chance of being inconspicuous than Kylie did of being bold. And Michael was no man to be easily lost in a crowd, either. Even one packed into tiny St. Brendan's. Kylie shifted as subtly as she could to increase the range of her peripheral vision.

Breege Flaherty, who had sat next to her, reached over and patted her hand. "All morning you've been as nervous as an ewe come mating season. Whatever's the problem?"

"No problem, none at all," she assured her friend, secretly amused and appalled at how close Breege had struck to the truth.

Widowed Breege was Kylie's closest neighbor, both in proximity and in her heart. When the rest of the town had turned from Kylie after her father's arrest for fraud, Breege had remained steadfast. The fact that her dearest friend was eighty-two years old didn't seem odd in the least.

"If you've no problem, then slide down, dear. You've left people waiting in the aisle."

Embarrassed, Kylie glanced back up and found herself looking straight into Michael Kilbride's unforgettably green eyes. Her heart did a low, lazy loop as she took in exactly how splendid this man was. He was wearing nothing grand—just dark trousers and a thick fisherman's knit sweater. Ah, but he wore it well. She'd not mind looking at him till time spun to a stop.

Breege's subtle nudge called Kylie back to her surroundings. She tugged her gaze away from Michael. Right behind him stood his sister looking none too pleased to be biding her time in the aisle. Kylie hastily moved closer to Breege, making room for the two Kilbrides. After giving what she hoped passed for a polite smile rather than the half-hysterical grin she felt painting its way across her face, she focused on the service about to begin. For a few brief minutes she even succeeded.

But inches away sat Michael Kilbride, seeming almost oblivious to her presence. The less he noticed her, the more she did him. Or so it seemed to Kylie, who had begun to hear only his deep voice as he sang, his steady responses. A crowd of hundreds and she had reduced it to one. Not once, though, did he glance her way. By neither word nor gesture was he anything other than impersonal. In fact, his disregard seemed to wave itself like a flag of challenge.

Lately, she had fixed upon the idea of committing an act so wild and unexpected that for a short while it would lift the weight of respectability from her. And for that short while, she could sink her teeth into life—not be proper on the exterior, ready to shatter inside, Miss Kylie Soon-to-Be-a-Saint O'Shea.

Here and now—in the middle of church—she'd like to shake Michael Kilbride by his broad shoulders and hiss, "Have you forgotten me already? Did that kiss mean nothing to you?" Sanity kept her in her seat. It was a blessing, too, considering Vi Kilbride's watchful gaze was upon her almost as much as hers was on Michael.

By the end of Mass, Kylie had herself firmly convinced that the man didn't even recognize her. And though she told herself she should be relieved, that he was far too rough and masculine for her to handle, she was sure her heart would break.

When Breege stopped to chat with a group of friends, Kylie kept her head down. She didn't know where Michael Kilbride was, and didn't want to. She'd not embarrass herself further. At least now her humiliation was a private thing. When Breege announced that she'd be staying in town for supper with Mrs. McCafferty, relieved, Kylie turned heel and fled.

With Vi's hand firmly anchored in the crook of his elbow, Michael saw no way of polite escape. He'd been trotted past half the citizens of Ballymuir and the other half appeared to be queuing up for their turn. All except Kylie O'Shea, who'd skirted the throng and stood with a group of women near the edge of the car park. And now it looked as though she was leaving.

Michael tried to shake free his arm, but Vi held fast. "Michael, I'd like you to meet Jenna Fahey. She's a grand friend of mine, for all that she's another blow-in Yank come to buy up our land. Jenna's opened a restaurant out Slea Head Road."

"Hello," he managed without turning his gaze from

the spot where Kylie had been. Then the heel of Vi's shoe came down in the middle of his foot. In deference to their location near the church steps, he bit back the oath that came to his lips. Settling for a meaningful glare at Vi, he turned his attention to the woman in front of him. She was a small thing, willowy with short chestnut curls framing a friendly face.

"It's nice to finally meet you," she said in a voice so crisp and American that he had to smile. "I'd love it if you and Vi could come to Muir House for dinner some night soon. I'll make something special."

"That would be grand," Michael answered out of politeness, then glanced back over the crowd to see if he could spot Kylie.

The American followed his line of vision and smiled. "If you're looking for Kylie O'Shea, she's gone already."

"How'd you know who I was looking for?" Michael asked, carefully reappraising the slight woman in front of him.

"Don't confuse me with your mind-reading sister. No second sight here," she said, raising a cautionary hand. She gestured toward the women still at the edge of the car park. "Kylie was the only one there less than eighty years old, and besides, what man in his right mind wouldn't be looking at someone that pretty?"

"Ah," Michael said with a returning grin, "then you'll be understanding if I move quickly to catch her." Prying loose his sister's hand, he said, "I need your car, Vi."

Her mouth curved into a complacent smile. "Buy your own car, love."

Michael frowned. "Blackmail, is it?"

"Whatever works."

Blackmail deserved no honesty. He'd give his sister the words she wanted and save the truth for later. After he'd seen Kylie O'Shea. "Fine, we'll open an account tomorrow, and I'll buy my own car. But right now, Sis, give me yours."

Vi dangled the keys in front of him, jingling them so they sang a cheery, tempting tune. "No dancing around me with half-truths on this one, Michael. I'll have your word. You'll take the money—all of it."

Even after the years apart, she knew him well. But then again, taking the money and spending it were two distinct matters. He could promise one without doing the other.

"You have my word," he growled, using just the right measure of defeated frustration. Vi tossed him the keys. Michael caught them with a victorious laugh.

"It was a pleasure meeting you," he said to Jenna Fahey as he backed away, "And I'll take you up on that dinner soon—before sweet Violet, there, starves me to death."

Her appreciative laughter rang over his sister's less hospitable response. Michael chuckled to himself as he jogged to Vi's car. He'd have hell to pay when he returned to her house tonight. Fitting, though, since he had a wee bit of hell to pay this afternoon, as well.

● ● ●

The miles to Kylie O'Shea's couldn't have seemed longer. Michael immediately learned that it was one thing to commandeer Vi's car, but another to drive it. He was thankful that this time of year he stood little chance of running into a poor sod of a tourist who'd strayed to the wrong side of the road. It was struggle enough to keep true to the curves and hills without hopelessly grinding the car's gears.

Rounding the last torturous bend before the little track to Kylie's home, for the first time he asked himself what exactly he was doing. He owed her an apology, perhaps two. That much was certain. Yet he wasn't truly sorry for the kiss—shocked that he'd done it, and a bit mystified, too. But sorry? No, he was too selfish to feel regret. All he could bear to give was an excuse. The honest truth was that the sight of her took away his good sense and what few words he'd ever been able to string together. And he expected this meeting to be no different.

As she had been the day before, Kylie was at work in her field. Knowing no one else would come their way, Michael parked the car in the middle of the track and climbed out. Since his Sunday best and his everyday were one and the same, he didn't hesitate before joining her.

She had changed from the simple blue dress she'd worn to church. The oversized sweater he'd seen yesterday hung to her fingertips. Her long, slender legs were now covered by khaki-colored trousers tucked into muddied black wellies. Her hair, though, was the same as it had been in the too close confines of St. Brendan's. She wore it pulled back from her face in a neatly woven style he vaguely recalled the girls all those years ago saying was a French braid.

Whatever the name, he'd sat through Mass with his fingers burning to loosen the strands of the plait, to feel its silken length. Because he knew he wasn't beyond temptation—he'd proven that well enough the night before—he'd pretended that Kylie O'Shea wasn't there at all. And hurt her by it, he knew.

"Hello," he said.

She murmured a greeting in reply but never stopped working. He had wondered whether she would make this easy on him. Now he had his answer.

"Fine day to finish clearing the field," he offered as he fell in step next to her.

She spared him a chilly glance from under her lashes. Filling her arms with jagged rocks, she stalked off to the fence and began setting in her load. Torn between frustration and the sure knowledge he was getting a warmer reception than he deserved, Michael stood and watched her for a moment.

Then with a shake of his head, he bent down and jimmied a large rock free of the earth. Using hands and the occasional foot, he rolled it in a zigzagging path to the fence. And all the while he considered his next move. Honesty seemed the only way out.

She still stood at the low line of fence, scowling at it as if by sheer force of will she could make it grow. Michael moved behind her, wanting to rest his hands on her slender shoulders but not daring to touch her. Not deserving to.

"I'm sorry."

She swung round to face him. A hot flame danced in those cool blue eyes, making him realize that his sister wasn't alone in the ranks of warrior.

"Sorry for what?"

Jamming his hands deep into his pockets he muttered, "For kissing you. It was wrong of me . . . stupid. I should have warned you . . . or something."

"Kissing me? You're sorry for that? There's nothing else you've done that you think might be worth an apology?"

A recitation of that list would stretch long past sunset, not that the woman in front of him looked inclined to let him slip in a word.

"Well, I'll admit the kiss was unexpected," she said. "And not invited, either. But I want you to take a look at me."

As though he'd be able to look away from such shimmering beauty.

She held her hands out to her sides. "I might seem a child to some, but I'm twenty-four years old and capable of knowing when I want to be kissed. And equally capable of telling a man to stop. Not that I stopped you last night. And not that I'll need to worry about stopping you, with you all but offering to send an engraved announcement before you try again."

She moved close enough that if he took his hands from his pockets he could haul her up against him. Tempting, so tempting.

"What amazes me, Michael Kilbride, and makes me doubt for my sanity, is that I'm beginning to think you've had less experience with the opposite sex than I have. Though looking at you, I can't imagine how that could be true."

He didn't think she'd like the answer, so he gave her none.

"Now, will I be getting that apology for the way you acted this morning?" The rueful shake of her head was something he was sure she'd practiced on her students time and again. "Not so much as a neighborly nod or hello."

Michael had promised himself that he'd give her the truth. Slipping his hands from his pockets, he stepped closer yet. He cupped her hand—so small—in his palm.

"For this morning, I'm truly sorry," he said, savoring the feel of her cool skin. The fact that it was a bit work-roughened somehow made her seem all the more appealing. "I'm not much good at social matters."

He turned her hand so that, palm upward, it still rested within his. She didn't fight him, just gazed at him through cautious eyes. It astounded him—humbled him—that she would welcome his touch. With his free hand he pushed back the heavy wool of her sweater until the inside of her wrist was exposed.

"Don't think that I ignored you, Kylie O'Shea, because you filled my morning, not whatever words Father Cready was offering up."

With one fingertip he traced the slender blue

veins beneath her translucent white skin. The intimacy of it made him swallow hard and hesitate before speaking again. But it didn't make him stop touching her. Never that.

"So think I'm a boorish sod, but never, ever think that I didn't notice you."

Kylie couldn't look away from the long finger so intimately stroking her skin. This was no kiss, she thought. But it might as well have been, for the quicksilver thrill his touch sent chasing through her. She imagined that caress traveling further, up to the sensitive skin at the inside of her elbow and to the upper curves of her breasts where no man—

She shivered, and as she did, an ugly memory gave voice deep inside. *Ah, but one man has,* it whispered. *One man.*

Kylie tugged her hand from Michael's, and the uninvited thought faded. She drew in a ragged breath and met his eyes. He hadn't meant to, but he'd shaken her. She didn't want him to know exactly how much.

"You are a man to seize the moment, aren't you?"

He gave her a crooked smile. "Are you looking for another apology?"

Not for his touch, she wasn't. Just for the ghost he'd—actually, *she'd*—unwittingly conjured. And that wasn't his apology to make. Fussing with the lopsided hem of her sweater she answered, "No more than I was last night."

His smile was wry and teasing all at once. "Good, because the well was running dry. I've given you more apologies this morning than I've managed to force out in my entire life."

Still breathless, she stepped away and set back to work.

"So how long are you in Ballymuir?" she asked, though not certain she really wanted to know.

"I'm not sure. I'm thinking of settling here," he said, sounding almost startled at his own words.

Kylie's first thought was that she couldn't have wished on a star and done better.

"Truly?" she stammered. She scrambled for some inane question to mask the confusing sense of elation and something much darker that whispered across her skin, leaving the downy hairs at the back of her neck dancing in its wake. "And you're moving from where?"

Michael paused. "I've family in Kilkenny."

"Ah. Well, if you need help finding a place or settling in, just let me know." The words slipped out, and how Kylie wanted to swallow them back. Glancing at Michael, she wondered whether it was her imagination or if he truly was inching closer to his car. She felt half-ready to run, herself.

"I expect I'll be staying with Vi," he said. "At least till I'm more sure about things."

"I see." Kylie gathered up a few more rocks and tossed them onto the pile. She'd do well to stop the personal questions now, she knew. Before she found her thoughts too far down a path she knew she shouldn't take.

When clouds blew in to cover the sun and a chill rain began to spit from the sky, Kylie gave up on field clearing for the day. She turned to Michael. "Would you like to come inside for a while? I started some bread just before you—*the bread!*"

Forgetting manners, Michael, everything but her two precious loaves of bread no doubt blackened to cinders, she flew to her house. When she reached the oven door, she already knew it was too late. Grabbing a pot holder she pulled out the loaves and dropped the pans on the stove top where they landed with a metallic clank. Though she wasn't one for swearing, she tried on one of her father's favorites for size.

Low laughter rolled from the doorway. She turned to see Michael framed in the entry, and experienced a mixture of embarrassment and pleasure.

"I've never heard anything more halfhearted in my life. If you're going to use talk like that, you've got to give the words power. Like this—" Loud enough to ring in the rafters, he launched the same profane phrase she had. "Now you try it."

A hot crimson blush climbed her face. "I couldn't. I've scarcely thought words like that, let alone used them."

He laughed. "I'd noticed. But this would be our secret. Here in the privacy of your home, no one need know what you're saying. Though I don't suppose you should get so accustomed to those words that they slip out while you're teaching the young ones."

"You can't imagine what I've heard from a few of those eleven-year-old boys when they think no adult's listening."

Moving out of the doorway and closing the door behind him, he grinned. "Oh, I can imagine, all right. I was about that age when I had a bar of soap for supper one night after Vi told Mam what she'd heard me saying. I belched bubbles for a fortnight."

"You did not," Kylie replied, laughing in spite of herself.

"A day, then. But my first point's the same. Relax in your own home, Kylie. It's one of the few places on earth you're free to be as you really are."

Kylie looked down at the burnt loaves. Michael had homed in on her personal sorrow: not allowing herself even that bit of freedom. She couldn't afford it, any more than she could more flour for bread. And for the lack of both, she wanted to hate her father, but knew she was more to blame.

It had been her choice to accept the job at Gaelscoil Pearse. "The next worst thing to being a nun" the other teaching students had sniped when she'd told them where she was going. True, the school held a very conservative philosophy and expected its teachers to be above reproach.

To Kylie, it had seemed a perfect fit, especially since the school paid better than any other in the area. She didn't mind wearing her skirts below her knees and was certain she wouldn't enjoy the local nightclub, anyway. As she'd focused on the struggle to repay her father's endless debts, she'd scarcely thought about what she might be missing. And being able to stay close to Breege was worth almost any sacrifice. But lately . . .

She cut off that thought, too.

Looking back at Michael, she saw a passing expression on his face that seemed to echo her emptiness. Burdened with her own regret, she had no time to wonder why he should look that way. It was enough to find the composure to gloss over the moment. She stepped away from the stove and toward the hearth where two bricks of peat still glowed, their scent competing with that of the well-cooked bread.

"I can hardly offer you the bread." She paused to tug her damp woolen sweater over her head and smooth down the worn cotton shirt she wore beneath. "Are you wanting some tea, though? Wouldn't take more than a minute to get the kettle going."

At his answering silence, she turned to face him. Just looking at him, feeling the odd, intense current that seemed to envelop them both, sent a shiver through her. Gooseflesh raised on her arms and she rubbed at it.

"What I'm wanting has nothing to do with food," he said in a voice so quiet and low that she had to strain to hear it over the pounding of her heart. "What I'm wanting is to come to you and undo each of the buttons on your shirt till I find what waits for me beneath. Then I'm wanting to put my mouth against your skin and learn the feel of you till I know you so well that you're part of me."

More words than she'd yet had from him. Small wonder he saved them up, what he could do with them. She didn't look away from his green eyes. Mesmerized, she didn't blink, couldn't have if she wanted to.

"But since all that would surely call for an apology, I'll be leaving now." As he walked out the door, he called back over his shoulder, "Though if you like, you can consider it your engraved announcement for our next time together."

Their next time. Kylie flopped into the worn armchair she'd been so fiercely gripping. *Their next time.* Her heart had scarcely survived this one.

Chapter Four

It is better to exist unknown to the law.

—IRISH PROVERB

Michael came downstairs at six-thirty on Monday morning. Already dressed, Vi sat at the kitchen table gingerly sipping a steaming mug of tea.

Setting aside the mug she said, "My studio's not far from the bank. You can come with me now or join me later—after the bank's open."

"You're going to work this early?"

"I've someone coming over from the States next week to look at my work. Some nonsense about doing fabric design for them."

"Nonsense?" he repeated in a teasing voice, amazed that she seemed so uncomfortable with her own prosperity. "People don't generally cross the ocean on a whim."

He could have sworn his bold sister was sporting a blush. "Don't go making more of this than what's there," she said. "I've things I need to see done, that's all." She stood and settled her hardly touched mug with the others nesting in the kitchen sink. "Now are you coming with me?"

He opened the cupboard and found it as bare as a pauper's. "I might as well." One last hopeful peek in the refrigerator yielded nothing. Shrugging on his jacket he asked, "What exactly do you eat, sister, fairy dust and summer dreams?"

"More like yogurt and the occasional bit of granola." Pausing from her efforts to secure Roger to his leash when he appeared more in mind of a game of tug-of-war, Vi grinned up at Michael. "Mr. Spillane down at the market is usually filling the shelves about now, and he's not against letting a customer in a bit early."

He followed on his sister's heels. "So I'm to go to market for you?"

"If you plan to do any eating, you are."

Vi dropped him off at Spillane's without so much as an introduction. Peering in the front window of the market, Michael saw a burly, silver-haired man busy stacking boxes of soap. He rapped on the glass, and the man looked sharply his way. Michael worked up a casual smile and wave, hoping that would get him through the gates to this paradise.

The man opened the door just enough to stick out his head. "We open at eight, as the sign on the door would have told you—had you come when there was light enough to read it."

Michael gazed at the neat rows and narrow aisles just beyond the door. "Vi—my sister—said you've let her in early now and again."

"Vi? Then you're Vi Kilbride's brother Michael come to visit? I'd heard you were in town." The door opened wider and one enormous hand ushered him in. "I always let Vi shop when the whim takes her. If I didn't, she'd forget to eat altogether."

Michael stepped into the store. Almost reeling with pleasure, he inhaled the combined scents of fruit, flowers, and food. Paradise it was.

"I'm Seamus Spillane," the storekeeper said, extending his hand. "Welcome."

Michael shook the man's hand. "Vi mentioned that she had an account here."

"She does, and because I'd hate to see the girl starve to death, I also have my son run the groceries to her house when she thinks to buy any."

"Your son hasn't been up her way in some time," Michael commented, then reached out to heft an orange in one hand. The color was incredible, almost tempting enough to have him biting into the bitter skin.

The grocer held out a basket. "Fill this, and when you're done, take another. You have the look of a man who likes his food."

Smiling, Michael took the basket and dropped the orange into it. "More than you know," he said.

It wasn't gluttony overtaking him. It was the sweep of hue, scent, and texture that he'd been deprived of for so long. Though he meant to have an eye to price, he had soon loaded the basket with a rainbow of produce: blood oranges from Spain, tomatoes from Holland, grapes so perfect they hardly seemed real.

In the next basket went goods from around the world: pasta of every conceivable shape, cereals screaming with sugar, and tins of soup that he was sure would be the difference between starvation and not.

Looking at the wealth of food in front of him, it hit Michael how prosperity had come to the Republic. He'd missed so much in his time gone. So much to make up for. So much to learn.

His gaze settling on a tub brimming with bunches of fresh cut flowers—God knew where they had been jetted in from—he pulled two bouquets and added them to his pile. This he'd pay for out of his small stash of pocket money. It wouldn't do to have Vi buy her own flowers, or Kylie's, either.

Grabbing the flowers, a bunch of grapes, and a sweet pastry sealed in crinkly plastic, he left the remainder of the purchases to be carted to Vi's by Seamus Spillane's son. After thanking the grocer, Michael strolled down the steep hill toward the harbor. While popping grapes into his mouth with all the relish of a Roman at a banquet of old, he nodded greetings to the few people out and about.

In spite of the wind's sharp teeth, Michael slowed and gazed in shop windows. Pubs with bicycle rental counters, bookstores, and bakeries tucked in the same small space, this town was a tribute to creativity and survival. And freedom.

Freedom, it was a heady thing. He could scarcely

understand—or believe—that it wouldn't be pulled from him. But he had to believe, for as Vi had said, it would surely kill him to go back there again. These money problems, needing work and a home, all were small compared to what he'd been through.

As he walked by the solemn stone front of the bank, he recalled yesterday's promise to Vi. He would open the account and buy the car, all the easier to explore this wonderful new world. But he would also keep a record of his expenses and pay her back as soon as he found a job. Stubborn Kilbride that she was, if she wouldn't take the money, he'd save it for the children she was sure to have one day.

He rounded the corner to the arts village and quickly spotted Vi's studio. As he stepped through the door, the breath was hammered from him. If the market had been a riot of textures, this was a damned war. Vivid flowing colors battled for his attention. Fluttering banners, fabric sculptures that breathed with life, abstract paintings so hungry and demanding. He dropped the flowers and pastry on the nearest surface that didn't seem to be alive and bolted from the room.

"Enough," he muttered after dragging in a breath of cold air. Leaning against the rough, whitewashed outer wall of the studio, Michael rubbed a hand over his eyes as if trying to wipe away the overload of images.

"Are you all right?" he heard his sister say.

Hitching a thumb over his shoulder, he asked, "How do you sleep at night, with all that in your head?"

"Sometimes I don't. It's too much, and all of it fights to get out at once." She reached over and smoothed a hand through his hair, a sign of affection he remembered from Nan a lifetime before. "Perhaps I should have fed my art to you in small doses."

He shook his head. "It's more a cumulative reaction. These past few days, all the people, the places. And then your art—"

Vi grinned. "Enough to send a customer running screaming into the street, you think?"

"Not this lifetime." Michael pulled away from the wall and stood straight again. "Your art's as you are—uncompromising. And if people lack the eye to see your talent, the hell with them. Now let's go inside, I have a gift for you." He gave a rueful shake of his head. "A pale one, I'm thinking now."

Back in the studio he handed her a bunch of flowers. While she arranged them in a vase, Vi made all the proper noises about the sweetness of his gesture and the beauty of the blossoms, but she kept eyeing the remaining bouquet on her display counter. Having learned that volunteering information was a sure path to trouble, Michael remained silent.

Finally, Vi swooped up the other flowers and settled them into a white enameled pitcher. "I don't need to be asking whom these are for, do I?"

Michael took the indirect route. "Gaelscoil Pearse—do you know where it is?"

"I do," she said sounding both resigned and unwilling. She returned to her workbench and began toying with a large, exotic seashell, something that would never find its way to Kerry's rocky strand.

"Have you thought, Michael, that this attraction you have for her shouldn't be trusted. You've been out scarcely a week, and it's been so long since you've—"

Michael's hand sliced through the air between them. "There are some parts of my life I deserve to keep private. If you're wondering whether I plan to drop onto one knee and propose marriage to a woman I met two days ago, I'll tell you the answer's no. Anything else I intend to do—with Kylie or any other woman—is my business, and mine alone."

His anger began to fade as quickly as it had risen. After all, Vi had said no more than he'd been thinking since he'd first seen Kylie. "Give me some room, Vi, and I'll give you the same with your men."

Her eyes sparkled with humor. "Men? I don't have even one."

"Not one? Amazing." He moved closer and ruffled her already wild hair. "Then I've made myself an easy bargain, haven't I? Now tell me where to find Kylie's school."

"After the bank, I will, and not a moment sooner." Kylie probably wouldn't be free till lunchtime, so Michael didn't bother to object.

"And until then," she said, pointing to an old apothecary's chest, gap-toothed with missing drawers, "you can give me a hand with this. I bought it for storage but it's never lived up to its purpose."

Michael walked to the jumble. As he touched the first piece of wood, memories spun back at him. Summers at Nan's spent fixing odd bits of furniture that had languished in a shed for decades. Building her a kitchen table and chairs from an idea so clear in his mind that he'd never felt the need to put pencil to paper. The hard work, even the cuts and gashes as the body grew too tired to keep up with the mind. All of it joyous.

Michael smiled. He'd gone too long without this sort of pleasure. In prison, he'd taken a great number of correspondence courses, things like business and literature and mathematics. Anything to keep his brain active while he was caged. He'd wanted to work on his carpentry, but the authorities weren't particularly receptive to activities that could arm prisoners with awls and chisels.

Hands almost itching with need, Michael began sorting through the broken parts in front of him. Oak, and a century and more old, he guessed. A fine piece. Handmade, and deserving of restoration.

A grand job it would be. With nimble fingers he fitted together two dovetailed pieces. Almost as natural as spending time with Kylie O'Shea, Michael thought and smiled. And if he couldn't be doing one, he'd just as well be doing the other.

"There's more than a morning's work here," he said to his sister. "But it's fine craftsmanship—too good to waste for storage."

Vi gave the chest a skeptical look. "That you'll have to prove to me."

"It's been years since I've done anything like this." Digging through his sister's toolbox he muttered, "No clamps at all. No point in putting it back together if I can't make it stay."

"Stop over at the hardware. I'm sure they'll have whatever you need. Besides, I hear they're looking for help." Never once looking up from the soft mountain of yarn she sorted, Vi added in a breezy voice, "But in your spare time, perhaps you could think about building me a bench for outside the shop. I thought it would be a nice touch. And maybe a new display case or two. If you've a mind to, that is."

Some forms of prodding were more tolerable than others. "I might," he said in an offhand way, while mentally ticking down a list of tools he'd need. And space to work, he thought, glancing around Vi's crowded studio. But if he moved aside that pile of canvases, and perhaps that bench over there . . .

"Don't even be thinking of it," Vi warned, now looking at him through narrowed eyes. "Not a thing moves in this room. If you're needing more space while you work, I know of some a bit out of town."

He felt himself being led down a path, complacent as any sheep. "A bit out of town" probably translated to miles and miles away from Kylie and the danger Vi seemed to think she posed.

"I'm sure you do. But all I've promised to do is repair that chest," he reminded her.

"You'll be doing more. Grand things," she murmured with a faraway sound to her voice.

"Whatever it is you're seeing, keep it to yourself."

Looking almost muzzy with sleep, Vi shook her head, then gave him a broad smile. "Seeing? I'm seeing no more than you are, Michael Kilbride. A future long put off and ready to be taken. And a chest to be mended," she added.

With a smile of his own, Michael turned to the work that he'd loved as a youth, and time flew by.

Just before lunch, Vi and he walked the few blocks to the bank and conducted their business. Account open and feeling almost a proper citizen, Michael stopped back at the studio and retrieved Kylie's bouquet. He doubted that she'd be free to have lunch with him, but she should be able to take flowers from an admirer. Following Vi's grudging directions, he soon found himself where he wanted to be.

Michael stood next to Kylie's rusted car, just out front of Gaelscoil Pearse. The school was more an arrangement of trailers than the building he'd expected. In a broad field to the side of the trailers were swing sets, a slide, and other random bits of playground equipment obviously pieced together from donations. It was lunchtime, and the children were out to play. Their laughter and shouts to one another came to Michael, lightening a mood that was already nothing short of uncharacteristically optimistic.

He saw her then, standing in the middle of a ring of children, as though she were the sun and the children basked in her warmth. On the boys' faces, he could see something near adoration, and they were nowhere near old enough to recognize the full impact of Kylie's appeal. Ah, but he was.

Michael had never thought himself a romantic man. In that moment, though, he felt romantic. If he were a poet, he'd give her the words. But he wasn't rich with verse, and the best he could offer was a bunch of flowers well on the way to wilted.

But even giving her flowers seemed a bit much, what with a dozen and more curious pairs of eyes looking his way. He glanced at the trailers. An older woman wearing a stern dress and an even sterner expression stood on the steps of the building closest to Michael. He worked up the same sort of wave that had gotten him into Spillane's this morning, and got the same semi-welcoming response. Chafing under the woman's gaze, he set the flowers on Kylie's car. He promised himself he'd come back for them when he felt less conspicuous.

As he neared her, he realized that she was singing for the children. Her voice rang clear and sweet. Michael smiled as he recognized the words to *Óró sé do Bheatha Abhaile*, a folk song about Galway's legendary pirate queen, Grace O'Malley. The children joined in for a rousing chorus, welcoming Grace home from her fight to keep Ireland free of marauding foreigners.

Just as Michael reached their little circle, the last notes of song had drifted off in the breeze. His applause quickly drew their attention.

"That was brilliant," he said.

"*Gaeilge, le do thoil,*" Kylie directed in a voice he supposed was meant to be stern. Her glorious smile rather softened the effect. Her hair rippled in the breeze, swirling around her shoulders, and her long skirt—blue with a scattering of pale flowers—danced, too.

"In Irish? You want me to speak in Irish?"

"That's the sole language permitted on school grounds," she replied in English, for which he was thankful. "We're not called All-Irish for nothing."

"Well, then I'm afraid you'll be calling me silent."

The children laughed. Using one hand to push her rich brown hair away from her face, Kylie asked them something in rapid-fire Irish. He picked up the word *Bearla*, meaning English, and easily interpreted the children's enthusiastic nods.

With a smile of pure mischief, she looked back to Michael. "They've agreed to show a little mercy on a visitor. You may speak your English, and we'll keep to our Irish. If you miss anything we're saying, I just might translate for you, if you make it worth my while. . . ."

He could think of many ways in which he'd love to make it worth her while, but he suspected her mind wasn't traveling quite the same path.

"And what would that take?" he asked, letting a bit of what he was thinking show in his eyes.

Color rose in her cheeks, but her voice remained level. "A story, of course. You'll tell us a story, and I'll pass it along in Irish."

A story. He could recall a tale or two his grandmother had told. Looking at Kylie's slender form and hair so sleek he longed to touch it, one story came to mind. "Then it's about Oisin's mother you'll hear," he said, "for she reminds me of you."

One of the young girls closest to Kylie raised her hand. Kylie nodded, and the girl murmured something to her teacher.

Kylie laughed. "Well, Niamh says if that's the case, she wants to know whether you knew me when I was a fawn, or only since I've taken human form. And she is a bit concerned you might leave me to an evil druid when you're done breaking my heart."

Perhaps he'd not thought through his choice of story quite carefully enough. "Well then, how about the story of—"

His words were cut short by shrill screams coming from nearby. Michael looked over to the play equipment. A child was dangling off the top of the slide, caught by a cord at his jacket's collar. Clearly panicked, he gripped at the clothing pulled taut around his neck. His mates stood on the ground, pointing and screaming.

"Dear Lord," he heard Kylie cry, but he was halfway across the flat field by then.

Michael was up the slide in what seemed one great leap. He gripped the boy by the shoulders of his jacket, and using both hands, hauled him to safety.

"Steady, now," Michael said. "I've got you."

The jacket's cord had lodged tightly between the floor of the slide and a metal bar meant for the child to hold onto as he readied to go. The boy had seen a few too many rich meals, and his weight had worked against him. He was still gasping, even though his breathing was now unrestricted.

"It's a bit of a scare you've had," Michael said as he finally worked the boy free, "but you'll be fine." He glanced to the base of the slide and saw Kylie standing there, her face still pale with alarm. "I'll be sending you down to Miss O'Shea. You ready?"

The child managed a weak nod.

Michael looked down at Kylie. "Ready?"

"Yes."

Michael waited until the boy was in Kylie's protective grip before backing down the steps. His own heart drummed with the residual alarm coursing through him. He walked to Kylie and settled a hand on her shoulder, as much for his comfort as hers. When she looked up at him, he was humbled by the gratitude shining in her blue eyes.

"It was a near thing," she said. "How can I ever thank you?"

"I did no more than anyone else would have done."

She smoothed the boy's dark hair. "I'm sure Alan, here, thinks otherwise. As do I."

They were joined by a cluster of adults, including the stern woman Michael had noticed earlier. She was clearly Kylie's superior, and took charge immediately. The Irish flew too fast and furious for Michael to follow. He glanced away, thinking it might be time to make his escape. The bright bundle of color on top of Kylie's car caught his attention. He'd entirely forgotten the flowers.

"Be right back," he said to Kylie, who managed a distracted nod, while still comforting Alan and fielding whatever questions her employer was sending her way.

Once back at the car park, Michael delayed a bit, hoping the stern woman would go back inside. Watching Kylie, even from a distance, was such a pleasure that he didn't mind the wait. He scarcely noticed when a white car pulled up on the other side of him. He did notice, though, when a uniformed officer stepped out and headed his way.

The sick feeling in the pit of Michael's stomach

had nothing to do with guilt or innocence. Then again, none of his few but memorable contacts with the law did either.

"Fine day," the officer said, ginger-colored brows raised at a quizzical angle as he took in the bouquet Michael held in a white-knuckled grip.

"Fine enough," Michael returned, instantly mistrusting the man—no, boy—with his smug face, which scarcely needed to be shaved.

The officer glanced across at the schoolyard. "Looking for anyone in particular, Kilbride?"

Michael exhaled in a slow, even gust. He shouldn't have been surprised that the authorities knew he was here, but he was. He'd begun to feel welcome and let down his guard. A mistake. Keeping his expression impassive, he said, "I've brought flowers for a friend."

"Then you'd best deliver them and move on. Standing in front of a schoolyard like this, it's a sure way to draw our attention. A fine target it would be, hmm?"

"Target for what?" Michael returned, sounding calm and level. Amazing, considering the horrific images spinning out in his head. Anger ratcheted tighter and tighter with each beat of his heart.

"We're watching you, Kilbride."

"So watch," he said, adding a silent *you bastard*. After tossing the flowers back on the bonnet of Kylie's car, he walked off.

Nothing had changed. Not a miserable, goddamn thing.

Chapter Five

*There are two sides to every story,
and twelve versions of a song.*

— IRISH PROVERB

Kylie had been watching Michael, her heart still beating a wild dance beneath her breast. When the Garda approached, the rhythm had changed to something thick and knotted. She knew Mairead, the school's principal, was asking her something, but Kylie honestly didn't care what.

She watched as Michael walked down the road in long, angry strides. The lovely flowers that had been no doubt meant for her lay in a heap atop her car. The officer—Gerry Flynn, heaven help her—flashed her a dark look, climbed in his car, and drove off.

"Five minutes till class begins," she reminded her students. "You'd best play while you can."

She gave Alan one last hug and turned him over to Mairead, so that his parents could be contacted. Kylie was sure he'd be fine once the last of the fright wore off, and he owed it all to Michael. She'd never seen a man move with such determination.

"On with you," she said to the rest of the children still milling about. They scattered like spring lambs on a fine morning.

But much of the shine was off the day for Kylie. She went to her car and gathered up the flowers, feeling sorry for them. Touching a fingertip to the bruised blossoms, she looked for Michael. She could see him far down the road, heading for open country.

A terrible thought struck her. Had Gerry warned him off? After all, she and Gerry shared an ugly past. Not that he was likely to raise something that stood to harm his reputation far more than it ever could hers. It would be easier for him to simply mention that she was Black Johnny's daughter. Her father had destroyed more lives and dreams than just hers.

Shaking her head, she walked back toward the school buildings. No, her father couldn't have been the reason for Michael's leaving. Even she couldn't spread the burden of her family guilt that far.

Then what of Michael? He didn't seem the type to have trouble with the authorities. But she hardly knew him, she reminded herself. And more than once she'd proven she was no great judge of character.

"Kylie!" Mairead, the school's principal, was hurrying her way. "That was some bit of wildness with

Alan, and quite a guardian angel the boy found himself. Is the man a friend of yours?"

Kylie nodded. She was about to give Mairead his name when some odd feeling made her stop. Brows arched, Mairead waited.

"He's new to town," Kylie offered as a sort of compromise.

"I see," her employer said, clearly not quite satisfied. She cleared her throat and said, "Well then, before Alan's mishap, I'd been coming out to tell you I had the most marvelous call!"

"What was it?"

"A local artist proposing a long-term special project with the children. I want you to follow up on this. I've told her that you'll be contacting her."

A woman artist. There were plenty in Ballymuir, an arts-loving town. To think that it was Michael's sister was sheer paranoia. Still, Kylie could feel a snare tightening around her. "And who is it I'm to contact?"

"Her name's Vi Kilbride. Do you know her?"

"I do," she said, imagining the final tug of the line binding her to a fate that seemed more designed than coincidental. Three days ago the name Kilbride had been one Kylie knew only as part of the community; now it was winding its way through her life.

"Good enough. Stop by her studio after school and the two of you can talk."

Kylie nodded, her gaze drifting to the road Michael had taken. Quite a talk that could be.

At four-fifteen, Kylie stood outside the door of Kilbride Designs. Though she had no solid reason to be nervous, she felt as though she were about to beard a lioness in her den. But there was only one way to face conflict, and that was head on. Putting on a bright smile, she stepped inside.

"Welcome," Vi said. "I've been expecting you."

Kylie smoothed her palms against her wool skirt, then shook Vi's offered hand. The artist's grip was firm, and her expression polite and blessedly impersonal.

Seeing that this meeting just might be survivable, Kylie relaxed. "Thank you for offering to work with our students. It's a wonderful gift you're giving us."

"This is far more a gift to me. I love children."

One thing in common, Kylie thought. Two, if she permitted herself to consider Michael—a dicey proposition at best. "Well then, what do you have in mind?"

They spent half an hour discussing the project Vi proposed. The longer they talked, the more Kylie came to like Vi Kilbride. She was animated and charming—hardly the imposing figure Kylie had seen in church the day before. Her proposal was ambitious, tied in with the children's study of the bold warriors, Fionn MacCumhaill and CúChulainn, and ending with an art exhibition. Kylie would have expected nothing less grand from the woman who had created the beautiful things in this studio. And she wanted no less for her children, either.

"I'd like to work closely with you on this," Vi added just as Kylie was getting ready to leave.

The comment was casual and not especially notable considering what they were to begin. Still, there was the other unspoken link they shared. Another reason Vi might want to spend time with her. And if she didn't raise it, Kylie knew she'd never feel truly comfortable around this woman.

"About your brother," she began.

Vi raised a hand, palm outward. "I've been told in no uncertain terms that what's between the two of you is none of my business. And while I'm of a different opinion, he's an adult, and so are you."

Just as Kylie felt the tension begin to seep out of her, Vi's gaze grew challenging. "But since you raised the subject, I will tell you this. . . . Michael's not the hard man he likes to appear. He's suffered his share and more of pain and betrayal. And if anyone should hurt him again," Vi said in a low, fierce voice, "they'll be answering to me."

Courage, Kylie reminded herself. She met Vi's gaze with a steady calm. "You're right. Michael and I are both adults and able to care for ourselves. And you're getting ahead of yourself, thinking that we have anything more than the beginnings of a friendship. I can't fault you for loving him, but he doesn't need your protection."

"He needs it more than you know."

"What do you mean by that?" Kylie asked.

"I've said all I'm going to. Whatever you want to know about my brother, you'll have to ask him." Vi turned to a small loom sitting on a table. "Now I have to be getting back to work. Call me when you have the project schedule approved."

Dismissed. The Kilbride family certainly knew how to end a conversation when they chose to. If she weren't so annoyed, Kylie might have been amused by Vi's high-handed tactics.

"Fine then." Noticing for the first time a bouquet similar to the one she'd received from Michael, she added, "And if you don't consider it meddling, tell your brother I thank him for my flowers. Oh, and tell him that Gerry Flynn has no spine at all."

Vi's head shot up. "Gerry Flynn? Michael was talking to Gerry Flynn? What about?"

"I'd be asking your brother," Kylie finished, then swept out of the studio. O'Sheas were known for liking the last word, too.

All the way home, Kylie thought of Michael. With each bend in the road she looked for him, hoping she'd see him, his long stride covering the ground. She didn't, though. The road was empty, its stony gray color met by that of a rain-heavy sky.

She stopped to check in on Breege, and found her cooking a supper of lamb stew. Not ready to face her empty house, Kylie accepted Breege's offer of a meal. They chatted about town events, then after a while fell silent and listened to the drumming of the rain on the slate roof.

Breege sighed and shifted in her chair. "It settles in my bones, this weather. Reminds me that I'm no longer a girl." She smiled, showing teeth still even and white. "Though I had promised Edna McCafferty I'd meet her for the *sessiun* at O'Connor's tonight. I'll not let a few aches stop me from enjoying good music and company."

Frowning, Kylie glanced at the window; it was sheeted with rain blowing straight at the house. This was no night for Breege to travel alone, not that she'd take kindly to such an observation.

"I'd been planning to go to the pub, too," Kylie announced in a bright voice. She glanced down at her long skirt and prim white blouse. More suited to a convent than a pub. "I'll just stop home to change."

The furrows in Breege's forehead grew deeper with her broad grin. "The pub? You? How grand! I've not seen you in there once in all the time I've known you. And I've spent too many nights worrying that if you don't get yourself out for the young men to admire, you'll end up being the last bride in Ballymuir."

"I'll be having a pint, Breege, not a husband," Kylie corrected as she stood and gathered the plates and cutlery to take to the kitchen.

Breege followed. "We'll see what you say after we get the pint in you. I'm betting that later tonight, I'll be making some lace for your veil."

It was Kylie's turn to laugh. "Now you're making lace? I've never even seen you knit!"

"For your wedding, darlin', I'd plant the mulberries to feed the worms to get my silken thread. And then I'd learn to tat the lace."

Kylie chuckled, then added the last line of their newfound poem. "And so the last bride shall wed."

A church. Of all the places Michael thought he might find himself twice within two days, a church was the last. Yet he'd walked empty roads and gained no peace, then gone home to find that the comfort of his sister was also missing. What was left to him but church? Nothing, he thought, pulling open St. Brendan's weathered door.

Feeling it would be impolite to do otherwise, he glanced away from the few people in line at the confessional. He genuflected before settling in the last pew, amazed that even that vestige of religion lingered somewhere in him. Once seated, he stared up at the empty altar, meditating on the question that stretched to the end of his life: What next?

Michael knew the Garda's hostility this afternoon had been a paltry offering compared to what might have been delivered. In the eyes of the local authorities, he remained a guilty man—and one who bore watching, with the continuing unrest in the North. He understood this, though he'd damned well never accept it. And he'd never stop hating the people who had trapped, then betrayed him.

Even the dim light and serious quiet of his current surroundings weren't enough to calm his internal clamor for revenge. Or the guilt that sickened him.

Revenge. It sounded a sweet word, a lover's word, with its sigh of satisfaction purling off the end. He didn't want to feel this way, so hungry for it that he could howl. And he didn't know how to kill off the need.

Michael stood and walked to the end of the confessional line. While he waited his turn, he told himself that this was useless. Absurd. But he didn't leave.

The little closet he soon entered probably had stood through the murders of rulers, rebels, and innocents. He knelt, conscious of the cramped space and of his own doubts and fears.

"Bless me, Father, for I have sinned. It's been . . ." He hesitated, counting back the years to the last time his mam had dragged him spitting and swearing to confession. "It's been twenty years since my last confession, and whatever else I'm supposed to be saying after this, I just don't remember."

"Well, twenty years is a long time gone. I suppose I'd be forgetting a few things, too," the voice the other side of the screen said. Michael knew it was Father Cready. Vi had said he was the only priest in town. "What brings you here, now?"

Brian Rourke, he almost answered. But saying the name would be putting a face on his target, renaming Satan. "I've been thinking about revenge," he said instead. "About how good it would feel to just once even the score, to kill someone who has killed. Someone who has destroyed me."

The priest paused before speaking. "Even in the twenty years you haven't been visiting, that rule hasn't changed."

Michael scrubbed a hand over his face. "No, I didn't expect it had. Look, I don't know what I'm doing here, except that I need to find some way to . . . God, I don't know. To get to tomorrow and the day after that without wanting to hunt a man down and take what he owes me," he finished in a rush.

"And if you do? Will that bring you peace?"

He closed his eyes and thought hard a few moments before answering. "No."

"Perhaps you should be visiting us a bit more often. You're not alone, son."

But he was. He was so horribly alone that he

thought he might die. And the idea didn't frighten him as it should. Without saying another word, he escaped the confessional and the church.

He ended up in O'Connor's, intent on getting drunk. It seemed, though, he was failing at even that. Shoving aside his empty whiskey glass and lighting a cigarette, he looked around. Far too fine a place for a man like him. He'd have preferred one of those ill-lit pubs with the dank smell of stale beer soaked into dirty carpets. But he'd landed here, and once the first drink was down, had lost the will to move on. Besides, after cutting off early attempts at chat, he had been left alone.

He jiggled his glass at the bartender. "Another."

"It's getting near to supper," the man said, neatly ignoring the demand.

Michael drew in on his cigarette; the smoke burnt less now that he'd worked his way through half a pack. The television chattered in the background, and the bartender moved to joke with a group of men at the other end of the long counter.

"Bookmaker's sandwich, chips . . . and another," he said in a loud voice, edging the glass closer to the inward lip of the bar.

The bartender came back with a cup of coffee. "Drink this, have your food, then we'll get to the other."

Michael finished his cigarette, stubbing it into a black plastic ashtray with an advertisement for some beer on its sooty face.

"Pint of Guinness, Rory," a woman's voice called from the door.

Michael watched in the mirror as Evie Nolan fluffed her fingers through damp auburn hair and tugged at a clinging dress that seemed to have started an inevitable climb upward. He knew the instant she spotted him; the predatory gleam in her eyes cut through his numbness. They watched each other in the mirror as she approached.

"Well, you're here early," Evie said, pulling a bar stool so close to his that they touched. At his blank expression, her eyes grew harder. "You were to meet me here, remember?"

He did. Now. The bartender set a platter of food in front of him, the greasy scent of the chips tickling his nose.

"The pint, Rory," Evie snapped as the man turned away.

"It's settling out, same as always."

Amused, Michael watched as the man slowed his pace to a snail's on the way back to the taps. After bolting down a bite of the thick sandwich, he asked Evie, "Meeting friends tonight?"

Her glance flicked over him. "Just one."

She ordered food and they ate without much talk between them. At one point or another his whiskey glass was refilled and quickly emptied. Time passed but his mood stayed as dark as ever. Eventually they played a few games of darts, came back, and drank some more.

Michael's concentration began to slip. The pub was starting to fill, but it wasn't just the noise and laughter rising. Evie's hand kept traveling insidiously up his thigh. With unwelcome results, too. He frowned at her and she gave a smile as content as a cat with cream. She'd probably been teasing men since she'd first popped breasts. He knew it—hated it—yet parts of him didn't care. Not one damn bit.

"I want to dance," Evie said, leaning closer. Even over the thin whitish curl of his cigarette smoke he could smell her cloying perfume.

"There's no music."

She stood and tugged him off his stool. "Doesn't matter."

He supposed it didn't, and if this small thing would make her settle down and leave him be, he was all for it. But then she towed him to the long, narrow hallway between the men's and women's washrooms.

"Here?" he asked giving a dubious glance at the close quarters.

Wrapping her arms around his neck, Evie launched herself against him. Unprepared, Michael staggered back against the wood paneled wall. As her mouth anchored over his, he discovered that he hadn't managed to drown his sense of discretion, either. He reached back to untwine her hands from his neck, and wrenched his mouth free at the same time.

"Don't tell me you're not wanting this," Evie said nudging her breasts up against him.

He clamped his hands around her upper arms and tried to fend her off. He'd have better luck holding an eel. "There's wanting, and then there's doing."

She worked her way in closer. "Then you do the wanting and I'll take care of the doing."

Persistent, she was, and too busy with her seeking

hands and attitude. But he'd been raised never to insult a woman. "That's a fine offer, but—"

He was cut off by the sound of someone clearing her throat with loud intent. He glanced up and saw Vi bearing down on him. Inconsistent as it was, he was delighted to have her come tidy up this bad moment for him. He wasn't drunk, but he was staggering tired.

Giving the clinging Evie a scathing glance, Vi said to him, "You might think of having that removed."

"I've been trying to. Stubborn, though."

"This isn't a laughing matter."

"There you're wrong, sweet Vi," he said. Miss Nolan was laughable indeed when measured against the rest of his woes. He unreeled Evie and patted her on her round bum. "Go on. Time for a family meeting."

With a toss of her head, Evie sniffed, "I don't like being treated this way."

"Then you'd best learn to behave, yourself," Vi chided her. "Now run along, Evie, before you make me lose my patience."

Evie spared Michael one last pouting face, then sulked her way back to the front room.

Michael leaned against the wall to let a woman edge by on her way to the loo. He gave his sister a long, curious look. "Not that I don't appreciate being rescued, but what are you doing here? I thought we'd agreed no spying."

"I'm not spying, you big oaf. I come an hour or two most Monday nights for the *sessiun*. Though why is it when you're left to your own devices, I always find you with a woman in your arms?"

"The Kilbride charm?" At her frustrated hiss, he came as close to laughing as he had since the Garda's visit. "No?" he asked. "But I have to point out that I was in Evie's arms, and not the other way around."

"Whoever was doing the holding, have a care." Vi glanced back up the hallway. "Anyway, that's not why I'm hiding back here with you. Tell me what went on with Gerry Flynn—the Garda—today."

"How'd you know about that, with you not spying on me?"

Vi waved aside the question. "Kylie O'Shea, but we haven't time to discuss that right now. Flynn, what happened with him?"

"Just a friendly greeting," Michael said with a bitter turn of his mouth. "Let me know they'd be keeping an eye on me."

Vi gave another glance up the hallway. Slowly the message came to Michael that she was nervous about something.

"What is it?" he asked.

"Flynn walked in the door the same time I did. If you were anyone other than a Kilbride, I'd suggest that you be on your way now, but I know better than to commit that sin. Just be careful, Michael. He's not been with the Gardai long, and is arrogant with power."

Masking the fury—and the guilt—that his life had come to this again, Michael shrugged. "He's got no power over me. I just want to finish my drink and leave."

"I'd rather you left now," she said, her love for him plain in her eyes. "No good can come of this."

"Don't you see? If I'm to cower every time Flynn comes around, I'd just as well go stick myself back in that cell. Now meet with your friends, and if you're of a mind to do anything for me, sing me a song. It's been years since I've heard you."

Vi went up on tiptoe and brushed a kiss against his cheek. "You smell of whiskey and cigarettes," she said, wrinkling her nose. She leaned closer, then with a disgusted little sound stepped back. "And Evie Nolan, too. Even a walk home in the rain won't wash that away."

"And those are the lesser of my sins today," he joked in a half-hearted manner.

"Then don't tell me about the rest," his sister ordered.

Michael followed Vi back to the pub's main room. The local musicians had drawn themselves into a circle just beneath the half-curtained front windows. Elderly women with their hair fussed and lacquered sat shoulder-to-shoulder with plain-faced farmers. The serious musicians sat head down tuning their instruments. The more congenial laughed with their mates.

Nowhere did Michael see Flynn, though today he'd focused more on the uniform than the face. Evie was easier to find; she waited for him at the bar. He pulled out his stool and bought a few inches of space between himself and Evie's wandering hands.

"She's a meddling bitch, your sister."

"She's—" Ready to defend Vi, Michael trailed off when he spotted a willowy figure at the end of the bar.

• • •

Kylie wasn't sure what got her attention, there in the unfamiliar laughter, noise, and smoke. It might have been Evie Nolan's shrill voice carrying her way, or the feel of Michael's eyes on her. Whatever it was, she wanted to turn and flee.

She wasn't meant to be in this foreign world. She hadn't missed the surprised and disapproving comments when she'd arrived. And she wasn't meant to watch Evie lean toward Michael and tug his face in her direction as if she owned the man.

But she couldn't leave without ruining Breege's night. Resigned to staying, Kylie sipped the pretty colored drink she'd ordered, then winced at its dreadful taste. No wonder Rory O'Connor had asked her if she might not be wanting something a bit plainer. Too late now, just as it was too late to pretend she hadn't seen Michael. But there was some merit in a tactical retreat; she'd just slink back over by Breege and the others.

Kylie was halfway to the front of the pub when she saw that the others included Vi Kilbride. She turned back to the bar. While she aimed for the far end, the press of people around her sent her toward the only open spot. Right next to Michael Kilbride.

Keeping her eyes averted, Kylie set down her drink. A large, warm hand closed over hers.

"I know you saw me."

She tugged her hand free. "I did, but you were looking busy."

She nodded to Evie Nolan, who had leaned forward on the bar to scowl at her from Michael's other side. Their homeland might be lacking snakes, but it held its share of venom, Kylie thought as she took in Evie's flat eyes.

"Never too busy to say hello to a friend," Michael said in a way that sounded as though he'd put in a long day drinking. The thought unsettled her even more. Far too many of her mornings had been spent nursing her father back to the living after one of his infamous "investor meetings."

"I won't be keeping you from . . . well, whatever," she said, trying very hard not to glance Evie's way. "But I do want to thank you for what you did on the playground today. You're quite the hero for rescuing Alan . . . at least, that's what the children are saying," she stumbled on.

"Thank the children for me." His green eyes remained perceptive, unclouded by whatever he'd spent his day doing. Maybe she'd been too hasty, assuming he'd drunk more than his share.

"Would you sit with me a while?" he asked. "Please?"

A note in his voice—yearning, yet hesitant—tugged at her notoriously soft heart. She was about to say yes when she noticed Evie's crimson-painted nails possessively curled around his arm. It was too much for her, one more confusing detail in this odd landscape.

"I'll leave you to your friend," Kylie said, then pushed her way back through the crowd and away from Michael Kilbride. As she neared Breege, a hand settled onto her shoulder. Praying it wasn't Michael, she spun around.

"We need to have a word, Kylie," Gerry Flynn said.

This was all the night needed.

"Another time," she answered, then tried to hurry past. He stayed her, keeping his hand wrapped around her upper arm. She was forced to stop and look at him.

It amazed her how a man could change while his face remained essentially the same. Gerry still had hair that was not quite red, yet not quite blond. His eyes were the same almost-gray they'd always been. What had changed from the boy she'd known was the light that used to dance in those eyes.

He'd always been full of laughter and smiles, just a bit of a devil when they'd been in school together. Now he was hard. From the grip of his hand to the set of his mouth, he had no lightness about him.

"That man—Kilbride—you need to keep away from him."

After seeing Michael with Evie, she hadn't considered doing anything else, but Gerry's tone angered her. "Are you giving me an order?"

"More a word of friendly advice."

"You're not looking very friendly this evening, Gerry," she said as sweetly as she could. "But thank you just the same."

His thick brows drew together over eyes carrying an edge of possessiveness that frightened her. "I'm telling you this for your own good. He's evil, and you don't want to be dragged down with him." His fingers closed tighter. "You need someone to take care of you. To watch over you."

She wrenched free, but kept a forced smile on her face. "I can take care of myself."

Gerry muttered something under his breath and shoved off. As her heart slowed, she wondered what incomprehensible quirk of the human mind allowed Gerry to think she'd ever let him care for her. Not after he'd so thoroughly abandoned her years before.

Relieved to see that Vi was deep in conversation with others, Kylie sat down on a tall stool next to Breege and waited for her frayed nerves to settle. The music began, slow at first as one musician then the next picked up the tune. She tried to take pleasure from it, but her gaze kept returning to Michael.

It was no hard thing to spot him now that the crowd had settled. Though people were tight up to each other all the way down the bar, there was a telling gap around him. Even Evie had wandered off somewhere. From her vantage point at an angle from him, Kylie watched as he used the broad mirror to observe the activity around him. A whisper of sorrow touched her soul at the lonely sight.

Her attention briefly slid back to the musicians. Showing all the concentration of a virtuoso, Breege played a brisk rhythm with a pair of spoons. The music grew more raucous, and even the patrons at the bar turned around to give an ear. All except Michael, Kylie noticed. He still watched through the mirror.

Gerry Flynn nudged in next to him. When Michael recognized him, he tucked his elbows into his sides and closed himself off, staring down at the ashtray in front of him. Kylie watched as Flynn did the talking, a nasty sneer shaping his lips. Music and laughter prevented her from hearing what Flynn was saying to Michael, yet she knew it was no warm welcome.

Flynn glanced around surreptitiously, then with one quick brush of his arm, he sent the ashtray and glassware in front of Michael flying across the bar. The music straggled off at the sound of shattering glass and raised voices.

Incredulous, Kylie watched as Flynn shoved Michael off his stool and sent him sprawling onto the floor. Rory O'Connor rounded the bar and stood over the two of them. Kylie pushed through the crowd with a strength she didn't know she had.

"I've got him, Rory," Flynn called up from the floor. Michael lay face down, his arm twisted back and upward at a horrible angle and Flynn's knee digging in the middle of his back. "I've no idea what got into the stupid bastard."

Michael didn't struggle at all. He lay there, passive and silent. Rory nudged Michael with his foot. "You'll be leaving now, and not coming back."

Kylie looked frantically at the circle of faces around her. Surely she wasn't the only one who'd seen what Flynn had done. Surely someone would step in. Someone else, please God. But almost to a person, they watched the action on the floor with avid and amused interest. All except Vi Kilbride, who gazed at her with a look of calm expectation.

"Tell them what you know," her green eyes seemed to say. *"Stand up for the man."*

But she couldn't. She didn't dare. Standing up for Michael Kilbride would be branding Gerry Flynn—a representative of the law, for God's sake—a liar. And it would be attaching her name to Kilbride's. Pub-brawlers—even those who rescued the occasional child—weren't the sort of men welcome in the conservative fold of Gaelscoil Pearse. She'd fought so hard for her job, her little corner of this world, and she wouldn't risk it now.

Kylie turned and pushed through the crowd.

Chapter Six

A Kerry shower is of twenty-four hours.
—IRISH PROVERB

The rain had slowed, and fog hung thick and silvery in the air. Shaken and still feeling lost in her own land, Kylie drove from town. With Vi Kilbride's disappointed gaze heavy on her, leaving the pub had seemed to take an eternity. She'd had to stop and be certain that Breege's friend Edna could get her home later in the evening. Breege's reassuring words that the pub wasn't usually visited by troublemakers, such as the man Gerry had tossed out, only deepened Kylie's remorse.

She had betrayed Michael Kilbride tonight, and if faced with the same choice, she'd do it again. Weak, she was. Weak and selfish, all over a job she couldn't afford to lose and a reputation she'd sacrificed everything to salvage.

Dazed, with forbidden tears blurring her vision, she navigated a sharp bend in the road. Suddenly a tall figure loomed a heartbeat ahead. With a panicked cry she swerved hard to the right, waiting for the sickening thump she knew was to come. It never did, though. The little car spun on the slick road, skittered sideways, and stalled out. Other than the rasp of her own terrified panting, she heard only silence. Her mouth dry and coppery-tasting with fear, Kylie rested her forehead against the steering wheel and willed her stomach to stop lurching.

A sharp rapping sounded beside her head. "Are you all right?"

She lifted her head and stared incredulously at the face on the other side of the glass. He had a grand way of putting himself in harm's path, this man. For one incredibly lucid moment thoughts of fate and impossible coincidence whirled through Kylie's head. Then the heat of anger settled over her.

Set on giving Michael Kilbride the sharp edge of her tongue, she grabbed the window crank and wrenched it downward. The knob came off in her shaking hand and for an instant she stared at it, nonplussed. Then riding the crest of the adrenaline wave that follows any truly dreadful event, she sprang to action.

At least the door handle still worked, she thought with a sense of triumph as she flung herself from the car. "What were you thinking? Do you have no common sense, or is it some sort of mad death wish?" She clenched the thick weave of his sweater in two fists and shook him, though she seemed to be the only one moving for the effort. "Walking down the middle of the road like that, I could have killed you, you big, bloody fool!"

"But you didn't," he said closing his hands over hers. His touch was strangely calming, considering he was the one who'd put the fright into her in the first place. "You didn't," he repeated. "There's not a scratch on me. In fact, all things considered, I seem to be doing a far sight better than you are at the moment." He untangled her fingers from his sweater and gave her hands one last gentle squeeze. "Now let's get your car set right on the road before some real damage is done tonight."

As his words sunk in, guilt consumed Kylie's anger. The real damage had been done back at O'Connor's, well before she'd almost mowed him down. The tears that had been forgotten with the scare fought their way loose. She held one knotted fist in front of her mouth and spun away from him.

"Kylie?"

Slipping back into her car, she slammed the door without answering. She wanted to be home, to have this wretched night at an end. Fumbling with her keys, she tried to restart the engine, but it wouldn't even turn over.

"Hurry . . . come on," she urged.

The car door opened, letting in the bite of the wind and Michael's low voice. "Kylie?"

She stared forward into the fog, wishing herself anyplace but here. Broad, strong fingers stroked the side of her face.

"You're crying," he said, surprise in his voice as his palm cupped her wet cheek. "Out." With a firm yet gentle hand he ushered her out of the car and around to the passenger side.

"I'll be doing the driving," he added before closing her door.

Overwhelmed, defeated, and knowing that the night hadn't reached its end, Kylie slumped low in her seat. Michael closed his door and after muttering, "Still in gear," started the car and turned them back around.

On the drive home Kylie fervently wished for a handkerchief. Unwanted tears slipped silently down her cheeks, but the sniffling she couldn't quiet. Outside, the rain picked up again.

"Would it help to tell me why you're crying?" Michael asked.

It was tempting but very wrong to seek solace from her victim. "N-no," she answered in a hoarse voice. "I'll be fine in a . . . in a minute."

Kylie caught the movement of his head as he looked her way. "Sure you will."

"I don't do this often, cry like this," she offered as they pulled up beside her house. "And I don't do it very well."

She heard him mumble something about her sounding like no amateur at crying, either. He switched off the car and came around to open her door, leaving her touched by this bit of gallantry she hadn't seen practiced in aeons.

For an awkward moment they stood looking at each other in the pelting rain. "Well, I'll be leaving," he said at the same time she began to thank him for seeing her safe home. They both straggled to a stop, Kylie realizing that he now had several miles more to walk in the dark of a wet night.

"I'll run you back to town," she said.

"Hold out your hands."

"What?"

"Both of them. In front of you, like this." He held out his own steady hands to show her.

Kylie copied the action, but hers trembled like a sapling's leaves in a strong wind. She quickly tucked them behind her back.

"I'd be safer standing in front of your car again."

True, unfortunately. And she knew there was only one thing to be done for it, even if it did step outside the bounds of respectability for the local maiden schoolteacher. She took solace from the fact that, other than Breege, her closest neighbor was over a mile off.

Tipping her face skyward, she said, "You can't be walking home in this. Come inside, you can sleep on the couch. I'll run you back to your sister's early in the morning—before I go to work."

He shifted uncomfortably, whether from the rain or her suggestion, Kylie wasn't sure. "I can't be staying here. It's not right."

"And you can't be walking home, either." She refused to add being the cause of a case of pneumonia to her night's sins. When he stubbornly refused to follow her to the front door, she added, "Please, Michael. I'm out of strength to argue with you. Besides, no one will know but us."

"Famous last words," he muttered.

She stepped into the house. Her mouth curved into a fleeting smile as she watched him look about for spying eyes before following her. Once they were both inside, for want of anything else to calm her suddenly dancing nerves, Kylie started a kettle on the stove. Michael had slipped off his shoes at the door and laid his soggy sweater over the back of a kitchen chair. His timeworn U2 tee shirt was blotched dark with rain.

She frowned. "I've a few of my father's clothes stored away. He's not quite your size, but they should do."

Before he could answer, she hurried to her bedroom. There she unearthed a shirt and pants out of the back of her large wardrobe. She shook out the trousers and gave them an assessing look. Too short to be sure, but Michael was a fit man and Johnny liked his food, so there should be room enough, anyway. She grabbed an extra blanket and pillow, then returned to her guest.

"Thank you," he said, accepting the bundle. "You've been kind. One of the few tonight who have."

Kylie flinched at the unintended sting of his words. Stronger than ever, the need to confess was on her. Faced with either hurting him or being dishonest, she retreated. "I'll be taking care of myself now," she said, waving one hand at her wet hair and clothes. "Have an eye to the kettle, if you could."

The sounds of comfort, Michael thought as the kettle's whistle gained his attention. Before that, it had been the music of running water as Kylie showered—just one rickety door sagging loose on its hinges between them. A feast for a starved imagination, the woman on the other side of that door. The imagination and nothing more, he reminded himself. He was beginning to sense his place in this town; it looked to be nose down on the barroom floor, and not at Kylie O'Shea's side.

By the time he heard the rusty protest of the shower valves being closed, he'd put together a pot of tea and found a couple of scones to add to the feast he could have.

Sitting on the edge of the spring-shot sofa that was to be his bed, Michael waited for Kylie to reappear. His left shoulder still pounded from Flynn's rough treatment, and his head was beginning to feel the aching effects of the whiskey he'd drunk. One hell of a day it had been, he thought as he absently scrubbed his hand over his eyes.

When he brought his hand away, she was standing there. Slender bare feet peeked out from beneath a white nightgown covered by a too short blue velvet robe. Though it had seen wear, it looked to have been one fine garment in its day. Michael pictured a fifteen-year-old Kylie opening a gift box wrapped in beautiful paper while her loving parents looked on. Sitting in front of a grand marble fireplace they would have been, all rich and cozy, no worries at all.

But no, he thought, shaking off the dream, that was his wish for her. Of the reality, he knew little— just that her father was a cheat, and she now lived poorer than he'd ever imagined a schoolteacher doing. He glanced up at her face, kissed pink from the heat of the shower or perhaps the intimacy of the moment.

"Tea?" he asked, then at her nod leaned forward to the low table in front of the couch to pour out a cup. "I've borrowed your father's shirt," he said, "but the trousers didn't fit."

She perched next to him on the couch. The scents of soap and clean, flowery shampoo wafted his way.

"There's something I need to tell you," she said, her words rushed and anxious.

Michael briefly tried to imagine what sort of confession could come from a woman who looked so pure and perfect, her damp hair pulled back into a schoolgirl's thick braid.

She looked down at her hands clenched together in her lap. "I saw tonight. I saw what Gerry Flynn did to you, blaming you like that, and I did nothing."

He paused, swallowing this bit of information. He'd rather she thought him a brawler than weak. And he'd die before accepting her pity.

"I should have done something, stopped him somehow," she said.

He tried for a light tone. "Just what would you have done, collared him and dragged him to the door with him twice your size?"

"No," she answered fiercely. "I should have defended you, told Rory O'Connor what Gerry did." Her chin went out a notch. "I'll do that. I'll tell Rory tomorrow."

"You'll not," he said, working to control his embarrassment and anger. Anger at his circumstances, not at Kylie. Never that. He took one of her hands in his, tracing her delicate bones. "This is my matter to settle, and in my own way."

"That's the thing of it . . . It's not just your matter. Gerry went after you because of me," she said, holding one hand to her heart. "I feel terrible for having drawn you into this. He's had this—this obsession with me for years. When he turned on you I should have stopped him, but I was too afraid of what the others might think of me. It was selfish, and I'm sorry."

She hadn't cornered the market on selfish. Michael kept silent about Flynn's other motives for giving him a hard time. "You're worrying yourself over nothing, a bad moment and no more. I don't want you to defend me, Kylie. I don't care what they think." He paused, looking at the beauty before him. "But you, has no one ever stood as your hero? Has no one defended you?"

Her blue eyes went wide and dark, and a sheen of moisture came over them. He could have drowned in her softness.

"I—" She started to speak, then trailed off as she looked down at his hand still wrapped around hers. "There are no real heroes anymore," she said in a near whisper.

"Do you believe that? Really?"

She nodded, her eyes meeting his. "I do. It's easier that way."

The heart that he was sure had hardened till it

was impervious to pain clenched tight within his chest. Releasing her hand, he cupped her face between his palms. *I want to be your hero*. If he could say those words, it would be the greatest truth he'd ever spoken. It would also be the greatest impossibility.

But he could kiss away the hurt and sorrow. He brushed his mouth once, twice, gently against her full lips, closing his eyes with the intoxication of touching her, feeling his heart ease with her indrawn breath of surprise and pleasure. He'd lied to himself, he thought, as he moved to linger against her. This kiss was for him.

At the shrill ringing of a telephone he pulled back with a guilty start. Kylie moved away, nervously smoothing the folds of her robe. She answered the phone, a bright blush staining her face as she spoke to the caller.

"For you," she said, holding the phone out to him.

He could think of only one soul who'd know to look for him here. And only one soul who cared enough to call, too.

"Hello, Vi," he said with wry resignation.

"You might have thought of ringing me up and telling me you were safe, after the way you left the pub."

"So much for giving me some room."

"I've been worried, that's all. You're safe now, and I'll let you be."

Michael relaxed; it appeared he was to be spared prods at his conscience.

"She's a pretty thing, though, isn't she?" Vi added

in a bright tone. "Innocent as a child, I'm thinking."

His laugh was deep and wholly involuntary. "Very subtle, Sis, very subtle."

She laughed in return. "Subtlety is of no use where you're concerned. But a mallet to the head is."

"No blows to the head are needed. You can consider the message received," he said, glancing over at Kylie, who sat on the couch desperately trying to look as though she couldn't hear his end of the conversation.

"Good. Now stop by the studio in the morning. Word about what happened in O'Connor's tonight is traveling fast," she said in a troubled voice. "We need to talk, to decide what to do."

Michael knew what he intended to do: nothing at all. After all, the tongues couldn't be unwagged once they'd started. He said a quick good night to his sister, then rejoined Kylie.

Even when he sat next to her, she kept her eyes downcast. He hated the distance that had grown between them. The weight of the night was too heavy to be ignored, their private time gone. He wanted it back, that quiet intimacy, the feeling that they could push away the rest of the world. They couldn't, though.

"Well then," Kylie said, "you know you've never exactly mentioned your line of work. If you settle in Ballymuir, will you be able to pick it up again?"

What she asked was harmless, the sort of chat one might use to fill an empty moment. Except in his case, any details would only beg questions he didn't want to answer.

"It should be no problem," he said, then offered nothing more.

"I see."

Searching for some part of himself that he could safely give her, he settled on family. "Do you have any brothers or sisters?"

"None," she replied.

"Then let me tell you about Vi." Michael knew of no topic better to remove the uneasiness that hung over them like a somber gray pall.

"When I was young, Vi was my very best friend," he began, then launched into stories of the marvelous days they'd had at their nan's, and the mischief they'd made at home.

After a time Kylie relaxed, laughing when he told how their one attempt at shearing a sheep had resulted in Vi's being clipped instead. In time, she eased into sleep, and her head rested against the plane of his shoulder. He held her, and wondered that such a simple intimacy between a man and woman could mean so much.

He'd have spent the night there, holding her, feeling the softness of her hair against his cheek, except that he worried for her comfort. She was a light thing, he thought, after he'd stood and scooped her into his arms.

Though he felt like an intruder, he used his elbow to push open her bedroom door the rest of the way and carry her inside. A small lamp glowed on a nightstand beside what had to be the most incredible bed he'd ever seen. He shook his head in amazement as he took it in, all fanciful carved mahogany and lush draped curtains. This was a fairy princess's bed, and worth more than the rest of her tattered belongings put together.

"When you're awake you might not believe in heroes," he murmured to the slip of a woman asleep in his arms, "but I'm thinking you still dream of them."

Chapter Seven

May our enemy not hear.
—IRISH PROVERB

⚭orning had begun with a call from Mam. In Vi's book that was a portent only slightly less dismal than finding a grackle perched outside her front door. And unlike the bird, she couldn't just shoo Mam away.

Nothing said in a straightforward way, that was Mam, Vi thought as she finished the last of her morning tea and considered—then rejected—the idea of washing up the dishes. Mam and her cowardly talk of "not being able to mend the mistakes of the past" and "understanding what's important now."

It infuriated Vi, seeing Michael cast aside. Infuriated her, and made her doubly determined to help him regain family and friends. It seemed family would take care of themselves. The twins were already chomping at the bit to come visit, and Mam was having a holy seizure at the idea. Two Bus Eireann tickets in the post just might be enough to send her over the edge, Vi thought with a fiendish chuckle.

That left friends. She considered young Kylie O'Shea, smiling that she'd immediately appended *young* to her name, when the woman was not so far from her own age. Bending to fill Roger's dish with more kibble for him to bolt, Vi wondered how far the friendship between her brother and the school-teacher had progressed. And she hoped to God that Kylie O'Shea had the strength to hold fast in the teeth of the storm to come.

It had been a dark night at O'Connor's Pub, and Vi could see no prospect for clearing. At least not until the talk and rumors about Michael's past had expired under their own weight. And that could take years. The old folks in town still talked of the 1916 Easter Uprising as if it had happened yesterday, and a reference to the Queen could as easily mean Elizabeth the First as the Second.

And as for the younger people, most of them would prefer that the Troubles and the poor souls like Michael ensnared in them, simply be wiped away. Or chased away, if necessary. Northern political matters, after all, were bad for tourism. And tourism put dinner on the table each night. Oh, things looked bleak, indeed, for her brother.

The impatient jangle of the telephone cut short Vi's thoughts.

"Bloody thing," she said as she walked to it and steeled herself to lift the receiver, "you've already dragged Mam into my day. What have you in store for me now?"

"Hello?" she said, but no one spoke in return. She drew in a breath and tried again, this time in her most imperial fashion. "Kilbride's Asylum for the Artistically Impaired. Which inmate do you seek?"

She caught the low murmur of a man's voice. The sound was muffled, as though his hand was over the receiver and he wasn't speaking to her at all. Even that indistinct noise sent a message. A shiver chased down Vi's spine, and the fine hairs on her arms rose. The line disconnected from the other end. Shaking, she slammed down the phone and turned away.

Moments like this, when she brushed against evil, made her wish she could give back the Kilbride gift of sight. But she couldn't, any more than she could lose her height or her love of color. Vi rubbed her arms to restore some warmth and told herself that the call meant nothing.

"Courage," she admonished.

After giving Roger a few moments to snuffle the last crumbs of his meal, she snapped on his leash and announced, "Off to the studio with us, *a ghrá*. We've work to finish before the distractions begin. They're going to be plenty today."

An idea that Roger relished, judging by the spring in his step. Vi felt mightily less pleased with the thought. Whether it be Mam or grackle, bad tidings were afoot.

• • •

It was a morning for more subtle intimacies, waking and readying for the day in Kylie's tiny home. Michael had lived elbow-to-elbow before, but there had been no closeness to it, only a maddening lack of privacy. This was different; he liked it—too much, in fact. It made him think of waking with Kylie in that dreamer's bed, and of staying there until the day had slipped into night. Dangerous emotions, those were, and becoming harder to ignore.

After a breakfast filled with talk and laughter, he helped her pile an armful of bundles into the boot of her car. When he asked her about them, she fluttered off some embarrassed answer about things she no longer needed and help for a family in town.

But they'd just made it back to the main road when she pulled up in front of a cottage. Curious, Michael watched as she hurriedly dropped a bag on the stoop.

"And that was?" he asked when she'd settled back into the car.

"Reading materials." Her cheeks blazed crimson.

He grinned. "What kind of reading materials might they be?"

"Romance novels," she said in a way that just dared him to laugh. "Breege won't buy them for herself—she's too old, she says—but she's not against reading them a dozen times through if they just happen to show up on her doorstep."

Books for a friend named Breege, bundles for people in town. And she lived like a pauper. "I don't think you need look further than your own mirror to find a hero, Kylie O'Shea."

She gave him a startled glance. "I've done nothing out of the ordinary. No more than anyone who wants to be a part of this town would."

He weighed that bit of unintended advice. To his experience, books and bundles didn't open arms that wanted to stay closed. But taking in her shuttered expression, he decided to let the matter rest.

Hungry as always, he asked Kylie to let him off in front of Spillane's Market. With Mr. Spillane peering out the front window, he didn't kiss Kylie, though he sorely wanted to. She looked so smooth and pretty, a schoolboy's—and this grown man's— fantasy. Instead he took a clumsy step toward getting that kiss another time. "If I rang you up sometime, would you . . . that is . . . ah, hell . . ."

The corners of her full mouth began to curve upward. "Are you trying to ask me out?"

He nodded. "I think I might be."

"Well then, when you figure it out for sure, let me know." Her wink was sheer flirtatious promise, making him laugh at his own rusty skills. As he got out of the car she said, "And Michael, I'm sorry for what happened at the pub. I'll be a better friend to you. I promise."

He stood on the curb and watched her pull away. In fact, he watched even after the little car was gone from sight. Moonstruck. He was past thirty and embarrassingly moonstruck.

He turned back to Spillane's, where the grocer still stood in the front of the store. Michael waved a greeting and came to the door, mentally savoring all the food he meant to buy. But Spillane didn't move or acknowledge him with anything more than a flat stare.

"Closed," he mouthed through the thick glass, then turned away.

Michael could feel the darkness gather around him, the anger at knowing this was how things were to be. After last night he'd still hoped he could make some headway before his past rose to claim him. Another dangerous emotion, hope.

He stood at the front door to Spillane's intent on making life no more comfortable for the man on the inside than it was for him, out there. Finally, ten minutes after opening time, Spillane unlocked the front door and hovered nervously by the cash register.

His hunger dull and dead, Michael grabbed the first bit of breakfast food he found and made his way to the grocer. When he reached into his pocket, he saw Spillane flinch. Spitting an obscenity, Michael slapped a few bills on the low counter.

"I've not yet killed a man over a box of cereal," he said, then left without waiting for his change.

Halfway down the block he realized that he had no idea where he was heading. Not that it really mattered. Glancing at the box of sugary cereal clenched in one hand, he turned toward Vi's house. Milk to top his cereal wasn't much of a reason to keep putting one foot in front of the other, but it was all he had.

Half an hour later, showered, dressed, and hungry again, Michael poured himself his third bowl of cereal and dug in his spoon. The problem, he decided, was in his expectations. Somewhere deep inside, he was still waiting for an apology from everyone at that bloody farce of a trial. He was waiting for that bastard Brian Rourke to tell the truth. For that he'd die waiting, too. They'd set him free, and that was as good as he was going to get. Maybe as good as he deserved.

Michael gave a disgusted scoff, then crunched another shovelful of sweet cereal. Before he had abandoned his faith—or it him—the part he'd rebelled against was the guilt. And it seemed that was all that stayed with him.

And what did he really have for this start on a life? A sister who loved him fiercely, enough money to last a time, and . . .

He chomped through the last of his breakfast, drowning out thoughts of Kylie O'Shea. There was no having her now, not without harming her forever. And wittingly or unwittingly, he'd done harm enough in his years.

After he scrubbed the teetering mountain of dishes in the kitchen sink, Michael made his way back to town. Recalling his sister's words about help being wanted at the hardware, he stopped there first.

The store owner—tall, skinny as a walking stick—looked familiar, probably one of the men Vi had introduced him to after church the other day. His expression looked familiar, too. It was the same blank stare he'd gotten from Spillane.

A sick feeling curdled in Michael's gut. He turned down one of the narrow, cluttered aisles. Take the worst chin up, his nan had always said. And that was what he intended to do. As an excuse to be there, he grabbed the clamps, wood glue, and sandpaper he'd need to start on Vi's apothecary's chest.

After paying, Michael said, "I saw the sign in the window, and was wondering—"

"Not hiring."

"But the sign says—"

The man walked to the window, pulled out the sign, and tucked it under the counter. "Not hiring."

Michael nodded his head toward the sign's hiding spot. "And when I walk out?"

"After that, I might be hiring."

Nan had her favorite curse, too: *Go hifreann leat*— the hell with you. In her honor Michael used it, and got a harsher one in return. There was no mistaking the direction of the wind that blew through town. Pure northerly and icy cold.

"Just what are they saying about me?"

Michael's sister looked up from her work. "I didn't stay long enough last night to hear all the particulars," Vi answered slowly. "And I'm sure even those have been well embellished by now. Where have you been?"

He slapped his bag onto the edge of her worktable, making a framed bit of painted silk rattle and dance. From beneath, Roger growled in warning. Michael gave a narrow-eyed snarl of his own. "I've been trying to find food and work. Spillane all but slammed the door in my face, and at the hardware—"

She raised a hand. "I don't need to hear about the hardware. Clancy, the owner, was at the pub last night, his mouth flying faster than any but Flynn's after you, ah, left. Incredible tales that Flynn was weaving, based on the few spoken loud enough for me to overhear." Riffling through the contents of the sack she commented, "I'm surprised Clancy took your money."

"It'll be the last time I offer it to him."

"Then consider yourself blessed that there's another hardware one town over," she said, flashing a quick grin before her face grew serious again. "But why don't you just tell people the truth of your past?"

He dragged a hand through his hair. "What am I to do, call everyone for a meeting in the village hall? Or post flyers on every corner? What good will it do? They won't believe me, not a one of them!"

"Not even Kylie O'Shea?"

Would she? And could he bear to see her face when she learned what kind of man he was?

"Kylie's not a part of this, and none of your concern!"

Vi pushed back from her stool and came around the table to face him. "Whether you want to hear from me or not, anything that has to do with you is my concern! I love you and want to stand by you. You're not making it easy, though. What are you going to do now, pack up your things and move on?"

"No." He drew a deep breath, then repeated a weary, "No. It really doesn't matter where I move. I'm smart enough to know that I can't outrun this. Even here, all this distance from the North . . . " He gave an ineloquent shrug, nowhere near enough to express his anger and frustration.

She brushed a tender touch against his arm. Her love and empathy humbled him. "Give it time."

Time was one thing he knew about. Wasted time.

"And until things settle, I'm hoping you're smart enough to defend yourself, too. Or at least not to plant yourself in the thick of it."

"I know my place. I'll stay on the outside, where I belong." And where he wanted to be, too. Screw the lot of them, he thought.

"Outside," Vi murmured, tapping one blunt-cut fingernail to the side of her jaw. "Hmmm . . ." Michael didn't like the speculative gleam in her eyes, not one bit. She gestured to a newspaper article taped to the wall not far from the antique cash register. "Have you seen this?"

He gave an amused grunt that she'd ask whether he'd noticed one yellowed clipping in this broad stroke of color. "Missed it."

"Take a careful look. You'll be going there this afternoon. Remember Jenna Fahey from out front of the church?"

He did, but knew better than to step enthusiastically into one of his sister's schemes. "Maybe."

"She's a chef—runs Muir House, a fine new restaurant."

Now that gained his interest. Michael walked over to the article, skimming it while half-listening to his sister. An undiscovered gem run by a dynamic young American, the article said.

"She's needing a bit of help."

"I can't do much more than boil water."

He glanced up to see his sister pacing the room. "She'd not let you into her kitchen, anyway," Vi said. "But she needs a carpenter. The bloody house is falling down around her ears."

Food aplenty and carpentry to be done. Also enough to keep putting one foot in front of the other, Michael thought. Enough for now, at least.

"Stop out to Muir House this afternoon," Vi said. "I'll tell Jenna you're coming. Oh, and straightaway you need to see Padraig, the silversmith two doors down. He has a car he's looking to sell. But go easy on him for price. He's got no head for business."

Turning heel, Michael escaped before more orders could be thrown his way. He'd swallowed quite enough for one day.

Gazing longingly at the imported tomatoes—too dear when out of season—Kylie didn't even see Evie Nolan approaching her in the narrow aisle of Spillane's. And if she had, Kylie thought as Evie sidled closer, she'd have run screaming from the store.

Evie flashed sharp teeth in what Kylie supposed was to be taken as a friendly smile. She took it more as being sized up for the kill. From that long-ago day Kylie had arrived in town, a lonely thirteen-year-old who'd just lost her mother, Evie had tormented her. And taken pleasure from it, too.

"Near miss we both had last night, wasn't it?" Evie said in a chipper voice, tugging the vee of her dress back into the range of merely slatternly.

Patience, Kylie schooled herself. Patience and kindness, even if it bloody well killed her. "What are you talking about?"

"You know—that Michael Kilbride. It surprised me at first hearing about him, but then I got to thinking about that sister of his. She's always been an odd one, too, with those clothes she wears and that trash she makes. Sometimes a whole family just runs bad, if you know what I mean." Her eyes widened with feigned embarrassment. "Not that I'm saying anything about yours, of course."

"Of course," Kylie echoed with precisely the same amount of sincerity. "Now what is it you're trying to tell me about Michael Kilbride, or am I to guess?"

"You don't know? Left early last night, did you? It was all over O'Connor's." She leaned closer as if about to tell a secret, but raised her voice. "That Kilbride's an escaped prisoner. From the North," she added in dire tones.

Kylie just barely stopped from rolling her eyes. "Evie, did you see Gerry Flynn in the pub last night?"

"Yeah."

"He's with the Gardai, isn't he?"

"Of course he is," Evie snapped. "But what has that to do with Kilbride?"

"If Michael were truly escaped from the North, don't you think Flynn might have detained him?"

"Oh." Kylie bit back a smile as she watched the air go out of the overpainted Miss Nolan. But malice had always sprung eternal in Evie's heart. "Perhaps Gerry's just waiting for some help. They say Kilbride's a dangerous man—blew up an army barracks outside of Derry, with plenty killed."

Mr. Spillane came around the laundry soap to stand by them. "I heard it was a pub in Belfast."

"Could it be both, do you think?" Evie asked, sounding far closer to aroused than repelled.

Kylie kept her voice level. It wasn't easy, not with her heart grinding to a stop and her stomach churning. Talk came loose and free, but not without some seed of truth. "Knowing how word grows in this town, I'd say he once crossed a street against the light."

"But Flynn was telling everyone—" Mr. Spillane began.

Kylie could take no more. "The same Flynn who didn't arrest him?"

Mr. Spillane gave her a paternal pat on the shoulder. Ironic, since that wasn't quite the same kindly attitude he'd shown when he'd demanded that she pay back the thousands he'd invested in her father's scheme.

"Now Kylie, with your da in prison and all, I'm thinking that you need some guidance, so I'll say what Johnny would if he'd seen you this morning. Michael Kilbride is a bad man, not at all the one for you. But that young Gerry Flynn has been sweet on you for as long as I can remember. And just the other day, Breege Flaherty was saying how she's worried you'll be the last bride in Ballymuir. Gerry's the sort you need, and you should be starting a family soon, the way you love the young ones."

It hurt to smile when all she really wanted to do

was stamp her foot down on his scuffed black shoe as hard as she could.

"Thank you for your concern, Mr. Spillane, but Michael Kilbride is just an acquaintance." She glanced at her watch and feigned surprise. "Oh, my, look at the time. I'd promised to run Breege home ages ago." She made good on her escape.

Evie, of course, was hot on her heels. They'd both just reached the sidewalk when she started in. "So you were with Kilbride this morning? Must have been early, what with the time you start work."

Kylie drew to a halt. Lying to Evie Nolan didn't seem such a big sin. "I saw him on the road to town, and offered him a lift. If that's all right by you!"

"From out your way? Strange, since his sister lives in the other direction." She paused, rubbing her hands up and down plump arms. "I wonder what he might have been doing?"

"I drove the man to town, Evie, I didn't interrogate him!"

"Maybe you should have. But then maybe you know him better than you're letting on. Much better."

Kylie resorted to the last bit of protection she owned: her saintly image in town. "Do I look the sort of woman to take up with a man like Michael Kilbride? Putting aside these absurd stories of yours, would a man of his looks waste a moment on a schoolteacher like me?"

Evie assessed her with knowing eyes. "It seems to me you might be exactly his type. He was friendly enough with you in the pub last night."

"And with you," Kylie shot back. "You should be

more concerned with preserving your own reputation. Such as it is," she added, wincing as the costly words escaped.

Evie let out a long hiss, turned heel, and left. Standing on the empty walk, Kylie knew she would pay dearly for this.

Kindness and patience. Was it such a lot to ask of herself, and of this town?

She was beginning to think it was.

Chapter Eight

Taste it and you will get a desire for it.
—IRISH PROVERB

It wasn't bad, going back to life as it had been before Michael Kilbride came blazing over the horizon, Kylie decided; it was bloody awful. Three weeks, and she'd not heard a word from him. Three weeks, and she was ready to do the unthinkable and hunt him down—her reputation be damned. And it would be, based on the whispers and worse in town.

Just yesterday she'd caught Mr. Clancy from the hardware store ripping down the flyers Michael had posted on the lightposts around town, offering handyman services. When she'd asked him what he was doing, he'd said he was keeping the place tidy. He hadn't been very pleased when she'd pointed out that he'd left plenty of flyers from other people behind. According to Mr. Clancy, thieving, murderous bastards deserved no home in Ballymuir.

Even if she taught at a school less stringent than Gaelscoil Pearse, she'd still be risking a lot to associate with a reputed killer.

Kylie sighed and continued polishing her tiny bit of kitchen counter with a towel. As she realized what she was doing, her mouth crooked into a half-humorous smile. Cleaning had become her Saturday ritual, and the house was already as orderly as a nun's quarters. Her life, too. Orderly and dull. Before, that had been the way she wanted it. Dullness had been an antidote for the horrible part of her life when she'd felt too much, and hurt too much.

Now, though, she knew at least part of what she was missing. The heart-stopping whirl of nerves and excitement that the sight of Michael brought was indelibly imprinted upon her soul. And the rest—to know what it would feel like to have her limbs tangled with his—God help her, as frightening as she found the idea, she was beginning to think about that, too. What she didn't know was whether he thought of her at all.

With a wordless sound of self-reproach, she tossed aside the towel and began to pace in front of her cold hearth. Pride and that damned caution, they kept her from calling him, kept her from asking his sister about him. They didn't keep her from sleepless nights, though, or from making a futile search of the crowd at Mass each Sunday.

It was as if Michael had been erased from every-place but her thoughts. There, and in the town's wild stories of murder and mayhem. For all the tales, each more blood-curdling than the last, she couldn't forget him, or believe he was evil. Those few souls she felt sure enough about to ask a few discreet questions had known nothing of his past. And the night he'd slept on her couch, he'd been willing enough to talk about his childhood with Vi, but had said nothing of his adult years.

She couldn't forget him, but it seemed he had forgotten her. So she would learn to let go, and accept it again, this dull life of hers. And she would be thankful for what she had.

Grasping for a bit of inspiration, she settled on the empty time she now had to finish righting her father's wrongs. That was the true sting of Mr. Spillane's demand for repayment; she would have done it anyway. The ledger would never be wiped clean, but she would be satisfied that she'd accomplished what she could. Over five years Johnny had been gone, and too soon he'd be a free man.

Free to return and foul her life again.

Kylie repressed a shudder. Father Cready once told her that God never gave more troubles than a soul could bear. In this instance she sincerely hoped the Divine Being might reconsider the nature of her burdens and give Johnny an overwhelming longing to live in Sligo, or better yet, even further north in Donegal.

She'd fought hard for her tentative place in Ballymuir—sometimes more tolerated than embraced.

If that was all she was to have, she'd cling to it till the bitter end.

The phone rang, the sound as startling to Kylie as if a flock of tropical birds had perched outside and begun to chatter. Pausing a moment to smooth her hair, then shaking her head at the odd impulse, she lifted the receiver.

"Hello?"

"Kylie, Vi Kilbride here. It's time we met on our arts project." All business Vi was, brisk and chilly as a hard wind curling off the mountains.

"That would be fine. Your gallery today?"

"No, I've appointments elsewhere. Meet me at Muir House for tea this afternoon. Do you know where the place is?"

"The one run by the American girl—out Slea Head Road," Kylie answered automatically, still half-waiting for a "please" or other evidence of courtesy from Vi. Not that she deserved it. Vi saw her for what she had been that night at the pub—a coward.

"Muir House then," Vi said before hanging up.

"Well, the food should be good even if the company will need some warming," Kylie replied to no one at all.

Just after four, Kylie pulled down the narrow lane to Muir House. Even on a dreary afternoon, the house was a dignified, if down-at-the-heels, sight. Noting that there were only three other cars, Kylie pulled into the gravel lot and parked.

She gingerly walked the rain-slick path, then climbed the steps to the front door. She was about to pull it open when she saw the small placard bearing

Muir House's hours. Saturday tea in the last days of February wasn't among them. That, at least, accounted for the slow business. She paused, wondering whether Vi Kilbride had sent her on a fool's errand, or if perhaps she'd misheard her. Not that there was much chance of mistaking Vi's bluntly issued orders.

Working up her courage, Kylie pushed the buzzer. Nothing happened. She tapped the button more heavily. Still nothing.

"Broken," she murmured, and somehow wasn't surprised. She reached up for the large cast-bronze door knocker. Enough to wake the dead, that was.

Nose pressed to the glass beside the door, she watched as booted feet came down the sweeping staircase and a man rounded into view. Her breath came out in a sharp puff of shock, delight, and sheer nerves as she realized that Michael Kilbride had trapped her in his deep-green gaze.

The door swung open.

Only a man like Michael Kilbride wouldn't look out of place wearing faded work clothes in the midst of the rich wood-paneled walls and faded splendor of the front hall. She knew a moment's urge to fling herself into his arms.

"So you've taken a job as butler?" she asked, was rewarded by a slight twitch of the mouth she chose to take for a smile.

"I'm here to meet your sister. . . . Vi," she added when he said nothing.

The corners of his mouth turned upward into a real smile. "I've only one sister."

Kylie fought for composure instead of blurting out how bloody much she'd missed him. "Tea, we were to meet for tea."

"I haven't seen her." He gave a disgusted snort. "No doubt she got caught up in one of her projects. Probably off counting the scales on fairy wings or some other such nonsense." He looked at her, and the warmth of his expression kindled a fire deep inside her.

"Perhaps I could step in and wait," she suggested.

"Of course," he said with a slight wince at his bad manners. "I'm sorry to leave you standing here." Then he moved scarcely enough to let her through. It took only the brush of her woolen coat against his side to send a tingle chasing to her fingertips.

Michael closed the door. "You're looking well . . . beautiful, in fact."

"Thank you." If she weren't so utterly thrilled by his compliment, she would have been laughing at the way they were dancing so carefully around one another. Perhaps if they focused on something other than themselves, they'd make it out of the front hallway.

Kylie looked around. "It smells glorious in here," she said with an appreciative sniff. "Almost as I'd imagined it, clean and full of spices simmering, and—" She trailed off at his bemused look.

"You'd imagined how the place *smelled?*"

"I do that," she murmured while she busied herself with her coat's fat buttons. "Don't you?"

Gesturing at the ridge of an old break running across the bridge of his nose, he said, "I've been spoiled for that sort of thing." He brushed at some dust clinging to his sleeves. "Well, you smell the spices because the owner's at work in the kitchen. Never leaves the place. She probably won't even notice when the rest of it falls down around her."

As he spoke, Michael turned and started down a wide hallway. Not knowing what else to do, she followed. "And the clean," he said over his shoulder, "that goes only as far as the restorations. You'd be smelling something else entirely on the second floor."

"Restorations—is that why you're here?"

"Well, it's not to cook." He stepped into a library filled with volumes of books and framed photographs. "You can wait here. I'll have a word with Jenna and see if she's heard anything from that fly-about sister of mine."

After Michael left, Kylie dropped her coat over the back of a chair, then settled onto a couch by the fireplace, where peat glowed orange and red and smelled like the comfort of home. Not any home she'd ever had, though. Certainly her father's opulent tribute to poor taste—sold off to satisfy bilked investors—hadn't been this welcoming.

Not letting herself consider the coincidence—or plan—that had landed her in the same house as Michael Kilbride, she gazed at the fire, feeling her lids grow heavy and her mind calm.

"Vi rang Jenna just a few minutes ago and asked that she make you at home." Michael's voice closed in on her as he drew near. She glanced up to see him holding a tray. "She wanted me to bring you tea. She's busy wrestling with some grand, puffy affair."

"A soufflé," Kylie provided.

"You know about them?"

"Enough not to try to make one." She laughed at his poorly hidden look of relief. Tugging a low table closer to the couch, she motioned for him to set the tray down. "Do you think you could join me for a while? We've left matters, er, open between us." She could feel her color rising as she spoke, but it was too tempting, having him here, not to ask.

"I suppose we have." He sat on the edge of the sofa and somehow managed not to look ridiculous though he was far too tall for the low, old-fashioned piece.

"You haven't been around town," she began.

"No, but I'm sure the stories have."

"I want to ask you something, and since I'm really little more than a stranger to you, you've every right to turn me down." She gathered her courage. "Will you tell me about yourself, where you were just before you came to Ballymuir? In town, they say that you've done everything but cast spells to make the sheep barren. And that I'm expecting to hear no later than next week."

Silent, he stared down at his hands—an artist's hands, Kylie thought, for all their rough skin, nicks, and scars. She shook off the fanciful image. It was Vi who was the artist. And Michael, she had no idea at all what he might be. Farmer. Businessman. Lover. Killer.

"It's not something to tell over tea," he said.

The need to know who he was, and what he had been, was as basic and insistent as the need to breathe. "Then tomorrow after Mass. I'll meet you out front of the church and we can—"

"I won't be attending."

Kylie leaned back against the sofa's soft cushions. "I see. I've asked too much, haven't I?"

"I'd guess in your entire life you've asked for too little. And now you start asking, here . . . with me." He gave a weary shake of his head. "I don't have the heart to turn you down, Kylie O'Shea. One 'please,' one look from those beautiful eyes of yours and I'm a lost man. I'll come to your house tomorrow evening, if you'll have me, and tell you then."

"Tomorrow?"

He nodded. "And when I'm through talking, I'll leave it to you to decide if you want to see me again."

A moment passed before Kylie found what was implicit in his words. "So you want to see me?"

He seemed to speak almost unwillingly. "I've tried not to, but I can't seem to turn away. It's wrong of me, though."

"And why is it wrong?"

"You deserve better."

"Really? How would you know what I deserve?"

"It's not so much knowing that, as it's knowing myself. And you should be more careful in your choices. I'm not the sort to take home to Mam and Da."

She'd been through too much in her years to tolerate being spoken to like a child. "Since my father's hardly available for visits, and my mother died some years ago, I'll not be worrying about that. And I'm growing very weary of being preached to. I know my own mind, and I know what I want."

In the face of her anger, his mouth curved into a full, honest smile. "And what is it you're wanting right now?"

"To take you by that ragged shirt of yours and shake you," she answered, actually enjoying this opportunity to let her emotions run free. "Though it would do me no good at all, with the size of you."

He looked her up and down, sending another type of primal tingle through her. Taking one hand, he uncurled her fingers and measured them against his own much larger hand. "I might have the edge on size, but you seem to have me beat in determination. I'd not bet against you in a fight."

Slowly, lazily, he rubbed his thumb in the middle of her open palm. As he lingered, she could feel her eyes grow wider, rounder, and the breath leave her body. "In fact, I'm sure I'd soon be begging for your mercy."

She came closer, her free hand drifting of its own volition to touch his dark, thick hair.

"I'll tell you what I want," he said, his voice low and raspy. "I want to kiss you again."

His lips brushed her palm. "And I don't mean one of those, but a real kiss."

She swallowed hard.

"I'm out of my bloody mind with wanting, but that kiss—the real kiss—won't happen until we've had our talk. And then if you still want me . . ."

"I— I—" was all she could seem to manage to get out.

"Hello, Kylie. I see you found some company while you were waiting." At Vi Kilbride's voice sounding from the doorway, Kylie hastily pulled her hand away from Michael's. She scooted over on the couch, the wool of her skirt tugging beneath her.

Michael, on the other hand, sat where he was. "You've been busy today, haven't you, little sister?"

Vi settled herself in a wing chair at an angle to the couch. "I'm a bit late, if that's what you're meaning."

He smiled at his sister, and Kylie marveled at how much younger and more carefree he looked in that instant. "You know well enough what I'm meaning." He stood and nodded at the two of them. "I'll leave you to your tea." To Kylie he added, "Tomorrow, and I'll bring dinner if I might."

Thinking she'd not have been more amazed if he'd offered to take a hand to her mending pile, Kylie murmured her thanks and a good-bye.

After he'd left the room, Vi spoke. "And that's why I asked you here."

Still struggling to gracefully reseat herself, and to get through the delicious haze that spending time with Michael brought, Kylie said, "I'm not following you."

"One smile." Vi put a sugary raisin scone on a plate, then poured herself some tea. "He hasn't smiled in weeks. Oh, he puts on a good show, coming out here and working, then walking his miles. But not one smile until today. You're good for him, Kylie. I should be feeling some guilt for dragging you back into his troubles, but I don't. He's family, and I'll do what I must to see him happy." She paused and took a sip of her tea. "And I think you know that sooner or later you'd have ended up seeing him again."

Kylie didn't argue the point.

"The two of you have far to go, but if you decide to do this, to stand by him, be sure that you stand strong. We both know I saw what happened at the pub that night. To turn your back on him again, it would be beyond cruel."

"I know, and I'll never betray him again."

A shadow, a whisper of some ineffable sadness, passed across Vi's face. "That's a fine promise, and one far more easily made than kept. But I'll be holding you to it."

"No stronger than I'll hold myself," Kylie answered, suddenly feeling cold. So very cold.

Chapter Nine

Two-thirds of foolishness is youth.
— IRISH PROVERB

Michael bolted upright in bed. Clammy with sweat and shaking, he tried to sort dreams from reality. The luminescent hands of the old windup alarm clock next to his bed told him that it wasn't much past two in the morning. His lurching stomach carried the news that he'd been dreaming of *her* again. Dervla.

Switching on the light, he rose from bed and walked to the bathroom sink, where he filled, then quickly drank, a glass of cloudy tap water. He'd had these dreams before. Too often, in fact. In prison he'd awaken, hard with wanting, hating her and hating himself even more for being aroused by the image of the woman who'd destroyed him.

He supposed it was progress of sorts that his dreams were no longer of the touch of her hands against his skin. But having her there at all—still inside his head—God in heaven, how he resented it. She was a ghost now, dead these fourteen years. Couldn't she leave him alone?

After setting the glass back on the shelf above the sink, he turned and made his way back to bed. There, dreams became reality. Instead of finding sleep, Michael found himself eighteen again, sweaty and panting in Dervla McLohne's rumpled bed, trying his best to get the one thing he desired above all else.

"Please, Dervla. Just this once," he moaned, insinuating his fingers under her skirt.

She squirmed away. "It would be a sin, you know that."

A sin he was almost certain she'd committed at least once in her twenty-five years. "I'm sure they'd forgive you in confession."

She kissed him long and hard, and no one was a more skilled or exciting kisser than Dervla. He toyed with the buttons of her blouse, overjoyed when she let him free them. She reached back and unhooked her brassiere. He pushed the red fabric out of the way and cupped her full breasts in his trembling hands.

It still amazed him that a woman so much older and more sophisticated than he was would be interested in him. He was beginning to think he might love her.

"Oh, Mickey," she gasped as he ran his thumbs over her rosy nipples.

"Michael," he corrected.

"You know I want to let you, but it just wouldn't be right."

He kissed her, then pushed her dark, curly hair away from her forehead. As he caressed his way down to her breasts, he said, "Ah, but I'm not quite through persuading."

She arched and gasped as he closed his mouth over one nipple. "And you are quite the persuader."

Later, when the need was pounding through him so hard he could hear little else, she rolled him onto his back and worked down the fly of his jeans.

"Can we compromise?" she offered, running her fingertips over his erection.

Mouth too dry to speak, he nodded, then closed his eyes as she peeled his clothes away.

Afterward, when he'd calmed, and she lay against him, one leg draped across his thighs, she said, "Remember my brother Brian from Derry? You met him here once." Fingers drifted downward and softly sifted through the hair at his groin. He couldn't help the moan that escaped. "I'm going this weekend to celebrate his birthday. Drive up there and be with me, Mickey. We'll have a room of our own, and I promise this time. . . . "

Michael wrenched himself from a bed miles and years removed from Dundalk, Dervla McLohne, and her compatriots. Not quite far enough, apparently. Two showers later he felt almost clean.

At four in the morning, having read the last of the books in his room and discarded the possibility of sleep without Dervla there to haunt him, Michael crept downstairs. He'd just made the landing when he was greeted by the click-clack of Roger's toe-nails across the tile floor. The dog trotted over to the hook where his leash hung and waited expectantly beneath it.

"There'll be no peace if I don't take you out, will there?" he muttered to the dog.

As they walked the still-dark streets of town, Michael thought of the evening to come. He had to believe that telling Kylie the truth of his past was the surest way to send her running. Still, he hoped—no, prayed, in his fashion—that he was wrong, for Kylie O'Shea was beginning to mean more to him than he dared admit.

"God help me," Michael said, the words echoing down the narrow, empty street.

Roger, who had been trotting happily alongside him, halted dead in his tracks and lifted his leg.

"And that's pretty much what God's been telling me, too." With that, they turned back toward Vi's house, where a certain beast could be shut into his owner's bedroom.

By the time Vi wandered out of bed and into the kitchen, Michael had read through, then hidden back in his car, the raft of cookbooks Jenna Fahey had loaned him. It was sheer self-defense, his sudden interest in the culinary arts. He couldn't face another of Vi's dead-by-neglect meals, or one of Kylie's, either.

"You'll be coming with me this morning, won't you?" his sister more demanded than asked. "Father Cready's been asking after you."

"Tell him my soul's too black for cleansing."

Vi gave a disgusted growl and turned her back on

him. Muttering about clot-headed men, she pulled open the refrigerator and gasped. "What in heaven's name is all of this?"

"It's called food," he helpfully supplied. "Yesterday after I left Muir House, I drove to that bloody huge supermarket in Tralee."

"And did you leave any food in the market?"

"Enough to tide them over."

Vi didn't comment. She was, Michael saw, too busy stuffing her gob with strawberries he had plans for. He wrenched the container from her hands, tucked it back in the refrigerator, and closed the door.

"So you're planning a regular feast for that O'Shea girl?"

He arched his brow. "Feeling deprived, are you?"

Vi shoved her hair out of her eyes and squinted threateningly, not that he was the least impressed by her show.

"Just hungry," she clipped.

"In that case when you come back from church, I'll have a full breakfast waiting for you. Eggs, toast, and maybe I'll even pop over to a neighbor's to see if I can chase up some rashers and a nice blood pudding." The last was a brilliant touch, perfect to keep his strictly vegetarian sister away from the kitchen. He hid a smile at her answering shudder.

"I'll be going straight to the studio. And you can keep an eye on Roger for me," she added over her shoulder as she hurried from the room.

Michael felt a wet nose nudge his ankle. He looked down and could have sworn the little dog was smirking at him.

Several hours and many failed recipes later, Roger wasn't smirking anymore. In fact, he lay under the kitchen table, belly distended and a replete expression on his furry face.

"Lucky for you I got it right this time, or you'd be exploding, you little glutton." Hating to see anything go to waste, no matter how misshapen or gelatinous, Michael had offered his disasters to the dog. Whatever internal mechanism a canine should have to tell him when he's eaten his fill was sadly lacking in old Roger. Confirming that, the dog let loose a resounding belch.

In a case of survival of the simplest, the meal for Kylie had come down to roast chicken, salad, and a platter of fresh fruit for dessert. Rather sparse for what Michael was personally tagging as their Last Supper. He hoped that she would accept his offering in the spirit it was given. One of desperation.

"Drink, then talk," his nan had always said. But Kylie had taken no more than a sip of her drink that rotten night at the pub. And though he hadn't much experience to base it on, Michael didn't think he was a drinker himself. Tonight was to be "Eat, then talk." If the food was good enough, maybe she'd later overlook one or two of his sins.

As Kylie watched Michael's car pull up, she thought she must have been crazed, agreeing to see him alone, out here in the middle of nothing much. If she believed even a fraction of what they said in town, she should be seeking armed guards. The best she had was Breege down the road, God bless her soul.

But justified or not, Kylie had faith in Michael. Whatever sins he might have committed, she believed he'd never harm her. Her common sense, the only thing she'd ever possessed in overabundance, seemed to have taken flight.

Kylie drew in a sharp breath. So impossibly tall, square-shouldered, and handsome, Michael walked toward the house. When she was little—before she knew better—she would often dream of bold and daring heroes, a sugar dusting of fantasy sifted over the old legends learned from her mother. And now, looking at Michael, his serious eyes stormy green and his jaw set firm, Kylie wondered, had she somehow foreseen this man? For when she dreamt, her heroes had all looked like him.

Mindless of the cold that hammered its way in, she opened the door well before he reached the stoop. As it had yesterday, the need to touch him shimmered over her.

"Can I take that from you?" she asked, hands extended outward to grasp the hamper he carried, hoping for even the brush of his fingers against hers.

He stepped in, hand still possessively wrapped around the basket's wooden handle. "I have it."

She couldn't help but smile. "I know I haven't made much of an impression on you with my cooking, but I don't think I can harm the meal by carrying it."

"I'll be taking the blame for this one," he said as he set the basket on the counter, then shrugged out of his jacket. Kylie noticed how much smaller her tiny home seemed with a man in it. It pleased and surprised her that she found this intimacy appealing; she'd always been concerned that she was damaged beyond repair.

She took his jacket and quelled the impulse to hold it to her face and breathe deeply the scent of him. She wanted to fix this moment in her memory, to hold it since she couldn't hold him. Turning away, she carried the jacket to the rack by the front door and allowed herself one fleeting brush against rough wool that smelled faintly of cigarettes and more of an honest male scent.

She turned back and watched with interest as Michael slipped a covered container into the oven, then set the temperature. "You look comfortable, there in the kitchen."

"I've had some practice today," he said.

"And before today?"

"None." His blunt answer left no room for exploration. As if sensing the sting she felt, he came to her and cupped her face in his hands. "We'll get there. I promise we will. But I need some time to work into this. It's not an easy thing for me, talking or thinking about where I've been. And what I've done. Give me this meal with you, and then I'll give you my past."

It was a small thing to ask. At her nod of assent, he gently followed the line of her jaw with his fingertips, then set back to work in the kitchen.

Kylie pulled her only linen tablecloth from its place in the sideboard. One of the few links she had to her past, the tablecloth had been her mother's, and her grandmother's before that. As she shook out the heavy ivory fabric crisp with starch, she gave them a silent plea to send her the wisdom she'd need this night. She fancied she felt a soft caress against her cheek. Comforted, a warmth burgeoned in her heart.

The meal itself—simple, delicious, and a touching gesture on the part of this quiet man—passed quickly. While they finished washing up the dishes and then went to settle together on the couch, Kylie was wise enough to give Michael his silence. This was his moment, and should be done in his way. Promising herself that she'd listen and accept with an open mind, she pushed away everything but the faith she had in Michael Kilbride.

"I don't suppose there's any sense in delaying the inevitable," Michael said, though he was thinking that delay did hold a certain amount of appeal. He would sell what was left of his soul for a few more minutes of Kylie looking at him with no accusation in her beautiful blue eyes, no hatred on her face. He wasn't fool enough to think that even her generous heart could hold him after this night was done.

"When I was twelve, my parents sent me away to boarding school in Dundalk. It was a third-rate place, filled with pretentious little assholes who weren't bright or well-connected enough to go to Queenstown, or someplace like that. No matter, though. I'd been sent off more out of expediency than any aspirations my parents had for me. See, I'd become a bit of an ass myself, making trouble in town, judging just how far I could push things at home. Getting thrown out of a school or two before Dundalk."

He paused and gave a brief smile in spite of himself. "Judgment . . . I've always seemed to have trouble with that. Anyway, each summer I'd come home and show them all what a sullen little beast I'd learned to be. And everyone believed it. Everyone but Vi, that is. No matter what I'd do, she'd just look at me with those grown-up eyes she had, and say I wasn't fooling her one bit. That she knew me and loved me for who I was."

Kylie's laughter warmed him. "Then she hasn't changed at all, has she?"

"Oh, she's changed all right. She's got the years and the size to go with the attitude, now. But even back then, I knew she was the only one in my family who really cared. When I was away at school, I'd write her every chance I got. She was—and is—my only true friend."

"I'd like to think that I'm your friend," Kylie offered in a husky voice. The sound of her pulled him back from those lonely school days.

"Wait until we're through this. Then decide."

Her answering look held mild reproach, as if he should know better than to doubt her.

"By the time I was fifteen, my parents had found a way to be rid of me when school wasn't in session, too. A second cousin of my mam had a farm outside of Dundalk and it was arranged that I'd work for him over the summers." Michael tipped back his head and gazed blankly at the ceiling. He could still see the old bastard in perfect detail, and smell the stench of his rotting teeth.

"You couldn't tell me from a slave, those days. I hardly left the farm all summer long, and had no mates to come visit." In retrospect, it had been fine practice for his years in prison.

"And you didn't get word to your parents about this?" Kylie sounded so incredulous that Michael knew for all her father's faults, at least he'd paid attention to her.

Michael shrugged. "I didn't see the point. They'd stopped listening to me long before. And at least it made the prospect of classes each fall one hell of a lot more tolerable. And then, my last year in school, I met someone. Her name was Dervla McLohne and she was several years older than I."

Not that Dervla had had any idea that first night she'd come up to him in the pub. With his size, he'd easily passed for a man in his mid-twenties, a fact he'd used to his favor in more than one late-night excursion off school grounds. It was only when he'd turned into a red-faced stammering fool over one of her more explicit comments that she'd asked his age. He'd been too distracted by his pounding erection to even think to lie.

"So she wasn't a student?" Kylie asked with a guilelessness that Dervla couldn't have matched even when still in nappies.

"No, she was a clerk at a store in town. The set she ran with was intense, wild. Brawls over political matters I'd never spent a second thinking about. Affairs . . . break-ups . . ." He trailed off, then bitterly finished with, "I was so damn thrilled to be a part of all this adult life."

She tucked a stray strand of hair behind her ear.

"It seems to me that you'd have been thrilled to be a part of anything."

"I suppose," he muttered, knowing that no matter how lonely, Kylie would never have permitted herself to be drawn in the way he was. She possessed too much integrity.

"Dervla and I became more, ah, involved. And it just so happened that my father, in the only stroke of generosity I've ever witnessed from him, got me a car as an early graduation gift. That made it all the easier to slip away and spend time with her.

"One weekend, I met a man she said was her brother Brian, down from Derry. He was the first of the group who made me genuinely uncomfortable. He teased Dervla about being with me, but he didn't really seem to be joking. There was too much malice to it." He paused, shifted his weight on the thread-bare sofa. "After that, when Brian came visiting, she didn't invite me over. Two or three times that spring, though, she did ask me for a ride north. Since I was in my last year at school, there weren't any particular restrictions on where I went. On Fridays, I'd pack into Dervla's flat with everyone else staying there, then early in the morning we'd cross the border and visit her friends in Belfast or wherever. I didn't much like her friends."

Kylie's head tipped to a quizzical angle. "Then why did you agree to go with her?"

"I was eighteen, thought I was in love, and knew I wanted her. I'd have agreed to do about anything she asked."

Kylie's cheeks grew bright crimson. She stared down at her hands, primly folded in her lap. "I see."

Judging by her color, Michael figured she did. "On the last weekend before I was to take my Leaving Certificate and be done with school, Dervla asked me to drive her north to see her brother. I agreed, of course. The trip was nothing out of the ordinary."

Without even closing his eyes he could see the two of them in the front seat of that car, Dervla distracting him from the road, and from thinking at all, with her hand moving upward to toy with the button on his jeans. *We've been waiting so long, Mickey, and Brian's promised me you and I will have a room of our own.*

"We got to her brother's house. It was in the thick of the projects, and I was sure my car would be stripped and put to use for local political causes by morning. That night, there was a party. I still don't know if I just drank too much or if something had been slipped into my drink. All I know is I woke when the front door was kicked in and a group of men stormed into the room."

He didn't tell Kylie about watching Dervla and Brian being dragged naked from the bedroom. Her brother who was no brother at all.

He didn't tell her how at the cost of a broken nose and jaw, he'd fought the officers who'd tried to grab him. Not because he feared whatever was to happen next, but because he'd wanted to kill. Kill Brian. Kill Dervla.

Not that he'd had the chance.

He didn't tell Kylie of the gunfire from the kitchen, of Dervla with the top of her head gone and a Royal

Ulster Constabulary officer drowning in his own blood. He carried the brutal scene with him every step of every day, but that wasn't why he was certain he deserved death himself.

Michael fixed his gaze on an idyllic print above the fireplace. Ireland through the eyes of a tourist, he decided. And while he told the rest of his story, he kept his eyes pinned to that idyllic green and placid place.

"I was arrested with the others in the house. When I was interrogated, I asked them to contact my family. The message came back that I now had none. No money, no family, no hope of any help. I kept thinking that the authorities would come to see I was telling the truth, that I was a bystander to whatever Dervla and her friends were doing."

"But they didn't?"

"No. It seems I'd been helping Dervla smuggle materials used to make bombs. Brian was more than happy to implicate me. They impounded my car. Taped inside the boot was enough Semtex to put a huge, damned crater into the earth. The authorities were amazed that we hadn't managed to blow ourselves up well before that. I spent the next fourteen years wishing I had."

"And were you guilty?"

"I was responsible. And because I had no one left, I admitted association with Dervla's group. You see, in the Maze—where they were going to put me—you were either on one side or the other if you wanted to survive. I picked the poison I knew. Family," he said, practically choking on the word. "I was jailed with my new family."

And the rest, he should have practiced saying it. Words came to him in jagged chunks that ripped at his soul as he tried to force them out. "When they were questioning me, I learned that a family living above a Belfast pub had died in a bombing attack . . . a little boy and girl. . . . They'd connected the explosion back to the group Dervla and Brian belonged to. It happened a week after we'd paid a visit there. Two children died," he repeated, then mentally finished the thought that hadn't left him since that night: *They died because I was a fool who couldn't tell love from deception.*

Steeling himself for the contempt he knew he'd see on Kylie's face, he looked at her. And what he found was even more shattering. He saw her tears, and it nearly killed him. Michael was out the door and down a dark road before his own tears came. Fourteen years, and finally they came.

Chapter Ten

God between us and all harm.
— IRISH BLESSING

If the man had to bolt out of the place, at least he could have had the common sense to take his car, Kylie thought. But no, Michael Kilbride had gone on foot, and left his jacket hanging beside the door, too. Three cold hours he'd been gone. And here she stood peering out into dark swallowed by more dark.

"Come back," she whispered. She ached for him, for what he'd been through, for the burdens he carried. He'd been a fool, people had suffered . . . and died.

Kylie pushed aside the image and sorted through what she knew of the man. He felt remorse, this much was true. Beneath the impassive, damned-if-I-care mask he wore, it weighed into his every word, his every action. He needed to heal. If forgiveness were hers to give, she could forgive him his youth and stupidity. She wondered, though, whether he would ever forgive himself.

"Home, Michael," she urged.

She knew he couldn't hear her, of course, wherever he was, tangled in his knot of guilt, grief, and self-hatred. As much as she wanted to search for him, there was no point in having two fools wandering in the dark. Eventually, Kylie changed into her nightgown, combed her hair, brushed her teeth, then curled up on the couch to wait. And later—much later—she fell asleep.

A beacon in the darkness, Michael wearily thought as he closed in on the soft, glowing light at the top of the hill. Numb from the cold and wrenching night, he willed himself forward. Just a few more steps and he would retrieve his jacket and car keys, then never see Kylie again.

Never again.

The confines of his old cell were more welcoming than the sentence he'd just given himself. He could have done his full bird of twenty-five years standing on his head before he could do this.

Feet making crunching sounds on the hard dirt path, he walked to the front window and peered in the smudged pane. The light next to the couch still shone, but everything else seemed still. He went up on the balls of his feet, trying to see over the back of the couch to the fireplace. If the peat was no longer smoking, he'd know she was asleep. But even at his height, he couldn't see clear of the couch.

Figuring that trying his luck at a quick escape was better than freezing to death, he edged toward the door and lifted the latch. Like everything else in Kylie O'Shea's house, it worked only halfway. Jiggling it a few times, he finally got it to open. One hand feeling the wall just inside the door, and the rest of him shivering outside, he finally touched the worn canvas of his jacket. Lifting it slowly from the hook, he froze when a soft hand settled on top of his.

"Are you going somewhere?"

He leaned his forehead against the hard, stuccoed side of the house, feeling it press sharply into his skin. He closed his eyes. There was no denying it; God had it out for him. Showing him the way to Kylie, then taking her away, but only after one last, tantalizing touch.

"I'm going home."

The hand pulled at him. "Then come inside."

It was the cold—it had slowed his brain until even the simplest words were too much for him to understand.

A second hand reached out and grabbed at the neck of his sweater. "I asked you to come inside, and do it before the last bit of heat escapes, if you please."

One hard tug had him stumbling over the stoop. The door closed behind him before he even knew what happened. Michael steadied himself, then looked down at her. He'd never thought of flannel as a sensuous material, but he'd never thought of it caressing Kylie O'Shea, either.

"I knew never to wager against you in a fight," he said.

"Leverage, nothing more. You've had me worried." She gestured at the couch. "Sit down."

He didn't consider disobeying. In a matter of minutes, she had stoked the fire, ordered him out of his shoes, buried him in a blanket, and tucked a mug of tea into his hands.

"You thought to just leave, didn't you?"

"Didn't see much in the way of a choice," he muttered, then took a scalding sip of the tea. Gasping, invoking a few of the saints, he set the mug down on the lamp table.

"Too hot?" At the concern in her eyes, he eliminated torture as a possible reason for being brought back inside.

"It'll cool," he managed to get over his burnt tongue.

She sat next to him on the couch, slipping her slender bare feet under one corner of his blanket. "While it does, let's get to my part in that little talk we were having."

He supposed it was better to be done now, while he was still numb and wrung empty from the grief he'd finally set free.

Kylie wasted no time in getting in her first blow. "You didn't have much sense back in those days. But then again, most young people don't."

"Most aren't lethally stupid, either," he pointed out.

She raised one hand in an abrupt arc. "You've had your say. It's my turn now. The choices you made, I'm not saying they were right, or even wholly understandable to me. But I don't think you made them meaning to hurt others, did you?"

Lord, he was bone-weary. He'd asked himself these questions countless times. And the answers never changed. "They were hurt just the same. Children no different than the ones you see in your classroom every day—"

Her eyes closed as if she tried to force back tears. He wondered if she was putting a face to the children, giving them identities. God knew he had, down to the minutiae of their budding lives. Long before he'd seen their photos at the trial, he'd known them. And tonight he'd finally mourned them. And himself.

"But did you know you were smuggling—" She trailed off with a wince. He could almost see her mentally picking up then dropping ugly, truth-laden words like "explosives" and "bombs" before she finally settled on, "—the things that you were?"

"No, I had no idea I was carrying anything at all. But—"

"A 'no' will do," she directed, sounding very much like a prosecutor he'd had the bleak fortune to meet. Kylie leaned forward to tug a bit more of the blanket off him and over her legs. "You were led, Michael, and far too easily. But you're no youngster anymore, and you've paid a heavy price for your poor choices. Don't you think it's time you let it go?"

This was not the kind of thing one could get free of. He could never grant himself absolution for his acts. Lives had ended, and his had changed irrevocably. But tonight, in the midst of the ache and chaos, he had felt something shift deep inside. A door rustier and more ill-sprung than even Kylie's had begun to open. He saw now that he could learn to move on. However horrible his mistakes, he had a life to pick up. One on the fringes, but a life nonetheless.

"Even if I do let it go, others won't."

"You can only take care of yourself." He wondered if she recognized the irony of those words coming from a woman who did nothing but care for others. "As for the rest of the world, they'll come around in time."

She spoke with such sincerity, such utter trust in a universal good he simply didn't believe in. There was nothing he could say in return without hurting her.

Color rose in her cheeks. Tugging the blanket the rest of the way off him, she cocooned herself in it. "You left it to me, whether I want to see you again. Nothing tonight has changed my answer. I-I want to be with you." She let out her breath in a relieved sigh. "There now, I've said it."

A profound relief rolled through him. He hadn't lost her yet. "I want to be with you, too," he said, then shook his head over the embarrassing inadequacy of his words. "I'll treasure you, Kylie, I swear I will. I'll see you don't come to harm."

She reached out and traced the line of his jaw. He fought not to show how much her simple touch affected him. Showing too much, caring too much, meant one day hurting too much.

"I'm safe with you. I've always known that," she said softly.

He didn't mean to pull her to him, any more than he meant to close his mouth over hers. Or to demand that she give her all. He didn't mean to, but even while knowing he couldn't give the same in return, he did.

At the first taste of her, the first touch of tongue to tongue, he was lost to his need. The feel of Kylie's lithe body in his arms only fed the hunger, as did the low moan of pleasure that drifted from her throat. Her throat . . . vulnerable, white as a virgin's thighs, and tasting sweet, so sweet.

It was physical, this wanting, slamming through him and leaving him breathless. But it was more. So much more that he couldn't understand it. Pushing aside the blanket, he cupped her breast in his hand, and took her surprised gasp into his mouth. Her fingers clenched tighter into his back, then relaxed. He didn't move, just felt her heartbeat— a flight of startled birds—beneath the thin fabric of her gown.

He fought the need, relentless though it was. He would not frighten her.

"My treasure, *mam stór*," he whispered, trailing kisses down to the tender curve where her neck met the sweep of her shoulder. At her sigh, he shifted their position just enough that he could turn his attention to the soldier row of tiny buttons marching down the upper part of her nightgown. Their eyes met, hers wide, smoky blue, and trusting, so trusting. His fingers fumbled and shook, but finally he slipped his hand against her skin.

"Like silk," he murmured.

Her eyes drifted closed. He caressed the valley between her breasts, then gradually feathered outward. Kylie's breath came fast and shallow, and she said something in Irish he couldn't understand. He stroked her, dusted the night with kisses and nonsense words. He honored her.

Soon it wasn't enough, this touching without seeing. The last few buttons gave way with ease. He pushed the fabric aside. Transfixed, he gazed at her lush beauty. After a moment, she made an embarrassed sound and tried to cover her breasts.

"No, you don't," Michael said, taking her hands and spreading her arms wide. "It would be a sacrilege. And a near impossibility," he added with a quick smile. He dropped a kiss on the pulse still fluttering madly at her throat. "You're beautiful, you know."

"I'm just . . . me." Her voice was thready with self-consciousness.

"Beautiful," he reaffirmed, then brought his mouth to one peak.

Kylie jumped as if kissed by fire. He touched her as no man ever had.

No man. Rough, terrifying images wavered in the shadows, then gathered substance. For a moment they succeeded in becoming her reality even though she knew they were ghosts.

Hurtful, evil ghosts. She was stronger than this, and smarter, too. Kylie lifted her hands to run her fingers through Michael's thick hair. She held him to her, focusing on the feel of his wet mouth against her hot skin, on the drawing pressure that brought an answering tug deep and low inside her.

This was Michael, the man for whom she yearned, the man who needed her as much as she needed him. Tightening her fingers she urged his mouth upward to hers. Their eyes met. The fierceness in his green eyes frightened her for an instant, then elated her. His need was tempered with such restraint.

Because she was safe with him, she was free to kiss him the way she wanted to—passionately—as an aggressor.

Not a victim. Never again. She learned the smooth feel of teeth and firm cushion of lips, the rough stubble of beard and the strength of him. Lord, the strength. Half passion, half something darker, she shivered yet tried to get closer.

"Your sweater . . . off," she managed to work free from a mind whirling with touch and texture and scent. He didn't hesitate, and she could feel his arousal pressing into her as he levered his weight up to rid himself of the sweater.

This is Michael, and no other man, she reminded herself as the vestiges of old terror again gathered strength. She closed her eyes and focused on the desire Michael had built in her. When she looked up at him again, he was tugging off his shirt, too. Her breath hitched harder at the sight of his broad, muscled chest, at arms strong enough to force her to his will.

"Kylie, do you want me to stop? All you need do is say it."

With her fingers she tested the strength of those arms, then trailed over his chest and followed a narrow line of hair downward. His muscles tensed beneath her touch. She rested her hand over his heart. It beat a mad rhythm, but in his eyes she saw patience and kindness. She could do this. And she would.

"No, don't stop," she whispered, then gave herself over to the moment.

Michael took his time, treasuring the trust that rested in his arms. He reveled in the soft fullness of her breasts pressing against him. Skin to skin, it was glorious, sacred. Like nothing he'd ever felt.

Moving so they both were on their sides on that narrow little couch, left with scarcely enough room to breathe before he'd roll off the edge, he let his hand skim over the dip of her waist and around to the small of her back. Sliding lower, he closed his hand over her bottom and pulled her even closer. She started at the intimate contact, and truth be told, so did he.

While he had a very clear image of what he wanted to happen this night, he was somewhat vague on how to accomplish it. Tenderness and caring were foreign to him. He knew two things. He wanted Kylie, and he wanted their coming together to bear no resemblance to times with Dervla. So he lingered over the details and allowed some of the strangeness to drift away with the minutes that they held each other.

When she had again softened in his arms and begun to kiss, touch, and explore on her own, he gave in to temptation. Hands splayed, he learned the sleek feel of her ribs, the narrowness of her hips, and finally the slight curve of her belly. Sliding his hand downward over her rumpled nightgown, he rested his fingers against the mound at the vee of her thighs. And with that touch everything changed.

Kylie sat upright so quickly that Michael tumbled to the floor. "Stop. I'm telling you to stop now." She scarcely sounded like herself, her voice high, thin, and quavery. Bracing himself on his palms, he watched speechless as she buttoned her nightgown, then tried to fight her hair into a hasty braid.

"I'm sorry," she said with the flash of something not very much like a smile. "It's all been too much for me, I suppose. The talk, you walking out . . ." She trailed off, then dragged in a ragged breath. "I'm just feeling overwhelmed."

God help him, she was going to cry. He swallowed hard and thought fast for words to stem her tears. "I was clumsy with you, but you see, it's been a long time since I've been with a woman." *Like never.*

The words didn't help. Tears spilled over her lashes. She brushed at them with one shaking hand. With the other, she gathered up the blanket that had been shoved to the end of the couch and clutched it like a shield.

"I'm sorry," he said. "I won't touch you again. Not unless you ask."

She sat, knees pressed to chest, rocking like a child trying to comfort herself when no one else would. Or could. "I'm just tired, so tired." Her face strained and pale, she said in a low voice, "Morning will be here soon. Stay with me, for what's left of the night. I've been alone too much, and you, too. Let's not be alone anymore."

Confused, still hurting with unappeased need, Michael scrubbed a hand over his face. He understood what she asked now, for a platonic companion to chase away the dark hours. What he didn't understand was how they had ended up here. Or how to extricate himself from what his body clearly felt was an unreasonable demand.

It was his own bloody, boorish fault, though, scaring her as he had. And if comfort was what Kylie wanted, comfort she would have. Even if it killed him. Which, judging by the hard knot in his blood supply, it just might.

He moved back onto the couch and drew her closer, taking care not to bring her into contact with such obvious evidence of his untrustworthiness. "I'll stay with you."

"So much . . . too much," she murmured, then turned her face into his shoulder. Trusting. So damned trusting. And he was to be her hero?

Giving his discarded shirt and sweater no more than a passing glance, he stood and scooped her into his arms. Carrying her to the bedroom, he swung Kylie down to her feet beside her fantasy of a bed, then tugged away the blanket she still clutched in stiff fingers and tossed it to the bottom of the bed. He pulled back the covers on her side. Her expression questioning, she slipped into bed, and he tucked her in.

"I'll be sleeping on top of the covers," he said as he walked around the foot of the bed. Sitting, he reached across her to switch off the light. Trying his hardest not to react to the way she had practically cringed as he leaned over her, Michael stretched out and covered himself with the spare blanket.

Kylie stirred. In the starlight passing through the thin curtains he could see her turn to look at him. She still didn't speak. It was as if she waited for him to ease them past this discomfort, and he could think of no worse person for the job.

At a loss, he reached out and fingered the billowy material pulled back from the bed's canopy. "Tell me about this bed of yours."

Settling in with a sigh, she answered, "My father always said it once belonged to a beautiful Princess of Tara. When I was a child, I'd imagine a daughter of Brian Boru asleep in here, dreaming of the future." She paused, and he could feel her gaze rest on him. "When I was older, I learned that it had been my mother's bed when she was young. And my mother, she was always Da's beautiful princess. After she died, things started falling apart. Knowing the mouths in town, you've probably heard the story by now," Kylie added in a tentative voice.

"Pieces," he answered.

"Well, for tonight, I think pieces are just enough." She yawned and curled up. After a long silence she whispered, "Thank you, Michael, for understanding."

He nodded into the darkness, and lay there listening as Kylie's breathing slipped into the regular pattern of sleep. His last thought before he, too, slept was that he understood nothing at all.

It was before sunup when Michael realized that even when asleep, the two of them had turned to each other. Still beneath her covers, Kylie had moved to fit herself to his longer frame. And his arm was wrapped over her as though he intended to never let her go. He satisfied himself with holding her that way, with the hope that once he'd learned to lose the roughness, she would come to him willingly.

Watery morning light was just beginning to push its way in when she stirred. "Where is she now, that Dervla woman?" she asked as though half the night—his running and her pushing him away—had never happened.

"She died that night," he said, offering nothing more.

Kylie raised herself up on one elbow to look down at him. "And the brother?"

It took a moment to understand that she meant Brian Rourke.

"I don't know where he is. He escaped before trial, and as my nan used to say, 'Another stone on his cairn.' "

Her eyes widened a fraction. "You wish him dead?"

Michael couldn't stem the bitterness. "Given the chance, I'd see him dead."

Together, silent, they waited for the sun to rise.

Chapter Eleven

There is no strength like unity.
—IRISH PROVERB

Kylie crumpled her father's letter and threw it in the general vicinity of the hearth. Then, not quite done inflicting torture on herself, she retrieved the paper and let the last few daggers find their mark. "'Looking forward to a fresh start in Ballymuir,'" she angrily quoted. "'Peace and solitude with my daughter.' That's grand, Johnny, expecting peace in the middle of the people you did your level best to ruin."

It was too much, the way the past was creeping forward to poison her present. Too much the way one awful event over six years gone had come back last night to claim her. Months spent with priests and counselors seeking healing, seeking closure, and for what? To see it all slip away the first time she moved toward intimacy with a man.

"Don't you think it's time you let it go?" she had asked Michael. A fine piece of advice coming from her. She absentmindedly tucked her father's letter in the small box filled with others containing his schemes and excuses. Nothing was ever Johnny O'Shea's fault. And sometimes it felt like everything was his daughter's.

"Live what you preach," Kylie told herself with a disgusted shake of her head. "Let it go."

But what had happened six years before wouldn't be shaken free quite so easily. One night when a simple "yes" might have purchased her father's freedom. One night when a hard-fought "no" had instead made her unable to accept a man's touch. Even a man she cared for very deeply.

She had let Michael believe that her emotional collapse last night had been his fault. Another wrong, another measure of guilt to be borne, for truly, he'd been gentle and patient. His tense body and ragged breathing had told her what it cost him, too. In repayment for that kindness she had turned from him again.

Twice now, she thought. Once in the pub when she might have salvaged his reputation, and again last night when she might have saved . . . *them.* Well, it wouldn't happen again.

She wouldn't wait for his call, either. She'd wasted too much time letting others determine her fate. With trembling fingers, Kylie paged through the phone directory until she came to the number she sought.

Vi stood with her hand cupped over the phone's mouthpiece and a peculiar look of glee on her face. "Michael, it's Kylie O'Shea, and she's sounding for all the world like she's never rung up a boy before."

Michael's mouth quirked at the idea of being a boy. Putting aside the materials list he'd been jotting down, he rose and took the phone from Vi.

"Do you have somewhere you could go?" he asked, hand safely over the mouthpiece as he gestured at their close quarters.

"Why, right here in front of my own fireplace, as I do every evening." At his growl she added, "Unless you're suggesting I move the fire."

Stretching the phone's cord around the corner as far as it would go, Michael reflected on the particular pains of being kept on a short leash.

"It must be true love," Vi called from her perch. More like unrequited lust from his side of the affair, Michael thought.

Keeping his voice low enough, he hoped, to escape his sister's acute hearing, he said hello and asked Kylie how she was feeling.

"Fine. Well, actually tired, quite tired, now that you ask," she said, piling one word on top of the next. "It was a long day at work. A cold's going 'round the classroom and it was a chorus of sniffles." Michael smiled as she drew in a breath. Vi would have little to overhear if Kylie kept chattering like a magpie too long deprived of its company.

"Anyway, I was glad to be home and have a quiet dinner, but now I'm feeling sort of . . . well, lonely, and I was wondering if you'd meet me at O'Connor's Pub this evening?" she finished in a great rush.

His hand tightened involuntarily on the phone. A vision of Evie Nolan, sharp, nasty-tongued, and vindictive, loomed in front of him. He'd promised to treasure Kylie, to keep her safe. As far as he was concerned that included protecting her from gossip.

"Michael, are you still there?"

He cleared his throat. "I am. I was just thinking that a night of noise and too much smoke doesn't sound quite the cure for loneliness. And besides, O'Connor's not very fond of me." If not the pub, then where? A visit to her house? He wouldn't survive the night without touching her, and that was another promise he'd made—not to, till she asked. "Why don't you come here, to Vi's house? We can, uh, play cards . . . or something."

His offer was met by a howl of laughter from in front of the hearth and a momentary silence on the phone.

"Cards?" Kylie eventually echoed.

He leaned his forehead into the door frame with a solid *thunk*. "Or something. I'll come around and get you if you like."

"No . . . no, I can drive myself."

He imagined her little car with its distinctive rust patterns—junkyard camouflage—sitting square in front of Vi's house. So much for cutting off the talk. Michael considered telling her to park down the road a way, but he knew that she'd take it as a slight. He'd hope for a dark night and quiet streets.

"Fine then," he said, "I'll see you in half an hour?"

"Shall I bring anything?"

"Cards," he answered, and smiled at the laughter in Kylie's voice as she said good-bye.

After he'd hung up, Vi came to give him a loving smack on the head. "You're set on running me out of my own home, aren't you? No great matter, though. I'll just pop over to O'Connor's for a pint and some company."

Michael reached out his hand and stopped her from moving off. "No. Stay, please."

Vi grinned. "Are you afraid of that bit of a girl?"

"I'm trying to maintain proprieties."

"And proprieties are worrying you after spending last night at her house?"

"Since her nearest neighbor is almost a mile off, and your neighbors snoop through the curtains morning and night, yes, I'm worrying."

Vi paused, her brow arched at an inquisitive angle, and a smile playing about her mouth. "I don't think it's just proprieties we're talking about. I think you're feeling nervous. Nature hasn't precisely taken its course between you two, has it?"

"Whatever course it's taken is none of your damned business. I'm asking you, as my sister, to stay here tonight and be nice to Kylie. No prying questions, and get that smug look off your face!" he finished, pounding his last order with heavy emphasis.

She reached up and patted him on the cheek. "If

you're going to be so skittish about a matter as natural as sex, you'd be just as well off entering the priesthood."

She'd tease him until he was as maddened as a bull, if he let her. But he wouldn't. "Only if I get to hear your confession, sweet Violet," he said with an answering tweak of her nose. "I'm willing to bet it would be a ripe one."

"That you'll never know. I'll play chaperone to you and your young miss for as long as you wish. You already have enough to unload on Father Cready the next time you see him."

"I'll save it for my meeting with the Almighty, Himself, if you don't mind."

"Actually, I do. But I'll hold that harping for another time, when you're not so besotted. Now I'll put on some tea for our guest, and you go see if you can make yourself look civilized. You've enough sawdust clinging to you to be declared a fire hazard."

Michael brushed his hand through his hair and winced at the shower of wood shavings that came free. "Nothing wrong with a little mess after hard work."

"And there's nothing wrong with presenting yourself like a proper suitor. Upstairs with you, Romeo."

And upstairs he went before Vi could land another dart. Being called "boy" and "Romeo" had been quite enough for one evening.

"Primping in front of the mirror, who'd have ever thought it?" Michael muttered a few minutes later, showing a self-disgust he more thought he should feel than actually did. In truth, caring about his appearance and whether his manners were intact made him feel a step closer to being alive.

A promise shimmered out there, one that was fragile and giving. He felt slow and clumsy as he reached out to grasp it. This waking up was a difficult business, but one he meant to accomplish with as much speed and grace as a man his sort could.

"Showered, teeth brushed, shaved," he ticked off the items on his hygiene list. The doorbell chimed. "And nowhere damn near ready," he admitted, then made his way down the stairs to see if he could survive an evening without further mucking up things with Kylie O'Shea.

An irresistible attraction. Even under Vi Kilbride's amused eyes, Kylie found herself moving nearer to Michael, closing the gap of electric-blue sofa between them.

And Michael, he was an immovable object. Though he sat close enough that she could reach out and trace the slight bump on the bridge of his nose, or that curve to his mouth that set her heart dancing, he was as distant as the stars.

She could hardly blame him after last night. This was no time to explain that it had been an aberration, some mysterious, cosmic folding-over of time she was quite certain would never happen again. At least, not while she had a breath left in her body to fight it. No, now was decidedly not the time, though Vi looked to be an avid audience.

Instead, talk lazily meandered its way through Vi

and Kylie's progress on the Gaelscoil arts project and the children's recent renderings of the mythic hero Fionn MacCumhaill and his bold hounds, Bran and Sceolang, then on to the coming promise of spring. From there, the ritual was completed with chat about common friends.

After a moment's companionable quiet, Vi popped in with, "And your father, Kylie, is he well?"

"Well enough." She paused, then added, "He'll be released in several weeks," wondering why she'd even volunteered such information.

"That must be a difficult thing for you."

Kylie focused on her hands clenched in her lap. "I'd imagine that it will be more difficult for my father."

"I'm afraid my sympathy lies more with you," Vi said in the softest of voices.

"Thank you, but I don't need your sympathy," she replied, knowing it for the lie it was.

"Well, Nan always said . . ."

Nan. Kylie flinched at the echo of her morning's conversation with Michael. So much alike, these siblings, yet so different, too. Both with a bolder spark of life than most souls carried. But even then, one so world-weary, so without hope. She glanced at Michael and saw the last shadow of discomfort ease from his features. So *Nan* held resonance for him, too. He shifted restlessly, and Kylie let her heart guide her words.

"Would you like to take a walk, stretch your legs a bit?" she asked him, knowing that it was like asking the sea if it would like to return to its shore.

"I would," he said, rising at the same time.

Stretching like a cat waking from a long nap, Vi lazily asked her brother, "Would you like me to join you?"

"Not bloody likely." Michael hurried Kylie toward her jacket and the door. "Keep the fire burning for us, Violet. We won't be gone long."

The chill bite of wind, the distant sound of a dog barking, the clasp of a hand large and warm. Some of life's moments crystallized so vividly, so vitally that they lived forever. For Kylie, this would be one of them. She wished she could close this magical sphere around the two of them for eternity. Since she couldn't, she gripped tighter to Michael's hand, satisfying herself with that, at least.

They walked to the very fringe of town. The moon, golden ripe, shone low in the sky. At the edge of the drive to one of the grander houses sat two large stones. One leaned against the back of the other, creating a place to dally. A place to talk.

Kylie stopped. "Do you mind if we rest a minute?"

"I'm sorry, have I been moving too fast for you?"

"Well, your legs are a great deal longer than mine and you move with such a sense of—" She searched for the proper word. "—purpose. But, really, I just wanted to stop here." She gestured at nature's bench with her free hand. "Lovely, isn't it, under the moonlight."

Michael agreed, but Kylie noticed he didn't look away from her face as he said it.

"Come sit with me," she offered, tugging him

toward the stones. "There's something I should have told you last night, and I don't want another day to pass without doing it."

"Out here, though?"

"There are some things your sister doesn't need to know." She paused, then chuckled. "Though looking at her, I get the sense that she knows most everything in the world already." She sat on the lower of the two rocks, patting its hard surface with her hand. "Just a few minutes and we'll be on our way."

Michael sat, then drew in a hissing breath. "You'd best be quick or we'll both be numb."

The cold beneath her was fine incentive to hurry the truth along. "Last night, when I—I panicked, it wasn't your fault. I knew what you were thinking— that it was—and I let you think it. It was easier, you see, than telling you about something that once happened to me."

"Kylie," he began, and she knew he was going to try to cut her off.

"Let me do this. If I don't, we'll never see our way clear of it." She drew in a breath and gave him the words with no prettiness about them, for there was no prettiness in what had happened to her. "The summer I turned eighteen—the summer my father got in trouble—I was raped."

She could feel Michael tighten next to her. His hand over hers was as hard and inflexible as the rock they sat upon.

"You don't need to dredge this up."

"Yes, I do. And I've dealt with it already. Mostly, at least," she added, feeling the fingers of last night's fear curl around her. "I've spent enough hours being counseled that it should be behind me."

She waited until her eyes and Michael's had met and held. "What I'd like to have is an exorcism of sorts. I want to tell you the whole thing, so you'll know, then I want it to go away. Will you listen?"

He nodded, a slow and deliberate movement.

Kylie grasped both his hands in hers, forging a physical link to get her through this. "My father came up with a scheme for a resort on a parcel of low coastline not far from Dingle. He wanted it to be the next Wexford, a seaside resort with hotels and cottages for families to come and vacation for a summer fortnight. He sought financing, negotiated with landowners, brought in people from town as partners. Everyone was so excited, it was going to be brilliant.

"One problem, though. Da was more fond of living the grand life than following through on plans. The first thing he did was build himself an enormous home on the one parcel he'd managed to acquire. He told everyone that it was to be operated as a country guest house once the project was up and running. He took more and more money, and nothing but that house ever materialized."

Taking the comfort she needed, she shifted on the cold surface, moving closer to Michael. "Oh, I think he meant to follow through. At first, at least. But it was like everything else since my mother died. Nights out with his friends were more important, traveling and the drink were more important. On my eighteenth birthday, he took me out to dinner and told me that times were going to be troubled, but I wasn't to worry because he had a plan." She shook her head. "Da always had a plan."

"The next day, a business associate stopped over at the house for a meeting. This man was no one I'd ever seen before. From London, Da said, and he was very smooth looking, expensive suit, shiny shoes, and just so polished. He caught me staring at him—I couldn't help myself. I was eighteen and hadn't been further away from home than Killarney and he was so . . . different looking, like someone out of those glossy magazines. Anyway, they left for lunch and didn't come back for hours."

It had been close to the time that Gerry Flynn was to pick her up for a special birthday dinner.

When she'd first arrived in Ballymuir, he'd been her protector, fighting off the childhood bullies who'd been pleased to have a shy outsider for a new target. Later, they'd started dating. He'd been the first to kiss her, the first—and last—to say he loved her.

That night, which she'd been certain was going to be magical, she'd even put on her mother's pearls. She wanted Gerry to see her looking like the princess he always called her.

"When they got back to the house, Da was barely able to stand he'd had so much to drink. I helped him upstairs and got him settled in, something I'd done plenty before. I figured Mr. Keefe, that man, would be gone by the time I got back downstairs. He wasn't, though. I tried to usher him along, but he just poured himself a drink and stood there watching me. He asked me if I knew of my father's financial difficulties. I said, yes, I knew something about it."

Kylie paused to draw in a bit of courage. "He moved closer and put one finger under my chin, bringing my face up to his. I noticed that his nails were all polished and smooth, just like the rest of him, and for some reason this frightened me."

She had sensed that something was terribly wrong. She'd considered running out of the house, but she was so unaccustomed to the heels she'd put on, she knew she wouldn't make it far. Glancing at the grandfather clock ticking away in the corner, she had comforted herself with the fact that Gerry would be there any minute now.

"He told me how pretty I was. Then he told me how wealthy he was, and how he'd like to help my father out, given the proper incentive. I was so naive, I had no idea what he was saying, at first. When he made himself plainer, I was furious. I refused him, and he shrugged, telling me that my father's fate would be on my conscience. I told him I didn't see that as being any worse than what he proposed. He smiled then, and said that willing or not, I'd be having the chance to compare those sins."

She had turned on her toes and run toward the door to the enormous salon. Feet slipping on the parquet floor, she wasn't fast enough. As the ability to fight was brutally stripped from her, she'd heard the sound of her mother's broken strand of pearls pinging against that hard, hard floor.

"He forced me," she finished.

"God. Oh, God," she heard Michael whisper just beneath his breath as he drew her onto his lap. He held her so tightly that it seemed he tried to absorb her body into the strength of his.

Gerry had eventually arrived, late as always. She had tried to scream for him, but could get no sound past the hand that made her teeth cut into the tender skin of her mouth. She heard him calling for her, heard his footsteps on the marble entry hall, then the wood of the salon floor. Then she heard his inarticulate cry, and his footfalls clip away when Keefe ordered him to get out.

He left. Simply left.

Kylie burrowed even closer to Michael. "I know you're not Keefe, and that I'm no longer a stupid little girl." She quickly silenced Michael's objections to what she'd called herself. "But last night . . . last night was the first time since then that a man's done more than kiss me."

Curled up on him with the sound of his heart drumming beneath her ear, she felt brave enough to tell him what he needed to hear. What she needed to say. "When you touched me, I gloried in it. I wanted you to touch me, and I wanted so very much to touch you. I still do, but some last bit of guilt and fear over what happened that night has gotten wrapped up in all the good feelings."

"Guilt?" he interrupted, sounding almost angry. "Guilt?" His arms came even tighter around her. "You haven't a thing in this world to feel guilty over."

She smiled sadly into the rough fabric of his jacket. "I know, and the first thing I had to learn to do was forgive myself. It was the hardest thing, too. I kept thinking if he hadn't caught me gawking at him, if I'd been more sensible about having a stranger in the house—"

"If your bastard of a father hadn't passed out," Michael offered. "Have you considered that one?"

Kylie nodded. "I have, and I've managed to forgive him. He doesn't know what happened, and God willing, he never will."

Michael didn't comment, then after a silence asked, "What happened next?"

"I took myself to a clinic in Tralee that night, and was home well before Da rejoined the world. Keefe, of course, was gone. Other than the people who've treated me, I've never told anyone."

"I'm thankful you've told me," he murmured into her hair. "I'd take it all back for you, if I could. If I had known you then, I would have protected you. I'd have never let you come to harm. And even now, I'd like to hunt down the son of a bitch and give him what he deserves."

Another stone on his cairn.

Kylie felt a primal surge of emotion, pure, hot, and so close to lust. All of Father Cready's talk of forgiveness had carried only so far. Though it was wrong, she wanted Keefe damned, wanted him to suffer. And she still felt a horrible, heartbroken pain over Gerry Flynn—the boy who'd said he loved her and then left her there in her own blood and shame.

"It's in the past," she said, willing it to be so. Willing the moment's hatred that had seized her to slink back into the darkness.

"It is," Michael agreed in a soothing voice, his

hand making a broad sweep over her back. "And now I'll keep you safe."

"And I'll do the same for you," Kylie replied, at first meaning it a joke, a way to lighten the moment. But the words had no sooner escaped into the night than she was overwhelmed by a fierce protectiveness. She'd face down anyone—even the specter of Keefe—for this man.

Laughter rumbled in Michael's chest as he stood, staggering slightly, moaning about the cold, and holding her tight against his body. "I'm sure you will, Kylie O'Shea."

He let her slide down the length of him until she found her feet. "Laugh if you will," she admonished him in her best schoolteacher's voice. "But believe in me, too."

"I do," he said as he brought his mouth to hers. "I do."

He kissed her then, his broad hands cupping her face, his mouth firm and wonderful. Wrapping her arms around him, Kylie gave herself up to his strength. And in doing so, she found a strength of her own.

Moonlight flowed over them, blessing them, she thought. Even when a car drove very slowly past, its headlights adding to the wash of the moon, she didn't stop kissing him. Fate owed her nothing, but if it was kind, it would give her this man.

Chapter Twelve

When the dance is at its hottest, that's the time to stop.
— IRISH PROVERB

Kylie had just turned onto the main road toward Gaelscoil Pearse when she noticed a Garda's car rapidly closing on her. She glanced at the speedometer, then recalled it had given up the ghost weeks before. Still, it didn't *feel* as though she were speeding. Just to be sure, she slowed and drove as sedately as she did when taking Breege to Sunday Mass. No easy task since she was scarcely going to make the morning bell as it was.

She hummed to herself and studiously tried to avoid looking back in the mirror. Then a short burst of siren gained her attention. The Garda was right behind her—certainly close enough to be recognized.

"Gerry," she groaned, then drew to the side of the road.

His face was set in hard lines as he came to her car door. Since the window crank was also still broken, Kylie stepped out.

"Was I doing something wrong?" she asked, knowing full well she hadn't been.

"You didn't come to a complete stop before turning."

"A complete stop for whom? In case you hadn't noticed, there's no one around."

"I'm around."

She gave in to exasperation. "If what you're looking for is a confession that I counted only to two-and-a-half instead of three before proceeding, you won't be getting one."

He looked down at the road beneath their feet then back up at her. "You can't help yourself, can you?"

Jolted by the mixture of anger and some other indefinable emotion blazing across his face, Kylie backed off a step, bumping against her car.

"What do you mean?" she asked in a carefully neutral tone.

He jutted out his jaw. "I mean the men you choose."

In an instant she recalled the prior night, and the car that had slowly passed by as she and Michael kissed. It had to have been Gerry. "You certainly are around, aren't you?"

His face turned a bright crimson at her sardonic words, but he didn't retreat. "You could have waited and had a good man, a man such as—" His jaw flexed as he cut off whatever he'd been about to say. "You could have had a man who'd honor and marry you, but instead you let that . . . that evil bastard touch you!"

Time seemed to be playing fast and loose with more than just Kylie. She drew in a slow breath. In the years since that horrible night, they'd never discussed it. She'd heard nothing at all from him for months. Then had come the calls while she was away at school. He'd never said a word—just hung up—but she'd known it was Gerry. And since she'd been back in Ballymuir, he was always there—visible, but just far enough away she couldn't precisely say he was watching her. She could feel it, though. And feel his anger. An anger she simply couldn't understand.

"Are you referring to the night of my eighteenth birthday dinner, or to last night with Michael Kilbride?"

He shook his head slowly, reminding her of a fighter reeling under a ringing punch. "I mean Kilbride!"

"Do you really? Somehow I doubt it." She looked somewhere over his shoulder, off into rolling fields where the morning mist still clung like a silvery blanket. "You know," she said in a low voice, "I've spent a lot of years wondering how you could have done that. How you could have left me there with that man."

"I don't want to talk about it."

Sheep dotted the high slopes. At a whistled signal from an unseen farmer, a dog crept low and stealthily toward the flock. "Of course you don't. After all, what's the point in dredging up the past? You turned away from me that night, and you've never shown a moment's remorse."

"Turned away from you? I've always watched over you. Always! Even when you were away at university—after your father proved to be the thief he is—I got word of how you were doing. You don't know what I felt then, or what I'm feeling now. But look at me!" He pulled her face toward him when instead she tried to keep her one link to the here and now, that dog earning its day's feed.

"I said, look at me!" Unwillingly, Kylie did. Gerry waved a hand at his dark uniform. "I have official responsibilities, now. I have duties to uphold and a reputation to preserve."

Her laugh was bitter. "Gerry Flynn, member of the *Garda Síochána*, a guardian of the peace. That's hardly a fitting title. You didn't guard me with much care that night."

It was his turn to look away. His hands were pulled into tight, white-knuckled fists. "That night, you were willing. I know you were."

Kylie let the sight of him drift off. The dog had turned the flock back down the hillside. She watched its every move as if her life depended on it. And in some odd way, she knew that it did. *Forgiveness*, echoed the old refrain in her head.

"It helps you, believing that," she eventually said, once she was able to draw breath without the stabbing pain of that old wound. "Well, I won't deprive you of your comforts. I know too well what that feels like." Then the fierceness that had been born last night came back to her. It was a pure, primal feeling, and she embraced it. "But I will tell you to leave Michael and me alone. We're none of your business."

He ignored her warning with the same unblinking determination that he ignored the truth of their past. "He's killed people, did you know that?"

"He's no murderer."

"Ripe for an easy line, aren't you? He's killed and who can say he won't do it again?"

"I can."

"Don't be a fool. You've made a proper, decent life for yourself. And now you're going to toss it away, aren't you?"

"I'm tossing nothing away!"

"No more," he said, then walked away, the sound of his heels on the hard road an echo of that night so long ago. He was almost back to his car when he stopped and turned to look at her, his expression flat. "I'll be free of you now."

I'll be free of you now. As if she'd somehow held him in a spell, as if by saying those words, he could undo the past and move on. She hugged herself for warmth, for comfort.

Gerry pulled by slowly, his eyes cold and straight on, never once moving in her direction. With the gait of an ancient, Kylie got into her car and turned back toward home.

Michael sat at an old oaken table in Jenna Fahey's kitchen, the cookbooks he'd borrowed piled in front of him. She chatted amiably as she bustled about, never slowing from her tasks. He asked her a few questions about America, a country that had always intrigued him with its vitality and confidence. She mentioned that she was originally from Chicago.

"So, why did you leave?" he found himself saying.

Her smile was bright. "I'd done all the damage there a girl can do." She looked down for a moment, then back to him. "Actually, I left to train in France. After working under a few different mentors, I decided it was time to be on my own."

"But in Ballymuir? It's hardly on the beaten path."

"To me, it's home," she said. "When I landed in Ireland for the very first time, I had a sense that this is what had been missing from my life. The mountains, the green . . ."

"Even the rain?"

She laughed. "Even that. This house is where I was meant to be. I can't think of a place with better atmosphere for a restaurant."

"You know," he mused, thumbing through one of the books, "I'd always thought of cooking as some sort of genteel pastime—ladies making tea cakes and fussy desserts."

"And now?"

"Now I think you chefs are a violent lot." He held up the book. "All this talk of carcasses and skinning!"

She laughed. "You've been living in your sister's house too long. She's turned you into a vegetarian."

"Not exactly, but you know I've never given too much thought to where those tasty cuts of meat come from."

"Well, if you're weak-stomached, don't."

Their shared laughter faded away to the sound of someone nervously clearing her throat.

"I'm sorry if I'm interrupting anything—"

Michael looked up to see Kylie in the kitchen doorway. "Vi had told me that I'd find you here, was all, and I—"

He subtly pushed aside the cookbooks. No point in having the woman think he'd gone soft in the head. "You're not interrupting anything. I was, well," he trailed off with what he knew was a foolish grin, "taking a break." At Kylie's lack of an answering smile, he began to worry. "Why aren't you to school by now? Are you not well?"

Kylie hovered in the doorway, and the American woman moved to greet her. "You must be Kylie O'Shea. I've seen you at church, but you've usually got a little more color to you than you do right now. Come in and sit down," she said, ushering her toward the table before Kylie could object. "Can I get you some tea?" At Kylie's murmured assent, Jenna turned and busied herself in the kitchen.

Michael stood and pulled out a chair next to his own. After Kylie sat, he moved close to her. Her face was drawn and her mouth had thinned to a sad curve. He wanted to hold her.

"What happened?"

She just shook her head.

"Michael, I'll leave you to finish putting the tea together," Jenna said from the doorway. "Since it doesn't involve skinning or carcasses, I'm sure you can handle it. Oh, and after Kylie's feeling more, ah, energetic, why don't you show her what you've been up to around here? I'm sure she'll be as impressed as I am."

He nodded his thanks and turned back to Kylie.

"Hang on, let me get you a bite to eat. I don't like the way you're looking." Rummaging about, he found some brown bread and a pot of strawberry preserves. By the time he had that together, the water for the tea was ready and he set it to steep.

Michael sat down again, and slathered the preserves thick on a piece of bread while he talked. "It's not that I'm not pleased to see you, because I am. But I need to know what happened." He handed Kylie the bread and waited for her to take a bite, then chew and swallow. "Now tell me."

"I called in sick. First time since I started to work there," she added, "so I'm hoping they'll forgive me."

He found it no great surprise that she'd feel guilty. She could find a way to feel remorse over the clouds in the sky.

"And are you sick?"

She took her time in answering. "Heartsick, I suppose."

"Why?"

She ran a finger around the rim of her plate. "I don't want to talk about this. I don't want to stir things up."

"Judging by your appearance, things have been stirred already."

Her shoulders slumped even lower. "Gerry Flynn—you know, the Garda—I think he's been following us."

No news there.

"It's not surprising," he said calmly. "A man with a past like mine is bound to attract some attention. Don't let it worry you, though. It's not as if I plan to do anything wrong."

"I know . . . I know." She paused, worrying at her

lower lip with her teeth. "It's just the thought of having eyes on me, even when I don't know, and in my most private moments."

"It's a hard thing," he agreed, recalling how dehumanizing it had been to live that way. Something—please, God—Kylie would never experience. "But I don't think they'll be doing more than driving by now and again."

"But aren't you angry?"

"More resigned." He nudged at the bread to remind her that it waited for her.

"Well, I'm angry for you. It's not right, the way you're being singled out."

"I did that for myself over fourteen years ago. And even though I've been released, I hardly fall in a class with petty criminals. Jesus, I'm sorry, Kylie," he quickly added, chagrined at how close to her heart he'd struck. "I wasn't meaning your father."

"Da's crimes were hardly petty. And it's not Da I'm worrying about, it's you."

"Don't, then. I can take care of myself."

"That doesn't stop me from caring for you," she replied before turning to her bread.

He poured her a cup of tea. "So that's all that has you heartsick, then? Worry for me?"

"That's enough, isn't it?" she answered after a moment, eyes focused on her cup as she stirred in a fat lump of sugar.

It wasn't. Not for a woman like Kylie, with her innate strength and resilience. But he wouldn't press things, wouldn't look any closer at this gift of her presence.

"Spend the day with me," he urged.

"But your work, won't Ms. Fahey be angry?"

"I'll get enough done. Stay, and I'll teach you how to be a carpenter's assistant."

"All right," she said, and he was pleased to see that some of her color was returning. After one last bite of bread, Kylie added, "But we might be better served if I stayed here and had your employer teach me how to cook."

He laughed. "All too true, but I'm keeping you to myself."

He led her to one of the second-floor suites, which was finally taking form. The plasterers had come and done their part, leaving him with details like the cove moldings and baseboards.

Kylie smiled as she walked about, peeking in corners and admiring the view from the bank of windows overlooking the bay.

"Pity Jenna Fahey's not married," she said. "This little alcove would make a perfect nursery."

Her expression grew dreamy. In that instant, Michael saw her with children of her own—loving, living, laughing with a vitality that made his heart turn over.

Of all his regrets over the blows life had dealt him, perhaps the greatest was that he'd never know the joy of a child of his own. His gaze settled on Kylie. She found life difficult as the daughter of Black Johnny. How would the daughter of an even blacker soul, *his soul*, survive? Better not to come into the world at all than to arrive the daughter of a killer.

He cleared his throat. *Back to the present. You've enough to deal with already.*

"Well then, here's what we're to do," he said in as level a voice as he could find. "Pick up that pad of paper and pencil over there, and I'll call down measurements to you. We'll rough-cut the moldings and prime them today."

"*We'll* cut the moldings? Are you expecting me to use that beast over there?" She pointed at the table saw, with its radial arm and rigged out to be any man's dream.

"I'll do the cutting, thanks, but you're not sneaking away before the painting's begun. Speaking of which, go look in the back of my car. You should find a shirt big enough to cover those fine clothes of yours."

"They're not so fine, but they are all I have. I'll be back in a minute."

"Make it no more, or I'll dock your wages," he replied with a growl.

Kylie paused in the doorway. "I don't want your money."

"Then what do you want?"

"Why, whatever other favors you might be willing to give." She finished with a wink and a suggestive little bump of her narrow hips, then flew from sight.

It was some time before Michael worked his slack jaw shut. Soon after that, he gave in to laughter. Pure, joyous laughter.

Kylie walked into the bedroom suite, a fine men's dress shirt in her hands. Surely this couldn't be the garment that Michael had sent her for. She knew little enough about men's clothing, but recognized quality when she held it.

"This was all I saw, and it hardly seems the thing to be painting in."

"It's exactly the thing," he said. "Vi pulled it from a box the other day, and tossed it my way. I think it must have belonged to one of her men, because she muttered something about opinionated Frenchmen. It's too small for me, but I thought it might make good rags."

Kylie clutched the shirt tighter. The man was mad. "Rags?"

"No?" he asked, obviously unimpressed by the hand-tailored work he'd discarded.

"It's mine now," she announced.

Busy running a tape measure from corner to corner in the sunny room, Michael nodded absently in response to her declaration of ownership. When he called a measurement to her, she put aside the shirt and jotted a note on the pad after confirming the number. On they went until he had all that he needed.

He switched on the saw and began cutting pieces of wood to the lengths he'd called. Kylie would have thought he was oblivious to her, except for the quick glances she felt come her way. That, and from the warmth and contentment that filled the room, cheery as the sun itself.

At loose ends, she picked up the shirt and tugged it on over her own proper blouse and skirt. After buttoning the cuffs, and then from top to bottom, she chuckled at the whimsical picture she made, elegant business layered over frayed schoolteacher.

Looking down, Kylie frowned. Her dark-blue wool skirt still peeked from the bottom of the oversized shirt. Much as she hated the skirt, she would even more if it were dotted with paint. It had to go. Glancing at Michael, she saw that he had his back to her. No loss of dignity if she were to just slip her hands up under the shirt, like so, and quickly unbutton and unzip the blue wool, then slide it off.

With a last wriggle and a sigh of relief, she accomplished her task. She folded the skirt and tucked it in a relatively debris-free corner of the room. All she was showing was a little knee and only a few inches higher where the tails of the shirt cut upward. Besides, she still had her stockings and shoes on. Hardly enough to inflame a man, now was it?

When she again looked at Michael, she saw that at one point or another he had turned to face her. Mouth agape, he stood with his hand poised in midair over the last piece of wood. Best to brazen it out, she decided.

"I hope you don't mind my getting rid of my skirt. The shirt didn't quite cover it, and I've a feeling that I'm going to be rather sloppy."

His hand just hovered there as his eyes traveled from her face downward, then lingered at her knees.

"Sloppy," he echoed in a thick voice.

"With the paint." She tried not to laugh at his dumbfounded expression, rather like one who had been slipped a shot or three of whiskey in his morning tea.

"Ah." He stared over at his hand as if he wondered what it was doing out there. Quickly dropping it to his side, he said, "Well, I want my workers to be comfortable."

"I'm comfortable enough . . . for now," she added, throwing a cheeky grin his way.

The choked noise he made was everything she'd hoped for. How grand it felt to be a bit of a flirt. And a bit of a fraud, too, Kylie admitted to herself. Knowing they were well chaperoned by Jenna Fahey gave her a boldness she wouldn't otherwise possess.

Michael opened a paint can and began stirring. After a moment or two, he cast a considering look her way. "I'd be worried about those shoes, if I were you."

"My shoes?"

"Paint thinner is hell on leather. You'd have no hope of saving the shoes if you got paint on 'em."

"You think?"

"I do," he affirmed.

"Well, then there's only one thing to be done for it." Kylie slipped out of her shoes. "But now my stockings will never survive," she said with just a hint of a regretful sigh. "They'll have ladders all the way up if I walk shoeless on this rough floor."

A smile played at the corners of his mouth. "You think?"

"I do. Now turn your back."

He did, but not without a muttered objection. And she wondered just how much he was picking up anyway, while he faced the windows with their fine reflective qualities. She'd not deprive him of his little game. After all, he was playing so nicely with her. A little roll of the waistband downward, then some awkward tugging and she was free of her stockings. All dignity, she carried them and the shoes over to the corner to join her skirt.

"You can look now," she said, smiling at his own smile in the window.

Whistling a cheery tune, he pulled two paint-brushes out of a box filled with a jumble of tools. "Ready to work?"

She nodded, taking a brush from him.

"Now, you don't need a heavy hand when you paint," Michael began directing before she'd even dipped her brush in the can. "All we're doing is seal-ing off—"

Truly the take-charge sort, she mused. And in need of a reminder that this game was being played according to *her* rules.

"Oh, no," she murmured, shaking her head rue-fully at the sliver of white blouse that peeped out from beneath one shirt cuff.

"What's the matter?"

"My blouse," she said gesturing at the smidgen of exposed fabric. "It's not quite covered, and it's my best one, too."

Michael's green eyes widened and grew brighter with humor. "Are you suggesting that—" He fin-ished the thought by waving his brush in the direc-tion of her clothing pile.

Kylie nodded. "It would be a shame to have any-thing happen to it, don't you think?"

"I do. Shall I turn my back?"

She hesitated a heartbeat, then purred out her answer. "Only if you want to."

His mouth worked soundlessly for a moment, then he finished with a shaky, "I don't."

For a woman with no experience in sheer brazenness, Kylie was finding she had quite a taste for it. After a dramatic pause, she slowly unbuttoned the dress shirt's cuffs. Biting her lower lip with feigned nervousness, she brought her right hand to the top button of the shirt, toyed with it for a moment, but then shook her head and left the garment chastely buttoned. She thought she heard Michael make some sort of low growl in response.

"This will only take a sec," she promised, knowing the noise he'd made had nothing to do with impatience. "I don't want to keep you from your work."

Holding the shirt's right cuff firm in her opposite hand, she tugged free, then did the same for the other arm. Now she wore it rather like a tent buttoned around her, with her arms able to move beneath its protection. Safely covered, she set to work on her blouse.

Kylie allowed her eyes to meet Michael's. Humming a merry tune of her own, she quickly unbuttoned the blouse, slipped it off, and let it drop from beneath the shirt and onto the floor. All the while she reveled in the parade of emotions crossing his face: surprise, frustration, and finally, what looked to be amused respect.

She scarcely had her arms back through the dress shirt's sleeves before he hauled her up against his hard, warm body.

"You're a smart one, aren't you?"

She had no chance to agree. All hot persuasion, his mouth settled over hers. Here, drawing up on tiptoe, snuggling in closer, wrapping herself around him, Kylie was just where she wanted to be. Lord, he tasted dangerous. Forbidden. Perfect.

Breaking the kiss to send his mouth on a fiery trail over one cheek, against her jaw, and finally to the sensitive spot beneath her ear, he murmured words of praise and encouragement. Not that the desire singing inside her needed any prompting.

Slipping under the fabric of the shirt, he cupped her bottom with his big hands, lifting her. She moaned with pleasure.

"Silky," he said before bringing his lips to hers again, and she knew that he wasn't referring to her plain cotton undies, but to the skin beneath them, that he stroked with his thumbs.

Kylie's head whirled with the wonderful decadence of the moment. The taste of Michael, the feel of the sun shining through the windows on them, and her with nothing more than a shirt to cover her. It was the wildest thing she'd ever done.

She loved it.

She wanted to tug off his work shirt and run her fingers over the hard rises of muscle on his chest. She wanted to trace lower to the arousal she could feel insistent—but, no, not frightening—against her belly. A quiver, then another ran through her, decidedly not fear. She wanted, trembled with wanting, practically keened with wanting.

Michael abruptly set her back on her feet. "You're shaking. I'm scaring you, aren't I?"

Hands still braced on his chest, sure she couldn't stand on her own, she tried to pull together words. "No . . . no you're not," she managed, thinking that she was the one who sounded muddled now. "Just hold me."

He did, rubbing his hand up and down her back. "We're best not left alone," he said. "At least not until we're both ready to, ah . . . see this to its natural end."

Kylie nodded, the side of her face pressed into his chest. His heart was slowing now, and she could sense his tremendous struggle to rein himself in. Michael, patient, kind, and infinitely desirable Michael. He was right, though. She wondered if she'd feel this grand, sweeping need if she were in a place private enough that it could be satisfied.

Minutes slipped by as they held each other. Eventually, she stepped back and found that she could stand on her own. "I'll help you with the painting now," she offered.

"One promise, first," he said with a crooked grin. "You'll keep the shirt on. I'm not sure I'd survive that dropping to the floor as well."

"The shirt stays on," she agreed, doubting she'd survive the consequences of taking it off. But she was beginning to want to find out.

Chapter Thirteen

There's trouble in every house, and some in the street.
— IRISH PROVERB

Michael knew he was no saint. Yet watching Kylie walk about half-undressed and knowing that to touch her again would be as incendiary an act as he could imagine, he felt a kinship with those martyred souls. Saints, though, never fell to temptation. He was falling, and falling fast.

He glanced around the room, racking his brain for just one more task that would have her up on tiptoe, giving him a tasty peek at pink panties. Ah, temptation, those panties and the skin beneath. Skin that he now knew for certain was firm and silky and that he believed must taste of paradise. He closed his eyes, reveling in a vision of pale white skin and fine, slender legs hugging tight around his. . . .

"Michael . . . Michael, you're dripping paint all over the floor!"

"Sweet—" He cut off the oath, and swung his paintbrush back over the can. Giving painting up for now, at least, he wiped the brush and lay it in a tray.

"Perhaps it's time I take over as supervisor," Kylie said, her eyes shining with amusement. "You're not earning your wages."

In truth, he wasn't, but he was earning something of far greater value—Kylie's trust. There was an ease to their togetherness they hadn't managed before. If the cost was a certain discomfort below the belt, he'd lived through worse.

"Well then, supervisor, I'm at your mercy." Which, indeed, he was. "Tell me what you want."

She swallowed once, and a blush crept upward from the collar of that damned shirt and began to paint her face.

"I want you to have dinner with me. Tonight. In town. Someplace fine." She blurted out the words quickly.

Frustration and vile, acid emotions he couldn't begin to name swallowed him whole. Dammit, it wasn't so much to ask, that meal someplace fine. That is, if he could eat—hell, walk down the street—without the hard stares and comments not quite out of hearing. If she could be seen with him without destroying her reputation. She asked for the moon, and it killed him not to deliver.

"Are you forgetting you called in sick today?" he

prompted, relieved that the excuse had even come to him. "It wouldn't do to be running into one of the parents, or worse yet, your boss."

Kylie's shoulders slumped. "I'd forgotten. I make a dreadful liar, don't I?"

He worked up a smile. "That's no sin." Though it was a sin to be playing so mercilessly on her sense of duty.

She sighed, then turned to look out the window. After a moment she swung back to face him. "I don't want this day to end. It's silly, I know, to think I'm so special that time would stop for me."

He walked to her. Heedless of the paint smears on his hands, he cupped her face between his palms. "You're a thousand small wonders, Kylie, love, adding up to one grand miracle." He softly kissed her, a tribute to her and a promise to both of them that he wouldn't destroy what they were so carefully building. "Let's get this room cleaned up. Then you drive on home and I'll come for you later. What do you think of dinner and maybe a show in Tralee? You should be safe enough that far from home."

Her smile returned. "That sounds grand."

An hour later, Michael stuck his nose into a barren refrigerator. For a woman who claimed to live on only a bit of yogurt, his sister had a mysterious way of making food disappear. He wanted just the small-est nibble to tide him over until Tralee, and he wouldn't be having even that. Unless he did what he hadn't in weeks—made a trip to town without Vi to shield him.

Wincing, Michael slammed the refrigerator shut. God, what a coward he'd become, standing behind his sister. His future came to him in an ugly vision—years of slump-shouldered, tail-tucked scurrying.

Since Kylie's sensitive ears weren't present to witness the act, he loosed a string of oaths. The hell if he'd let this town starve him out. The hell if he'd live like he was under siege. He'd rather take the blows and face them alone than hide anymore. Only one thing in his life would he hide, and that was his time with Kylie. Michael wrenched on his jacket and readied for war.

He marched through town meeting each expression of distrust with a bold grin and an exaggerated nod of his head. And behind that smile wide enough to swallow the River Shannon, he thought, sodding old biddies whispering behind their hands and not knowing shit.

He swung open the door to Spillane's making the bell chime with frantic alarm. Whistling loudly, he took a basket and filled it at his leisure. Spillane followed four paces behind, stopping each time Michael did. After the third aisle he'd had enough. Michael swiftly turned the corner, then hauled to a stop. He wheeled around as the grocer came up on his heels.

"Is there something you're wanting to say to me, Spillane?"

The man actually wrung his hands. "I was just wondering if . . . if . . . you're finding everything you need?"

"Were you now? How charitable. I'm doing fine,

thank you. That is, unless you might have some explosives hidden behind that row of Puffy Oaties. A man can never be too prepared, if you know what I mean."

Spillane's mouth worked in a round, gaping "O" with no sound to match the motion.

"What? None at all?" Michael gave a regretful shake of his head. "Then after you take my money—and you *will* be taking it—I'll just have to visit the hardware. I can work bleedin' miracles with a few boxes of nails and a bit of plastique, you know? Top in my class at terrorist school."

He ambled to the counter and set down the basket. "Hurry along, Spillane. I've got business to attend to."

Michael's smile was meaner as he strolled back through the village streets. Meaner, but also one hell of a lot more genuine. Doing penance had never been one of his favorite pastimes, and doing it for those who didn't deserve his apologies was repugnant. What he repented for—and he *did* repent—was between himself and that God who had looked the other way at so many crucial times in his life.

Stones and glass houses, Michael thought as he took the steps to Vi's front door. Plenty of stones hereabouts, and some strong arms to heft them. All he could do was snatch the missiles from the air and fling them back at their senders. Imperfect justice was better than none at all.

To Kylie, Tralee was a wonderful, almost exotic place. It amazed her that she'd have the choice between spicy Indian cuisine or sturdy Irish meat and potatoes, and between live theater or cinema. After all, choice wasn't something she'd experienced often in life.

As she and Michael cut through the pathways of Town Park on their way from dinner to a movie, he held tight to her hand. Kylie smiled, wondering if he thought she'd wander off in the soft twilight if set free. Silly, because there was no place she'd rather be than by his side. Especially here. She imagined that after imprisonment a man would value solitude, but it was such a pleasure to walk next to him in the busy park, with couples and families all bustling from one place to the next.

Dormant now, in summer the park's roses would be in full, glorious bloom. She drew in a deep breath, imagining their scent and practically seeing the riot of yellows and crimsons.

As she indulged in this walking dream, Michael slowed. "Am I moving too fast for you?"

"No, I was just smelling the flowers."

He made an amused noise, sort of a cross between a growl and a laugh. "Like you imagined how Muir House smelled?"

She nodded. "Exactly."

"I'm beginning to worry about you, love. For a practical woman, you don't seem very well anchored in the here and now."

It wasn't so much that she didn't know where she was. Over the empty years, she simply had fallen into the habit of embellishing life. Gazing at Michael, she realized that the here and now was finally enough.

"I like it, that you're worrying," she said. "But don't waste much sleep over me. Not for that, at least." Flirtation was coming easier and easier, too.

He chuckled and gently tugged her hand. "You're becoming just a bit of a tart."

"That's not so bad, is it?" She had meant the question to be joking, but its tentative tone gave away her concern. The rules, the boundaries, those lines one simply didn't cross when dealing with matters of a sexual nature, it was as unfamiliar to her as the mulligatawny soup she'd tried—and loved—at dinner.

They stopped, and he took both her hands in his. "It's not. At least if you don't loose your new-found talents on anyone else. I want you to be comfortable with me, and know you can say or do anything. Between us, away from the others, anything, Kylie."

This gift held only the value she was bold enough to give it. She was braver now, stronger than she had been that day Michael first stepped over a low stone wall and into her life. She knew what she wanted, though she still wasn't quite brazen enough to give it words.

"Thank you," she said, then went up on tiptoe and brushed a kiss against his mouth, chilly but welcoming in the evening air.

They walked to the cinema without sharing any more talk. Kylie was accustomed to his silences, but still wished that she could slip inside his mind and see what he examined with such intensity when those quiet times came.

Turning the corner, they found that a small group had already queued up for the night's shows. As they took their place at the end of the line, she offered up some teasing chat about how kind it was of him to agree to the Shakespearean movie instead of the action thriller she suspected most everybody else would be seeing. As she spoke her gaze brushed over the crowd, then flew back to one head of auburn-colored hair. A shrill, unpleasant laugh carried back to her.

"Evie," she muttered just under her breath, thinking how unfair it was that even miles away from home she would be haunted by Evie Nolan.

She watched as Evie took a last drag on a cigarette, then stepped a bit out of line to toss the butt onto the sidewalk and grind it under the toe of her black, sharp-heeled boot. Just the sight of her was enough to dim the bright evening. Kylie unconsciously slipped closer to Michael.

"Are you all right?" he asked.

"Grand. Couldn't be better," she lied, then added, "I'm looking forward to the show." Particularly because Evie would as likely be caught translating Attic Greek as she would watching Shakespeare. "I haven't been to the cinema in ages."

"More recently than I have," Michael said with just a hint of a smile.

"I doubt that it's changed so much. Just to bring back memories of your youth, we'll sit in the back row and kiss."

"If it's my youth we're trying to conjure, we'd do better by pelting the audience with hard candies."

"One of those, were you?"

"Trouble from beginning to end," he said.

Almost in answer, Kylie again heard Evie's harsh laughter.

"Sometimes I wish I'd been a bit more trouble myself. Just a spot or two of mischief to keep Da on his toes," Kylie said, trying to drown out thoughts and sounds of Evie. It didn't work.

Kylie knew that if she were brave, she wouldn't care who saw them together—Evie, the Gaelscoil teachers, or the entire village. She shouldn't care, but an unpleasant churning in her stomach told her that she might, after all.

Lies and evil were Evie's forte. A night at the cinema would become a tryst at the hotel when Evie was through refashioning events. And once a story was out in town gossip, it was as good as fact. Better, actually.

Kylie smoothed a lock of flyaway hair with one shaking hand. She'd been naive to think that she and Michael could walk the village streets without a wave of malicious but oh-so-sanctimoniously-delivered gossip following: *Did you hear about the schoolteacher and the child killer?* It seemed they couldn't even manage a night out in Tralee.

She forgot what she'd just been talking to Michael about, where they were, everything but the tension that was making tiny beads of perspiration form on the back of her neck. She felt ill, physically ill.

She opened her mouth, intending to come up with some good reason for the two of them to leave. "Ah—"

At that moment, Michael's hand tensed, then just as quickly relaxed.

"I—" he said, then hesitated before asking, "You were saying something?"

"Dinner's suddenly not sitting too well with me," she said barely able to voice the lie above a whisper. "Would you mind too much if we went home?"

He tipped up her face and looked at her with obvious concern. "You're looking pale. Maybe it's best if we came back another night."

One when Evie's back home making someone else miserable, Kylie thought. "I'll make it up to you," she said aloud.

Michael took her hand again and led her toward the car. And away from Evie. "You've got nothing to make up, love."

At that last word—*love*—warmth flowed over the frozen edges of Kylie's guilt. He'd been calling her that more often—*love*. She wasn't vain or even hopeful enough to think it meant he really loved her. Or even so sure that beneath the hard anger that held him, Michael knew how to love. Still, he cared. And she cared for him.

She'd done right by protecting them from Evie tonight. It didn't make her weak or selfish. She was simply looking out for their well-being. Practically noble, she was. Her stomach rolled again. Kylie ducked her head and watched her feet and Michael's close the distance to safety.

Michael saw Kylie safely inside her tiny home, then sat in his car and watched as a light flickered on in

her bedroom. He leaned back against worn uphol-
stery and released the breath he felt as though he'd
been holding for the past hour and more. It had been
a close thing tonight, avoiding Evie Nolan. Kylie
might think herself strong, but she was too inher-
ently good to survive what Evie could deliver.

Thank God the Indian food hadn't set well.
Thank God they'd gotten away before she had seen
Evie. Kylie would have insisted on facing her
down. Michael knew that as surely as he knew his
own name. And as surely as he knew that Gerry
Flynn was waiting for him down at the main road,
ready to tail him back through the village, as he
had all the way to Kylie's. Small-town life at its
finest.

A large city like Dublin or even Cork had a certain
amount of appeal. A man could get lost there, simply
fade into anonymity. And anonymity was something
he craved more than a good meal, or mates to share a
pint and a laugh with. But a large city didn't hold
Kylie O'Shea, and Michael was afraid that she held
him.

One battle to the next, he thought, starting the car
and readying himself for whatever Flynn had in
mind this night. Once Michael made the main road,
the Garda followed him steadily to the edge of the
village, then flashed his lights. Michael pulled over,
his jaw so tense that the ache crept down his neck.

"Evening," Flynn said as he gazed into the car's
open window. "Would you mind stepping on out?"

"A pleasure." He hated sitting beneath the man's
gaze. It brought back memories of how it had felt to

be slammed into the pub floor and have Flynn sneering down at him with an oddly intense expression of hatred. Even older memories of hard, concrete floor, brutal hits, and humiliation slithered forward to claim him. Michael shoved them back. He was a free man now, free to be hunted and harassed.

Glad for his inches and muscle in excess of Flynn's, he got out of the car and leaned casually against its fender. In the steady shine of the Garda's headlights, he caught Flynn's hostile expression. "Time for another friendly chat, is it?"

"You left town tonight."

Michael shrugged. "That's not a crime."

"It might be if you were meeting old friends."

"I was entertaining new ones," he answered, knowing that the smugness he hadn't quite been able to suppress would just tie Flynn all the closer to his tail. "You know Kylie was in the car with me, and you know I just dropped her back home."

"What I don't know is where you went."

"And you're looking for me to tell you? Not too bloody likely. You'll just have to start wandering further afield."

Flynn clenched, then unclenched his jaw before getting words out. "It would be in your favor if you were cooperative."

"Balls. I was cooperative before and all it bought me was a cell in the Maze. Besides, what do I have to be cooperative about? My life's none of your concern. Christ, I work as a handyman, live under my sister's roof, and don't know more than a handful of people who willingly speak to me!"

"Brian Rourke . . . does he speak to you? Or you to him?"

The name had all the subtlety of a knife in the back. "Rourke?" Michael spat. "What the hell would I know about him?" *Except that I wish him dead*, he added silently.

"You might know where he is," Flynn said. "Word is he's back in the country—Sligo or Galway. You can tell him it's just a matter of time till we get him."

If he were here at all—which Michael refused to believe—it would be Galway. Rourke's group had always had strong connections there. In prison, Michael's padmates had mentioned more than once a backstreet pub that was their meeting point. Not that he gave a good goddamn where Rourke was. Unless it was six feet under Galway's rocky soil.

"I'll be cheering when you find him," he said aloud.

"Will you? There are those who have their doubts."

"With you being one of them, right, Flynn?" Michael stood to his full height. "I've been patient with you, Gerry, me boy. I've tolerated your little game of following me about, but that patience of mine—it's wearing thin. You do your job, boring as you'll find it following the village pariah, but keep your distance. From both me and Kylie. Understand? Now, unless you have an official reason to be stopping me, I'll be on my way."

Michael brushed past him. Flynn moved an instinctive step backward, and didn't stop him from getting back in the car.

The Garda's voice quavered. "You've had your

say, but know this, you murderous filth. You'll be going back to prison, where you belong. If it's the last goddamn thing I do, I'll be the one getting you there. And I'll be doing the cheering then."

A challenge, was it? Before he rolled up his window and drove off, Michael tossed one of his own. "If you can accomplish that, feel free to cheer, you stupid bastard."

Chapter Fourteen

Possession satisfies.
—IRISH PROVERB

Feet slamming down the stairs, Michael bellowed, "Vi, pick up the damn phone!" Five rings now and she hadn't bothered to stop singing long enough to answer it. "Taking after Father, are you? Deaf as a post?"

By eight rings, he loomed over his sister. Vi lounged in her overstuffed chair in front of the empty hearth, singing an old song about family far across the sea. She paused only long enough to arch a brow in his direction.

"It's not for me."

Michael bit back an annoyed remark about the grim fate of witches. He'd settle for wiping that complacent grin off her face. Once he'd answered the damn phone.

"Hello."

"Ah . . . is that you, Michael?" The voice was male—a young one trying to sound adult. City noises played in the background.

"It is. Who's this?"

"Pat." Relative silence was followed by the sound of nervousness being gulped back. "Your brother . . . Pat."

Michael shot an incredulous look Vi's way. Her smile grew until she found the good sense to hide it behind her morning mug of tea.

" 'Lo, Pat. Were you looking for Violet?"

"Uh, no . . . actually, I was looking for you."

For *him?*

"I see," he said. But he didn't see at all. His memory of Pat was one of two matching carrot-headed boys crying, whining, and generally being dual pains in the ass.

"Tell him I'm here, too," he heard someone shouting not far from the phone.

"I . . . uh, we—Danny and me—were wondering how you are."

"Fine, and you?"

"Expelled from school for the rest of the week, but if Mam doesn't catch wind of it, we should be right enough."

Michael almost smiled, recalling his own early efforts to sneak behind Mam's back. "I won't be telling her."

"We didn't figure you would, especially since every time we mention your name, she tightens her lips down to nothing. I keep hoping that one day when she does that, her mouth'll seal shut. Life would be easier then, wouldn't it? Anyway, we were thinking maybe this is a good time to come visit. We picked up the bus schedule and so long as we're careful we could be to Ballymuir and back before Mam ever knows we're missing."

Michael gazed down at the cold tile floor. The chill under his bare feet wasn't nearly as uncomfortable as this call. He didn't want to hear about his mother. He knew her well enough. The twins, though, were strangers to him. Worse, they represented another link to the mother and father he wanted to cut from his life. As they had cut him.

Michael tried to keep his anger behind his teeth. "I'm working now, busy all day."

"We don't want to be entertained. We just want to see you."

Couldn't the boy take a "no" with some measure of grace? "If you go sneaking off without your mother's permission, you can be damned sure it'll be the last time you see me. Hell, you'd be lucky to leave the house for another year."

"We're seventeen years old and free to go where we want."

"Then why are you calling me from a pay phone? If you have all this freedom, why not go home and ring me up from there?"

Pat didn't answer. An uncomfortable knot grew in

Michael's gut and traveled outward, leaving him tense. "Look, it's not that I don't want to see you, but the time's just not right."

"Yeah? When will it be, Michael? You don't want to see us at all. It was pretty soddin' stupid of us to think you would."

"Wait—" But the line was already dead. Telling himself it was for the best, Michael hung up, too.

"Royally screwed that up, didn't you?" Vi commented.

"Why don't you just go back to your singing?" He kneaded at the back of his neck where the guilt seemed to have settled.

She stretched, then stood. "I've got nothing to sing about." As she padded toward the kitchen, mug in hand, she added, "Would it have killed you to see them?"

He followed, nearly tripping over Roger, who'd come to associate him with a buffet of failed cooking experiments.

"Not now," he murmured to the dog, then turned to his sister. "What would I say to them? What the hell do they want?"

"They want a brother. And as for what you'd say to them, say whatever. You, more than anyone, know it's not the words that matter, it's welcoming them into your life."

"Maybe I don't need them."

Vi's empty mug clattered onto the counter. "You really can be a selfish bastard, can't you? Did it ever occur to you that Pat and Danny need *you*? That Mam's been as horrible to them as she was to you?

Have you thought beyond your own troubles even once since you got out of prison?"

He opened his mouth to answer, but she wasn't quite done.

"And don't be telling me you don't need your family! Is your life so rich and wonderful? Now, I'm glad for Kylie and for your work at Muir House, too. But is it all so grand that you can afford to shut out the rest of the world?"

It was a blessing that he loved Vi, because at that moment he didn't like her very much. "Can't you ever leave me alone? Isn't anything I do enough?"

Her expression softened, and he thought maybe he saw a hint of tears shining in her eyes. "Everything you've done is wonderful, and I know that healing yourself is no easy thing. But you can't stop now. Weeks ago I would have held off Pat and Danny, told them to wait before they spoke to you. It's different now—you're ready. You can be what they need, and you just might get something back in return." She paused. "It's been that way with Kylie, hasn't it?"

"Yeah, but I could no more have turned away from Kylie than I could from—"

"Your own brothers?"

She had a tidy way of making him feel small. Of forcing the truth on him. Michael made a show of getting a mug and throwing together a cup of tea.

"If they call again," he said over his shoulder, "tell them . . . tell them that I'm asking after them."

"Good enough."

It had better be. It was all he was willing to offer.

"I'm expecting that you'll be out at Kylie's this evening," Vi said after a tactful silence.

"I will."

Over the past few weeks, two routines had become part of his life. Michael liked the first one far more than the second. Each night he slipped off to Kylie's where they would share dinner and talk about their day. Then they'd spend time holding each other, edging closer to the point where there would be no turning back. Where need would push past her lingering hesitance. Soon, he thought. Soon or he just might die from wanting her so badly.

The second routine was his nightly drive home with Gerry Flynn staying just far enough back that he couldn't do a damn thing about it. With luck, Flynn would tire of the game—or find some better way to spend his nights—before he was forced to spread the boy's nose from ear to ear.

He pulled out of his thoughts to see Vi digging around in the velvet sack he privately termed her sorcerer's bag. She drew out an envelope with a victorious "Ah!"

"When you see Kylie, give her this, will you?"

Michael took the letter. "What is it?"

Vi laughed. "None of your business." At his threatening look she added, "What do you think, vain man, that we're passing notes about you?"

"Kylie, I trust. You, Sis, take a little more watching."

"Me? You'll be steaming open that envelope the second I turn my back. And just to find out that I've managed to secure Village Hall for the Gaelscoil student art show, too."

"That was grand of you. Kylie will be thrilled."

His sister shrugged off the kind act. "It was nothing."

"To think that I was doubting your motives," he teased, "nosing into Kylie's life like you did."

"All right, so I wasn't exactly pure-hearted when I started this project, but I like my time with the children. I like watching Kylie, too. She's a natural with them, you know. I wouldn't be surprised if she wanted a brood of her own."

"Now you get your own words back. It's none of your business."

"It's not, but it's something you'd best be considering."

He preferred to consider the step preceding parenthood. Much preferred it. "You sound like one of those talk programs on the radio. But I haven't rung you up and I'm not looking for advice."

"Then just store that bit away for when you are," Vi said before disappearing back to her bedroom.

Left in the kitchen with just Roger for company, he said, "Keep an eye on her today. She's up to no good."

The dog peered up at him as if to ask, *What's in it for me?*

"You'll be getting a true dinner tonight," Michael answered, no longer concerned that he'd fallen into the habit of talking to the homely beast. "It's my night to bring food to Kylie's."

Seduction. Kylie rolled her eyes at the thought. No woman had ever been less equipped to carry off the act. But seduction was all she had left—a flat-out luring of Michael into her bed. For days now he'd been noble and not gone beyond the kisses and touches that left her weak-limbed and knowing that there was something absolutely marvelous shimmering just beyond her reach.

How she wanted him! One dreadful night in her past was nothing against the here and now. Nothing against her need.

Seduction. He'd never take that last step before she asked, and the idea of asking filled her with panic. Kylie peered down at the silky top and tweed trousers she'd put on. They were a bit more alluring than the drab convent blue skirt and white blouse she'd worn to work yet again today. Better, but hardly how she had pictured this moment.

Soon he'd be knocking at the door. She had mere minutes to go from schoolteacher to seductress. Kylie flew back into the bedroom. Fingers fumbling, she tugged out of her tweeds, then stared into the gaping doors of her wardrobe.

"Well, what then?" she asked, shoving aside her only two dresses. And there it hung, the man's shirt that Michael had tossed to her weeks before. She smiled at the memory and felt her fear begin to fade.

"Of course." She'd been a seductress that day. She slipped on the shirt over her conservative undies, which she didn't even consider taking off. One could carry a role only so far. Kylie walked to the front room. She pulled aside the curtain and looked out the window, hoping Michael would appear soon.

Before her courage fled.

She drew in her breath as his car made its way up

the track. Wiping her palms on the soft cotton of the shirt, she fought the impulse to grab her robe and delay this seduction business.

"Coward," she chastised herself, then swung open the door. A cold wind eddied around her bare legs, at least giving an excuse for her shivering and goose-flesh, she supposed.

Juggling a bottle of wine, a casserole dish, and a sack, Michael didn't look directly at her until he reached the stoop.

"I brought—" His eyes widened, then his gaze skittered back to the bundles he carried. He cleared his throat. "I . . . ah . . . brought—"

"Dinner," she finished for him. Feeling a complete fool, she crossed her arms over her breasts, as though the act would somehow make up for her scanty clothing. She stepped aside as he entered, then closed the door behind him.

Michael rattled about in the kitchen, doing, it seemed, everything he could to avoid acknowledging that she was in the room. And wearing nothing but a shirt.

Seduction? Hardly. She should have known she'd be a failure at this. Not that the blame was entirely hers. How thick-headed could one man be?

He poured some wine. "Would you like something to drink?"

"Nothing for me, thanks," she said, leaving him to offer the glass to the spot just to her right where he seemed to be staring.

"Well, dinner, then," he said and bolted for the table.

Kylie bit back a frustrated sigh. "Did you notice anything different about me tonight?"

He put the wine at her place, then sat and peered down at his empty plate. "Different?"

"Yes, different." Standing above him, she laid her hand on his shoulder. He tensed beneath her touch. "Surely you don't think I wore this to school today."

Busy nudging at his silverware, he still wouldn't look at her. "I figured you had a bit of a lie-down when you got home."

"Really?"

"Or you're not feeling well, is that it?" he ventured, picking his words so gingerly that Kylie had to smile.

She tugged at his shirt until he stood. "I don't suppose you'd like to help me, here? You're making me do all the work, and truthfully, I'd rather be out in that field moving rocks than trying to find some way to tell you that I want you to—"

"Thank God," she heard him say just before his mouth settled over hers.

He kissed her long and hard, nothing held back, and Kylie gave a silent "Thank God" of her own. It was easy to set aside the shyness—to stop worrying—when Michael held her. Hot, demanding, and so very right, he was, Kylie thought just before thinking became impossible. She had put herself in the hands of an obvious expert, after all.

The sweet taste of her, the feel of her tongue meeting and mating with his, the knowledge that tonight—*now*—he would make her his, Michael was wild with it. Wild, spinning, and losing what small bit of control he still had.

Wrapping his hand around Kylie's wrist, he was intent on getting them both into that fantasy of a bed. But, no. It was too damn far. He'd starve if he couldn't see her first. After two steps he stopped and set shaking hands to the buttons on her shirt. She murmured words of encouragement—at least he thought they were—and shrugged her way free as he finished. Pale silken skin covered only by prim white underwear. He smiled at that. This was the Kylie he knew—proper, tidy, and somehow still bold enough to greet him at the door wearing only that damned shirt. She'd knocked him reeling, and he'd scarcely righted himself yet.

"I'm too skinny," she whispered as he took in her beauty.

Michael cupped his hands over her breasts. "Are you, now?" he teased, then with his tongue traced the plump line where her breasts were no longer covered by white cotton. "Plenty there."

He knelt before her and rubbed his thumbs over her hipbones, where their points sat just under her skin. "As for the rest of you, you've only your cooking to blame."

She gave a shaky laugh that turned into a shiver as he brushed his mouth against her mound. He peeled her panties down. She stepped out of them, hands clutching at his shoulders. He wanted to look his fill, and to touch, too, but she whispered his name in an embarrassed little voice.

He stood, then reached behind her to slide the

elastic off the end of her braid and comb his fingers through her hair until it rested in waves over her shoulders. As he kissed her, he fumbled with the tiny hooks on her brassiere. God, what he'd give for a little more finesse, for the endurance to hold her.

The hooks came free, and he managed to rid her of the bra. She moved closer to him. He knew that it was as much to shield herself from his eyes as it was for the physical contact. Michael wrapped his arms around her. He tried to keep his touch comforting, but somehow his hands settled on the curve of her bottom. Another wave of absolute, mindless need rolled over him.

He swung her up into his arms. "I'm trying to go slow, here," he said, and it practically hurt to speak. "I'm trying, love, really I am, but it's just not going to work that way."

"I trust you."

She trusted him, and all he wanted was to get out of his clothes. He set her on the bed, noting that she'd turned back the blankets sometime before he'd arrived. It was a good thing they'd both been thinking about this evening for some time, because he was afraid the act itself was going to be over in short order. Michael stripped with a single-mindedness that bordered on ferocity. He tossed his wallet on the nightstand and covered her body with his own. Skin to skin, they both shook.

"I'm a bit frightened," Kylie whispered.

He supposed it would do neither of them any good to admit that he was, too. "Just let me hold you," he said instead. And for a while, he managed to do just that. He held her until the uncertainty faded, until they both trembled with excitement, not fear. As one, they began a slow dance.

Hands gliding over sleek curves, finding spots he had dreamt of but never touched. Mouths seeking and holding until the need to follow hands grew too strong. Her cry as she arched beneath him. Hours, minutes, a lifetime.

Reaching over to the nightstand and the waiting condom, he readied himself, then moved back between her thighs. In that instant before union, he looked into blue eyes, wide, smoky with need, and so trusting. God, so trusting.

"It's all right, Michael."

Slow, now. Slow, now, he told himself. Tight, wet heat closed around him. Perfect, so incredibly perfect that he couldn't imagine anything finer. Once, twice, he rocked his hips into hers. She gasped and wrapped her legs about him. Michael's head dropped as he fought for control.

Slow, now. He repeated the internal chant in time to his slamming heart. It was no bloody use, for he'd found oblivion. Pure, perfect oblivion.

Chapter Fifteen

Do it as if there was fire in your skin.
—IRISH PROVERB

Kylie tried to wriggle from beneath the dead weight that was her love. "Michael, you're smothering me . . . I can't breathe." Face-down in the pillow he said something that sounded like "Mmrphll," then shifted his weight and rolled onto his back.

She was able to draw air into her lungs, but missed the intimate contact. Then one long arm wrapped around her waist and drew her close. Kylie sighed and snuggled in. Being held this way eased some of the tension still shooting through her veins. Some, but decidedly not all of it. Just when she'd worked up the courage to ask a few questions about what had happened between them, he brushed a kiss on top of her head.

"I'll be right back," he said as he swung his legs over the side of the bed, then sat there a moment as if gathering the strength to stand.

After he left the room, Kylie reached down and pulled the covers up to her chin. She heard the sound of running water from the bathroom and immediately cozied up to the idea of having another soul in the house. Smiling, she reached over to switch off the light—something they'd never gotten around to doing. Her gaze settled on the empty condom packet on the nightstand.

Forgetting the idea of settling in, she scooted closer to the edge of the bed. Two more packets peeked out of Michael's wallet. It seemed bad form to be poking around in his billfold, but . . . Curiosity won. She took one of the little packages, turning it over and flexing it between her fingers. Interesting, really, and something she'd never had the opportunity to inspect. Just as there had been no time to revel in lovemaking before it—actually, Michael—was done.

Kylie sighed. It simply hadn't been what she'd expected. She knew she carried a large burden when it came to these matters, and she shouldn't expect perfection from the first. Still, she had been close, so very close to feeling something brilliant. Something that she knew was as right and natural as her love for Michael. And it was love, or she wouldn't have found the courage to put aside her fears. To give herself to him, body and soul.

"I thought maybe you'd like some dinner," Michael said from the doorway. "That is, unless you have something else in mind." He gave a pointed look at the forgotten condom packet still between her fingers. Kylie quickly tossed it back to the nightstand and focused on him.

"Ah—" Whatever brilliant response she'd planned to give disappeared. He was naked. Beautifully naked. The ache low in her belly that had never quite been satisfied returned with a vengeance. As her gaze traveled over his broad chest, then downward to narrow hips and strong, muscled thighs, it became apparent to her that neither of them was interested in food.

She turned back the covers to welcome him. Michael eased in next to her. The feel of his warm skin, coarse with its dusting of dark hair, sent a hungry thrill through her. Embarrassed by its intensity, she tried to hide her reaction. It was no use, though.

Leaning over, Michael cupped her chin in his hand. "I'm sorry about earlier, love. This time . . . this time it will be slow," he said, pausing between words to kiss her temples and the tip of her nose. "And no matter how much begging you do—or I do, for that matter—I promise I'm taking my time with you. Very . . . thoroughly . . . slow," he finished in a whisper that sent an erotic thrill chasing through her.

Bracing on both hands, he settled his open mouth over the hollow at the base of her throat. His tongue played against her sensitive skin, and Kylie moaned— both with the pleasure of what he was doing, and with her imaginings of where else his talented mouth might travel.

Michael proved to be a veritable artist in promise keeping. Her hair was damp and clinging with perspiration by the time he turned his attention from her mouth to her breasts.

Later—much later—when he slipped lower in the bed and traced her hipbones with his lips, she clenched the sheet in knotted hands, feeling as though she were about to go spinning into the night. Unable to help herself, she cried his name. His answering chuckle held an edge of pure male satisfaction.

"You're not begging yet," he said as he ran his fingers up the insides of her thighs, stopping just short of the deep caress her body demanded.

A brush of his mouth here, a stroke there . . . Kylie wanted to beg, and would have, too, if she had been able to put words together. Since that was impossible, she took a page from Michael's book and gave him the same attention he'd been giving her. His body was a grand new world. She smiled at the crisp texture of his hair beneath her fingers, relished the faintly salty taste of his skin as she flicked her tongue against his hard male nipple.

And she felt great satisfaction when he was the first to beg. Kneeling above him, Kylie reached for one of the two little packets waiting on the nightstand.

"Put this on," she said, wanting to sound all smart and take-charge.

The look he shot her way brought to mind a pasha with one of his favored women. "You do it for me."

She'd been bested at her own game. Tugging at

her lower lip with her teeth, working to still trembling fingers, she gave a valiant try, but Michael's hands quickly replaced her own.

When he was deep within her and skillfully teasing her to the edge of sanity, she gasped, "I'm glad one of us has some idea what they're doing."

He paused and an odd smile crossed his face. "But you're my very first, love."

Just like that, Kylie reached the edge of the world she knew and arched into the hot, dancing starlight beyond.

Leaving Kylie and returning to his own lonely bed struck Michael as madness. Madness, but also very necessary. Rubbing his hands together to fight off the cold, he took one last look at her bedroom light, still shining golden and inviting. Kylie, wrapped in her threadbare robe, appeared in the opening between the sagging drapes. She shouldered aside the hangings and pressed her palm flat to the window. Her smile, rich with lovers' shared secrets, drew him to a stop.

An icy wind hammered at him, the beginnings of rain needled his exposed skin, yet he was wrapped in warmth from the inside out. He returned her smile even though he doubted that she could make out his features in the inky darkness. She was the most beautiful thing he could imagine, and he wanted her more than he did his next breath. He watched her smile grow to a laugh as she shooed him in the direction of his car.

He gave one last wave, then dug his keys from his

pocket and climbed into the mile-weary sedan. As he drove down the narrow lane, an incredible thought settled on him: For the first time in his bleak, god-and-family-forsaken life, he was truly welcome and wanted. Michael smiled, then sobered as he imagined the reaction of his old prison padmates to this new, soft and needy Michael Kilbride.

They'd laughed enough at the reading he'd done and the studies he'd pursued while they spent their days doing as close to nothing as they could. Well, damn them all. Damn Brian Rourke and the rest of those driven, devious bastards who had put hatred above human life. And damn himself for letting them steal so much as a second of his thoughts. He had finer things to think about. Much finer, now.

Soon after he pulled onto the main road, another car's lights shone behind him. It would have meant nothing, except that just there, he knew of no drive, not even the smallest track for the car to have come from. He slowed, and the follower did, too. He slowed more. The car lagged enough to be conspicuous.

"Flynn, of course," he muttered. "A slow learner, that one." Any other time, Michael would have been angry to see the man creeping along behind him. But this wasn't any other time; he'd just finished loving Kylie. He could afford generosity of spirit, something he wagered Flynn knew nothing about.

"If it's a morning's drive you're wanting, that's what you'll be getting, me boy."

So on he drove with no purpose other than giving Flynn his day's exercise. Eventually the rising sun washed the dark from the sky. As it did, Michael got a bit of a surprise. Gerry wasn't in his official-issue white vehicle, but an older, pale-tan one. Off duty, was he?

Keeping a decorous pace, Michael crept past tumbled fences, stone skeletons of long-dead farms, craggy earth, and blank-eyed sheep, their rumps painted bright blue with their owner's mark. He reached the top of a narrow pass. A small gravel car park sat next to a stream that tumbled down the mountainside before disappearing beneath the road. He pulled over, switched off the car, and climbed out.

"Just stretching the legs, Gerry," he called to Flynn, who hadn't bothered to pull onto the gravel. "And I thought I'd freshen up, y'know?" He grinned, then finished with another one of his grandmother's favorite curses, pure Irish and anatomically accurate.

Flynn's brows shot together, and his mouth pulled tight. A slow learner, but not a bad lip-reader, Michael thought.

Michael followed the rain-heavy stream uphill, then bent down. Cupping his hands, he filled them with a shock of icy water. He splashed his face, used his tee to sluice himself dry, and checked on Flynn. Engine idling, the officer waited.

Before returning to his car, Michael picked up a bottle that had been left roadside. He hated the mess someone would leave in the midst of pure beauty, hated the feeling that his land was becoming crowded. He glanced back at Flynn. Too crowded.

He walked to Flynn's window and rapped on it. After hesitating just long enough to give Michael pleasure in knowing he had the boy rattled, Gerry rolled down the window.

"Grand one, isn't it?" Michael said as he tossed the bottles among the food wrappers and other detritus taking root in the back of Flynn's car.

"Grand what?"

"Why, day, of course. But then again, you might not be thinking that," Michael commented. "After all, a night spent sleeping in a car—which you must have done in order to follow me—doesn't put a man in the mind to enjoy a day like this.

"Now, me, I've had sleep enough to be feeling generous, so here's what I'm going to do for you. My schedule, Gerry, in dull, deadly boring detail is this. . . . I'll be taking myself back to my sister's house for a real cleanup and a bite to eat. Then I'm off to work at Muir House, out Slea Head Road, though you've followed me there before, I'm sure. Tonight, I'll be going back to Kylie's—and here's the part I want you to listen to very carefully."

He leaned in the car window. "If, when I'm looking out Miss O'Shea's windows, I catch sight of you in either this piece of shit or your official vehicle, I won't be a nice man, Gerry. You might say hostile, even. And since I'm beginning to see you have no idea where your official duties leave off, I'll be happy to show you. And I won't be rolling over and playing dead for you like I did in the pub that night. Understand?"

Flynn's knuckles shone bony white where he

gripped the steering wheel. "You were with her all night."

Guilt arrowed through Michael. It wasn't wrong, being with Kylie, but it wasn't precisely right, either. He shook off the feeling, and reminded himself that none of this was snot-nosed Flynn's business. "And what of it?"

"If—" He swallowed convulsively. "If you—"

"If I what?" Michael spat. "Don't send your thoughts or your imagination creeping past Kylie O'Shea's front door."

Flynn stared out the front window of his car. Something primal in his expression, in the way his chest heaved as though he'd run up the mountain rather than drove, startled Michael. He'd seen that set of face a dozen times and more in prison—sometimes in his own mirror. Hatred layered over frenzy, a murderous rage.

Flynn turned his glare to Michael, then his hand shot out and grabbed hold of Michael's jacket. Gerry's voice was low, hoarse. The words weren't coming clearly . . . until the last.

"If you've dirtied her," Flynn forced through a clenched jaw, "if you've touched her, I'll kill you for it. This time, I swear I will."

This time? An image—or was it someone's half-memory?—seared Michael's brain. *Kylie's cries, and a sick, seizing panic.*

He wrenched out of Flynn's grasp and staggered back from the car. An angry buzzing sounded in his ears, and the metallic taste of shock and anger sat on his tongue. Eyes half-closed, he tried to draw in a clean breath and find his bearings. It was still morning, they were still miles from town, but the landscape had grown confusing, threatening. He looked back at Flynn.

Gerry gave an inarticulate cry, jammed his car into gear, and left. Gravel spit over the edge of the cliff in his wake.

Michael wiped one shaking hand over his face. It came away wet with sweat and colder than the mountain water he'd washed in. Carefully placing each foot, still not really feeling the ground beneath him, he made his way back to the stream. There, he sat on the hard earth and fought to calm his roiling gut.

Jesus, was this what Vi felt when she saw or sensed evil? This icy sickness, this empty, silent scream welling from somewhere just beneath conscious thought? If so, then God be with her. He'd rather be struck dead than feel it again.

In time, he worked his way to his feet and stared at the water as it raced by. His thoughts raced, too. Had Gerry been with Kylie that night? Had he left her there to suffer? Michael's muscles knotted at the unbearable thought. If so, it was a wonder she'd speak to any man, let alone honor him with her trust. Impossible. She couldn't have survived so much, and come out of the fire so . . . pure. So giving.

Michael shook his head, clearing it of the last of that awful buzzing. Was he sensing a meaning to Gerry's words where there was none to be found? He wasn't Vi, praise the saints. He didn't sense, or feel, or whatever the hell it was his sister did.

Did Gerry and Kylie have more of a past than Kylie had told him? He might well never know the truth. Unless she told him willingly, it was none of his business—even if it was his concern. But if Flynn had been there . . .

Michael looked at his clenched fists. He was better off never knowing. And Flynn was safer that way, too. Much safer.

Kylie allowed herself the luxury of an extra cup of tea before dressing for work. After settling at the kitchen table, she thought of the night before. She felt deliciously tired, and so very pleased with herself. Smug, almost . . . if that weren't such an arrogant thing to be. She smiled at the way she was cloaking herself in humility when she'd done a smashing fine job of tossing it into the ashbin last night.

A humble woman wouldn't have demanded the way she had, wouldn't have reveled in the things she and Michael had done together. A humble woman wouldn't want to do it all again. Now.

Kylie looked at her watch, then stood. Muscles she didn't even know she owned protested the quick action. She stretched, slow and easy, happy for the reminder of last night's passion. Well, then, she thought in answer to the lingering ache, perhaps she wouldn't do it all again this instant, but soon. Very soon.

She walked to the cluttered kitchen counter. For never actually sitting down to dinner, Michael and she had managed to make a very impressive mess. She gave a sorry shake of her head at the remains of the salad Michael had brought. She'd been carried away with herself, indeed, to let good food sit out all night. Pushing aside plates and half-finished glasses of wine, she came upon an envelope addressed to her.

Kylie opened it and unfolded the note inside. In a bold, angular scrawl Vi Kilbride had written that she'd secured the Village Hall for the art festival. Kylie's smile grew to a jubilant laugh. It was a fine pleasure, bringing her students the chance to shine in front of the village. Joy sifted down like glittering fairy dust upon all of the other pleasures—great and small, lasting and not—that she'd experienced over the last several days.

She hummed as she tidied the kitchen, sang as she made her bed, then buried her nose in the blankets for one last bit of Michael's scent. For so long she'd pretended to be conducting her life out of the shadows, pretended that the ugliness with her da—and with Gerry—had little bearing on her present. Perhaps finally now, that game had grown into the truth.

As she showered, energy seeped back into her bones and marvelous plans came to her. Why just a children's art show? Why not dance and food and celebration? By the time she'd dried and dressed, she had mentally dissected the affair into committees, subcommittees and decided whom to approach for what. She felt as though she could take on the world, and win.

Still with a few minutes to spare, she stopped to share her new plans with Breege, and enlist her help in prodding the notoriously slow-moving village council into a quick decision. Standing on Breege's tidy whitewashed stoop, Kylie rapped at the door. Her friend's hearing wasn't what it had once been, though she'd never say that loudly enough for Breege to hear.

After counting to an ambling, lazy "twenty," Kylie knocked again, surely loud enough to be heard over the jovial noise of Breege's telly, which yattered away in the background.

Still, no one came. Kylie opened the front door just enough to stick her head inside.

"Breege? . . . Breege, are you in there?"

When no one answered, Kylie stepped the rest of the way in, and made her past the empty sitting room and to the kitchen at the back of the house. "Breege . . . it's Kylie. Have I caught you at a bad—"

The rest of her words died, for Breege Flaherty lay facedown on the kitchen floor.

Chapter Sixteen

*The health of the men. And may
the women live forever.*

—IRISH TOAST

Kylie hated hospitals. She hated them for their antiseptic smell and for the undercurrent of distress that eddied through the hallways. She hated them for the waiting and for the times people she loved had entered, then never came out. She wasn't ready for it to happen again. But, *Not Breege, please, not Breege,* was the closest to a prayer she'd been able to form.

"Does she have family nearby?" Michael asked. Looking every bit as uncomfortable as Kylie felt, he sat on the hard plastic chair one away from hers. Even though she understood why he kept the discreet distance, she wanted to curl up in his lap and let his strong arms push away her fears.

She shook her head. "Her children emigrated years ago. One daughter lives in London, and the rest are somewhere in Canada. She's never talked of anyone else."

Michael fell silent, then reached across the empty chair between them and took her hand. His thumb stroked slowly over her bones. She closed her eyes and let herself relax.

"Her friends in town?" he eventually asked.

"I called Edna McCafferty," she said without opening her eyes. "She'll be here as soon as her son can drive her over."

They sat another hour before a Sister stopped to tell them that the doctor would be by to speak to them "straightaway," which proved to be another hour, yet.

The doctor cut right to business. "We have Mrs. Flaherty stabilized, though we haven't been able to do anything for the fractures yet."

Kylie's hand crept up to rest at the base of her throat. She could feel her heart slamming. "Fractures?"

"Ankle and leg," he said as though checking off items on a market list. "And she was quite dehydrated. Though the fall wasn't far, apparently she'd been down a day, at least. At her age, that's how we lose them."

The look he gave Kylie wasn't in the least accusatory, but she still felt guilty. "I try to stop in on her every day—" she began, then trailed off as the doctor glanced at his watch.

"You can go in and have a visit," he said, "but keep it brief. She needs her rest. This evening, we'll be able to tell you more about when she can be released."

As a matter of propriety Michael insisted on waiting in the hallway, but Breege was already asleep when Kylie entered the room. She pulled up a chair next to her friend's bed and sat. For the first time, Breege, farmer's wife and mother to half a dozen, looked fragile. A plastic line snaked to her arm, her hair was mussed, and her skin so thin and pale that Kylie could see the veins just beneath the surface. She wished she could give Breege a magic elixir of her own youth.

Time slipped by. Conversation drifted over from the folks on the other side of the curtain, bits and pieces about medication, who'd died, and who'd won the lottery.

Breege's eyes fluttered half-open. "They'd best not be talking about me," she murmured. "I'm not ready to be going."

Kylie softly laughed, then wiped the tears she'd just noticed running down her face. "And we're not ready to have you go," she whispered. She smoothed back Breege's hair, then stood to leave.

Michael guessed the iron-haired woman had to be Breege's friend, Edna. Not that the thought made him want to cozy up to her. Edna, if indeed that was who the woman was, kept shooting him hostile looks. Worse yet, not so much in appearance as in attitude, she reminded him of his mam. He had enough making him break into a sweat without adding the chilly stare that was his mam's trademark.

He stood and moved to the far end of the row of chairs. He didn't want to begrudge Kylie her time with Breege, but he also didn't know how much longer he'd last without suffocating. When Kylie called, he hadn't hesitated. He truly wanted to be here for her. He just didn't want half of Ballymuir knowing that he was, then going back and whispering it to the other half. Old Edna looked to be just the sort to relish a nibble of gossip.

And then there was the more insidious reason that he wanted to hide, the one that ate at his soul. He felt as though a thick, inflexible wall of glass separated him from the rest of the world.

It was more than his stay in prison still holding him captive. He had no idea how one was supposed to behave—or react—at a time like this, and it shamed him. It angered him, too, that he'd been raised by his mother to be so distant. He didn't know how to change. Not at this late date.

From her end of the row, Edna cleared her throat, stood, and turned his way. He considered bolting down the hallway, but was saved the run. Kylie was approaching.

"Edna," she cried and hurried to the old woman. Michael took his cue and disappeared.

Kylie grasped Edna McCafferty's broad, gnarled hands. "I'm so glad you're here. She's sleeping now, but I know she'll feel better just seeing you once she wakes."

Edna pulled Kylie into a hug, then released her. "Poor child, you look knackered. Tell me what happened."

Kylie gave Edna a quick version of finding Breege, and the doctor's prognosis.

"It's lucky that you found her, then," came Edna's brisk response. "And they're taking care of her, so you can quit looking like the world's gone black on you."

Kylie nodded, not trusting herself to speak without tears.

Edna smoothed out her rumpled dress. "Now then, I'm going to settle down for the wait, then give that old bird the sharp side of my tongue for refusing to move to town, as I've been begging her to do for the last twenty years. You go on back home and have a cup of tea, or something even stronger, if you know what I mean," she added with a broad grin. "You need to get your feet back under you."

Edna gestured down the hallway. "I'm assuming that big, hulking one's here for you." She paused, looked in the direction she'd been pointing and gave a shake of her head. "I could have sworn that was the Kilbride man I saw lurking about. You know, Violet Kilbride's elder brother . . ."

Kylie glossed over Edna's speculative question. Gathering her coat from the chair where she'd left it, she said, "I'll get home right enough. And your son will be back to get you?"

Edna nodded, still looking down the hallway, her brows knit as if she were trying to mentally recreate a crime scene.

"Well then," Kylie said as she buttoned her coat, "I'll be talking to you later, Edna."

Kylie took the lift to the ground floor and found Michael outside. He was sitting on a concrete bench, his hands tucked into his jacket pockets, and his face tipped up to catch the bit of sun that had fought its way through the clouds. She called his name and closed the distance between them. His broad smile made her feel less bleak and tired. Unable to resist temptation, she brushed her fingers through his crisp black hair. He took her hand and kissed it before standing.

"It's time we get home," he said. "We'll leave your car till we come back this evening."

Kylie tucked her arm through his as they walked toward his car. "I'd like to stop over at Breege's. She'll be wanting her own gown once they let her wear it, and a book or two."

He closed a hand over hers. "You're a good friend."

She didn't feel like a good friend. A good friend would never have left Breege alone long enough for her to lie there like that on the kitchen floor. A good friend would have—

Michael's low growl interrupted her thoughts. "Sweet Jesus, you're at it already, aren't you?"

"Whatever do you mean?"

He stopped and set her close enough to him that her neck bent at an uncomfortable angle as she met his eyes. "I mean you're busy punishing yourself over Breege's accident. 'I should have been there sooner,' " he mimicked in a tone close to her own dark thoughts. " 'I should never have left her alone at all.' "

His loose grip on her upper arms tightened. He shook her with just enough force to gain her full attention—which he already had. "You'll stop this now. You are a good friend, and a fine neighbor, and I won't watch you do penance."

In the face of all that bluster, she laughed. Small wonder she loved him. He had her pegged, down to the last Act of Contrition.

Michael's hands dropped to his sides. "This isn't a laughing matter."

"Of course it's not," she said, fighting down the last of the laughter. "You know me too well, that's all." She wrapped her fingers through his. As they walked the rest of the way to the car she tried to explain a welter of emotions she could scarcely understand herself. "I was feeling guilty for Breege's accident, like I somehow caused it, and I'll admit that was silly. But I still feel *responsible* for her."

His forehead creased with a full-out scowl. "I can see where this is going." He opened her door, and she slid in.

Once he was settled behind the wheel, Michael looked at Kylie with one brow raised in a resigned sort of slope. "We're off to Breege's house, I'm guessing. And for more than the gown and books you mentioned."

How anyone could overlook this man's compassion was beyond Kylie. Sometimes she wondered whether all of Ballymuir had fallen under a spell, and could see nothing clearly.

"You're a good man, Michael, and a good friend, too," she said in an echo of his own words. She smiled when he cleared his throat and stared straight out the windshield. She could have sworn he was blushing.

An hour later, Kylie could find little else to smile over. While Breege's house wasn't dirty, neither was it the orderly haven it had always been. There was little food in the kitchen, and the preserves Breege must have been getting from the shelf when she fell were old enough to qualify as a National Treasure.

Scrubbing the kitchen floor to get up the last of the sticky fruit, Kylie announced, "She's staying with me."

Michael, who'd just finished walking Breege's cow to a neighboring farmer, said, "Till she's on her feet, of course she will."

"No. Forever."

His sigh was weary. "How did I know you'd be saying that?"

Kylie stood and rinsed out the rag. "Look at the ladder she was climbing when she fell, and I promise you that being in plaster and bandages up to god-knows-where won't slow her any!" The thought of what might happen sent a shiver through her.

"And when she's well," she continued after drawing a breath, "Breege'll be back out trying to patch a roof or whitewash the barn. She needs to be with me. At my house."

When he opened his mouth, Kylie raised her hand palm out, the same way she silenced her students. "Don't you dare say I'm doing this as penance, or you'll be sorry you spoke."

He sent his gaze up to the ceiling, and rolled his

shoulders like a fighter readying for a match. "I wasn't planning on saying a thing."

"Good."

"Except what about the daughter in London?" He sounded like a man grasping the last straw, and knowing it's the short one.

"I'll ring her up, of course, but I'm not hoping for much. She and Breege don't speak often."

Michael took the rag from her hand and tossed it into the sink. He drew her into his arms and rested his chin on top of her head. His broad hand rubbed comfortingly up and down her back. Kylie wrapped her arms around his waist and settled her cheek against the solid wall of his chest.

"Darlin', I know you're doing this with the best of intentions, but had you noticed that you're just the smallest bit short of room in that house of yours?"

"We'll make do."

She heard a smile in his voice when he answered, "I'm sure you will, love. You seem to have an unholy talent for it."

In the end, it took all of Kylie's powers of persuasion, and a few threats, too, before Breege agreed to her offer. Less than a week after the accident, she was released from the hospital, and with Michael's help, settled very nicely at Kylie's. Even then, it was "just for a while" and "only because Edna's rooms are too small to change your mind in."

Kylie was content that she'd done the right thing. It was well worth all of Michael's grumblings as he moved furniture and ferried over Breege's essential belongings. Kylie regretted the loss of privacy every bit as much as he did, but there were some things that couldn't be helped. And looking at Breege, with the color beginning to return to her cheeks and the sparkle to her watery blue eyes, while privacy didn't seem a small sacrifice, it seemed a worthy one.

Breege patted the covers on either side of her and laughed. "Well now, who'd have thought you've been hiding a bed like this, Kylie O'Shea? Quite a secret you've been keeping." She sent a cheery smile Michael's way, and Kylie noticed that he moved back to the threshold.

"The bed was my mother's. I know it's a bit much for a place like this, but I haven't had the heart to get rid of it."

"And you shouldn't either. It's glorious! But it's not right, me taking your bed," Breege said, one hand stroking the silken duvet. "Especially with you left on that little bed of mine pushed close enough to the fire to singe your toes."

Kylie tidied the stack of paperbacks on the night-stand. "It's an adventure, like having a new house sleeping out there."

Breege looked past her. "Michael, be a dear and see if I left my eyeglasses in the car. I can't seem to find them."

Kylie raised one brow at Breege's glasses, sitting next to the books, just where her friend had left them. Michael muttered something about being back straightaway, then disappeared.

Breege sighed, then leaned back against the pillows. "Between the doctors, the visitors, and the way that man sticks by you like he'd forget to breathe if you're not in the same room, we haven't had a second to talk, just the two of us."

"Michael? He's not like that at all," Kylie protested.

Breege's smile seemed to hold private memories. "He is, and you should be glad for it." Her smile smoothed out and her expression grew serious. "I don't want you to think I'm ungrateful, because I'd want my daughter over from London taking care of me about as much as I'd be willing to put myself back in the hospital. But I don't feel right about this. You and Michael need your privacy. The way he was moping about in the doorway, I don't think I'm the only one who likes this bed."

Kylie felt fiery color climbing her throat and burning her face. "He's—he's—" she stammered.

"If you haven't used the bed, more's the pity for you."

If Breege were younger—say, by fifty years— Kylie might not have been shocked. She opened and closed her mouth once, then again, feeling as if the wind had been knocked from her.

Her friend laughed outright. "Why is it the young always think they're the only ones to have ever felt passion? Do you honestly believe that you're the first not to have waited until your wedding day? If I told you the names of Ballymuir's fine citizens—including a certain Garda who drives up and down this road too many times for my peace of mind—who were born less than nine months after the ceremony, even your hair, straight as it is, would curl."

Even sanctimonious Gerry? Impossible. Kylie felt compelled to say something. Anything. "I ... I, ah ..."

Breege waved aside her effort. "I don't mean to be turning you that interesting shade of red. I'm just telling you not to forget about that man of yours while you're fussing over me. If you have any intention of *not* being the last bride in Ballymuir, he needs his attention, too."

"Erm ... well ..." Lord, what had happened to her powers of speech? Kylie settled for a nod, then went to the window and pulled aside the drape.

"It's beautiful weather we're having," she said, falling back on chat so old that she was sure it had been trotted out as soon as the first caveman formed words. "Spring is truly on us."

Breege chuckled. "Then I expect my barn would be warm enough for lovers. You might mention that to Michael ... when he comes back from not finding my glasses."

Kylie choked down her embarrassed exclamation and fled to make a pot of tea. Having family could be very unsettling.

Outside Kylie's small house, Michael milked the reprieve Breege had granted him down to its last drop. He searched his car from top to bottom, knowing her glasses lay on the nightstand. Then he inspected the crumbling shed at the back of Kylie's property.

The lack of a roof meant it couldn't hold feed for Martin, Breege's ill-mannered peacock whom even the farmer down the road wouldn't take. He had, however, suggested that Martin might be tasty in a stew if all else failed. Michael snorted. Knowing Kylie's soft heart, the damned bird was probably going to get its own cushion beside the fire.

Since the sun was shining and the air smelled rich and fertile, Michael took to the fields. The earth was still soggy with the weight of spring rains, and it squelched beneath the solid weight of his boots. That was one sound he'd never heard in the cell block, and hearing it now made him think of how incredibly his life had changed. As he thought, stone by stone he cleared the land where he'd first met Kylie months before.

Only months. It felt a lifetime, and in some ways it had been. He'd lived more since landing in Ballymuir than he had in all the years before. He'd developed patience, too.

He was pleased that Kylie had Breege for an adopted grandmum, of sorts. She needed family in a way that he didn't. Still, he could see where the present circumstances were going to prove ... uncomfortable.

Michael gave a wry shake of the head at the total inadequacy of the word he'd settled on. Uncomfortable, hell. It was going to be bleedin' torture. And after seeing Breege settled in like Ireland's answer to the late Queen Mam, he'd never look at Kylie's bed in quite the same lust-ridden light again.

All in all, though, he had to admit that life was better than what he'd been expecting. His continuing spite campaign of posting handyman bills around town was beginning to produce an odd job or two. A small blessing—infinitesimal, actually, since Jenna Fahey had told him that just now, she couldn't afford to finish what she'd started. As he jimmied loose a muddy rock, he considered his options. Work, real work—that's what he needed if he meant to care for Kylie after they married.

Michael lifted the heavy stone, then came close to dropping it square on his toes as he realized what he'd been thinking. Telling himself he was next in line for the village eejit, and that he might as well just bash in his thick skull with that rock, he brushed his hands off on the worn denim of his jeans.

He was more likely to be made Prime Minister than he was to bury his past and marry Kylie O'Shea. He should take the sunny day, the soft breeze, and the taste of Kylie's kisses and be content.

Somehow it was no longer enough.

Chapter Seventeen

What is in the marrow is hard to take out of the bone.
—IRISH PROVERB

Kylie pushed aside the piece of old lace that served as a drape over the kitchen window. Looking out the ancient glass, she felt a sudden and surprising burn of tears. Michael stood in the field, staring at the house as though he didn't recognize it. She didn't understand half of what went on in his head, and wished that he'd open to her enough so at least she could give a fair guess. Not very likely, she admitted to herself. He gave up nothing—not even guilt—without a battle.

He was so stark and male and beautiful that she hungered for him. Physically, to be sure. But also from someplace even more intimate, someplace where heart and soul melded into a yearning so strong that she wanted to weep from it.

That was the trouble with having wishes come true. Once fate had granted her one favor, she had begun to build her expectations. Having Michael as even a secret part of her life was more than she'd ever dreamt possible. To be asking more, for all of him and to be able to give all of herself in return, was nothing more than greed. And nothing less than impossible.

Kylie let the curtain drop, then put together the tea tray to bring to Breege. Once her friend was settled, and Kylie was certain that she could handle the tea without scalding herself, Kylie found her coat, slipped out of her shoes and into her wellies. If she couldn't have Michael forever, she'd steal what moments she could.

He was attacking the field with a ferocity that would have been amusing if she had any idea what motivated it. She waited until she had pulled abreast of him before speaking.

"Breege's glasses were on her nightstand."

"I saw them."

She thought she heard a bit of humor in his voice. That gave some comfort since he still threw rocks with an effort just skirting violence.

"It's grand of you to finish clearing the field for me, but it really doesn't have to be done by sunset."

He stopped to slant a sidelong look her way. "Just working off steam. Sorting through some matters."

"Such as?"

"What to do with that fool peacock of Breege's, for one."

She pushed back her hair where it flew wild in the breeze. "Breege says he'll forage well enough, or adopt himself into another family, as he did with her." Now wasn't the time to tell him she already considered Martin part of her new clan. "And the other matters?"

He hurled a rock to the far corner of the fence line. "Nothing that talking about will make come any clearer."

She laughed, then stood on tiptoe to brush a kiss against his cheek with its dark stubble of beard just beginning to show. She smiled as it tickled her, loving his feel, his scent. Loving him. "Well, I'd be a fool to suggest otherwise when I'm getting my field cleared in the bargain. But if you ever want to tell me what's truly bothering you, I'll be waiting to hear."

He nodded in response, as if he deserved no less. Annoyance nipped at Kylie. Like the high king, himself, she thought. "It helps to be good at waiting where you're concerned, doesn't it?"

His eyes narrowed as though he'd just spotted trouble. He didn't know the half of it.

"Trouble is," she continued, "I've spent my whole life waiting for one thing or another . . . for Da, for happiness, for forgiveness. I've decided that I'm through with it. So you can stand here and hurl rocks, or you can tell me what's bothering you and get on with the day."

His squint hardened to a scowl.

Kylie waited, this time liking it, this time relishing the coming clash of wills. That in itself amazed her. Before Michael, she'd have fled from the first sign of discord as fast as her feet could carry her. Before Michael, she'd been so frightened of stepping even the smallest bit out of line.

"You're becoming just a bit of a harridan, aren't you? I can see you sixty years from now smacking your poor husband with a cane—" His brows lowered and his jaw clamped shut on whatever else he'd been intending to say.

"Quiet so soon?" she challenged. No walking away now, neither emotionally nor by foot. "All those stormy looks and nothing else to say? I don't believe it for a minute."

"Believe it." He kicked a rock and sent it skittering. "Shouldn't you check on Breege? She might be needing something."

Kylie crossed her arms and stood her ground. "She's in finer shape than you are. And she's far clearer in what she's wanting and not wanting. What you need is someone to take you by the shoulders and shake you until that tongue of yours loosens."

His mouth opened, then closed. He made a huffing sound that was so out of character she struggled not to laugh. A small snicker escaped.

"Are you laughing at me?"

Though she knew she was already caught, she put her hand over her mouth to hide her smile.

"I asked if you were laughing at me."

When she was sure she'd regained her composure, she let her hand drop. "Not at you, exactly . . . more with you."

"I'm not laughing."

"But you should be. And you should be talking, too."

He moved closer, so close that her heart jumped.

"Or you'll take me by the shoulders?"

Kylie danced back a step, then circled, sizing him up. Michael was a big man, and she'd noticed time and again that he was all the more careful for it. Now he loomed over her, using physicality when he couldn't chase her off with silence. She rolled her eyes. Dangerous indeed.

"A little thing like you, I wish you luck in trying," he scoffed.

All bluster, she thought, smiling again.

He didn't slow. "I'll see a field full of flowers in this rock heap before I see you taking hold and shaking me. And—"

She darted in and settled her mouth over his. A low sound of surprise echoed from deep in his throat, and his hands clamped onto her shoulders like he was readying to push her away. Twining her arms around his neck, she held on for all she was worth. No running, she willed him. Just wanting.

She knew the moment when he accepted her and understood she wouldn't be bullied or placated. She didn't let go. His hands, cool and gritty from the work he'd been doing, cupped either side of her face and held her. She could feel the streaks of mud now painted on her skin, and didn't mind in the least.

Kylie welcomed him, his tongue even hotter in contrast to the cold hands cupping her face. His taste was indisputably Michael, singular and elemental, and she wanted more. Her tongue stroked his, ventured to taste more, and still it wasn't enough. On the kiss spun until she finally realized she'd forgotten to breathe altogether.

Kylie ended the moment and drew in a ragged breath. She didn't let go of him for fear of sinking to the wet earth. He curved his hands on the backs of her thighs, just beneath her bottom, and tugged her closer.

"You loosened my tongue, all right. Straight into your mouth," he murmured into her ear. "A damn lot more fun than being shaken, too."

She froze at this—the first blatant sexual banter she'd ever shared.

"Good, now," she said, not quite brave enough to meet his eyes, "since that tongue of yours is nice and loose, perhaps you're ready to tell me what's got you flinging rocks and scowling at nothing in particular."

"I can think of other things I'd like to be doing with my tongue." He bent closer and whispered words so intimate and delicious that a resounding *yes!* echoed though her imagination even as she pushed away.

"Just a thought," he said in an offhand way that didn't at all match the hot sexual intent of his expression.

Kylie turned from him and rubbed the slight grit that had transferred from her face to her fingertips. She'd underestimated him, and it had nothing to do with his size. One whispered picture and all thought of getting to the bottom of his unhappiness flew. Sharp man, Michael, she thought, then turned back to face him.

"A thought you'd best be saving for later. Now talk."

He wore the look of a hunted man. "You won't be letting this go, will you?"

She shook her head.

"Right, then . . ." Instead of continuing he gazed off into the countryside, miles and miles unbroken by town or tree. He cleared his throat, glanced at her, then looked back to the horizon. "The summer I was fourteen, I asked my mam if I could be apprenticed to a furniture maker in Kilkenny. I was sick to death of the boarding school she'd pitched me into, and they were damned sick of me, too. And the furniture maker, I'd gravitated to his shop from the time I was old enough to slip away from home. He made a fine living of it, and you see his pieces in glossy magazines these days. But you'd have thought I'd asked to work in the sewers the way she acted. Why couldn't I plan to go into business with my father, she wanted to know."

He jammed his hands into his jacket pockets even though the day was warm. "Insurance." He spat the word like an oath. "Can you imagine me in a suit and tie, cell phone attached to my ear, spouting actuarial tables?"

She couldn't. He belonged to a solid, simpler time, one that had ended long ago.

"Anyway, Mam refused to do it, and my da—as usual—wouldn't cross her. As it turned out, it didn't matter. There was no great calling for woodworkers in prison." His smile angled sharp with irony. "For some reason they found it inadvisable to equip terrorists with awls and screwdrivers and the like."

"So I'd guess." She marveled that he could find

any humor—even the painful sort—in his past. Unfortunately she also saw where this was leading, and her heart ached for him.

"I got myself fourteen years of book education, the best Her Majesty offers her prisoners. I can tell you about Homer and Plato and formulae and business plans, not that anyone would hire me. Fourteen damn years and the only useful thing I walked out with was a one-hundred-pound clothing allowance. I've got no skills, Kylie, nothing to offer."

"That's not true. I know the work you're doing now isn't as grand as you'd wish, but it's a place to start."

"A place to start," he echoed bitterly. "I'm thirty-two years old. Actually, thirty-goddamn-three soon enough." He paced away in long, angry strides, then swung back to her. "A place to start! I've got no place to go! I could start here, then throw every rock in Kerry. I might as well die doing it because that's all I'm good for."

He closed the distance between them and gripped her by the shoulders. "You ask me what's the matter. I want what I can't have. I want . . ."

His fingers tightened convulsively, then he let her go. Still his pain closed around her heart, squeezing until she couldn't draw a breath.

". . . and I've got no business to be wanting."

She reached out her hand, needing to touch, to comfort.

He stepped back. "Don't. Just . . . don't."

That hurt more than anything else he could have done.

He scrubbed his hand over his face, then stared at the ground. "I'll be going. I'm sorry."

Without answering—without knowing how to answer—Kylie turned and walked to her house.

He'd made an absolute mess of that, Michael admitted to himself as he retreated to town. He hadn't meant to say anything at all, but the woman had a way of working under his defenses. He'd tried to sidetrack her with talk of lovemaking, something neither of them could ever have enough of, but even that hadn't worked. No, she'd pushed him until what words he'd managed to scrape together were the wrong ones.

Silence. God—if there happened to be one—as his witness, he'd stick to silence from now till the bitter end. And bitter it would be. Bitter to see her marry another, and laugh and love with him. Most bitter of all to see her one day grow round with another man's children.

Michael clenched the steering wheel tighter, thinking he'd like to rip it from the dash. He wanted to howl at the injustice of life, but knew better than to bother. When it came to Kylie, he was a beaten man, and had been from the start of the race.

He glanced in the rearview mirror and saw that Gerry Flynn had taken up his appointed position. No point in making the effort to be angry.

Gerry drove slowly by as Michael pulled his car alongside the curb in front of Vi's house. Michael trudged to the front door, swung it open, then leaped back from the wave of sound blasting at him.

"What the bloody hell—" he began, then Vi

reached out and hauled him into the house. That he'd managed to miss the music before he'd reached the door only showed what a damned mess he was. Though he wasn't quite sure he should close off a means of quick escape, he shut the door behind himself.

"Bruce Springsteen," she shouted over the driving rhythm, then spun off into a dance that looked nothing short of pagan.

"That much I knew," he muttered, well aware no one could hear him. Not that anyone other than his sister seemed to be at this party. Roger, too, he amended, watching the homely dog bound after his owner, trying to grab onto the fringe from the purple shawl-thing she waved about like a harem veil.

Vi stopped to gulp from a glass full of some bubbling neon orange stuff. "Dance with me!" she urged after wiping the back of one hand across her mouth.

Michael inspected the contents of that glass instead. He sniffed it once, then again. No scent of liquor. He took a sip, winced at its cloying sweetness, then set the glass back down.

"It's orange drink, you big ninny. Orange Crush, all the way from America."

If his sister had to pick a vice, he supposed this one was harmless enough, though not as satisfying as a good, thick pint.

She shimmied in front of him, and he came damned close to being embarrassed. "I'm celebrating. Sold myself today. Lots of lo-o-o-vely Yank dollars will be flying my way," she announced while

Bruce sang about someone named Rosalita jumping a little higher.

It seemed that his sister was quite high enough. He took her by the elbows and tried to still her, not that he had much luck. She danced out of his grip and planted a great, smacking kiss on his cheek.

"I'll be designing fabrics for them," she said, leaning close enough to be heard. "We've been talking on and off for a year, but I never thought anything would come of it. Just surfing the Irish craze, I figured. But they want me, and they're paying fine for the honor, too!"

"You're worth it," he said, then wrapped Vi in a hug she suffered for all of two seconds, then spun away.

Half-breathless from her dance, she blurted, "Oh, I forgot you had a call today, too. Said he was an old friend of yours, but wouldn't leave a name. Not from prison, I hope."

Michael's stomach lurched. It sure as hell was none of his fellow "political" parolees, though he was quite certain they'd made a point of keeping track of him. They specialized in embracing their enemies.

Who, then? He'd written the correspondence teacher from his last business courses and told him where to forward his remaining tests and papers, but the man wasn't the sort to pick up a phone. Which left Michael hearing Gerry Flynn's insidious words about Brian Rourke, who surely wasn't fool enough to have returned home.

"You might as well quit scowling," his sister

ordered. "If the man calls back, he calls back. And if he doesn't, you've wasted a perfectly good dance."

She grabbed his hand and forced him into some semblance of moving with the pounding beat. He started out stubborn and intractable as any mule, but soon enough was pulling off his jacket and setting aside thoughts of matters he couldn't control. It felt good to let go to the music, though he couldn't call what he was doing dancing, exactly. And it felt beyond good to share in his sister's happiness, to push some of his own woes out of the way.

Then trouble came slamming through the front door.

After pounding over the din until her knuckles throbbed, Kylie gave up on good manners and marched into Vi Kilbride's house. She decided it must be a genetic flaw, this Kilbride madness. She paused for an intriguing instant to watch Vi move about in a way that shocked her, and made her more than a little envious. Vi waggled her fingers and mouthed a silent "hello," then danced on. Michael had stilled as soon as he saw her. His face lost its rare smile and took on that cornered expression she'd already seen once today.

Well fine, because he was a hunted man. She stalked toward him, and he froze in place.

"You go slinking off in a sulk, then not half an hour later I find you dancing like you're auditioning for *The Full Monty!*"

The corners of his mouth curved upward almost as if he were pleased at the thought. "I saw that one, you know."

"I wasn't meaning it as a compliment," she hissed.

"But I'll take it as one. And I'm shocked that you'd know about a movie like that, exotic dancers and all." His deep voice carried easily over the music, and Kylie felt all the more frustrated because she could scarcely hear herself.

"I'm not here to talk about naked men!" she shouted, then winced as the last two words echoed around her. Fine timing Vi had in turning down her stereo.

"No naked men? Pity, that," Vi commented, then flopped backward onto the sofa.

Kylie spared Vi an annoyed glance. Vi laughed in return. The woman looked as though she'd settled in to watch a show. Much as she wanted to ask Vi to leave her own house, Kylie knew better than to take on both Kilbrides at once.

She turned to Michael. He was grinning, too. "I suppose I should be happy you've given up on the self-pity," she said, not quite willing to give up on the good—and totally justified—anger that had fueled her drive into town. "It was getting a little wearing, all that 'poor me, I want and can't have' noise."

His eyes narrowed. "Don't start—"

"Don't you dare be telling me what to start or not start, Michael Kilbride! This time you won't stop me with either your threats or your . . . your *suggestions*." She could feel the color rising in her cheeks, but refused to acknowledge exactly how those "suggestions" had rattled her. "I'm sorry you didn't get apprenticed to the furniture maker years ago, but what's stopping you now? In case you failed to notice, there's a fine one next to your sister's studio."

"He turns bowls and candlesticks. Not quite furniture."

"And a fat lot better than nothing," she shot back, then took a deep breath and tried to calm herself. "At least you had noticed, even if you'd done nothing about it. There's a certain lack of . . . ah, what's the word I'm looking for here?"

"Initiative?" Vi supplied from her perch on the sofa.

Kylie nodded her thanks. "Yes . . . a lack of initiative, that I'm sensing in you. Not that it's so uncommon in the men I know," she added, and watched his brows lower like a thundercloud rolling in from the sea, "but I'd thought better of you. You want to be a furniture maker? Then be one! And don't go moaning about the poor lot you've been dealt in life because I can tell you from vast personal experience, no one wants to hear it. Take hold of that past and shake loose whatever's still got you frozen, then let it go!"

He couldn't have looked more shocked if she'd cocked her fist and landed one on his nose. She circled closer for the knockout punch. "And if you're worried about the money, don't bother with that, either. Even if I didn't teach another day, I could find a way to earn enough to keep food on the table."

He peered at her like she was speaking in tongues.

Exasperated, Kylie flung her arms around his neck and hauled his mouth closer to hers. "What I'm trying to tell you, you great fool, is that I love you."

She tilted her head and kissed him long and hard. For once, he didn't take over, but let her do as she would. And she did, until she reeled away starved for air.

Kylie pulled back her shoulders and stood as straight as she could. "So add that little bit of information into your wanting and needing, and see where you come out."

She turned heel and marched to the door. Pausing on the threshold, she swung back and added out of automatic, ingrained politeness, "Grand to see you again, Vi. I'll ring you up about the student art show."

Michael and Vi watched the closed door after Kylie left, almost as if waiting for a curtain call. When it was clear she wasn't returning, Vi sighed, stretched out on the sofa, and propped her feet on its arm.

"Sounds like she's willing to make a kept man of you, brother. That is, if you're so thick that you don't marry her, first."

In response to his blistering curse, she only laughed. Bloody awful rotten sister.

Chapter Eighteen

*The three things Aristotle couldn't understand:
the work of the bees, the coming and going
of the tide, and the mind of a woman.*

—IRISH TRIAD

Kylie wasn't surprised that giving Michael words of love would send him fleeing into the hills. What amazed her was that he'd managed to avoid her for nearly a week. Though she'd been tempted to knock at—or down—his door once again, she'd left him alone.

It was as much for herself as for him that she'd done this. Except for lesson plans, paper grading, and being sure she had a bit of food in the house, she'd never given much thought to the future. She'd simply let it take care of itself. Now, sheer uncertainty exhausted her. She was finding it hard to wake and work each day.

Worn down from a long school day followed by an interminable staff meeting and another stretch of time spent on the student art exhibition, she had just crested the incline between Breege's house and her own when she saw him walking her way. Her weariness evaporated, leaving anticipation in its place.

"Well now, if it isn't himself," she murmured.

Michael's hair was longer than it had been when they'd first met, and she loved the way the wind ruffled through its dark thickness, pushing it back from his brow. Even now, when her love was meshed in a great knot of frustration, her fingers tingled to follow the breeze's caress.

As she drew closer she could see that he was looking none too pleased. His hands were jammed into his jacket pockets and his mouth set in a hard, determined line. He was probably stewing on some way to slip by without offering so much as a hello.

Kylie pulled to the side of the road. She tried to roll down her window, then recalled she'd never had the blasted window crank repaired. She switched off the motor, stepped out of the car and closed its rust-raddled, groaning door.

"My house is back up the hill," she said as he neared. "Or is it just a grand coincidence, finding you here?"

He kept his expression impassive, but Kylie didn't miss how his gaze traveled over her, or the way he relaxed almost imperceptibly when she softened her question with a smile.

"I was having a visit with Breege. I made her a tea tray and rounded up some of those books she likes."

He had a way of astounding her with simple acts. Astounding her and leaving her wondering whether she understood him at all. Still, books and tea weren't enough to let him off the hook.

"And you had no thought of staying to see me?"

"I wasn't sure when you'd be back. I parked by Breege's barn," he added, as if that explained everything.

"And?"

He hesitated. "I need to be home before dark falls."

"So Vi has you on a curfew now, does she?"

He scowled, and Kylie knew that was all the answer she'd be getting. The wind was coming faster now; rain was on the way.

"Well then," she said, looping loose strands of hair behind her ears. "We've a few hours before night. Plenty of time."

"Time for what?"

"For whatever you wish." She tucked away her own wishes. If she voiced them, he would just disappear again. Before she got back in the car, she said, "I'll run you down to Breege's."

Michael climbed in. They were well down the narrow road before he spoke. "I finished up at Muir House today. Jenna Fahey's out of money at the moment, and I can't finance her."

Her heart tugged at his bleak expression. She turned between the boulders marking the entrance to Breege's property, then pulled up next to Michael's car and switched off the engine. They sat in tense silence as the first rain spat against the windshield.

"Well, if you're done at Muir House, then it's time to be looking at the possibilities, isn't it?" she eventually offered. It wasn't much, but it was all she could latch onto.

His laugh held no humor. "Considering my possibilities should take no more than a blink of the eye."

Something snapped inside Kylie. She almost heard the sharp *ping* as it let loose with lethal velocity.

"I won't have it! I won't have you tearing yourself down. I—I won't have you acting as though—" She couldn't get anything else out before the tears started. Not small, polite lace hankie sniffs, but a great breathless torrent stronger and faster than the rain hitting the window. She was beyond embarrassed, beyond anything but shock at the sobs wrenching free.

"Kylie?"

She wrapped her arms about her midsection and leaned her head against the chill, damp glass of the car door. It hurt terribly to cry this hard. Now she knew why she'd avoided it for so many years. And now she knew she would never—could never—stop.

"Love, I didn't mean to—"

She hunched down, trying to draw herself into a ball, to disappear altogether.

Two strong hands hauled her out of the corner she'd hidden in. She found herself wrapped in Michael's arms. She struggled to free herself, but he held fast.

She was filled with an impotent fury that she couldn't make him see his own worth. She had been through so much, sliced to ribbons by her mother's death, her father's sins, and the evil, soul-rending act inflicted on her by a stranger, but this man whom she loved with an intensity bordering on pain, he was going to finish her off.

She was finally, indisputably broken.

Kylie cried for her youth lost on that drawing room floor, she cried for Michael, for her mother, and for her weak, weak da, and the years she'd spent trying to right wrongs that weren't hers. Most of all, she wept for her bleak future, for the green-eyed babies she would never have.

Michael held her. His weight shifted beneath her as he fumbled about, then pressed a square of cloth into her hand. He offered soothing words that only heightened her grief, then told her to cry herself out, when she knew it was impossible.

But it wasn't, after all. A body could do only so much to set free a lifetime of sorrow. The tears left emptiness in their wake, emptiness and the knowledge that she'd just burdened him with more guilt.

She scrambled back to her side of the car, wiping her eyes with the crumpled white handkerchief she held clenched in her hand, then blowing her nose.

"I'm sorry," she croaked, then cleared her throat. "I shouldn't have gone on like that in front of you."

He raked his hand through his hair and stared up at the car's dingy interior. "You should be sorrier yet for feeling you have to apologize."

Kylie stared down at her hands, still knotted around the handkerchief. "I'm . . . I'm more tired than I thought. Perhaps it would be best if we pretended this never happened."

When he said nothing, she let her gaze travel hesitantly up the tense lines of his body to a face that was tight with checked emotion.

"I'm—"

He cut her off. "Don't tell me you're goddamn sorry again."

Nodding, Kylie tucked away his handkerchief. She'd wash it tonight, and tomorrow everything would be back the way it should be—neat, starched, and orderly.

He scrubbed his hand over his face, blew out a slow breath, then said, "You cried. It happened. You can't go about reinventing history to suit yourself."

Of course she could. Until just a moment ago, she'd been sure she was the high priestess of that particular feat.

He hauled her back into his arms. "Listen, dammit! Everything I've ever touched in my life has turned to poison. Plans, dreams, all of it." His lips brushed the top of her head in what she imagined was a kiss. "What you said the other night, that you—that you love me, it scared the holy hell out of me. I don't want to drag you down into whatever morass I'm to sink into next.

"I won't let go of you, but I don't want you making plans. I don't want you thinking that things are going to go well for us, because I can bloody damn well guarantee they're not."

She moved away slightly and tilted her face up to look at him. He must have seen the lecture just trying to slip loose because he gave her a resigned smile.

"That doesn't mean I'm just sitting about waiting for Flynn and his people to find the proper excuse to haul me back in. I've been thinking, making some plans. I spoke to Breege this evening. She knows she won't be doing any more farming, so she agreed to let me use her barn to start a woodworking business—assuming I can find any work. She's offered the space at a fair rent, and I've promised to fix up a few odds and ends about her house." He stopped and frowned at her. "Unlike your place—which I also plan to be fixing—Breege's electrical service isn't one spark away from a fire. I can run the tools I need and have space to store my work."

He drew back his arm so that it rested on the door. Kylie leaned on the offered pillow and smiled up at him. So much anger and self-doubt shadowed his eyes, so much more than he was willing to voice even now. Still, she saw something new. Something so small that it was nothing more than a glimmer. Kylie saw hope, and her heart grew warm at the sight. Small steps, she told herself. Small steps.

She drew his mouth closer to hers. Before their lips touched, she whispered, "You might be careful. You have me thinking my nagging's done some good."

He laughed, the sound free of bitterness. What heavenly pleasure, Kylie thought as laugh and kiss came together and made her whole. Whole and, a yearning voice whispered inside, just perhaps loved.

As Michael kissed Kylie, he knew this wasn't lust he felt. It burned too white-hot for that. Some animal-fast, unfeeling shag wasn't what he wanted. This was . . . this was . . .

He dragged in a breath. His heart slammed against the wall of his chest as she murmured to him in Irish, her voice smoky, smooth, and intoxicating as the best whiskey.

This was beyond comprehension.

He cupped her full breast in his palm and stroked his thumb over the nipple. He could feel it rise to him, even under the thick weave of her pullover.

Her back arched. "Yes," she whispered, making it sound more command than plea.

He tried to pull her closer, but hit his elbow against the dash with a hard smack. He blinked away the pain and concentrated on the warm and willing woman in his arms. He followed the taper of her waist down the line of her thigh and curled his hand around the firm curve of her bum.

Kylie wriggled on his lap, making the already uncomfortable fit of his denims agonizingly tight. She moved her long legs so that she straddled him, then rocked her hips. He surged upward in response, his body more than ready to reach the end of the dance right then and there. He tugged at her clothes, seeking even the smallest patch of soft skin to caress. When Kylie leaned back to give him room to maneuver, she cried out. He didn't think it was from pleasure.

"Darlin'?"

"It's nothing," she said, sprinkling frantic kisses over his forehead, down his neck, and on his chin. "Just barked the skin on my back a bit, I think. Help me with this blasted thing," she added, tugging at the hem of her fisherman's jumper. "Hurry!"

Blood roaring in his ears, panting like he'd just run the length of the Slieve Mish Mountains, he tried his best and rammed his other elbow into the window for the effort.

"Hell and dammit! Why couldn't you drive one of those tourist caravans with a bloody bed in it?"

Kylie collapsed against him and began to giggle. Since his face was more or less nestled between her breasts, he put aside any slight to his male pride. Truth be told, he wasn't above a cheap thrill.

"Maybe you'd like to show me the barn," she suggested. "Breege had a thought or two in that direction the other day."

"B-Breege?" he stammered, not quite able to absorb the idea.

She leaned back and smiled down at him. "For us, of course. Did you think she'd be luring a man out here, while she's encased in plaster from ankle to hip?"

He could feel his answering grin stretch from ear to ear. "She's a game enough old bird."

"Well, for tonight the barn's ours." She slid off his lap. Michael stifled a hiss of discomfort as she nudged close to places that felt hard enough to shatter. "We'd best make good use of it."

She was out of the car and around to his side before he had time to blink. She opened the door and gave him a sweeping bow. He joined her, and took one kiss in the soft rain to tide himself over. Then he led her the few feet to the spot that he'd chosen to stake his future—such as it was.

Inside, the light was dim, so he switched on the overhead bulb. It cast a glowing, golden circle. Kylie stepped into the light. Smiling, she ran her fingers through her hair, pulled out the clip, then tucked it in her skirt pocket. She shook her head, and silky brown tendrils tumbled about her shoulders. His heart drummed faster at the sight.

She plucked at her woolen sweater and wrinkled her nose. "I smell like a wet sheep."

She tugged the garment over her head. Standing there in her white blouse and blue skirt, a convent girl combination that he'd seen her wear time and again, she shouldn't have looked as tempting as a selkie, that mystical seal turned perfect woman, come to land to steal his heart. But she did.

He wanted to take her down onto the damp earth and have her there, where he could watch every expression that crossed her face while he loved her with all the ferocity heating his soul. Instead, he took the sweater from her and set it on a low bench outside the stall that usually held Breege's milk cow.

He needed to buy time to get hold of himself. He switched on the radio that sat on a dusty wooden shelf, then fiddled with its dial until he found music. Michael grimaced. All the talent God could bless an island with, and only "done my heart wrong" wailing semi-American ballads coming over the air.

He stayed to the fringes of the golden circle holding Kylie, closed his eyes, and inhaled the mingled scents of feed, hay, and dampness.

"I've got some money, y'know," he said over the twang and moan of the music.

A little line appeared between Kylie's brows. She

tilted her head. "Money? Are you offering to pay me for a tumble in the hay . . . or wherever?" she added as she glanced into the shadowed corners.

"Jesus, no!"

She crossed her arms under her full breasts. Riveted by the sight, for an instant he forgot what he was trying to tell her.

"So I'm not worth a coin or two, then?"

He was immeasurably thankful for her teasing smile. "Don't trip me up. I'm doing a fine enough job of that all on my own."

He moved closer, so that the light played on him now, too. "I meant what I said in the car. I've been thinking ahead. I've got some money that Vi says our grandmum left to me. I consider it a loan from Vi, but one I'll be taking to pay for what all I ordered from the tool supply catalog yesterday. A table saw, a lathe, a router with some really grand woodworking bits . . ."

He trailed off as Kylie's eyes began to glaze over.

"Well," he finished, "I just want you to know that—"

"I know all I need to," she gently cut in. "I wouldn't have told you I loved you if I didn't."

She paused, and he knew what she waited for. What she deserved. But he couldn't give her those words; he wasn't even certain he knew how to love. Shamed, he dropped his gaze to the tips of his shoes. He heard the rustle of old silage beneath her feet as she moved closer.

In an act that immediately drew his attention, she took his hand and settled it over the top buttons of her oh-so-bloody-proper blouse. Hurt still lingered in her eyes like a ghost, making pale-blue irises almost silver.

"I'm glad that you're thinking forward," she said. "But maybe we should take it one day at a time."

He nodded. His hand still rested on that fragile spot where her heart beat so very close to the surface. He didn't want to hurt her, to promise things he didn't know how to deliver.

"Kylie—"

"Unbutton it."

He blinked. "What?"

"My blouse, of course," she said with teasing patience.

He knew what she was doing, bringing them safe to the other side of a rough moment. He didn't deserve her, but damned if he'd let that stop him.

His fingers shook as he unbuttoned the blouse down to her skirt, then tugged it out and finished the job. She slipped the cuff buttons free and slid the cotton from her shoulders.

The radio began to play a dark and mournful dirge, and he grunted with amusement at the mix of irony and suitability.

"Strip," she ordered.

"Me?"

Her mouth curved into the true, Kylie-bright smile that was becoming his anchor in life. "I wasn't talking to Martin."

"Martin?"

She laughed and pointed to the peacock who'd just strutted in. The bird appeared cross and wet and ready to chase them from what he apparently considered his shelter.

He narrowed his gaze. "Stay where you are, you arrogant wee bastard."

The peacock looked at him with utter contempt, then with a shake of lax tail feathers, paraded to the grain bin.

"Strip," Kylie repeated, "then come keep me warm."

He left his jacket and his shirt on the ground, and pulled her into his arms, feeling hot enough to toast them both to a crisp. He kissed her once, twice, then followed the line of her scrap of a bra with his mouth.

Her fingers drifted though his hair as she cradled his face to her breasts. He wondered whether she thought he might walk away if she didn't hold him. Michael smiled against her soft skin, which was faintly scented of flowers and goodness.

He told her how beautiful she was, how the taste of her drove him to want more. He gave her all the words of praise he could think of, except for the ones he knew she wanted most. The ones he couldn't give.

He slipped the skirt from her, and set it on top of his jacket. Kneeling, he let his fingertips voyage up her slender calves, find the sensitive spots behind her knees, then trace the line of her white panties. She braced her hands on his shoulders and slipped off her shoes. He helped her out of her stockings, leaving the panties in place. As he worked his fingers beneath their elastic and cupped her bottom, he watched her face. Her beautiful mouth curved into an oval just wide enough to free a sigh of pleasure.

He brought his mouth to the silken skin of her stomach and kissed her, his hands still worshiping her, flexing and moving in time to an internal rhythm his body demanded be satisfied.

Kylie again settled her palms on his shoulders, her fingers kneading muscles tense with excitement. "I wonder what it would be like to make love in the hay."

He looked up at her, then around the barn. All the hay that hadn't left with the cow was one small, unbaled pile to the left of the bench that held Kylie's sweater. He stood, clasped her hand in his, and brought her there.

Michael bent and tested the meager stack with one hand. "It's a bit scratchy, and there's not much here."

She nudged the hay with her foot. "Maybe it's enough," she said with such yearning in her voice that he had to smile.

"We'll make do, love," he promised.

What he lacked in practical experience, Michael figured he more than made up for with determination. Cupping her face between his palms, he kissed her. As they kissed, he walked her backward until she was practically knee-deep in the sweet-smelling hay.

"Let me look at you," he said.

Kylie knew there was no need for false modesty, or shyness, either. She opened the distance between them, moving until she almost leaned against the wood-slatted wall behind her. Reaching back, she unhooked her brassiere, then let it drop into the hay.

Michael's groan of pleasure wrapped around her, warming her blood, making her shiver.

"Is there more you'd like to see?"

He nodded.

She looped her thumbs into the waistband of her panties, and took those off, too.

Dried, grassy stalks tickled at her calves as she straightened. Perhaps he'd been right about the hay. It wasn't quite the lovers' cushion she'd imagined. Maybe if they— Her thought was interrupted by her lover's voice. "I'm thinking I might need a closer view." Then his mouth was on hers, and his hands running possessively over all she'd bared for him.

Kylie's eyes slipped shut. She moved into a dark realm of taste and touch and scent, a place where sight no longer mattered. The sweet pull of Michael's mouth at her nipples, the firm brush of his knuckles at the vee of her legs, the hot urgency in his voice as he told her to open to him, to give him her all, that was her reality.

His kisses traveled down her body. She heard the rustling of the hay at her feet as he moved lower. She reached out and wound her fingers into his thick hair, holding his head close, not wanting to lose that magical contact of mouth against skin.

He settled his hands on the insides of her legs, just above her knees. "A little wider, love," he urged.

Because she could refuse him nothing, Kylie did as he asked. His fingers parted her. Warm, humid places felt the kiss of cool air. She shuddered.

"Beautiful," he whispered. "So beautiful."

Then the cool kiss gave way to the hot, wet slide of tongue.

Kylie's fingers tightened against his scalp. "Michael," she gasped, half in protest over an embarrassment she didn't want to feel, half in shock at the fire that shot through her.

"Let me," he asked.

And so she did.

Fire consumed any last bits of hesitancy. Soon, Kylie was sure her legs would hold her no more. She begged him to stop, please, before they both tumbled. He answered by sliding one finger deep inside her. She flew then, hard and fast, to a release she wouldn't have dreamt possible. But she didn't tumble, for Michael was there to hold her.

Kylie's heart eventually slowed. The sound of someone chatting on the radio drew her out of her own private reality. She realized that she sat cradled in Michael's lap. He rested against the stall's outer wall, his arms wrapped around her. Twining her arms about his neck, she sat upright and kissed him—with wonderment, with gratitude, but most all, with love.

He smiled. "Liked that, did you?"

She smiled back. "At the risk of sounding a total tart, yes." She paused and brushed another kiss against his lips. She'd thought herself too tired for more passion, but as the feel of him—the hard pounding of his heart, his clean, male scent—steeped its way through her sated senses, she knew she wasn't done. Not by a far cry.

Kylie shifted so that she straddled him, kneeling in hay that had become sadly flattened. "But grand as it was, I'm thinking we're not quite done," she said, pausing between words for more kisses.

The hay pile was out of the question for any serious lovemaking. She drew herself to her feet, then
glanced around their shelter from the world. There
was little in the way of creature comforts, though
Martin seemed to be pleased enough, busily pecking
at whatever ill-tempered peacocks snacked on.

Kylie, on the other hand, wanted a bit more for
Michael and herself. Then the beginnings of an idea
settled on her.

"Follow me," she said.

Michael rose, and she led him to the broad bench
that sat several steps away. She wasn't quite certain
how to go about what she was envisioning.

"So, love, what is it you're wanting of me?"

"Oh, I'm working on that," she answered, her
hands going to the fastening at the top of his denims.
He didn't ask or argue. He simply let her be the
aggressor. And for that gift of power, so healing to
her soul, she loved him all the more.

She had him gloriously undressed in no time at
all. He was so hot and alive and wonderful that Kylie
knew unless she was part of him, she'd never have
enough.

"I was thinking . . ." she began, then paused, her
courage still a fledgling thing. "I was thinking that I
want you sitting on that bench and that I want to take
you inside me."

His chest rose and fell hard beneath her palms. He
stepped back and sat. "Come here, then."

Their lovemaking wasn't free of awkward
moments, but that only brought a sweetness that
Kylie knew she would cherish forever. Soon enough,

she was just where she wanted to be. Michael holding her, in her, and she holding him, legs and arms wrapped tight, her body his shelter.

This time, her private world held two. They swayed and surged to a primal dance, his large hands cupping her hips, but letting her set the pace. Kylie thought it incredible, the absolute freedom in an intimate moment of dependence. Together they found the center of that world, their cries echoing to the rafters of the little barn. Then, boneless, replete, they held onto each other until the chill of the air became too much.

Michael groaned his protest as she unfolded herself from him, and he left her. He promised delights almost too tempting to refuse, if she'd just come back to him.

She made an apologetic little noise, then staggered, half love-drunk, toward her panties. Somehow, she managed to get back into them. Wrinkling her nose at her stockings—too much work—she moved on to her brassiere.

Having given up on luring her back, Michael stood and began to dress, too. Shirt gripped in one hand, and pants still unbuttoned, he came to her.

"So there's no persuading you to stay?" he asked while trying to tease her fingers away from her skirt's zipper.

She wrapped her arms about his waist. "It would be grand if we could be Adam and Eve," she said, then sighed. "But we both have things to get back to. And Martin isn't exactly the first creature I'd want in my Garden of Eden."

Michael's laugh was drowned by a raucous scream. They both jumped and held tighter to each other.

"I'll make stew of the bird yet," he muttered. "Bloody thing's louder than an alarm."

A flash of a movement drew Kylie's attention to the doorway. In that instant, everything changed. She clung to Michael, suddenly thankful for the peacock's shrill interruption. Peering around the muscled strength of Michael's arm, she locked eyes with Gerry Flynn.

Cloaked in gray evening twilight, he stood in the entry, battery-powered light in hand. She looked away from the angry hunger that had pulled his face into a drawn mask. She didn't want to think about how long he'd been standing there.

"Just leave," she said in a low, trembling voice. "Go on, now."

Michael chuckled and cupped the back of her head with a broad hand, almost as if he were protecting her. "It'll take more than that to get the damned bird out."

Flynn stepped all the way into the barn. At the sound of his footfalls, Michael swung around, taking Kylie with him. She held fast, fear for Michael's reaction overriding any instinctive modesty.

"Get out, Gerry," she cried as Michael snarled something far stronger. He didn't let go of her, though, and turned her back around so that his body shielded her from Flynn's eyes.

Michael edged closer to his shirt. "Put that on, then get in your car."

"Not a bloody chance." She snatched up his shirt and tugged it on. By the time she was adequately covered, Michael had started advancing on Flynn.

"What are you doing here?"

Flynn held his ground. "I saw the light and knowing that Mrs. Flaherty wasn't here, stopped to have a look-see."

"And when you saw my car—and Kylie's. What then, Gerry? And why are you still standing here, unless you're looking for that lesson on the extent of your official duties I promised you?"

"You've no right to be here, yourself," Flynn shot back, though Kylie noticed a certain thinness about his voice.

"I have all the right I need. I'm setting up business in here."

Gerry pointed the beam of light at Michael. It shone on the ridges of muscle across his flat abdomen, on the rope-like strength of his arms. Michael's mouth quirked into a smile. He didn't appear in the least uncomfortable with his lack of clothing. And he shouldn't have been. He was a man at the peak of his physical prowess, a fact that set Gerry at obvious disadvantage.

Flynn moved the light around the barn. "Business? You? We're too peace-loving to be needing your services."

Michael stiffened. "Kylie, love, go on home now," he said almost gently. "Flynn and I have matters to settle."

"I told you I won't be leaving," Kylie answered in a voice every bit as calm as Michael's. Quite an accomplishment, considering the way she trembled. "Unless you come with me."

He shook his head, but kept his gaze on the officer. "I can't do that, darlin'."

Kylie knew he was slathering on the endearments to goad Flynn. It was working, too.

"Unless you can show me proof of Mrs. Flaherty's permission to be here, you'll both leave now," Gerry snapped. "Or I'll arrest you for trespass."

Michael laughed. "Fine threat, but hollow. Everyone knows Breege is staying with Kylie, and that trespass charge would have you laughed out of town. Go on your way, now."

Gerry looked Kylie up and down. "Payment for services rendered, is it? You tend to Breege so you can use the barn to f—"

Michael had his hand about Gerry's throat so quickly that Kylie couldn't have cried out if she had wanted to. He forced the Garda backward and slammed him into a wall. Gerry clawed at Michael's hand. He would have had better luck at digging his way through the rough stone of the wall.

"This is between us," Michael snarled. "I keep telling you that, and you keep cocking up. What you said there, Gerry, that was the greatest cock-up of all time, and I think it's going to have you swallowing some teeth." He raised his fist.

Kylie jumped onto Michael's back and wrapped her two hands around his single large one. "No! You're doing just what he wants. He loses a tooth or two, and you lose your freedom." The words rushed out in a burst of pure terror. "Let him go. It doesn't matter what he said. Don't let him hurt us like this."

"Ah, love, but it does matter what he said." He frowned at Gerry, who was panting and looked pinched and white about the mouth. "It matters very much."

Michael glanced over his shoulder at her. She still clung to him.

"You won't be leaving without me?" He sounded almost teasing.

"No," she said as fiercely as a flea on a lion's back could manage. "Perhaps an apology will do?"

Michael pondered the matter while Flynn still squirmed within his grip. "You can get down now, love," he finally said to her.

Kylie unwrapped her legs and stood, her heart beating far too quickly with residual fear and dawning relief.

"On your knees, little man," he said to Flynn, enforcing the words with a shove that sent Gerry sprawling. "You'll give Kylie the apology she deserves, and tell her that you're nowhere near fine enough to stand under the same sun she does. Then you'll hurry your pasty white arse out of here before I change my mind and knock your teeth out. Understood?"

Gerry did exactly as told, his words strangled, ugly, almost frightening to hear. The message delivered was one of reprisal, and Kylie shuddered with it.

In the silence that followed Gerry's departure, Kylie unbuttoned Michael's shirt and slipped back into her own, using the mundane task to calm her nerves. Michael dressed, switched off the radio, then stood staring out the doorway.

After twisting her hair back into some semblance of dignity, she joined him.

"We made an enemy tonight."

Michael brought her hand to his mouth and brushed a rough kiss on her knuckles.

"No, love, you're just finally seeing him as one."

Kylie closed her eyes to whatever else in her life she'd missed. It was simply too much.

Chapter Nineteen

A shoulder without a brother is bare.
—IRISH PROVERB

Michael saw Kylie safe up the road to her home, then went back to the barn to work out the rage he hadn't been able to spend on Gerry Flynn's face. While the radio blared one of those mindless chat shows, he mucked out the already clean cow stall, swept the main floor, and would have taken on fixing the sagging window if it weren't so damned dark.

Still fighting a gut churning with anger, he flung the broom into a corner. The peacock squawked in protest. Michael quickly checked to be sure he hadn't accidentally struck the creature. The only one he wanted to hit was Flynn.

No, that wasn't true. He was pushing back the same thoughts he'd been fighting to ignore all day. He also wanted to hit someone he hadn't seen in over fourteen years, but was pretty damned sure he'd heard from the night before. Another phone call had come, and this time he'd been there to pick it up.

"Settled in, are you?" the man had said. *"Got something—or someone—to lose?"*

Nothing more. But certainly enough to make him sick.

Threats weren't unfamiliar to Michael. In prison, they'd been common currency among padmates and guards. He still saw them in the eyes of people like Clancy and Spillane in Ballymuir. But his caller—whether it was Rourke himself or one of his compatriots—had struck to the quick.

For now he had much to lose. A sister. The beginnings of work. And most of all, Kylie.

He hadn't been trying to frighten her with bleak talk of the future. He'd been trying to ease her expectations. Michael knew he couldn't stop living over threats, but he couldn't go to the local authorities, either. His personal prejudice against the justice system aside, any office that held Flynn was of no use to him.

Faceless, nameless threats. How to fight back against someone he couldn't see?

"Another day, another thing to be learned," he said to the peacock, who appeared to believe he knew it all, already. Leaving the door open just enough that Martin could escape, Michael headed home.

• • •

Vi's back was to Michael when he walked into the house, not that it stopped her from bossing him about.

"*Shh-h-h*, you'll wake them."

He looked around. Only Roger was in the room, and there was still just one of him. He moved between his sister and what seemed to be consuming her attention. She simply stretched out further on the electric-blue sofa and continued staring at the flames licking bricks of turf in the fireplace. Her brows were arched fiercely together, and her green eyes dark and fixed. Enough to scare the bejeezus out of most men living, his baby sister. Not him, though.

"Communing with the spirits, are you?" He opened his arms to encompass the small living space. "What have you got going here—a regular convention of banshees, pooka, and ghosties?"

She rolled her eyes. "No, it's your little brothers upstairs, fast asleep."

He took a second to swallow the thought. Here, and . . . "In my bed?"

She swung her legs around and sat up. "Don't you yell at me, Michael Kilbride. Where else was I to put them?"

"In your bed," he snapped. It was a selfish answer, but an honest one. The thought of Patrick and Danny snuggled into the bed he'd come to think of as his own was too much to take, especially after the series of atrocities recently inflicted on his privacy. "You asked them here, let them drool on your pillows!"

Vi gave a hoot of laughter. "They're not infants any more. Closer to giants, I'd say, and looking to be a bit beyond the drooling stage." She combed her fingers through her hair and shook it out all wild. "Besides, I didn't ask them here . . . exactly," she added.

No great shock since Vi was likely the least "exact" person walking the planet. "Well, what did you do . . . exactly?"

She cleared her throat before speaking. "I sent 'em two Bus Eireann tickets in the post, with a note saying that a little visit this summer might be in order."

"And?"

"Well, after having it out with Mam over a suspension from school—some nonsense involving chickens I didn't quite catch—they thought now might be the better time for some travel."

"Chickens," Michael muttered. "And have you rung their mother to let her know she needs to gather up her boys?" He asked the question with more bitterness than he wanted to own up to having.

"Mam—and like it or not, she's yours, too— doesn't want them back." Vi's generous mouth seemed smaller, like she was holding in a bad taste. "They'll stay here till this can be sorted out."

He laughed because any other response would have been an admission of how much power he still let his mother hold. "So you've got the lot of us now. Maeve's castoffs. Probably the only reason Da's not here is that he hasn't looked up from his newspaper long enough to take it in the teeth. And won't he be in for a shock when he does, only him left at the supper table."

The sympathy he saw in Vi's eyes burned like acid. She started to say something to him, but he shrugged it off and walked the stairs to his room. Or what used to be his room.

Michael stood in the doorway. He took in the two silhouettes bathed in dim light and felt his mouth twitch with something that might have been a smile. They damn near stretched from headboard to the mattress's end. The poor boys had been cursed, as he had, with a man's size before a man's wisdom had even the slightest chance to form.

A low, seismic rumble filled the room. He smiled outright. Pat and Danny might not drool, but they could work up some hellbending, resonant snores. He looked at the two of them, hulking squatters taking up the space he'd already begged for his own. He should be angry, royally irked. But for some stupid, incomprehensible reason, he suddenly felt pleased. He moved closer and tugged the pillow from beneath one twin's head, then watched him give the other a sleeping, retaliatory swat.

"Brotherly love," he whispered. He'd missed so much with these boys—his brothers. And he didn't want to miss any more.

Grinning like a fool, he made his way back downstairs to the blue sofa and its resident witch.

"Up with you," he said to Vi, then tossed the pillow at her to back up the order.

She caught it with absolute grace. "Are you evicting me from my own couch?"

"Fair play, Violet," he admonished. "After all, you've given away the only spot I have to lay my head. The fire's burning nice now, and I'm ready for a bit of sleep."

"Well, I'm not."

"Then go to your room and read a book, or putter around in the kitchen and see if you can ever learn to cook."

She called him a nasty name that he'd not heard since childhood, lobbed the pillow back at him, then stalked off to her bedroom.

"Then you'll not be learning to cook?" he called after her. "You've no hope at all of catching a husband."

"And what would I do with one if I did?" she growled just before slamming her bedroom door.

Upstairs, another mighty snore erupted. Chuckling, Michael slipped off his shoes and sprawled on the couch. He'd slept on worse.

"Family," he said, testing the word to see how it rolled off his tongue. Two brothers to love. Two brothers to protect. Two brothers to lose.

Kylie had quickly learned that Breege survived on little sleep. It wasn't all that unusual, Breege assured her. This was simply God's way of fitting time into the end of a life. She didn't like to think of Breege as elderly, and absolutely refused to contemplate the end of her life. She had so few true friends that panic consumed her at the thought of losing one.

Tonight, since Kylie was sleeping none too well herself, Breege's rustling sounds and anxious sighs seemed amplified. Kylie sat on the edge of her little cot and tucked her feet into slippers. She pulled on her worn wrapper and padded her way to Breege.

The light shone under the bedroom door. Still feeling oddly like an intruder, Kylie knocked.

"Come in, darlin'," Breege called.

Kylie opened the door and stepped in. "I heard you moving about and wondered if I could bring you something."

Breege smoothed the duvet over her tiny frame, then patted the bed beside her. Kylie took the invitation, sat, and held Breege's knotted hand, its knuckles swollen under silvery, translucent skin.

"Can you bring me something?" Breege echoed with an amused note in her voice. "A leg that works, the energy I had when I was thirty, or a healthy tot of whiskey—take your pick."

Kylie laughed. "Well, the leg I can't be helping you with, and the energy you still have, so we're down to the whiskey." She frowned and tapped her lower lip. "Hmmm ... with Black Johnny O'Shea as a father, d'you think I might have some whiskey still about?"

An odd look flitted across Breege's usually serene features before she said, "More than at Paddy's distillery itself, I'd be thinkin'."

Her friend's words held more than a nip of asperity. Kylie gave Breege's hand one last pat, then stood. "Not quite that much, but I think I can scare up a wee drop. Don't be nodding off on me while I'm gone."

Breege looked heavenward. "A soul should be so blessed."

When Kylie returned with the whiskey, Breege took an unladylike slug before saying, "You might want to get a glass for yourself."

Kylie wrinkled her nose. "Never could stomach the stuff. The scent is pretty enough, but it tastes like a mouthful of petrol to me."

Looking glum, Breege tipped her glass again, then waved it to Kylie to be topped off. After Kylie obliged, Breege said, "Trust me, it's far better to swallow than what I've to tell you." She swirled the amber liquid round and round before continuing. "I meant to say something when you came home tonight, but you were already looking as though someone had danced a hard hornpipe on ye, and I didn't want to be adding to your woes. Then afterward I lay here wishing I could move about enough to toss and turn instead of just count the cracks in the ceiling—and you have a fair few of 'em, you know—"

"The news," Kylie urged.

The deep brackets around Breege's mouth tightened. "Your da called. He'll be getting out Monday next."

Kylie gulped straight from the bottle, then choked and snorted. Feeling as though she were drowning in something far less palatable than the salty waters of Dingle Bay, Kylie smacked the bottle onto the nightstand.

Breege pounded her on the back with more strength than those worn hands should have. "There now, dearie, you'll be fine in just a moment."

"Holy Mother," she gasped. "It burnt a hole straight through to my toes!"

"As it's meant to."

Kylie wiped at her watering eyes and drew in a ragged breath. When she could speak in something above a croak, she said, "You're right. It's still easier to swallow than Da coming home. Did he give you any details?"

"None, really. He seemed confused enough getting me when he rang up. He'll be calling back tomorrow evening and hopes you'll be home."

"Best reason yet not to be," Kylie muttered. She didn't want to hear Johnny's voice. She didn't want to be forced to act pleased that he was about to come back and muck things up for her once again. As if matters weren't sufficiently mucked already, she thought with uncharacteristic bitterness.

Breege stroked her hair, and Kylie sighed at the comfort of the act. She felt the whisper of a maternal touch she scarcely remembered anymore. "Calm now, darlin'. This'll be hard on you. But you have friends who love you, and your da coming home won't change that."

Johnny's arrival would change everything, and they both knew it. Virtually no nest egg had gone untouched by the time her da had made the rounds.

If nothing else, the whiskey appeared to have cleaned her mind of clutter; it suddenly struck Kylie how misguided her attempts at restitution had been. Her acts had been a salve to her conscience, but had done nothing to resolve the town's feelings toward Johnny. And probably had added a drop or two of resentment toward her in the bargain. Small wonder so many had been annoyed by her efforts. Saint Kylie, sacrificing herself to tend to the defrauded.

"I'll deal with the changes in town when Da gets here," Kylie said. "No use in borrowing tomorrow's trouble when today's was enough already."

"Do you want to tell me about it?"

Kylie shook her head. "I just want to put it behind me."

"That's my girl. Just a sip more of the *fuisce*, then," Breege directed, holding out her glass. "And I'll sleep for certain."

Kylie laughed. "I'm putting this bottle up someplace good and high."

Breege's smile showed teeth that remained white and strong. "How d'ye think I fell to begin with?" she teased.

Kylie kissed her papery cheek, whisked the bottle away just to be sure, then wished Breege a good night.

Before tucking the bottle back in the cupboard, Kylie eyed the level of its contents. She sighed. She'd be needing this and more to survive the arrival of Johnny O'Shea.

Chapter Twenty

If you meet a red-haired woman, you'll meet a crowd.
— IRISH PROVERB

Pat and Danny swore they weren't identical twins, yet Michael was having the damnedest time telling them apart. Not that it really mattered which one was which. They seemed to share the same thoughts, one beginning a sentence, the other finishing it, and all so liberally sprinkled with obscenities that Michael felt like a saint.

Of course the morning hadn't started with this scattershot approach to conversation. Painful silence had reigned, the three of them cautiously watching each other from beneath lowered brows. It had taken Vi's late arrival, her offering of blackened toast, and subsequent refusal to cook anything else, to break the deadlock. Survival had a way of uniting strangers.

Michael took over at the stove and told the boys where to find the things he'd be needing. Soon, the salty scent of sizzling rashers filled the air, fried eggs took on the proper hue of faint gold at the edges, and the toast was declared done before it tasted of soot. Vi watched the entire affair in an apparent state of shock.

"You mean you can cook this well and you've not shared with me? You've bloody well betrayed me in my own kitchen."

Michael just looked back over his shoulder at her. "And how, exactly, did you think that dog of yours has grown fat as a sausage roll? And more important, how'd you think I avoided starvation? Though it was a near thing," he added before deftly flipping the eggs, leaving their yolks perfectly intact. "And as for sharing with you, you'll note I'm not much for tofu or whatever that gelatinous block of white stuff you live on is."

Vi grabbed a pot of raspberry preserves. "The stuff in the fridge? I don't live on that! I'm just keeping it till I remember what it is, or until it has a life of its own—whichever comes first."

Michael laughed. The boys first looked confused, then eventually joined in the teasing. He recalled how he felt when he'd first arrived in Ballymuir, a stranger in his own skin. He hadn't known what to expect, and didn't understand the love that simply seemed to exist in Vi's world. A love without expectation, without demand—well, perhaps a little demand. He would give the twins what Vi had given him, the time and love necessary to start healing.

Cupping his hands on the backs of two tousled red heads, he directed them toward the table. And so they sat and shoveled food in the ferocious way that only boys-not-quite-men can, and they talked. Jesus, how they talked about musicians he'd never heard of and people he was sure he didn't want to know, until Michael's head rang with it.

"Eat, then you're coming with me," he finally said.

"With you?" they howled in unison.

He tried on a big-brotherly voice for fit. "Did you have any other plans in mind?"

"Uh, we thought maybe we'd put our feet up for the day and have a rest," Pat—or was it Danny?—ventured.

"You're not lazing about here all day. To begin with, Vi doesn't even have a telly."

The twins' panic-stricken gazes shot about the corners of the room, then to their sister. She raised her mug of tea in silent salute. Michael tried not to smile at their acute disbelief.

"And beyond that," he said, "I won't have you doing here in Ballymuir whatever the hell it is you did with chickens back at home. I've given the family name enough to live down as it is. You'll come with me, do some hard work and get paid a fair wage. Understood?"

One of the twins muttered a string of words under his breath while the other pinned Michael with what he supposed was meant to be a threatening glare. Michael gave him the bared-teeth version of a smile in return.

"Enough," he ordered. "We can go about this one of two ways: either you come along like gentlemen, or I grab you by your balls—and don't think I can't— and persuade you upstairs to get ready." He cracked his knuckles and waggled his fingers as though preparing to seize the royal gems.

Freckles stood out on milky-white faces. Chair legs scraped noisily across the tile floor, and twin sets of gangly legs made their way upstairs. A few reverent curses drifted down.

Michael cleared the table while Vi observed him as if she'd never seen him before.

He cleared his throat. "I'd say we're off to a fair start, wouldn't you?"

"I'd say you're going to be taking over the cooking while they're here."

"To take it over implies that you've been cooking in the first place."

She arched her brow. "So you want their laundry instead?"

"By the time I'm done with them, Sis, they'll be self-sufficient enough to live on their own. Which is what they'll be doing anyway when they're back in Mam's claws."

She toyed with her empty mug. "True enough. I don't suppose we can really do wrong by them, can we?"

As he looked into her worried face, it occurred to Michael that for the first time in as long as he could remember, his perfect harridan of a baby sister was looking to him for guidance. Pride, love, and relief made him stand a little taller. He'd arrived at what he had always considered his rightful place. Not that he didn't love Vi, and not that he wouldn't be indebted to her forever. Now, though, he could stand on his own, and God willing, show Pat and Danny how it was done, too.

He slipped Vi's mug from her slack fingers, then took it to the sink. "We'll do fine by the two of them, I promise," he said. "And don't be in any hurry to ring up Mam and try to change her mind. We'll keep them here for as long as we can."

Vi came up behind him and wrapped her arms around his waist. "You're a man to love, Michael Kilbride. Truly a man to love." She hugged him, then began puttering about the small kitchen.

He ducked his head and stared intently into the sink. The bubbles from the washing-up liquid seemed more shimmery, and he was having trouble finding his voice.

"Well, then . . ." He stopped to rid his throat of an embarrassing tightness. "I'll keep the boys busy today. I want some time with Kylie tonight, and I can see that the only way I'll be having it is to knock those two off their feet."

Vi chuckled. "If that's your goal, I'd suggest a hard shove behind their knees. You're no match for seventeen-year-olds."

A challenge, if ever he'd heard one. "We'll see who's left standing at the end of the day, and who's down for the count."

"I'm putting my money on the wild reds," she announced with a shake of her own blazing hair. "Double or nothing, of course."

• • •

They'd scarcely made it into the car—a nasty tight fit—when Michael was wondering whether his sister wasn't on the winning side of the wager. The twins were hungry again, and this with breakfast just down their gullets.

"We'll have a stop and pick up a bite or two," he said as he pulled up in front of Spillane's Market. Knowing the grocer's greeting would be none too warm, he went on the offensive. "Stay by me," he ordered the boys.

"Morning, Spillane," Michael offered as they came into the store. Mr. Spillane's face had already eroded into a geography of anxious crags and chasms. "These are my brothers, Pat and Dan. To be making things easy on you, I promise we'll keep in a tight pack while we're here. No point in having you panic in three directions at once, now is there?"

Spillane stammered something that could be taken either as agreement or outright shock at the thought of having three male Kilbrides to contend with.

Michael gave the twins—who were busy staring at Spillane—a push forward. "Find what you're wanting."

As he trailed behind them, he said over his shoulder to Spillane, who tailed him, "Pat and Danny, here, will be staying with Vi for a while, and the way they eat, I expect you'll be seeing a lot of them.

"I'm asking one thing of you, though I expect you don't feel that you owe me much of anything. Judge the boys on who they are, and don't let your opinion of me fall into the mix." He stopped and turned to face the man. "Do it for Vi. She has strong feelings about family, Spillane, and I don't want to see her hurt. I don't think you do, either."

The tips of Spillane's ears grew pink. He shuffled his feet and aligned a box of pasta that had been nudged from its militarily straight row.

"Vi's a fine woman," he said, then went to stand by the register.

Michael knew that was as close to a concession as he'd be getting. And it was more than he'd expected, too.

"Vi would thank you, Spillane," he said. He didn't add his own genuine gratitude because he knew it carried no weight with the grocer. A fact for which he now knew some small regret.

After Michael had paid for the twins' haul, and Spillane had packaged it down to the last packet of vinegar-flavored potato crisps, Spillane said, "Have a grand one, boys." He met Michael's eyes for the first time in months. "And you too, Kilbride," he added in a voice not quite warm, but better than ice.

Feeling humbled, yet somehow elated, too, Michael nodded, then herded the twins back into the car.

"What the fu—" one of the twins began.

Michael cut him off. "I'll be charging for that particular word . . . say, fifty pence for each use. It shouldn't be slipping from your mouth like rain from the sky. Not at all the way a Kilbride should act. So unless you're looking to be working for free, I'd suggest you come up with a new word of choice."

The twin in the seat next to him swung around in absolute rage. "Screw that! You can't charge us!"

Michael raised one brow. "I can't? Now, how would you plan to be stopping me, Pat?"

"I'm Dan, dammit to hell and back. If you can't even keep our names straight, how the f—" His throat worked convulsively, oversized Adam's apple bobbing with the effort of swallowing the forbidden word. "How do you plan to keep track of who to charge?"

"I'll just charge you both."

Michael grinned into the faces of twin fits of apoplectic rage. "You each owe me two punts fifty so far. Keep 'em coming, boys, and I'm off to retirement before I ever have to work."

And hours later, he marveled how the elimination of one small word reduced conflict. He gave orders, and if the boys objected, it was done through guttural grunts and moans. Over the course of the day, Michael had learned that for all his mouth, Danny was a hard worker, and that Pat—a boy after his own heart—had a way of trying to negotiate himself out of the tough tasks.

Both possessed the Kilbride sense of justice in full measure, too. When Michael slammed his thumb with a hammer and voiced his displeasure, the twins had demanded fifty pence knocked off each of their accounts. He had, of course, agreed.

By the time the sun touched the horizon, the barn was as clean as the day it had been built, and the three of them were head-to-toe grime. Michael pulled out a length of hose and attached it to a spigot outside the barn. After peeling off his shirt and throwing it aside, he stuck his head under a stream of icy-cold water. He howled as it hit him, enjoying the shock.

The boys laughed as he shook his head, sending water flying.

"Your turn," he announced at the exact moment that he trained the hose on them. What had been meant as a quick clean-up immediately degraded into mud throwing with war whoops and bellows loud enough to bring legendary CúChulainn back from his hero's sleep.

Hard work and hard play—Michael wished like hell someone had shown him at age seventeen that both could be fun.

Kylie sat in her car, not quite certain she wanted to get out. She had stopped at Breege's hoping to find Michael and his strong shoulder to rest her head on. Not bloody likely, given the state of that shoulder.

The sight of Michael and two mud-spattered strangers laughing and grappling about had her mind traveling on odd tangents. She felt almost naughty watching them. Her mouth curved into a smile. For the first time today, she was blessedly free of worry. And it pleased her that she liked feeling naughty.

Even more than that, she liked looking at Michael with no shirt on, especially when he was coated with mud. As though he sensed her thoughts, he suddenly looked up, one stranger's head still locked into the lee between his elbow and body. Michael smiled, teeth white in all that dark. He released his captive and headed toward the car.

Still smiling herself, Kylie stepped out. The two men—quite young men, Kylie saw now—back-pedaled toward the barn.

"I didn't hear you pull up," he said.

"Small wonder. I heard you." She encompassed the strangers in her look. "Even over my car."

Michael laughed. "That loud, eh?" He glanced over his shoulder before saying, "I have somebody—make that two bodies—I want you to meet. Pat! Danny!" he called without looking away from her. "Come here."

They approached cautiously and stood one to either side of him. It was obvious they'd rather be back rolling in the mud than meeting her.

"Kylie, I want you to meet my brothers." He looked at one, then the other, and frowned. Muttering something under his breath, Michael ran his hand over the face of the person to his left, then wiped the resulting palmful of muck on his leg.

"Better," he said. "This is Danny, and that dangerous-lookin' fellow on the other side of me is Pat. They've come for a little visit.

"Boys, this is Miss Kylie O'Shea, and I'd suggest you be very nice to her. Kylie's a teacher, and though you're a bit older than her usual students, I'm sure she'd be happy to put together a lesson or two during your . . . ah . . . holiday from school."

"A teacher?" the boy named Pat said. "Can you believe it, Danny?"

"Jesus, if Mrs. McGilray looked anything like her, we'd never have locked the f—" Pat leaned across Michael and smacked Danny on the side of the head.

Danny winced, shook it off, then finished, "—the chickens in the loo with her."

Between the mud and the mystifying talk of chickens, Kylie didn't know how to respond. Not that anything the boys had said had been directed at her, anyway. She looked to Michael for help, but he was too busy laughing.

"Chickens in the loo?" he finally sputtered. "What the hell were you thinking?"

"I don't suppose that we were thinking at all."

"It's a pleasure to meet you both," Kylie cut in, seeing that the evening was about to devolve into a discussion of whether male adolescents ever thought. She held out a hand and bit back a smile when they glanced down at their own muddy paws, then at their brother. He nodded firmly.

Two gritty handshakes later, they scurried off to the hose and began cleaning up. Michael took the hand his brothers had already dirtied, brushed off the grit, and then drew it to his mouth. He kissed her palm; it was all she could do not to wrap her free hand beneath his jaw and bring his mouth to hers. But some remaining desire for cleanliness and knowledge of their audience stopped her. The boys—their hair as red as Vi's, she now saw—watched warily.

"I've missed you," Michael said. "A night and day apart and so much has happened."

She smiled. "So I see."

He looked at his brothers and pure pleasure shone even from under the streaks of mud painting his face. "I can't say I was thrilled to find 'em sleeping in my bed last night, but they're all right, those two."

His expression grew more serious, and he held tighter to her hand. "This will change things for us, not that events have been any too normal to begin with. It looks like they'll be about for a while. Their—ah, our mam doesn't want them back."

"Over the chickens?"

He gave a weary shrug. "And probably a couple of other things, too. Not that it's any excuse."

"No. None at all." A mixture of frustration and outrage—both as an educator and from some spark of maternal emotion—began to simmer. "So your mother thinks she can just parcel children off when they make a spot of trouble? You think she would have learned by now where that can lead." Kylie shut her mouth and squeezed her eyes tightly shut when she realized what had just slipped out.

Tentatively, she opened them to find Michael looking at her with an amused sparkle lighting his expression. "Amazing. You're going to apologize now, for speaking the truth, aren't you?"

She wished for a bit of that mud to disguise the color she felt burning on her cheeks. "I'll apologize for the way I said it, how's that?"

"You said it from the heart, and it's the kindest heart I've ever known. Truth is truth, love. And seeing the boys, being able to spend some time with them, maybe—just maybe—I'll be able to undo a bit of the damage their mam has inflicted. I don't want to see them half a lifetime from now struggling to learn what I've had to." He paused to take her other hand, too. "Until my mother changes her mind, or my father notices the twins are missing, I guess my days—and nights—have grown a little fuller. Do you mind?"

Now mindless of the mud, the boys, anything but the love she felt for this man, she went up on tiptoe and kissed him. "I don't mind any more than you did when I moved Breege into my house."

His smile was crooked. "I was just smart enough to keep my complaints to myself."

"Well, I have no complaints at all. They seem like fine boys." She choked back a laugh as she glanced at the sizable "boys" in question.

"Fine they are, and they're also hungry. They eat like young wolfhounds—swallowing rabbits whole." At her laugh, he added, "God's truth, I swear. And I think I'll get them on home, fill their bellies, then come have a visit with you this evening. If you don't mind having a visitor, that is."

Kylie tilted her head and took in the details that made her heart beat faster—the sensuous curve to his smile, the way he held himself as though he'd take on and flatten any evil the world threw his way. "I don't think you fall under the category of visitor anymore, do you?"

"Not a visitor and not quite a resident," he said with a teasing tone. "I should be thinking of picking up an injury or two, then maybe you'd find room for me under your roof."

Kylie fought to hide her instinctive flinch. Michael looked at her carefully, as though observing things invisible to the naked eye. Not for the first time, she wondered whether he didn't have a share of his sister's second sight.

"Struck a nerve, have I?"

She tried to smile, but failed miserably. "Just more birds coming home to roost, and the nest already full up."

He was silent a moment, then said, "Your da, is it?"

All she could manage was a tiny nod of her head. Anything more and she would either rage and roll in the mud or break down and weep. And whichever happened, it wasn't the sort of impression she wanted to make on Pat and Danny Kilbride.

Michael sighed. "I'm sorry, love, but we'll work our way through it. I promise."

Kylie smiled, this time for real. She loved being part of a "we," with all the unity and strength that the word implied. It was still more wish than reality, but it was all she had.

"We'll be fine, the both of us," she said. "And the rest of those wild Kilbrides, too."

He hugged her and laughed at her shocked cry as his mud became hers. He rubbed his face into the sensitive crook where neck met shoulder, and growled, "Wild, Kilbrides are? You haven't seen the half of it."

Kylie laughed, too. Pat and Danny merely watched, one commenting to the other, "Not half f—, uh bad, for a teacher."

Chapter Twenty-one

If it isn't better, may it not be worse.

—IRISH PROVERB

Vi Kilbride scrutinized the down-at-the-heels interior of Ballymuir's Village Hall. "A bit of paint, a few banners, and we'll be set—in a minimalist sort of way."

Trailing in Vi's wake, Kylie grimaced. Even with paint and banners, there was a certain ill-used air to the place she needed to address before it was ready for her students' show, which was just a matter of days away. She tapped her index finger against her lower lip as she considered the possibilities.

"I suppose you have the materials for banners at your studio. And the village council might be willing to pay Pat and Danny to do a little paint-up.

Assuming Michael can spare them, that is." He'd kept them running dawn to dusk for the week they'd been in town.

Just then, sharp heels drummed across the dusty wood. Kylie turned to see Evie Nolan closing in on them.

"So is it true?" Evie gave a little wiggle to settle her sausage-tight top.

"Is what true?"

"Your da, of course. I heard at the pub that he was coming back to town today. Didn't you go get him?" She looked around as if he might be lurking in a corner.

"I work. I've got no time to be driving all the way to County Laois."

"Then he's taking the bus? Do you think he'll be in tonight? It's nearly eight already."

Kylie knew neither when nor how her father was arriving, and had been struggling mightily not to care. He had called more than once in the past several days, and each time she had avoided him, using Breege as an unwilling shield. All because she couldn't bring herself to speak five blunt words: *I don't want you here.*

She spent the anger she felt toward herself on Evie. "Why the sudden interest in my da's arrival? Been sending love notes off to prison?"

"Just wantin' to know whether it's time to lock up my pocketbook."

Defending Johnny O'Shea to Evie, who'd been a petty thief for as long as Kylie could recall, bordered on the absurd. "Lock up your pocketbook? You wouldn't want to do that until you were through stealing from your da's till, now would you, Evie?"

Evie's plum-painted lips snapped shut. Her low growl was quickly lost in the chime of Vi's laughter.

"Kylie me girl, I'm liking you more every day," Vi said, accenting the words with a pat on the back that had the air escaping from Kylie's lungs with a whoosh.

As Kylie recovered, it occurred to her that she was liking herself more every day, too. Feeling plenty strong to face down Evie, she pinned the girl with a glare.

"Are you here to help with the art show? Because if you are, you're not dressed for it. And if you're not, leave us to our work. You could always go wheedle gossip back at the pub. Tongues are looser after a pint or two."

"As are some women, from what I've seen," Vi added.

At Evie's rude response, she cautioned, "Be careful what you say. Life has a nasty way of coming back and biting you in the bum."

Evie stalked away. Halfway to the door, she teetered on the slope of her ridiculously high heels, then fell off. Arms flailing, curses spouting, she righted herself.

Vi smiled brightly. "Bloody things'll kill you if you're not careful."

Kylie suspected Evie's fall had more to do with Vi's uncanny abilities than bad shoes. The slamming door signaled Evie's departure.

Vi gave a wry shake of her head. "That one will

never grow up." She ran her finger along the back of a worn bench, then said, "So your da's due back. Must be a bit of a shock even though you knew the day was coming."

"It'll be more of a shock for my da when he learns that Breege is living in my house, and her peacock in my shed."

The noise of Michael's power tools had sent Martin scurrying for a more placid location. Suddenly, Kylie wondered if she hadn't invited Breege into her house to attain exactly the same thing.

"You've not talked to your da, have you?"

"Not precisely."

Vi simply looked at her, brows raised in the inquisitive curve of a mother confessor's. She was obviously itching to say more.

Kylie watched dust motes drift and dance in the glow of the overhead light. The expectant silence grew too thick to be ignored.

"Go on then, before you explode."

"It's not my business to be telling you anything, but since you asked. You owe your father and yourself the truth."

She'd been short and sweet, at least.

"I've known I do, but it seems that every time I get a grasp on happiness, Da finds some way to wrench it free. He doesn't mean to hurt me, but he always does. As much as I can't bear the thought of having Da under my roof, I feel even worse for depriving him of a place."

"So scrabbling for a home of your own while trying to repay his debts wasn't quite enough?"

She shook her head. "He's my father. That's something, even if it no longer seems to be quite enough. And you're a fine one to be arguing this with me, anyway. You took in Michael, didn't you?"

"It's not at all the same thing. He's with me because it's where he's meant to be, how he's meant to start. Now, your father, he chose his path long ago, and stuck to it even when he knew it would leave you living in ruins. Michael, he's—"

The front door's rusty hinges squealed, drawing Kylie's attention. "Walking in the door right now," she quickly cut in.

"The hall hasn't seen this much traffic since old Aislinn Greavey's wake. Evening, brother," Vi called across the room. "And how are you?"

"Better, now that you're through gossiping about me," he replied before giving Kylie an all-too-quick kiss in greeting.

He kept his hand resting on the curve of her waist, and she leaned into that casual touch, imagining how it would feel against her bare skin. Elemental emotion jumped and sizzled between them, almost a palpable thing.

Michael swallowed once—hard—before adding, "And I'd be even better yet, Sis, if you'd kindly clear the room and leave the keys to the place."

Vi jingled a keyring between her fingers. "And risk having my first niece or nephew conceived in the Village Hall? On behalf of Miss O'Shea, here, I'll hold out for silk sheets at the Connaught following a proper ceremony in front of Father Cready." She nudged Kylie. "Quit your swooning or he'll think you're easy."

Easy didn't begin to describe it. A week of depri-
vation had done its work. She felt rounder-heeled
than Evie Nolan. She stepped away, but the current
between herself and Michael arced the distance.

Michael shot his sister a gimlet stare. "You'll pay
for this, sweet Vi."

"You'd best ask Kylie what happened to the last
soul who crossed me."

"He's not wearing spike heels," Kylie pointed out.

Vi's smile was positively feline. "But men have
certain inadequacies in their armor, so to speak."

Michael took a sharp breath and clutched Kylie's
hand. "To the door."

"And be quick about it, before I toss a bucket of
cold water over you both," Vi said.

Once they were safe outside and had finished a
good laugh at Vi's audacity, the pull between them
seemed stronger then ever.

"Walk with me," he said, and she looped her arm
through his.

The village streets were quiet, and the air damp
with the rain that had fallen all day. Kylie's fingers
rested against the hard muscle of Michael's upper
arm. Without paying any attention to their route,
they strolled down the hill and along the edge of the
quay. A breeze carrying the fertile scent of sea eddied
around them. The water lapping against the stone
seawall seemed to surge in time to Kylie's heart.

They reached the end of the pier. Michael cupped
her face between his palms. Just as she rose on her
toes, he leaned forward to kiss her. A chorus of male
laughter sounded from a boat in the harbor. They

both started, and Michael pulled away. He drew her from light they'd been standing near, and into the protection of last twilight. Kylie knew the laughter had nothing to do with them. Still, the moment was lost.

"We can't go on this way much longer," Michael said. "I'd sell my bloody soul for the chance to kiss you as you're meant to be kissed. And to get my hands on you. . . ." He drew a ragged breath.

Kylie nodded, her throat tight with emotion.

He moved closer, but didn't touch her. "I've been thinking about this for a while now. I want you to come away with me. Not some weak excuse for privacy like the cinema in Tralee, but someplace so far that we don't stand the risk of running into anyone from Ballymuir. I want to be more than passing acquaintances in public. I want to be free of all this—this—goddamn worry of what being seen with me might do to you."

He touched his fingertips to her cheek, and she shivered at the heat his caress carried.

"And those silk sheets Vi spoke of," he said in a low, thick voice, "I want to see you on them with nothing but my body to cover you. I want to make love to you until neither of us has the strength left to move. Then I want to sleep and do it all again."

Once, not so very long ago, he'd said things less explicit than this to her, and she'd been silent with apprehension. Now, she wanted it all. And more.

She found her voice. "When?"

"W-when?" he echoed, looking as though it had never occurred to him that she'd fall in with his plan.

"Yes, when?"

He raked a hand through his hair. "Well now, love, I guess that's the one part of this scheme I haven't exactly got down." His smile was endearingly crooked. "I guess I was too wrapped up in what we'd be doing."

"Understandably so," she said, then gave him a smile of her own. She sobered as reality came crashing in. "It's a grand idea, truly it is. But with the art exhibition coming up, and no break in school till June, I don't see much hope for us."

"Have faith," he said, then laughed.

"Care to share?"

A conservative slice of air between them, he led her back toward the low, sloping roofs of the village. "Well, I was just thinking how Vi insists if you want something enough, and visualize it down to the smallest detail, you can nudge it down the path to reality."

Kylie smiled at the fanciful idea, then considered its wise-beyond-her-years source. She stopped walking, hauling Michael up short. "Close your eyes."

She waited until he'd complied before closing her own. "Now give it a try."

They stood there at the edge of the quay, two village lunatics, eyes tight shut.

"Do you think we're visualizing the same thing?" Kylie eventually asked.

He chuckled. "Variations on a theme, I'd imagine."

Smiling, she opened her eyes, then immediately wished she hadn't. For one instant she wondered if through amateurish magic, she'd somehow conjured this specter.

But, no, it was just Johnny O'Shea, that last bird come home to roost.

She saw nothing of the dapper man she'd once known. Her father looked and smelled as though he'd drunk his way from prison to Ballymuir.

"Haven't you got a kiss for me?"

"Hello, Da," she said, and hated the way her voice wavered. She wanted to be strong, firm.

"I was telling the blokes down at the pub how busy my own child was. How she couldn't even come to the phone when I called. And now I see that you've been busy, indeed."

He eyed Michael, who had taken a firm grasp of her hand. Kylie held on as if he were her only lifeline.

"I'm Michael Kilbride, a friend of your daughter's. Welcome home."

"Did ye hear that, Kylie? A welcome from a perfect stranger and nothing from you. No welcome, no home, not even a place to lay my head."

"Sorry, Da, but—"

Michael squeezed her hand and cut in. "She's got nothing to be sorry for. Kylie's given up her own bed, caring for an ill friend."

Her father stuck out his chin and his eyes narrowed. She'd never thought him a mean drunk, but the possibility was evident.

"I'm better than a friend, I'm family. The only family she's got."

"Well now, Da, that isn't exactly true anymore. I have Breege Flaherty for a grandmum and Michael's sister, Vi, for my own. I'm sorry I don't have a place for you, but it's not as though I could afford much after trying to take care of your debts."

He looked truly shocked. "But I've already paid with years of my life and every pence I couldn't get offshore."

Explaining honor to Johnny was like discussing the sanctity of human life with an assassin. Kylie skipped the impossible and gave in to the inevitable. "I'll get you home, Da. You can have my spot in front of the fire."

"Well, if I can't be having a room, I suppose that will do," he said grudgingly. "Do I at least get a private bath? I could do with a little freshening up."

"I'm not running a bed and breakfast—"

"He'll sleep in Breege's barn," Michael cut in. "The boys left their bedrolls there. It's warm enough to get him through the night. And if he wants to freshen, he can use the hose."

Johnny puffed up like a bantam rooster. "Who are you to be giving my daughter orders?"

"The man who will see that you never take advantage of her again," Michael answered in a flat tone.

Kylie sensed a tension in the air she didn't understand. It seemed more than male territoriality, and whatever the source, it sent a chill curling through her.

Johnny slowly deflated. "A barn, you say. Jesus and Mary, I'm glad your poor, sainted mam didn't live to see this. What would she say?"

"I'd wager she'd think you're getting more than you deserve, O'Shea," Michael answered. "You'll come with me, and can visit Kylie tomorrow."

Kylie knew she should be objecting to this bit of

blatant, take-charge, know-it-all chauvinism, but all she felt was relief.

After Michael had finished questioning Johnny on the whereabouts of any belongings he might have, she drew him aside.

They both looked back to Johnny, who bent over to tie his shoe, then tumbled to the ground. Before Kylie could voice her concern, he gave a wave, stood, and stumbled to a bench.

"Just havin' a little sit-down," he called.

"Better a sit-down than a fall-down," Michael muttered, and Kylie laughed.

She tugged his hand and moved him a few more steps down the road for discretion's sake.

"You know that event we were envisioning?"

He nodded.

"I want you to envision me showing my gratitude for tonight in some very creative ways."

He grinned, then brushed a brief kiss against her cheek. "You won't know the meaning of grateful until I've had my way with you on those silk sheets, love."

Arrogant man, she loved him so.

Chapter Twenty-two

Drunkenness hides no secrets.

— IRISH PROVERB

Michael had decided he didn't like Johnny O'Shea long before the man puked in his car. The sour scent of vomit, though, wasn't helping matters.

"This time, O'Shea, you'll be cleaning your own mess."

Johnny moaned and shifted in his seat.

"And I get the feeling that you're not a man for the aftermath."

O'Shea told Michael to go commit certain indecent acts, then way bloody late, stuck his head out the window. It was tempting to swerve too close to the hedgerow lining the road and take the little bastard's head off. Only the fact that this was Kylie's father—a miracle of genetics, there—and that another little bastard, Gerry Flynn, was on his tail, stopped him.

By the time they'd pulled onto Breege's property, O'Shea seemed to have tossed himself dry. Gerry Flynn had faded away, probably satisfied Michael wasn't continuing up the road to Kylie's. Michael aimed the car's headlights at the barn, then hopped out.

Once inside, he switched on the lights, took a second to be certain that the boys' bedrolls were where he'd last seen them, then exited to gather up his charge.

O'Shea was asleep—or unconscious. Since leaning over the man wasn't worth considering, he walked to the driver's door, slipped in, and turned off the beams.

"O'Shea, wake up."

His mouth hung open and his eyelids were at half-mast.

"C'mon, little man, up with you."

O'Shea's head lolled to the side.

Michael scowled. There was no hope for it. If he had felt any compassion, he would have carried Johnny O'Shea to the barn and let him sleep it off. But more than the vomit stopped him. It ground at him, the way the man had treated Kylie tonight, as though she lived solely to serve him.

Michael thought back to when she'd told him of her rape, of Johnny off drunk, leaving her to fend for herself. Hearing the story, he'd had his doubts about Johnny's lack of complicity.

He looked at the man in the car beside him. Clearly, tonight was not the first time Johnny had used his daughter to suit his ends. His lines had been too well rehearsed for that. Even so, could the man truly have been evil enough to trade Kylie's innocence for debts forgiven? That it was even remotely possible sent a shot of pure venom to Michael's heart.

He climbed out of the car and slammed the driver's door, then stalked to the tap and filled the rusting bucket beneath it with water. Icy cold, please. Then he returned to the car, opened Johnny's door, and let fly without a moment's hesitation. O'Shea awoke gasping and sputtering. Michael looked at his car's interior and shrugged. A little water was nothing compared to its other contents.

"You're home," he said.

While Michael removed the standard prisoner's release duffel from the boot of the car, O'Shea staggered toward the barn. Michael pulled abreast of him in the entry.

Johnny squinted into the interior. "You really think I'm sleepin' here?"

Michael gave him a firm push. "And d'you really think I'll be driving you anyplace else?"

He tossed O'Shea's belongings onto a chair, then grabbed rags and detergent from a shelf. "The bucket's by the car. Fill it and get busy. And you'd best put on something dry after you've finished cleaning. Wouldn't want you to catch a chill."

O'Shea snorted. "How do you plan to make me clean your car?"

He had to give the runt credit for a huge set of balls. He rolled his shoulders like a fighter readying for the ring. "I've found that people never argue with me more than once."

O'Shea sized him up, then stuck out his chin. "And if I do, they'll find me beaten to a pulp in the morning?"

"No, just a bit worse for the wear." As he looked at the man, Michael felt a grim smile fight its way out. A bucket of water looked to be the gentlest greeting the little rooster had received tonight. "What the hell is that on your forehead anyway, a rug burn?"

"Nothin' at all," O'Shea muttered, then thrust out one shaking hand. "Just give me the goddamn stuff and let me get this over with."

When the car was at last cleaned to Michael's satisfaction, and sat doors open, airing out, he prodded O'Shea back into the barn. The hard work seemed to have had a sobering effect; O'Shea began to settle in with minimal complaint. Michael permitted himself to soften—marginally. This was Kylie's father, he kept reminding himself. And anyone who had contributed to such a wonder had to have some good.

O'Shea stepped out of a stall, dressed in dry clothes. Michael acknowledged him with a nod.

"It's not a far walk uphill to Kylie's," he said. "If you get there early enough in the morning, I'm sure she'll be glad to give you a bite to eat."

"And will I be finding you there?"

"If you're asking whether I live with your daughter, the answer is no. I will tell you this, though," he continued. "Don't get comfortable with the idea of not seeing me around. I know Kylie's wishes, and I'll do what I have to, to see that you follow them.

"And since I've got you alone, and you're not nearly as sotted as you were earlier, I'll add this, too. At the risk of your health, you'll do nothing to disturb your daughter's life. No complaining and whining until she feels honor-bound to let you live with her. No more references to her 'poor, sainted mother.' None of that shit or you'll answer to me."

O'Shea's brows rose. "Answer to you? Now, there's a rich one. Think I haven't had a word or two dropped about you already? Think I don't know exactly who I'm talking to? Christ, I might be a bit poor with the numbers when it comes to money, but I'm no murderer."

The blow scarcely hurt anymore, and Michael knew he had Kylie to thank for starting the healing.

"That'll teach you to listen to pub gossip, because I'm no murderer, either. And as for you, I'll grant you a certain amount of deference because you're Kylie's father. But for the very same reason, I need to know exactly what you are."

"I don't know what you're getting at, Kilbride."

"You'll know what I'm getting at when I'm ready to get there," he said. The man would show his true colors in time. "For now, be the soul of respect to your daughter, and I promise I won't rearrange your face. Sleep well, Johnny," he added over his shoulder as he left. "And be ready to find yourself a new roof come morning."

• • •

Full dark had fallen by the time Kylie neared Breege's property. Though she'd intended to leave straightaway and be sure her father was tucked away for the night, Vi had caught up with her outside the Village Hall. A minute of chat turned into more as they covered the last details of the art exhibition.

Kylie turned into the drive, then hesitated. Her da was probably asleep by now, and what a blessing that would be. As she fidgeted in her seat, debating whether to continue up the drive, the whitish glow of a pair of headlights came toward her, then stopped. Michael, of course. They climbed out of their cars, leaving engines on and headlights shining.

Kylie stepped into the circle of his arms and rested her head against his chest before asking, "How is he?"

"Better now that he's through fouling the inside of my car. Six pints of stout in the man, at least."

Pulling away, she winced. "Oh lord, did he . . ." She trailed off before giving the act its evocative name. "I'll clean it."

He drew her back into his embrace. "No. Your da and I had ourselves a chat. You're not cleaning after him, not the mess in my car and not anything else he might do."

Kylie sighed. She'd already learned that cleaning up after Johnny was futile.

"You're a wise man, Michael Kilbride. Where were you four years ago when I was starving myself and needed the sense knocked into my head?"

He laughed. "Getting some sense knocked into my own, of course." He paused and hugged her tighter.

"And you're still not treating yourself nearly well enough to suit me. I'm serious about us getting away. I was thinking the west—Connemara, maybe. Or someplace else if you're in the mood for a city."

She smiled and let her fingertips trace the line of his jaw, sexy with a day's growth of beard. "Wherever you want sounds grand."

He gave her a quick kiss, then set her away from him. "Any more and I'd be tempted to take you into that field, sheep and stray dogs be damned."

The deep timbre of his voice let her know his words were more truth than joke. She loved the feeling of power that gave her.

"Get some sleep, love," he said. "I'm sure your da will be knocking at your door come sunup."

"G'night," she replied, then murmured a softer *love* as he walked away.

He paused as if startled, then turned back. Kylie wished it were light enough to read his expression, because as usual, when she most wanted him to speak, Michael Kilbride said nothing.

Michael opened the door to Vi's house, then took a step back from the blue haze of cigarette smoke that reached out to draw him in. Frowning, he entered and hung his jacket on the hook next to the door.

"I liked it better when you celebrated with music and orange drink," he called to his sister.

No smart remark flew back his way.

"Vi?"

The sounds of scraping chairs and muffled voices came from the kitchen. He pushed open the door. Pat and Danny were hunched over the table. Each had one handful of playing cards, the other hand beneath the table, and a face that couldn't bluff worth a damn.

Michael nodded. "Boys."

"Didn't expect you home so soon," Pat offered.

"Been smoking, have you?"

"N-no," Danny stammered. "Nasty stuff, that."

"Might stunt our growth," Pat chimed in.

Michael raised a brow at the absurdity of that statement. "And is your belly bothering you, Pat? You're all folded over."

"Nah, just tired."

Michael came closer and settled a hand on his brother's shoulder. "Let me help you up, and we'll get you to bed." He hauled Pat from his chair.

Michael shook his head at the whiskey bottle that tumbled from Pat's lap. Pat bent down to retrieve it.

"You might as well get the glass and the ashtray while you're down there," Michael commented. "And you, Danny, put your glass on the table."

Pat dumped the contraband, then edged toward the door.

"Back here and sit," Michael ordered without looking away from Danny. Pat was smart enough not to try to run.

Michael pulled out a chair, then sat, too. "Cards, cigarettes, whiskey . . . What's the matter, couldn't you find a couple of willing women to round out the picture?"

He sighed, wondering whether it was the full moon that was making throats seem parched for a drink, or if it was just his stinkin' luck. "Here's the thing of it, boys. Most any other night than this, I'd be a bit more tolerant of your activities, but you've shown the Kilbride talent for timing. I'm not feeling inclined to mercy."

"Honest, it's the first time—"

"Don't be adding lying to the list." Michael hefted the whiskey bottle. Only a few inches remained, and he was damned sure the balance hadn't gone down the twins, or they'd be dead by now. "Where'd you find this?"

Jaws grimly set, the boys stared down at the table-top.

"You don't want to do this the hard way."

"In Vi's closet," Pat finally said.

"Well, I'll give you credit for meeting my eyes and telling me the truth. But I still have to say you're the stupidest pair to have come my way in a long time. Snooping and stealing from the woman who took you in?"

"She wouldn't take us to the pub like we asked, then Mam called and said—"

He ignored the second bit, though a call from Mam would put him in need of a drink, too.

"You're underage, you fools." He unscrewed the whiskey bottle. "Give me your glasses."

They slid them his way. As Michael divided the rest of the whiskey between the two, their eyes grew huge.

"One of the things I've had to learn is my way around the kitchen," Michael said as he pushed back his chair and strolled to the fridge. "No point in having a dull diet, now is there?"

He opened the fridge, then pulled out two eggs and whatever the white mess was that Vi had been keeping. "You two seem to be in the mood to try new things."

He set the bowl and eggs on the table. The boys, he noticed, were looking a wee bit washed out. He cracked an egg into each whiskey, then reached his hand into the bowl of moldy God-knows-what.

As he dropped globs into the glasses, he said, "You'll have to tell me if this bears repeating."

He shoved a glass toward each boy, hoping he was doing right, and admitting to himself that he didn't know jack-all about being a parent. "Now drink up."

"You're f-f- insane!" Danny howled.

"Fifty pence from you both because I know what you meant to say, Danny. And no, I'm not insane. Now drink up or I'll let Vi decide your punishment. She's a regular ball buster when she's got the mind to be. Hell, this'll look as tasty as a trifle by the time she's done with you."

"I don't see as we got much choice," Pat said to Danny. "And it'll be over with quick."

Michael smiled. "And boys, see that it doesn't come back up. I won't vouch for its flavor the second time down."

Half an hour later, the boys were sprawled on old blankets in the backyard—in case the whiskey ventured back up—and because a night outside their sister's roof might give them a finer appreciation of her privacy.

Michael was looking forward to a night spent in a real bed. Room to stretch out, room to roll, and room to dream. He was halfway up the steps when the phone rang. Mentally fining himself fifty pence for his muttered comment, he made his way back down.

" 'Lo?" he growled into the phone.

At the silence on the other end, he gave it a full, formal "Hello?"

"I paid Ballymuir a visit, size of a flea's ass that it is. Saw your teacher, too. She's really quite pretty. Seems almost a shame to put a bullet through her head."

The breath slammed from Michael's body.

"Who is this?" he managed to croak, even though he knew. God help him, he knew.

"You can't have forgotten me so quickly. I haven't forgotten you . . . *Mickey*."

"What do you want?"

"To be paid back for what you took from me. Time's come, my friend."

The line went dead.

"Goddamn you, Rourke," he whispered to a ghost. "Goddamn you."

Michael hung up the phone and leaned his head against the wall. He'd eaten little, which was a blessing because soon he was bent over the toilet losing everything he had. After a long shower, he lay in bed, hollow and horrified, almost afraid to sleep.

There was an answer to this ugliness, one so bleak he could scarcely let the thought form in his mind. But he had no choice. He rose, made a call to Galway Information, then stared at the ceiling, trying to find the grace to accept the unacceptable.

When exhaustion overtook him, he dreamed he was tumbling down a mountainside, a bloody fall with breath and heart and hope torn from him. Dervla McLohne and Brian Rourke cheered as he fell.

But what terrified him most was that Kylie was falling with him.

And he couldn't save her.

Chapter Twenty-three

Treachery returns.

—IRISH PROVERB

No matter how much he'd drunk the night before, Johnny O'Shea was an early riser. Until the rapping at the front door awakened her, Kylie had forgotten this. She pulled on her old velvet robe and staggered toward the noise.

After steeling herself for the inevitable, she opened the door. Johnny strolled in. He flicked a glance toward her wrapper. "Still own that, do you? Doesn't look fit for the rag bag."

"I haven't had money for extras."

Her father didn't comment. He made his way to the kitchen on what had to be sheer instinct. Kylie followed, marveling that it wasn't even dawn and already she was apologizing for something that was his fault. While he rooted around in the fridge, she looked out the kitchen window for any sign of sun.

"What time is it, Da?"

"Not quite gone six. Where's the eggs and rashers?"

"At this hour, the eggs are still with the chickens and the rashers on the hoof. Though you can feel free to start a pot going for tea, and I think there's some muesli in the cupboard."

"Muesli?" He spat the word as if it were toxic. "You call that food?"

"Yes, I do. I'm going to shower now and get ready for work. I'd say make yourself at home, but I think you need to keep firmly in mind you're a visitor."

"So you won't be fixing me a grand welcome-home breakfast?"

"No, but I'll give you a lift into town when I leave. You'd best be thinking about finding work and a place to stay."

"Work?" If muesli had been toxic, work appeared to be utterly lethal. "You mean work for someone—in a shop?"

"Or an office or a back room or sweeping the streets, if that's what it comes to. I won't support you, Da."

Mouth sloping in a mournful curve, he announced, "I'll go on the dole, then. If my own daughter won't care for me till I get back on my feet, at least my country will."

She rolled her eyes. A fine time to embrace patriotism. And even more convenient how he'd failed to mention the money he said he'd hidden away.

"Do what you must. Just make sure it's legal."

"I'll settle for not being caught."

And that, Kylie decided as she stalked off to the shower, was Mr. Johnny O'Shea's problem in a nutshell.

Despite his protestations that O'Connor's Pub was more centrally located, at seven forty-five Kylie dropped her da in front of the hardware store.

"If another pint's all you have in mind, you can walk to the pub and wait till opening time," she said. "The exercise'll do you some good."

"You've grown into an ungrateful woman. Hard and ungrateful." He curled his lip at the "help wanted" sign in the hardware window and turned in the direction of O'Connor's.

As Kylie watched him walk away, she recalled those childhood days when she'd thought her father gloriously strong and perfect, and believed that he could save her from death itself. She sighed, feeling melancholy and wholly inadequate to deal with Da as he really was. Likely, as he always had been.

Far down the hill, a uniformed man stepped from a doorway and stopped her da. Whatever the man was saying, Da didn't seem to like. He was all puffed up and thumping the Garda on the chest with one index finger.

She needed to move closer. The narrow stretch of street was lined with the cars of those who lived above the shops, so she left hers where it was and stepped out. She'd walked no more than a quarter-block when she realized it was Gerry.

"Da, not trouble so soon," she whispered. "And above all, not with Gerry."

She knew she should rescue her father. Still, she hesitated. It would be so simple—so painless—to turn back and pretend she saw nothing. After all, Gerry might go away all on his own. She winced at the path her thoughts had taken.

Might.

For too long, she'd let what *might* happen rule her life. If she had talked to even a single boy in her time at university, she *might* have been attacked again. If she had stood up for Michael in O'Connor's Pub, she *might* have risked her job. And for all those *mights*, all those illusory disasters, she had let herself become less than the person she knew she could be.

"You must have learned by now," Kylie told herself. "Jump in with both feet." Then she did.

"Da," she called as she jogged toward the pair, "I was wondering if you could pick up a few bits for dinner."

They turned to watch her. She pulled in front of them and rounded her eyes into what she hoped was a look of surprise.

"Oh, Gerry, it's you."

"And who did you think it would be giving me this welcome," her father snapped. "His Holiness all the way from Rome?"

Gerry's cheeks were mottled crimson. He looked somewhere past her and gave a curt nod.

Kylie ignored the unpleasant undercurrents and focused on moving her father along. "Well, Da, you'd best be heading toward the market. Mr. Spillane is in there early enough that you shouldn't have to wait long."

"Young Mr. Flynn and I need to finish our talk."

"Perhaps another time would be better." She brightened as she glanced down the walk. "Besides, isn't that Mr. O'Bannion down the way? I heard he got a job at the dog track in Tralee."

"Really, now? Working at the track . . ."

Johnny took off at a fine clip, leaving Kylie and Gerry alone. There was no fleeing now. And there was no pretending she could just skirt past the ugliness between them. Not without failing herself.

"About the other night," she began, with no idea where she might end up. Seeking a better handhold on diplomacy, she paused, then started again. "I know that it's going to be difficult, seeing each other after what happened—"

Gerry frowned. "What are you talking about?"

Kylie felt as though the world were slipping from beneath her. While she'd imagined hostility, outright denial had never been a possibility.

"At Breege Flaherty's barn?"

"I think you've finally gone over the edge." The red flush hadn't left Gerry's face, and his eyes never once met hers. "I haven't been there in years."

Tears of pure rage burnt at her eyes. "You want to pretend the other night never happened? Fine then, add it to your list, right after the night of my eighteenth birthday. But before you march off all full of yourself, answer me this. Do you even know the truth when you meet it?"

He shouldered his way past her. "Quite a question from someone who's sleeping with evil."

Kylie tucked her hands into her pockets, tipped

her face to the ground, and walked back to her car. She'd do whatever it bloody well took to get away with Michael. And with any money she had left, she'd put up a new sign at the village limits: "Ballymuir, Finest Accumulation of Loons West of Bedlam."

Fifteen minutes before the children arrived, Kylie sorted through papers she'd graded.

"Morning, Kylie."

Mairead Corrigan, the school principal, stood in the doorway.

"Morning, Mairead."

"Two things we're needing to discuss."

Kylie nodded.

"First, I've decided to give the children a holiday on Monday before the art exhibition opens. A chance to get a bit of rest before the premiere—which I'm sure will be brilliant." She flashed a distracted smile that quickly faded away. "And as for the next, well, it's not exactly as cheerful as all that. I've heard your father is back in town."

Kylie fought off a sense of impending doom. "He is."

"I've had a number of calls on the matter—starting about the time his bus pulled into town, from what I gather. The parents have been told it's not their concern."

Which was as it should be.

The principal cleared her throat, then scowled at the clock. "It's also being said that you've been seen about with Vi Kilbride's brother."

Thankfully, Mairead didn't seem to be seeking comment, because the words forming in Kylie's mind weren't the sort to assure long employment.

"If this job were about educating children and had none of the parents' nonsense, it would be heaven. Unfortunately . . ." Mairead trailed off, massaging the bridge of her nose between thumb and index finger. "Well, I feel a fool for saying this, but here it is. If you are involved with Michael Kilbride, I have to be sensitive to their concerns. I don't know the whole of his past, but what I do know—"

Kylie's stomach roiled. "Are you demanding I choose between my private life and my position here?"

"No . . . no, I don't mean that," Mairead said, though the way her eyes darted away from Kylie's sent another message. "If it is true—and I don't want to know whether it is—please be careful. Emotions have a way of getting out of hand around here, and whether it's his fault or not, Michael Kilbride has become a walking reminder of matters people don't want to even admit still exist."

She trailed off, then after a sigh, squared her shoulders, seeming to smooth out the mantle of authority. "I'm sorry," she finished. "I'll let you get on with your day."

Kylie stared at her desk. The papers on it wavered with the sheen over her eyes.

Mairead paused at the door. "I want you to know that I trust your judgment, and I'll support you the best I can. But I can't be guaranteeing my best will be good enough."

Kylie nodded. After Mairead left, she dug through her desk for a tissue, and wished herself anyplace but Ballymuir.

Michael bolted upright at the sound of someone clearing his throat. Daylight shone through the window at the top of the steps. He scrubbed a hand over his face, then looked at Pat, who stood at the end of the bed.

"What time is it?"

"Just past ten."

"Jesus." He couldn't recall the last time he'd slept that late. Not that last night counted as sleep.

"We've made you breakfast. And Vi, she's brooding about like a mother hen. She's been up here twice to check and see whether you were still breathing."

"Barely," he muttered, nerves jittering just beneath his skin. He'd made some decisions—or more accurately, faced the inevitable—sometime before the sun rose.

"Well, c'mon down and eat when you're ready."

When he made it downstairs, the twins were huddled in front of the stove. Vi sat at the kitchen table, a concerned expression tugging at her mouth.

"They're feeding me?" he asked in an undertone. She nodded.

"And did you witness them preparing the meal?"

"No."

On a morning when he least needed it, he'd been presented with a test of nerves. After the lesson he'd given Pat and Danny last night, eating whatever they'd cooked up would be a nasty gamble. But he also knew he had to show them trust. He just hoped they'd earned it.

"What's going on?" Vi asked. "Why were the boys sleeping on the stoop when I got home?"

"We'll talk about it later." Assuming he survived breakfast.

Resigned to his fate, Michael sat. "Bring it on, boys."

Danny settled a plate in front of him, and Pat provided the cutlery. Though his stomach objected to the thought of food, he tucked into his eggs and rashers. The boys were doing anything they could to avoid looking at him.

Between bites he said, "I'll be leaving town today for a day or two."

"Short notice, isn't this?" asked his too-perceptive little sister.

"The opportunity came up to do some business in Galway. Guess I forgot to mention it yesterday."

Her eyes narrowed. "You did. And what sort of business might this be?"

"Furniture and room repairs for a hotel," he lied. "It's one of those old townhouses all fitted out for paying customers. They're friends of Jenna Fahey, and got my name from her. Anyway, I had hoped to be here to help Kylie finish setting up for the art exhibition, but I can't. Boys, I need you to fill in for me."

"Sure," Pat said. Danny nodded his agreement as he set toast and juice in front of Michael.

"And Vi, keep an eye on Kylie, if you could. Her father's not going to make life any too easy on her."

"Only a few days gone, you say?"

He did his best to feign nonchalance. "I think I'm

allowed to worry over the details. After all, I haven't traveled much."

"Fine, then. We'll carry on for you."

"Grand," he said, ignoring her skeptical tone. He raised his juice glass, thinking to take a sip, then paused and set it back on the table. Last night's call had made time precious, and certain words needed to be spoken. Before it was too late.

"Pat . . . Danny, I know you think I've been hard on you, and maybe I have. But I want you to know I'm proud of you, and glad you're my brothers." He hesitated before going the full distance. "I—I guess all this is my roundabout way of telling you I love you."

The boys coughed and stammered, but words didn't matter because Michael already knew they felt the same way, too. Embarrassed after pitching all that messy emotion into the open, he concentrated on his juice. The glass was nearly to his mouth when Danny sent it flying.

At Vi's outraged howl, the twins bolted.

Michael cocked one brow at the mess before him. "My payback for last night. Something more than oranges in that juice, I'd be guessing. We'll leave the boys to do the cleaning."

Navigating around the spill, he led his sister from the kitchen. "Before you start interrogating me, I promise everything's fine. I've written out the name and number of the hotel."

"Now, that's big of you. This is nothing but business?"

"Nothing but. And I love you, too, sweet Violet."

Neither of which was a lie.

• • •

Michael reached Galway by midafternoon. He parked his car in a garage a block from the City Centre hotel he'd lied to Vi about, booked a room to calm any suspicions, should she call, and then set out on foot. He bargained with himself: *"Thirty minutes, just thirty last minutes of freedom, then down to business."*

Though it was early in the season for any tourists but the most avid, the sidewalks were full to spilling. It was a day he considered obscenely beautiful—skies blue, breeze fresh—too pure for the ugliness he faced. Bargained minutes ticking down, he walked past the shops and bars along the pedestrian area of Quai Street, through the "suits, ties, and cell phones required" business district, then to Eyre Square.

Hands jammed into his pockets, Michael focused on the details of his surroundings long enough to recognize that he stood in front of a jeweler's window. The irony was acid-sharp. If this moment had spun out just twenty-four hours earlier, he might be seeking an engagement ring.

His unwilling gaze swept past the Claddaugh rings, a Galway tradition of two hands clasping a crowned heart. Just before he turned away forever, he saw a ring with a center stone the silvery blue of Kylie's eyes. It was an elegant thing, no flash about it, just deep and quiet substance.

He couldn't have her, couldn't love her, but he could leave something for her to remember him by. Fighting back the emotion closing its fingers about his throat, he walked into the store.

"Can I help you?" asked a young woman from

behind the counter. The small gold stud from her eyebrow piercing glittered in the overhead light. The sight of it gave Michael strange comfort. She looked every bit as out of place in the posh surroundings as he.

"There's a ring in the window . . . some kind of bluish stone."

She smiled. "Ah, the aquamarine." Slipping a set of keys from a chain about her wrist, she unlocked the display and brought the ring to him. "This is an heirloom piece. We get them now and again. Pretty thing, isn't it? The stones on either side are diamonds—an old cut. Not modern enough to suit most women."

He knew one whom it would suit to perfection, and it pained him that he wouldn't be sliding it on her finger himself.

"In fact, the store owner's been pressing me to put the ring back into the vault. But I've had this feeling . . ." The clerk paused, then tilted her head and gave him a look that could have been Vi's, had it not been coming from a girl a full head shorter and with eyes of brown instead of green. "I've known that the right person would be coming for it. Soon, too."

A day too late, to his way of thinking, but he kept his sorrows to himself.

Ring all prettily packaged together with a note of love and apology he'd written, Michael left the jeweler's and wove into the crowds. Briefly settling his hand over the box in his jacket pocket, he walked on.

It was time. Past time, actually. He pulled a slip of paper from his pocket.

"O'Gara's Pub," he murmured, thinking of the meeting place his prison padmates had spoken of.

The terrorist's flavor of the month in munitions, money, whatever one fancied, they'd said old O'Gara knew where it could be had.

It took only a few questions of a man behind the counter at the corner bookshop, and Michael was on his way. Instead of taking the bus line that had been suggested, he walked, of course.

The streetscape gradually changed from urban to seedy. Shop stoops went unswept, paint peeled from doors and shutters. Slashes of gang graffiti scarred bleak brick walls. This might be another city and another time, but truth remained constant: He had walked straight to his own past.

Two men walked by, caps pulled low. Though they didn't slow, he knew he was being watched. These were the sort of streets on which one didn't stop, not without raising suspicion and risking a beating—or worse. Pulling on a cold, closed expression, Michael walked with absolute intent.

Not much farther down, next to a vacant shop front, stood O'Gara's. Its windows were painted over, cutting it off from the rest of the world. Trash littered the walk. It was exactly as he'd known it would be. He pulled open the door, walked in, and settled at the bar as if he'd been there a thousand times before. In a way he had, for in his days with Dervla, he'd seen plenty of places like it.

Four men sat to his left, each hunched over a glass, and each with a cigarette anchored in the corner of his mouth. None looked familiar, though with the dim light and heavy pall of smoke, his own brothers could be here, and he'd not know it.

The bartender, with his stained tee shirt and shaved head, was too young to be old O'Gara.

"A Paddy's," Michael said.

The drink arrived in a glass that looked as though it had never seen soap or water. He downed it, then cadged a cigarette from the man closest to him. As he sat there, it occurred to Michael that while Rourke wasn't a stupid man, he quite possibly was. Without old O'Gara to drop names with, no one was going to speak to him. He waved the bartender over, ordered another whiskey, and gave one last try.

"I'm looking for O'Gara," he said when the sullen man slapped down a refill in front of him.

"Dead."

No point in offering condolences, and no point in making chat. "Then what about Brian Rourke?"

The bartender's expression slipped from sullen to overtly hostile. "Don't know him."

It was a lie, but arguing would change nothing. Only finding Rourke would. Michael put a few bills on the counter.

"If you do happen to meet Rourke, tell him Kilbride came to spit on his grave."

He drank down the rest of the whiskey, then readied to leave. He knew he had the advantages of time and no other ambition. He'd walk the streets, find himself a hidden corner, then wait as long as it took to make Kylie safe. He trusted the job to no one else.

Just before Michael turned away, a door next to the bar swung open. The heavy figure in the entry was silhouetted by yellowish light. "You can't spit on a live man's grave, Mickey."

Michael froze. He'd thought he could handle this with the same icy coldness that had gripped his heart since last night. But he'd made one crucial error. It was fire that had seized him, not ice.

"The name's Michael," he fought past teeth clenched nearly as tight as his fists.

"Ah, but you were Mickey when I last saw you. 'Quick Mickey' is what Dervla called you. You're late enough getting here, though. I expected you after the first time I called."

Brian Rourke walked from the doorway beside the bar and stood in front of him. Michael would never have recognized him. Fourteen years. Fourteen years in which Michael knew he had aged, yet somehow had expected Rourke to remain as he'd last seen him. But the man had changed. Bulky muscle was going to paunch and hair disappearing altogether. He was still threatening enough, but not the figure of Michael's nightmares. Perhaps that man had been a creature of his own making—all the hatred and sorrow of his youth rolled into his own private demon.

"So what do you want, Mickey?"

"I've come to bring an end to it—to work a truce."

Rourke's laugh ended with a phlegmy cough. "An end to it? Just what kind of stupid bastard are you, to think there's an end to any of this?"

But there was an end, and Michael was ready to lure Rourke to it. He shrugged. "Not so much stupid as desperate."

"Take it from Dervla, desperate'll get you dead."

He eyed the man before him, face and belly bloated from drink. Eyes flat, already dead. Taking him the rest of the way would be almost a pleasure. "I didn't kill her, and I sure as hell don't mourn her."

"Well, I do." Rourke's fist connected with Michael's nose, rocking his head.

With a slow, deliberate motion, Michael used the back of his hand to wipe the rivulet of blood that worked its way from his nostril to his upper lip. "More the fool, you. Come outside with me, Brian. We've matters to discuss."

"And who do you have waiting outside, the Gardai? They've nothing on me, you know." He smirked. "Nothing yet, at least."

"I came alone."

"Well now, that's exactly what Dervla used to say about you. 'Too quick on the draw, that boy.' Did you ever really think she'd let you have her?"

Michael set his jaw, holding back ancient humiliations. "Meet me outside or spend the rest of your days looking over your shoulder."

Eyes fixed on Rourke, the bartender moved toward the ancient black telephone hanging behind the bar. "Do you want me to call Coyne?"

Rourke shook his head. "I've already got trouble enough with Coyne. Besides, this is nothing. I'll handle it myself."

First one outside, Michael glanced up and down the deserted street as he waited for Rourke. The wind blew stronger now. Maybe colder, too, though Michael couldn't feel it. He wiped at his nose again. The blood was slowing already. The fool couldn't even land a good shot on an open target.

Rourke stepped from the bar to the empty sidewalk. "So you think to end this?"

"You shouldn't have bothered me, Brian. And you never should have threatened those I love."

"You don't know shit about love, and you won't until you've seen someone you love with her brains half-gone. Rory was aiming for you that night, did you know?"

Michael offered a two-word answer. "He missed."

Veins stood out on a bull-thick neck. "You killed her as sure as you pulled the trigger yourself."

This was what he wanted—Rourke past thinking. He curved his mouth into a smile. "Dervla wasn't worth the stain she left on that rug."

Rourke barreled at him, his head catching Michael in the gut.

Michael rolled and pinned his attacker to the ground. "You think I don't know about love, you poor, pitiful bastard?" He closed a hand over Rourke's throat and squeezed. "I'm giving it all up—everything—to keep her safe. The second you threatened Kylie, you became a dead man." His breath came in hard gusts as he squeezed tighter. "Dead."

Rourke lay passive, so he loosened his grip, then felt his lip split under Rourke's fist. Never underestimate a killer, he reminded himself.

"Harder to crush than a cockroach, aren't you?" Using an anger that the older man could never match, Michael dragged him to the alley. Cursing and struggling, Rourke spat into his face. Michael hauled him up against the wall. Bracing one arm against the man's throat, he searched his pockets with the other. He tossed Rourke's revolver into a nearby trash bin.

"Never did learn to fight fair, did you, Brian? Explosives against children. Dragging down innocent women. Well, this'll be fair. I'm using nothing more than my fists."

And so he did, until he was forced to adjust his grip to hold Rourke upright. Then he saw it—a small blue box at Rourke's feet. Kylie's ring. Michael's breath whistled from his lungs in exhausted gasps as he took in the sacrilege of what he was seeing. Averting his eyes, he looked at his own fist, crimson with blood and somehow not a part of him. Yet it was. And that fist—and the rage driving it—was no better than his victim.

Ah, it would feel grand to kill Rourke. He'd fantasized about it for years. But to do it in the name of a woman who'd die before having harm done in her name? It would be the worst sort of lie.

Furious with himself, with circumstances, with life, he loosed his grip and watched Rourke crumple to the ground. He needed a clean, honest kill.

"A clean, honest kill," he repeated aloud to Rourke, who was alive but in no condition to fight.

A clean, honest kill. Another lie, because there was no such thing. Before Kylie, he'd have taken that kill, dirty and brutal though it was. But now? To do it would tear down everything he'd built, destroy everything Kylie had said he could be.

He hungered for that kill, but he would not take it.

After the strife, the anger, and the emptiness, Kylie had made him whole. If the best he could do was love her in return, he would love as no man ever had.

As he leaned down to pick up Kylie's ring, he heard Rourke stir and groan. "You're a dead man, Kilbride."

With his clean hand, Michael dusted off the box and tucked it into his pocket. "No, Rourke, I've just begun to live."

Chapter Twenty-four

Study the river before you go into the middle of it.

—IRISH PROVERB

It was Kylie's own slice of misery, having Da underfoot after a wretched day at school. Before she could even start an evening meal, he'd criticized her housekeeping, commented on her "drab" furniture, and shot a few volleys at Breege, who'd simply responded, "We're all praying for you, Johnny, m'dear."

More alarming, for all his complaints, Johnny seemed to have settled in, his worn bag parked in the middle of the sofa. Kylie frowned at the sight. It was time to give him a firm shove toward the door.

"Let's get you back to town, Da."

"Why'd I be going there when I've not even been fed?"

"To move into your room, or whatever accommodations you've found for yourself."

"Haven't made any. Couldn't seem to find a spot with any of my mates," he said, then finished with a mournful—and somehow expectant—sigh.

Ah, she knew this moment well, the one where she was to be rendered helpless with pity and obligation. Pity for Da she'd already spent her day's allotment on herself. Though the encounter with Gerry had been horrible, it was Mairead's warning about Michael that truly galled her. This afternoon, she'd found herself scrutinizing the mothers when they'd arrived to gather their children, and wondering who was whispering about her. Given the speed of sound in Ballymuir, probably all of them.

Before today, she'd always felt safe in her little world at school. Now it was sullied, too.

"Well then," she said as she pushed away from the table, "here's your chance to meet some new mates. I'm going visiting, and I'll be happy to drop you wherever you want in town. That is, if you're ready."

She jingled her car keys and started to the door.

"Of course, if you'd like to sit and reminisce with Breege, I'm sure the walk to town would be relaxing. It's not raining that hard, after all."

Breege didn't bother hiding her amused chuckle, nor did her da his displeasure.

"We'll be on our way, now," Kylie said to Breege. "I'll be back to get supper going."

"Don't be bothering yourself. Edna's coming for a visit and I expect she can open a tin of soup as well as any of us."

"Right, then. If you need me, I'll be at Vi's," Kylie said to her friend, then left. She wasn't especially worried whether her da followed. He did, of course, and they were no sooner in the car than he started.

"Visiting someone named Vi, you say? Anyone I'd be knowing?"

She snorted. "I couldn't begin to keep up with your list of acquaintances."

"You're really seeing that Kilbride man, aren't you?"

"If I am, you don't need to concern yourself with it."

Johnny was silent for a few minutes, then said, "I haven't been the ideal father, have I?"

That he'd even ask the question shocked Kylie. She took a moment to gather her thoughts. "You haven't been all that horrible. You never raised a hand to me, and kept a roof over my head. Well, most of the time, anyway."

"I've failed you often enough," he muttered.

Flashes of his drunken sprees hovered at the edges of her memory. As did a ghost of a face at the window on a night she would never forget. She pushed it back into the realm of the dead.

"If you've failed me, it's in the past."

"I'd be failing you now if I didn't tell you to stay away from Kilbride," he said after a few false starts.

She smiled, though it tasted a bit bitter. "You're standing at the end of a long queue with that advice."

"He's—"

Kylie cut him short. "Be careful what you say. I love him, Da, just as Mam loved you. It's as simple as that." And as horribly complicated, an internal voice whispered.

Johnny sighed. "I don't suppose you'll be changing your mind?"

"I don't suppose I will."

When Kylie arrived at Vi's house, neither Michael's nor Vi's car was in sight. She rapped on the door anyway. After a few moments a redheaded giant in sawdust-covered clothes answered. Kylie couldn't help but smile at the sight.

"Danny Kilbride, your sister will cook you alive when she sees the mess you've tracked through her house."

He grinned as he stepped aside and ushered her in. "She won't leave her studio long enough to cook me, and you're forgetting she's a vegetarian, anyway."

"Lucky for you," Kylie replied as she glanced around. "Is Michael here?"

Danny scratched his head, releasing a shower of wood shavings. "You mean he didn't tell you?"

"Tell me what?"

"That he's off to Galway City for a day or two. Said he had a business prospect to visit."

"Really?"

He nodded. "You're not to worry. We promised Michael we'd finish up the Village Hall for you. You'll be open for business come Monday."

The student art show had been nowhere in her thoughts. The idea that Michael would up and escape without offering to take her along was too enormous to leave room for anything else.

"I don't suppose he left a number where I might ring him?"

"Uh, yeah, he did."

Kylie's lips curved into a smile as Danny riffled through a stack of paper by the phone. She'd more than call, she'd show up at his door. It was either that, or lose what bit of sanity the citizens of Ballymuir hadn't already prized away from her today.

"Found it!" Danny crowed.

Kylie copied down the needed information, flew home, and told Breege of her plans, then drove north to her future. Dark cloaked the city by the time she arrived at the hotel.

She stewed up an absurd broth of marital lies for a hotel clerk who had neither asked nor cared, then shut her overnight bag in the lift door. Now she was confronting an ancient hotel room door that had no intention of giving way. Biting back a frustrated hiss, she leaned her forehead against the cool wood of the door and slowly counted to ten. From the other side, she could hear the sounds of running water and what must be Michael singing.

Singing? Now, there was a miracle, and she was ready for one. She'd sooner run naked through Galway's Spanish Arch than face that clerk's superior smirk if she had to tell him she couldn't get into the room.

She rattled the key again, then turned the knob and butted her hip into the door. It flew open. She staggered into the entry, overnight bag clutched in one hand, key fob left behind, clanking against that godawful door.

She hadn't even righted herself when Michael, towel slung low about his hips, burst from the bathroom.

"What the—" he snarled with a fury that made her drop her bag and take an alarmed step backward.

Her "I'm sorry—" collided with his oath in midair.

She'd never had the experience of being greeted by a mostly naked and thoroughly enraged male. Despite the jolt of fear that shot through her, she couldn't seem to tug her gaze from the dark line of hair arrowing down his abdomen into the towel.

"God, Kylie, I'm the one who's sorry for scaring you half to death, but what can you expect breaking into a man's room?" He paused long enough to draw a breath. "And what exactly are you doing here, anyway?"

Now that was the wrong question to ask a woman who'd just driven hours in a dying car.

"I could be asking you the same question, disappearing like you did. I stopped over Vi's for a visit and Danny told me you'd gone. Silly me, with all your talk of getting away, I thought you'd like it if I surprised you—"

"I do like it. Really, I do," he said, reanchoring his towel.

Transfixed, Kylie's eyes followed his hands. It had been so long, so very long since she'd had him to herself.

"When I heard the noise in the entry, I thought—" he was saying. "Well, it doesn't really matter what I thought, now does it?"

He walked around her, retrieved the room key, and

closed the door. "Fine greeting I've given you. Shall we try this again with more kisses and less shouting?"

At his words, Kylie's gaze drifted upward to his mouth, and her heart tumbled. His mouth—his beautiful mouth—was swollen and had a nasty split at the corner. Her cry of distress sounded sharp in the quiet room. "Whatever happened?"

"It's not as bad as it looks. A little fall, nothing important."

But she was the daughter of Johnny O'Shea and had patched cuts and bruises from any number of brawls. She took Michael's hands in hers, running fingers over his puffy and scraped knuckles.

"And I suppose you caught yourself on these when you fell."

When he nodded, she was thankful that at least he couldn't give voice to such a ridiculous lie. She traced her fingertips to either side of the bridge of his nose. He winced.

"Well, judging by your nose, you didn't do a very good job of catching yourself."

"Really, love, it's nothing."

Kylie let out her exasperation in a long breath. She turned away and busied herself by settling her overnight bag on a chair in the corner. "So you're asking me to believe that you did all of this by tripping over your own feet."

He came up behind her and wrapped his arms around her. "I'm asking you to trust me." His voice was deep and low in her ear. The sound washed through her, bringing comfort even when she knew it shouldn't.

She wanted to trust him, but couldn't let go of this. Not without the risk of stepping into the same role she had held for her father. A role she'd been able to see through unclouded adult eyes upon her father's return. She wouldn't aid another man down the road to disaster.

"Trust comes through honesty," she said.

His arms left her. Kylie faced him. She watched as he turned away, dug about in his duffel bag, then pulled out a pair of denims. He dropped the towel, exposing a somehow vulnerable stretch of muscled buttock and haunch. After pulling on the denims without consideration for niceties such as under-wear, he turned back to her.

"And you're thinking I'm not honest?"

Ripe that was, considering the way he was hiding the truth. "Tell me who hit you."

He scrubbed his hand through still-wet hair, leaving it wild. "I happened across an old acquaintance."

"Happened across?" she echoed, weighing the words with her vast disbelief.

"Fine, maybe I was doing a little research. But let's not get bogged down in details."

"And this—ah—friend, would he be looking much like you do?"

A smile hovered at the corners of his bruised mouth. "A bit worse, I'm hoping."

He sat on the edge of the bed and patted its white tufted spread. "Come sit."

She hesitated. It was too hard thinking clearly when Michael was close, and her terrible day had left her feeling muddled enough.

"Please."

Against her better judgment, Kylie joined him. He took her hands in his. Staring down at their clasped fingers, he began.

"I told you once about Brian Rourke, about what he and Dervla had done to me." His throat worked with the obvious difficulty of getting this out. She couldn't help but feel for him. "He's been calling Vi's house and saying things. Ugly things. Anyway, our friend Gerry Flynn's been dropping word for the past several weeks that I might find Rourke up this way."

He bloody well was trying to fix the world, and at the risk of his own life. "God, Michael! You might as well have served yourself up on a platter—"

He squeezed tighter on her hands. "Let me finish, love."

She swallowed her frustration and alarm, but still tugged her hands free. "Go on."

"I was doing what I had to. Rourke knew about you, Kylie. He'd been to Ballymuir and seen you. I couldn't let him . . . let him do what he said he was going to."

"And you couldn't have called the authorities, either?"

He snorted. "Flynn? And said exactly what?"

"Not Flynn, but someone else."

He stood and began to pace the room. "And still said what?"

At her silence, he wheeled on her. "What, dammit? That a man who might or might not be Brian Rourke and might or might not be in Galway was making threats? They'd have laughed themselves sick at that one, and I couldn't blame them. Don't you see? I needed to know for sure."

She nodded, for she did see. Through hard experience, Michael Kilbride had been led to believe that absolute truth was no defense, and sometimes an impediment.

He looked down at the floor, then back to her. "You want honesty, so I'm giving it you. He threatened to kill you, so I came here to kill him."

She was left feeling empty, old, and hopeless. "And did you?"

The pause before he answered stretched out endlessly. "I didn't, but I wanted to, which I figure is pretty much the same thing."

She tipped back her head, allowing her tears to track down the outer curves of her cheeks. "It's not the same thing at all. It's what separates you from Rourke and the rest of them, knowing the end never justifies the means."

He made a sound close to a laugh. "I'm not so different as you'd like to give me credit for. Sure, I felt good for a few hours, but now that it's night and I can't protect you from the shadows, I'm regretting not having killed him."

"I think we've all known a few regrets." She drew in a ragged, teary breath. "We'll call the authorities. Let them take care of this. Please, Michael. They won't fail us."

"I already called anonymously from a pay phone. With luck, they'll have some reason to hold him. And once we're back home, we'll try the Gardai in

Tralee, where hopefully saner minds prevail." He paused, cleared his throat, then said, "As long as we're going for honesty, I've never told you this straight out like I should—partly because I couldn't believe what I was feeling and partly because I was bloody terrified—but I love you, Kylie. I think I have since that night you almost ran me down on the road, then called me a damn fool for being there."

He knelt at her feet. She closed her eyes to hold back the tears she'd just tamed.

"I know I'm no great prize, and it's a world of grief I might be bringing you, but I can promise you this—no one will ever love you more than I do."

She was crying now, no more able to stop than she could stop loving this man. She wiped at the tears with her fingers, then tightly clasped her hands in her lap—holding some small part of herself together.

"Dammit," Michael muttered, then patted her knee. "I'll be right back, love."

He stood and dug around in his bag again. "There, now!" she heard him say triumphantly. He settled in front of her and nudged her hands with a tissue. She took it and wiped her eyes. Through a lingering sheen of moisture, Kylie could see that he was still holding a small box. Her heart pushed against her breastbone like it wanted to escape.

"I never thought I'd have the courage or the freedom to do this," he said as he fumbled with the box between his two strong—and usually steady— hands. He pried the lid open, crumpled a tiny square of paper in one hand, and tossed it aside.

"Will you stay with me for the rest of our days? Will you marry me, Kylie O'Shea?"

She had never known so many thoughts to fight for precedence. Was this the right thing to do? What about this Rourke person? What if she lost her job? How would they get by until his business grew? And finally, how would she ever live if she tossed aside this chance at happiness?

"Kylie?"

"Yes," she said, pushing back everything but this moment.

"Yes?" The uncertainty in his eyes battled with the smile beginning to tug at his mouth. "Are you saying yes, you'll marry me, or yes, you just noticed that I'm still kneeling in front of you like some kind of fool?"

"I'm saying, yes, I'll marry you." Joy whirled through her like a cloud of white doves. "Yes, I'll love you forever."

Michael's hands shook as he slipped the ring on her finger. "It fits perfectly," he said, sounding a bit surprised.

"Of course it does. As do you and I," she added before framing his face between her hands and settling her mouth over his. "Now do you think that you could possibly make love to me?"

She took his hungry growl for a "yes."

The sky was still a pale wash of early light when, wrapped in her old robe, Kylie pushed aside the drapes and gazed out the window. She turned back to Michael. Totally comfortable with his nudity in a way that made her just the tiniest bit jealous, he lay on top of the rumpled sheets. In his hand was a note that had been tucked beneath the door sometime during the night.

"It's not like Vi to call unless something's happened," he said. "And it bothers me the way no one's answering the phone. I keep thinking Pat or Danny might have been fool enough to head out to the barn and tangle with the table saw or . . ."

She hushed him, and came and sat beside him. He tugged her down until she was curled into his side, her head pillowed by his broad shoulder. "I'm sure nothing's wrong, or Vi would have called again. But if it's worrying you this much, perhaps you'd best head home."

"You wouldn't be angry?"

She stroked her hand over his chest and felt the tension seep out of him. "Because you love your family? Never. You do what you have to."

"I want you to stay here," he said, resettling her next to him before sitting up. "I'll order up breakfast to be delivered to the room." He settled a kiss on her mouth. "And I want you to promise you'll at least take a peek at the city." He stood and began riffling through his duffel bag for clothes. "And Kylie, I love you."

Smiling, she snuggled into the covers. "Of course you do."

Chapter Twenty-five

Every cock crows on his own dunghill.

—IRISH PROVERB

As Michael drove past Ballymuir's shops and homes, he worried. The boys were bright enough to work unsupervised, he told himself. He'd spent enough hours drilling safety rules into them. But then came the memory of what it was like to be nearly seventeen, all-powerful, and most assuredly immortal. His stomach rolled. This business of caring for youngsters wasn't for the weak.

Michael parked the car, grabbed his duffel bag, and dashed up Vi's front walk. Ironic how fourteen years in prison seemed inconsequential when compared to a few hours' drive agonizing over loved ones. It was time to rethink his objections to modern inconveniences, like cellular phones.

"Vi," he bellowed, stepping inside. Once in, he considered popping back out just to be sure he was in the right place. The house was empty, and cleaner than he'd ever seen it. Eerily so. There was obviously no great crisis afoot if his sister had found time to clean her home from top to bottom. As he was busy wondering what had become of her stock of half-finished projects, Roger came flying at him.

" 'Lo, guy. Miss me?" Michael bent down and scratched the creature behind his ears; he'd take what companionship he could, to ease the coming hours. He leaned closer, then shook his head. Odd . . . even the dog smelled antiseptic.

When he would have made for the upstairs shower, Roger tugged at his shoelace, trying to haul him in the direction of the kitchen.

"Has nobody remembered to feed you? Come on, then." He followed the dog, then chuckled as Roger danced around his empty dish. "Hard to believe that Vi was too busy cleaning." Perhaps his flyabout sister had decided to plunge into domesticity with the same passion she did her art. He laughed at the thought. Not bloody likely.

Michael first checked the kitchen table for a note—none, of course—then gave the dog food and water. Roger eyed his kibble with utter disdain, then trotted to the refrigerator door and gazed longingly.

"I've spoiled you rotten, haven't I? Well, you'd

best get used to poor food again, for I'll be moving along soon enough."

He'd spoken with Breege a few days ago about the possibility of renting her home, since she was set on moving in with her friend, Edna. Michael's vision of the future was clear. In that solid farmhouse, he and Kylie would raise as many children as she wished, and love each other to the last moment of time.

Reality remained a bit cooler about the edges. He still had matters like money and Rourke and acceptance to address. Still, as Nan used to say, nothing a cup of tea wouldn't help. Or in this case, a tall glass of whiskey. But since the boys had taken care of that, Michael filled the kettle with water and set it on the burner. He was switching on the stove when he heard the front door close.

"Michael, that you?" Vi called from the front room.

Well, at least he'd be to the bottom of this mystery. "Yeah, it's me."

"Can you come here for a sec?"

He adjusted the flame under the kettle, then joined his sister. She stood in front of the door, looking like she didn't know whether she wanted to stay or go.

Her eyes widened as she took in the damage to his face. So much for thinking he looked better this morning.

"Do I want to know what happened?" Vi asked.

"Not in any great detail."

"Right, then. We'll leave it for later. What are you doing back so early?" As she spoke, Michael noted that her gaze flitted from his. Unusual, from his direct, never-back-down sister. "I wasn't expecting you back quite yet."

"It might have something to do with the message that said nothing at all slipped under my hotel room door. Or the fact that it would be easier to raise the dead than get you to answer your damned phone."

"You were worried, then?" she asked, still leaning against the front door. The knob rattled. She covered it with her hand.

"Barring the door, Vi?"

She drew a deep breath, then sent a barrage of words his way. "Michael, Mam got here last night. She's come to take Pat and Danny home. We can't keep 'em, you know. Anyway, I called you, hoping to give you some warning, but . . ."

Another storm, Michael thought. A bucketful of troubles on a day that he wanted to be sunny.

Weeks after the fact, Maeve had made her way from Kilkenny. That, at least, explained the sterile house. She'd probably spent the night putting out every last spark of creativity.

The door shook within its frame.

"It would be easier to hold back tomorrow," he said to his sister.

"If you need time to adjust—"

He snorted. "Adjust? I'm not the poor sod having to go home with her. Let her in, and let's be done with this."

Vi let go, then stepped aside. Michael stood there, arms crossed over his chest, watching as his mam— one dried-up old bird of a mother hen—prodded the twins into the house.

Rourke had been unrecognizable, but his mother was frozen in time. A few more threads of iron gray in her hair, the brackets about her mouth deeper, but for all that, essentially the same. And bearing no more love for him than she ever had. Closing himself off from the pain, Michael turned to his brothers.

All clean and starched and sullen they were. Only in their eyes could he see that plea, that silent "Help us, somehow" that he had no way of answering. So he went to them and ruffled identical heads of red hair, leaving a random wake of tufts and waves— just enough to make their mam grind her molars.

"You're going home, I hear."

"She's making us," Danny said. Frowning, he added, "Did Kylie hit you with her handbag or somethin'?"

Now there was a thought far more entertaining than the truth. "She did," Michael said, working up a wink. "One hell of an arm the woman's got."

"Then we'll let her take on Mam so we can stay here," Patrick suggested.

There was nothing Michael wanted more—with the exception of Kylie at his side to help him lead these nearly-men the last steps to adulthood.

"You've got school to be thinking of," he said to his brothers, watching from the corner of his eye as Vi dragged Mam off to the kitchen. He found himself wishing for a bigger kettle on that stove. Big enough to stew her in. "You knew she'd be coming for you. Sooner or later, Da was bound to notice that you're missing. And before you ask, we'll not be fighting this, or I'll have no chance of getting you for summer holidays."

"You want us back?"

Michael blinked at the moisture burning in his eyes. "Want you back? Now who else do you think I want working with me? Business'll be too much for one pair of hands, come summer. Of course I want you!"

He looped one arm over each set of gangly shoulders, and drew the boys close. God, how he loved them. And how he loved Kylie for showing him the way to these riches.

"And if Mam gives you too much trouble before then," he said, "I suggest you try some more chickens in the loo. Seemed to do the trick last time."

Their grudging smiles were as good as Michael knew he'd be getting. "Now let me fix you a grand supper before you leave."

He ushered them into the kitchen, where Vi sat at the table with Mam. Since it would never occur to his mother to comfort the boys by showing some manners, Michael did the unthinkable.

"Good to see you, Mam. You're looking well."

"Michael." His name was squashed flat as it came through her pinched lips. "Still fighting, I see."

He had no saving response, so he forged ahead. "I thought I'd make a family supper, roast a chicken," he said, amusing himself with the mental image of Mam all trussed and squawking. "And maybe make the boys their favorite trifle."

"We have to be on our way," she said, bracing her hands on the table as though she meant to push off and be gone that very moment.

"Michael's a brilliant cook," Vi said in an unnaturally cheery voice. "Stay, Mam. A few more hours won't hurt anybody."

"No. We're—"

"We're staying, Mam," Patrick interrupted. "You haven't seen Michael in years, and now you're trying to leave after saying nothing more than his name. It's not right what you're doing. You go, and you go alone. Right, Dan?"

Dan planted himself in a chair. "Right."

Their mam stood. "I'll have none of this disrespect. Patrick and Daniel, you get—"

Seeing Vi wasn't going to be any more help, Michael stepped in front of his mother. "Don't do it. Don't make these boys turn from you." *As you did to me*, he didn't bother to add aloud.

"They're asking for a meal, just a damned meal," he said, his voice amazingly devoid of the intense hurt slicing through him. All he had ever wanted was one unconditional mother's embrace, one small nod of understanding. "For the sake of the family, you owe it to them. And if seeing me bothers you this bloody much, I promise as soon as the bird is roasting, I'll leave you till supper."

That jaw she held so tightly clenched finally came loose.

"You want the truth, do you? I hate seeing you. I'd hoped to go to my grave without seeing you again. Oh, I might have loved you when you were a baby, but that loving is so far in the past that for the life of me, I can't remember it."

Her eyes narrowed, and her hands closed into tight fists. "You've brought us shame. Nothing but shame, dragged our name so deep into the dirt that it will never come clean. And now you want me to chat with you? And tell you what? How you made it so I couldn't step out of the house without catching somebody whispering behind their hand? How your father blames me—*me*—for not bringing you up properly?"

It tore at him, the way he'd become fixed in her mind, a creature of equal parts ugly truths and uglier myths. And it tore at him—a man who could mend just about anything—that he couldn't fix this. She would never see him for what he was today. Now. She would never love him.

"I think you've told me enough."

She looked past him and said to the boys, "Four o'clock. No later."

After she swept from the room, taking the twins with her, Michael pulled out a chair and sat. His sister, he saw, was crying. What he'd give for the same luxury.

It had been a fine idea, to catch a few of Galway's sights before heading home. A fine idea, but a lonely one. Once Kylie had realized that nothing was as interesting without Michael, she'd packed up and readied to head home. Unfortunately, her car wasn't nearly as anxious to arrive as she was.

The old Renault chugged and heaved, protesting the uphill grade. She'd been nursing the auto along, growing more frustrated as each mile crept by. The roads were rougher now, and the land emptier, too, as she wound through the mountains toward Ballymuir.

"C'mon, you rusting piece of blight. Just a little further."

It answered by sending a belch of oily smoke from the front, then giving out altogether.

"Well now, that's just bloody wonderful." She coasted downhill, supposing she should be thankful that at least she'd made the top of the rise. She drew as close as she could to the jagged stone fence marking the road's edge, then switched off the already dead vehicle.

"No point in waiting for someone to happen along," she said to herself, then wrenched the parking brake into place.

Kylie slipped from the car, pocketed the keys, and pointed her feet toward home. Her heels were soon blistered and stinging from the silly little city shoes she'd worn to Galway. She'd been walking half an hour when she passed a white signpost reading, "Ballymuir 20 Miles." It might as well have been two thousand.

The bird was roasting, and Mam had come damn close, herself. All the time he'd been working in the kitchen, Michael could hear her in the next room sawing away at Vi's self-esteem and treating the boys as though they didn't own a brain between them. Through it all, he'd kept his mouth firmly shut, and the largest pot in the kitchen stowed. The best he could have hoped, anyway, was to have deflected her anger. But since she refused to acknowledge him, there was little chance of that.

When, as promised, he'd left the house, Vi was beginning to come back to life. The twin blazes of crimson on her cheeks were not-so-subtle warnings of the storm soon to blow. Bless Vi, not even Mam could keep her down for long. He wished he could be there to witness the end result.

It felt odd, walking when for once he didn't want to. The sky overhead shone a crystalline blue that didn't often visit these parts. With nowhere else to go, he decided to have a peek at the Village Hall. Though the exhibition didn't open until Monday evening, he knew his sister well enough to be sure that it was already perfect.

He rounded the corner. Evie Nolan stood in front of her father's shop, smoking a cigarette. He nodded a polite greeting, but didn't slow his pace. Evie gave no answering greeting.

Michael closed the distance to the Village Hall, then climbed the three steps to its entry. He cupped his hands and peered through a narrow window cut into the door. From what he could see, the exhibition looked grand. Vi had hung great sweeps of fabric from the ceiling, and the walls were alive with art. He leaned nearer, trying for a better view. The door creaked open.

He chuckled. "An invitation, I'd be saying." He closed the door after himself and switched on the lights.

"Not half bad, sweet Vi," he murmured. Knowing how bloody thrilled Kylie would be when she saw this made him all the more pleased. He wasn't sure how long he'd been strolling around, looking at the students' art, when the door opened again. A young couple walked in.

"We saw the lights on and thought we'd have a look about, if you don't mind," said the woman. "Una, our eldest, has a bit or two on display."

"Welcome in," Michael said. "And why don't you show me your daughter's work?"

And so it went as one person after another arrived. Michael milled about, greeting those he knew, smiling at the good-natured jokes about his bruised appearance, and feeling just a touch chagrined for having started the party rolling.

A friendly hand settled on his shoulder. "And you didn't invite your own sister?" Vi teased. "Here I expected to find you sulking about, and you've thrown a hooley."

"The door was unlocked," he said with an embarrassed shrug. "And then, well, I can't explain the rest."

"News travels fast in Ballymuir. Mam and the twins are with me. I wanted to show her what Kilbrides can accomplish when they stick together."

He landed a kiss on her cheek. "Grand things, Violet. Grand things."

Kylie waved good-bye to the elderly couple who had dropped her home. It had seemed almost divine intervention when they'd appeared on the empty road, then slowed and offered her a ride. She wouldn't have made it home without them. Her heels were a blistered mess, and there wasn't a part on her that didn't ache. She needed a long shower and then an enormous meal.

"Breege, I'm home," she called as she entered the

house, not wanting to startle her friend. She slipped off her shoes, wincing as her heels came free, then gingerly walked to the bedroom doorway.

There was no wondering whether Breege had been well cared for. She had a box of chocolates on one side of her and a stack of books on the other.

"And what might you be doing back so early?" Breege asked with affectionate sternness.

"A bit of trouble with Michael's brothers," she said. "Has he called, by any chance?"

"Sorry, dearie, no call from him." Breege looked her up and down, and obviously wasn't impressed by what she saw. "Well, if this is what leaving town does, I'm all for you staying. You'll be wanting to clean up before you head to the Village Hall."

"The Hall? Why?"

Breege crumpled a chocolate wrapper and made a neat toss into the basket by the nightstand. "It didn't matter much when you were all the way to Galway, but now that you're home, you might as well know that Mairead Corrigan called. Seems the art exhibition has opened a wee bit earlier than planned." She rolled her eyes and added, "You'd think the world was coming to an end. An unholy love of schedules that woman has."

Shower and food would have to wait. On the bright side, at least she could corner Mairead and schedule a meeting with the school administration. The sooner she had that part of her future settled, the better.

"Can I borrow your car?" she asked as she dug a pair of paint-spattered clogs from beneath the bed.

Her friend chuckled. "It's not as though I'll be using it."

"Good, then. I'll be back by supper."

"Keys are in the ignition," Breege called as Kylie flew from the room. "And have a grand time."

With nothing more threatening than a glare from Vi—which admittedly was ominous enough—Mam had managed to send a few impersonal comments Michael's way. Like fighters between rounds, they now stood in opposite corners of the room. Vi hovered next to him, uttering hopeful little comments like "It's grand she's meeting you halfway" and "I think age is softening her."

Michael doubted there would ever be true peace between himself and his mother, but he was willing to give it a go.

"Don't push it," he said to his sister, clasping her hand in his. "Let's enjoy the day."

A regular town event, this had become. Fiddles had been brought out, and a traditional ceili dance begun. Ladies wearing their Sunday best served cakes and scones. Soon, though, he'd have to go home and check on that bird. The party would go on without him, no doubt for hours yet.

Michael glanced across the dancers to see the door swing open again. Lips curved into a snotty smile, Evie Nolan entered the room.

"Oh, marvelous. Miss Congeniality's here," Vi muttered.

"You mean among your many dubious talents, you can't make her disappear?"

Apparently not, for Evie stopped in front of him, surveyed him like he was up for purchase, then laughed. "Perfect, just too bloody perfect. I wouldn't miss this for all the money in the world."

Michael squeezed his sister's hand tighter, then drew her back when she tried to take a step toward nasty Miss Nolan.

"What do you want, Evie?"

"It's not what I want. It's what you're getting."

The fiddle music died on a discordant moan.

"He's right here," Evie called over the sudden quiet.

Michael watched as the crowd parted, and Gerry Flynn led two cold-faced Gardai across the dance floor. Straight at him.

Sick fear engulfed Michael. Then came the awful, all-encompassing guilt for a sin he couldn't even begin to identify.

"You made this too easy," Flynn said as they neared. "No sport to it at all."

Just like before . . . Jesus, it's happening again.

"Oh my God, Michael, what's happening?" he heard his sister say.

Through the cold terror that sent the sound of his own ragged breathing echoing in his ears, Michael clung to one comfort. Thank God Kylie wasn't due back till later. At least he could keep her safe.

Galvanized by that thought, he grabbed his sister by the shoulders. "She was never with me," he said low and urgent into her ear. "I haven't seen Kylie in days. Protect her, Vi."

They were nearly on him, now, seeming to grow

larger with every step. A shoulder nudged close to his. Tearing his gaze from the approaching men, Michael saw that his brothers had lined to his left, and his mother and sister to his right. The sight almost brought him to his knees.

"Michael Kilbride?" asked one of the Gardai.

His mouth sour with the bile of fear, Michael nodded.

The crowd stirred as the door opened one last time. Voices raised. Though he couldn't make out the words over the roaring in his head, one voice he knew.

Please, God, not this.

"Let me through," Kylie cried.

Not this. He must have wavered, for he felt his sister's and brothers' hands support him.

"Michael Kilbride, I'm arresting you in connection with the murder of Brian Rourke," said the Garda. "I'm asking that you come with me peacefully."

Kylie's inarticulate cry tore through his heart. He couldn't look at her. Couldn't survive this moment without crumbling. And that he'd not do. Keeping his gaze squarely on the pair of Gardai in front of him, he stepped forward.

"I'll be all right," he said to his family, while deep inside he felt himself begin to die.

"Gerry, what's this about?" Kylie's voice was thick with horror.

"Your lover's been off in Galway plying his trade. A little murder, and—"

"No!"

"Are you saying he wasn't there?" Flynn's smile

was dark and ugly. "Or maybe you're saying you were with him?"

Sly bastard, Michael thought. Sly, evil bastard.

"Don't put words in my mouth. I'm saying—"

"What?" goaded Flynn. "No begging? No offers for the gentlemen here? I'm surprised, after the way I saw you that night—spreading your legs to clear your father's debts. And later your da drinking to his daughter, too. So now I was thinking you wouldn't be beyond suggesting a spot of whoring to free your lover."

He might not have killed Brian Rourke, but Michael was goddamn well going to murder Gerry Flynn. Breaking free of the Gardai who held him was no great challenge. They seemed almost inclined to let him get in a shot or two. Gerry wouldn't have been much in the way of a fight at all, except that someone else chose to dive into the fray.

"Stay back," he shouted at Kylie, grabbing Flynn by the shirt and ducking his flailing arms. "I don't want you hurt."

Before he could stop her, she had Flynn from behind, her fingers dug into his face. Then Flynn drove his elbow back with brutal force. Kylie's head hit the floor with a sickening thud, and Michael's world went black with rage.

Chapter Twenty-six

Necessity knows no law.

—IRISH PROVERB

Kylie drifted up from blackness. She felt as though she'd been ground to bits, with a mysterious ache in the back of her head throbbing especially hard. She opened her eyes, and her head rebelled at the introduction of light. When she tried to bring her hand to her forehead to ease the pain, something tugged at her. Squinting, she focused on plastic tubing biting the tender underside of her forearm. That brought her wide awake.

The hospital. Even dizzy and hurting, how could she have missed the hated noises and scents of this place? She was in the hospital. And Michael was—

She clenched the sheet with her free hand and felt

the band of a ring press into her skin. Dear God, it was coming back to her now in terrifying detail. Michael's arrest, the way she'd launched herself at Gerry Flynn, and the sharp pain in her head before blackness swallowed her.

"So you're back with us now?"

Her gaze shot to a figure at the side of her bed. Her da was there.

"How long have I been here?" She winced at the parched sound of her voice.

"A couple of hours. They say you fought like a real O'Shea. If you hadn't hit the floor quite so hard—"

She braced herself on her elbows and slowly sat up. For the effort, pinpoints of bright-yellow light shot past her eyes. "I don't have time for this. I'm leaving, I have to get to Michael." She fussed with the intravenous lines attached to her arm. "Find someone to get this stuff out of me."

Her da patted her shoulder, then took a hasty step back when she glared at him. "Now Kylie, you're not well. Not enough potassium in you, or something like that. The doctors say you have to stay the night."

"I'm leaving," she repeated, then began to pick at the tape holding down the lines.

"Darlin', there's nothing you can do for the man. They took him back to Galway as soon as they patched him up. And he did it, Kylie. He killed a man. Evie Nolan was telling everyone there's no doubt."

She'd never felt so close to madness, yet had everything so clear at the same time. "I don't care if Evie says she watched Michael do it. Just get someone in here, and get me unhooked. Now, dammit!"

Johnny retreated from the room.

After signing a bunch of bloody forms that said she was taking her life in her hands by leaving without the doctor's consent, Kylie was released.

Before leaving the hospital, she made a frantic phone call to Vi, who confirmed that Michael was in Galway, and that given his and Rourke's paramilitary connections, they could hold him for three days before charging him with a crime. The family was hiring a solicitor and an investigator. Beyond that, she offered nothing.

"Michael doesn't want you involved, and at present it's best to keep it at that," Vi had said in a firm voice, then hung up.

No, it wasn't best. It was Michael skewering himself on his own sword. And Kylie would have none of it.

Her da helped her into Breege's car, which he'd found outside the Village Hall with the keys still in it. As they drove back to Ballymuir, she shifted in her seat and looked at him. Gerry's taunts still whispered insidiously in her mind. If she could do nothing for Michael right now, at least she could free herself.

The day's troubles had given her no patience for subtlety, so she said it straight out. "Da, Gerry Flynn says I prostituted myself to settle your debts, and that you arranged for it."

Her father nearly swerved off the road.

"Watch out," she cried. After she'd calmed enough to pry her fingers from the dash, she asked, "So is it true?"

"Never," he said with such vehemence that she wanted to believe him.

"But you know what I'm talking about."

He was silent for a moment, then said, "Keefe."

The word hung in the air between them. Kylie knew if they didn't finish this now, they never would. And that any hope of finding her way with her father would vanish.

"Suppose you tell me what happened."

Her da gave in without a fight. He blew out a slow breath, seemed to grip the steering wheel tighter, then began.

"The night Keefe came to our house, I woke feeling fuzzy, so I went downstairs to drink a hair of the dog. I was walking across the salon with the decanter in my hand when my foot hit something. It was a pearl. Just like the ones you'd been wearing. They were everywhere. God in heaven, I was so scared for you, Kylie. I couldn't find you. I ran to the garage thinking I'd go looking for you, but my car was gone."

"I had taken it." Though she had never been willing to admit it to herself, she'd seen him—a ghost in an upstairs window—when she'd returned. And she had always wondered.

"I walked to the road, then sat there and cried and drank from that goddamn decanter. Gerry Flynn appeared, I don't know how much later, and helped me into the house."

Flynn. Always bloody Flynn at the bottom of her woes. "And what did you say to Gerry?"

"I don't remember. I plain don't remember, but I can promise you I didn't do what Flynn said."

The choice between Flynn and her own father was an easy one. "I believe you, Da."

"Keefe called a week later," he said in a ragged voice. "He told me I could consider my debt settled. Then, I knew. I knew and I hated myself for putting you in harm's way. And God forgive me, Kylie, it got so I couldn't bear to look at you, the guilt was so bad." He dragged a hand over his face. "The truth is that I'd give the world to take it all back. All of it."

That, at least, was a sentiment she knew well.

It was an old refrain, the same whether in the Maze or Galway City: Concrete walls, concrete floor, pride and privacy stripped, dignity gone. Michael sat on the edge of his cot, head dropped and hands hanging limply between his knees. When questioned, he had told them the truth about seeking out Rourke, about the fight, of his every step in the city. At least until the truth crossed path with Kylie.

It was no great risk, protecting her reputation. Even if it were, he would have done it without a moment's hesitation. Because truth, as Michael knew, meant nothing. And for the ultimate truth—that he had broken Rourke's face, but not caved in his skull—he had only his word to give. That, and the argument he'd hardly have given them Rourke's location if he'd killed the man. But in the eyes of the authorities, his word meant nothing, too.

He supposed there was some chance that Rourke's true killer would be found—if anybody cared to look. Sitting where he was, on the wrong side of the bars, it took an impossible leap of faith to believe they weren't already content. They had his fingerprints all over a gun, even if they couldn't quite come up with a bullet hole to match. He'd seen them overlook details before.

He might well die in a place like this. The first time he'd been jailed, that had been simply a matter of comparing shades of gray. But now, having loved Kylie, he was plunging into lethal blackness from a rainbow's embrace.

Michael stretched out on the mattress and stared at the drab plaster ceiling. If possible, would he give back the joy and the loving? Erase Kylie from his memory for the chance to live out his days in numbness, instead of the agony awaiting him?

No, he wouldn't trade a moment of it, neither the happiness nor the sorrows. But he would mourn.

God, how he would mourn losing Kylie.

Kylie had practiced her speech over and over until she was sure she had it down to an art. But confessing to a man who'd last seen her trying to rip out Gerry Flynn's eyeballs was a bit dicier than chatting up the bathroom mirror.

She'd been hoping for a more familiar face from the local ranks of Gardai. Not Gerry, of course. But since he was in the hospital with his jaw wired shut, he was no concern of hers.

So now she faced one of the Galway Gardai, still wrapping up loose ends in Ballymuir. As she stumbled over her tongue, the officer wasn't doing much to hide his disbelief.

Kylie cleared her throat and pressed on. "So, you

see, I never left Michael's side, not once the whole time he was in Galway."

There now, she had it out. And please God, let it be enough.

The officer took a sip of his tea, then fiddled with the papers in front of him. "Interesting, Miss O'Shea. We'll be in touch if we require anything more."

"Interesting? That's all you have to say?"

He leaned back in his chair and shot her an amused look. "What would you have me do, ring the jail in Galway and ask that they free Mr. Kilbride?"

That had been the general—if hazily-thought-out—plan. She had known it wouldn't be enough to say that she'd been with Michael for the hours they'd really shared. Only full measure would work. So full measure she had given, and would have handed over her life, if she thought it would help his cause.

"Well, no, I wasn't expecting him to be released this instant," she said aloud.

"Fine, then. Good day, Miss O'Shea."

And then she was back on the street, but not without other work to do. If Ballymuir's tongues were going to dance, she would orchestrate the motion.

Kylie marched to O'Connor's Pub. Inside, it was elbow-to-elbow talk. She borrowed a chair from the corner. Pushing through the whispered "she's here's" and "did you see's," she dragged it into the middle of the crowd and climbed atop it.

Now head and shoulders above everybody else, she called out, "Excuse me."

Since the place had quieted at the sight of her, it took nothing more for silence to fall.

"I know many of you were at the Village Hall this afternoon, and those who weren't have heard the story by now. But I wanted to add a few things Gerry Flynn might have missed, since he won't be talking for some time to come."

Heartened by the few approving chuckles, she dragged in a shaky breath and thought, here you go, girl, time to toss out your life and start again. Time to truly fly free.

"One of the things Gerry failed to mention was that I was in Galway with Michael Kilbride. I won't give you the details of what we were doing, but I can promise I didn't leave him time to be off killing a man."

There was more laughter, and for the first time in her life, she didn't care that it was at the expense of her precious reputation. All that mattered was easing the way for Michael's return. And he would be back with her, if she had to tear down every bloody jail in Ireland to make it happen.

"Now, I'm sorry if it offends some of you to hear that I'd have a bit of fun, and I'm sorry if I'm offending even more of you by saying that Michael and I have been . . . ah . . . together for some time. But you need to know he's no murderer. He's the man I love, and if you can't accept that, well then, the devil with all of you."

Kylie took one last look into the sea of faces that held people she'd considered friends. Then she climbed off the chair and clutched the back of it, willing her knees to stop wobbling.

In the silence, a single pair of hands started clapping. "That's my girl," she heard Black Johnny O'Shea shout.

"Thank you, Da," she whispered. "Thank you."

When more hands joined in, Kylie cried tears of joy.

But by midnight, she had received the word she expected from Mairead Corrigan. Mairead was terribly sorry, but it was out of her hands. Until the matters involving Michael Kilbride had been resolved, Kylie was officially suspended from her job.

And Michael was still in jail.

It was early morning. Even without a glance at the outside world, Michael's internal clock told him that. He still lay on the mattress, dry-eyed and sleepless, when he heard approaching footsteps.

The cell door swung open. Three men stood in the doorway.

"This way," said the center man. Since he had no choice, and no reason not to, Michael followed.

He was taken to the same interrogation room he'd seen the night before. The chair was still too small for his tall frame, and the lights still too bright. He blinked as his eyes adjusted.

"Is my solicitor here?"

"No," said the man apparently in charge. "But let me ask this one question, and you decide whether you want to answer."

Michael shrugged.

"Have you ever heard of Timothy Coyne?"

He began to say "no," then stopped as a recollection came to him. "The bartender mentioned a Coyne. Asked if he should call him."

"That's it?"

"That's all I know."

"Escort him back."

Once back in his cell, Michael resumed his vigil watching the ceiling. One question. Not much to build hope on, but more than he'd had last night.

The insistent ringing of a telephone woke Kylie from a drugged, leaden sleep. She made no move to answer it; she wasn't ready to face the world.

When the ringing stopped, and she heard Breege's "Hullo" from the bedroom, she focused inward and began to plan. Today, she'd drive to Galway and push matters along. And she'd talk to the authorities there, too. She had little faith that the officer she'd seen last night was doing anything at all. And—

"Kylie, dear, come pick up the phone," Breege called.

"I don't want to," she answered, not much caring that she sounded less mature than her students. Former students, she amended, and knew heartache at the thought.

"It's Violet Kilbride, and I'm thinking you should talk to the girl."

"Well, I'm thinking I shouldn't," Kylie muttered, but still dutifully rose, pulled on her robe, and padded to the bedroom. She knew Vi well enough to be sure that a visit would follow a refused call.

She took the phone from Breege, who buried her nose in a book and did her best to look as though she wouldn't be hanging on every word.

"Yes, Vi?" Kylie steeled herself for another blast of ice from the formidable Miss Kilbride.

"Quite a scene you must have made in the pub last night."

"Yes, well—"

"I've had no less than a dozen calls today," Vi said, then laughed. "Father Cready said he'll be looking for you at confession, though I have the feeling he'll be going light on the penance."

If she weren't so bloody tired, Kylie would have smiled. "Vi, I know you haven't always thought the best of me, that I've not stood strong enough for Michael—"

"I'd say you made your stand last night. And since you're now officially mad enough to be a Kilbride, I wanted to let you know we just had a brilliant call from Michael's solicitor. The Gardai think they've found the real murderer, and—"

The same energy that had pushed Kylie past dropping yesterday filled her again. She had never doubted Michael's innocence, but she had doubted the system holding him.

She cut into whatever Vi was saying. "Then they'll be letting him go, and I'll never make it there on time."

"It could be days, yet," Vi counseled. "And anyway, I was planning on heading up to Galway this afternoon, myself."

"No."

"No? You're telling me I can't go to my own brother?"

"He's mine to bring home."

Vi was silent a moment, then said with dawning surprise, "Right you are. Bring him home. And give him our love."

First, Kylie intended to give him her own.

Michael looked about a bile-green reception room lacking a single familiar face. Not that he cared so very much, just so long as he was free. The man named Coyne occupied a cell in the building Michael was now permitted to leave.

From what he'd pieced together from conversations with his solicitor, Rourke had been acting as an enforcer in Coyne's small-time drug business, and had gotten sloppy. Coyne must have figured it was time Rourke retired. He'd taken advantage of the fact that the man was down and committed the act Michael had turned from. Luckily, Coyne had been careless in the execution. He'd left the hammer he'd used in a trash bin the next block down.

Yes, the pieces had fallen together quite nicely. Michael couldn't say he had a renewed faith in the law, but he no longer saw it as his enemy.

He gave one more futile glance around the crowded room. He'd already tried his sister's house and gotten no answer, of course. And Kylie could be in no shape to drive, what with the blow to her head and exhaustion from stewing up the wild lies he'd been told she'd offered as his alibi.

Resigned to slow torture on Bus Eireann, he made his way to the jail's exit. As he pushed through the steel "Out" door, a familiar figure came barreling through the "In."

The smile that had been with him since he was freed grew into a fool's grin.

"Kylie," he called, but she'd already entered the building.

Michael followed. By the time he'd cleared the proper "In" door, Kylie was already at the front desk harassing the clerk. He came up behind her and settled his hand on her shoulder.

"Do you mind?" she snapped without looking back. "I was here first and you can bloody well wait your turn."

Never in his life had he felt this absurdly happy. He could think of only one moment that might soon top it.

"Ah, but I've waited a lifetime, love, and I won't be waiting any longer."

She spun to face him. "Michael. Thank God, Michael."

Epilogue

May your troubles be less
Your blessings be more.
And nothing but happiness
Come through your door.

—IRISH TOAST

Kylie woke early the morning of her wedding. She quickly showered and dressed, but not in the lovely gown she'd be wearing later. Still, she couldn't help but pause and admire it. She gently ran her fingers across the lace veil Breege had given her. Sewn inside the headpiece was Kylie's favorite part of all—the tiny bit of lace Breege had made before concluding that lace making was "bloody torture."

Kylie hummed to herself as she tugged on her old

sweater and work pants. Checking her watch, she hurried out the front door and through the field to the meandering stone wall she'd been building since spring.

It was a fine August Saturday. The sky above was free of clouds, and once the sun chased off dawn's chill, the weather would be perfect. So much in her life was perfect.

She'd regained her teaching position and looked forward to a new crop of students come fall. Gerry Flynn had packed up and moved on, which was the best for all concerned. Breege was recovering quite nicely from her accident. Just last month, she'd moved into Ballymuir proper, and Michael had bought the farmhouse and land from her. Kylie was honored to be making her new home in a place that had seen so much love.

Even Da had found his idea of heaven and taken a job at the dog track in Tralee. She doubted they'd be letting him near the till. As for Kylie's bit of paradise, he was walking over the rise just now.

Michael's stride was long and easy, that of a man who knows what he's about. He slowed when he spotted her, looked down at his clothing, then laughed.

"So you're wearing the same clothes you wore that first day, too?" he said.

She smiled because his heart so perfectly matched hers. "I am."

As he came to her, she held out her hands. He took them in his.

"Thank you for coming here so early," she said.

"Thank you for the invitation. You know I'd do anything for my almost-wife," he teased.

Kylie gripped tighter to his hands. "I want us to continue as we began . . . here, in this field. And I have some promises to make."

He opened his mouth to speak, but she said, "Wait—I need to get this out before I do something silly like cry." She drew in a breath. "I, Kylie O'Shea, promise that I'll do my best to make every day of our lives together as magical as the day we found each other." She blinked back the start of tears. "I promise I'll stand strong no matter what comes our way, and that I'll love you beyond the end of time."

He swallowed hard, and his green eyes shone. "That was beautiful, love. Now let me give some promises of my own. I, Michael Kilbride . . ." He faltered, then cleared his throat. After a moment he said, "Well, I'm glad we're getting the choking-up out of the way while it's just the two of us."

He began again. "I, Michael Kilbride, promise that I'll wake each morning and thank God for the gift I've been given in you. I'll rejoice in our family as it grows, and keep us safe and warm. But most of all, I promise that to my last breath and beyond, I'll love and treasure you."

He wiped the tears from her face. Then, gently and thoroughly, he kissed her.

That evening, as Michael and Kylie sat at a raised table in the Village Hall, Michael again took Kylie's hand in his. She was well and truly his wife now, a miracle if ever one had occurred.

The vows they'd made at St. Brendan's in front of friends and family had been joyous, but the morning's private promises were those of his heart.

Still, he was glad to share the day with those he loved. Kylie's choice of location for their reception had surprised him, but she'd said that the ill spirits lingering in the hall needed to be danced away.

Given the crowd filling the place, Michael was sure that would happen. The twins looked proud and handsome in their Sunday best. Even Mam had managed to put on a good face and not peck at Da too horribly. Not that Breege was giving her the chance to misbehave. She watched both Johnny and Mam with a sharp eye.

Michael had made his peace with Johnny weeks ago. Kylie had finally told him the full picture of what happened that terror of a night, years before.

It was an awful burden Johnny lived with, knowing what his schemes had cost his only child. But with Kylie's constant example of love and forgiveness, Michael could do no less than welcome Johnny as a father-in-law.

And then there was Vi . . . She'd sung "Ave Maria" at church, and there'd not been a dry eye in the place. Now she raised her glass, and the hall fell quiet.

"Before we begin the fabulous meal that our own Jenna Fahey has made, I want to say a few words. First, to Michael." She looked at him, pride shining in her green eyes. "I love you, brother. No man deserves happiness more than you. When you came to Ballymuir, I had one wish for you . . . that you'd find someone to open your heart. You did, and all of us in this room are the richer for it."

She turned her attention to Kylie. "Kylie, words for you were a bit more difficult to come by. After all, who could out-do your speech in O'Connor's Pub a few months back?" The crowd laughed and Kylie raised her own glass in salute.

"So," Vi continued, "I sat myself down with Breege Flaherty, and we had a chat. Now, Breege says that a great number of people in town had been concerned about you. It seems you were destined to be the last bride in Ballymuir.

"I'm a bit worried that all this fine Irish air has gone to their heads, for there are those among us, myself included, who have now managed to stay unwed longer than you. It's clear to me, the last sane woman in this town, what your true destiny is.

"A toast to my brother, Michael, and to his wife, Kylie—the most beautiful bride in Ballymuir."

Dear Reader,

I hope you've enjoyed Kylie and Michael's journey to their corner of paradise. Seasons turn in Ballymuir, and hearts open to new love. Sometimes the process is as gentle as a soft August afternoon. Other times it possesses the elemental flash and sizzle of a lightning strike. Please join me again in Ballymuir when chef and restaurateur Jenna Fahey clashes with sexy executive Dev Gilvane, a man as rare as Irish lightning, but far bolder!

Until next time,

Dorien Kelly

POCKET STAR BOOKS
PROUDLY PRESENTS

THAT'S AMORE

CAROL GRACE

Available in paperback July 2003
from Pocket Star Books

Turn the page for a preview of
That's Amore. . . .

She was lost. All the streets looked alike and all the street signs were in a foreign language. Perspiration dripped down Anne Marie's face as she pulled her Samsonite suitcase through the back streets of Sorrento. It was early September, but by ten o'clock the Italian sun was so hot her money belt was plastered to her waist. The guidebooks warned not of violent crime, but of petty theft. Thieves were everywhere, they said, looking for innocent tourists. Tourists like her, dragging suitcases, weighted down with visas and passports and Italian phrase books and still unable to say more than a few words to anyone. She heard footsteps behind her. With a swift glance over her shoulder, she noticed a man in a dark suit with a long loaf of bread under his arm following her.

She made a quick turn down a narrow cobblestone street with laundry hanging from a line above her and prayed he wouldn't come after her. But he was right there behind her, slowing down when she slowed, speeding up when she sped up. Her heart pounded. Even if she knew the word for help, who would hear her? He might take everything she had—cash, travelers' checks, and credit cards.

After all, there would be no witnesses. No one to see him drag her body away where it would lie in an alley for days until stray dogs gnawed at her bones, and who would ever find her and notify her family? Her family, which now consisted only of her eighteen-year-old son.

Two little boys in tattered T-shirts came around the corner, bouncing their ball off the cobblestones and casting curious glances in her direction. The man with the bread passed her by without a second glance. A man on his way home with bread, that was all. She was paranoid, that was all.

"Buongiorno," she said to the boys.

They stared. She hauled out her Italian phrase book to ask directions. She was not only lost, she was late. If she didn't find the station soon she'd miss the bus to the Amalfi Coast.

"Dov'e el termini?" she asked.

The boys burst into laughter at her accent and she felt her face turn red. With a glance at her watch, she repeated the phrase and they pointed back the way she'd come.

"Grazie." With her suitcase clattering behind her, she turned around and headed down the hill.

Ten minutes later she had a sinking feeling she was no closer to the bus station than before. She felt like giving up, like sitting down on her suitcase and giving in to tears of frustration. Instead she kept going. Block after block, street after street.

Suddenly, there it was—the termini! Swamped with relief, she checked her watch and saw that she'd missed the bus. When she went in to buy her ticket, she learned there would be another in an hour. She would still make it in time to meet Giovanni.

There was already a line outside across the street, but she didn't mind waiting. She was in Italy! If she could handle a ten-hour flight squished in a center seat between two Sumo wrestlers followed immediately by a second-class train ride from Rome to Sorrento seated in the aisle on her suitcase while the train swayed and lurched, an hour in line under the sun was nothing.

She sniffed the air, laden with the scent of lemon blossoms. She had to remember everything to tell Evie, who'd insisted she make this trip, even when Anne Marie said she couldn't afford it.

"Borrow money against your retirement fund," she'd urged. "You must have at least six months of vacation accrued. Do you think the library will close without you? Do you think people will stop reading, stop dropping in to use the Internet because you're not there?"

"No, but maybe I should just go to Oregon or Yosemite . . ."

"You've always wanted to go to Italy. Now go."

So she'd gone.

Though she wouldn't be here without her friend's encouragement, the person she had to thank most was Dan. Funny she could thank him for anything, after what he'd done to her, but she was no longer bitter about the divorce.

How could she be bitter about anything when she was in Sorrento, a gorgeous old town wedged between the mountains and the Mediterranean, where tourists had been coming for hundreds of years for the climate, the views, and the relaxed atmosphere of *dolce far niente*? The hills were dotted with lemon groves and olive trees. Her senses sang in the fragrant breeze that came up and cooled her face. She was here. She was really here. At last.

The guidebooks said to arrive early to land a seat on the right side of the bus, for one of the world's most spectacular drives along a winding road with views of the cliffs and the sea below. But she'd be lucky if she got a seat at all.

When the bus finally came, it belched diesel fumes that clouded the air. Just as Anne Marie feared, she didn't get a seat on the right side or the left. She stood between a solid German man with a mustache and a young Italian man who was listening to his walkman. With her suitcase at her feet, her hand wrapped around the strap from the ceiling, she felt the bus lurch and they were on their way.

The bus rumbled onto the coast highway and hugged the first curve, only inches from the cliff that dropped five-hundred feet straight down to the sapphire blue sea that sparkled below. She gasped and gripped the strap so tightly her knuckles turned white. She told herself no bus had ever gone over the side and crashed on the rocks before. But there was a first time for everything. She wondered if it would be front page news in the *Oakville Times*.

ANNE MARIE JACKSON'S VACATION ENDS IN DISASTER.

Just like her marriage, the gossips would say.

EX-HUSBAND ON HONEYMOON WITH NEW WIFE.

The bus went around another bend. While others brought out their cameras and leaned out the windows taking pictures, Anne Marie was too terrified to look. She pictured the tires exploding, she imagined the expression on the driver's face changing from calm assurance to the terrified realization that the unthinkable had happened. Maybe it was his first trip on this road. Maybe he was still a trainee, unused to the curves and the bends in the road.

Then the bus would go tumbling over and over until it crashed on the rocks below. She could almost hear the screams of her fellow passengers. Screams that would blend with the cries of the gulls which would pick their bones clean as their bodies lay broken and bruised on the sand. Her own throat was too dry to scream; her palm was so sticky it stuck to the strap above her head.

She turned her head, only to see the bus was so close to an oncoming car they were certain to scrape sides. By some miracle the driver avoided both going over the cliff and taking the paint off the Fiat. This kind of close call didn't just happen once, but about twenty-five times during the next hour, always accompanied by the honking of horns and shaking of fists. She resolutely stared straight ahead at the back of the bus driver's head, channeling her thoughts on something more pleasant. On Giovanni.

If he was surprised that she was coming to Italy to see him, he didn't say so in the brief note she'd received the very day she was leaving. He just suggested they meet at a hotel in San Gervase today, which had caused her to change her plan of spending her first night in Rome.

If he was afraid she'd expect him to be her tour guide, the way he'd promised so long ago, he didn't have to worry. She was a grown-up woman, on her own now. She'd gotten herself this far, she could get herself all around Italy, too.

She didn't know if he remembered the way she'd clung to every word he said about Italy, when he was an exchange student back in high school. He wouldn't know that she'd kept every post card he'd sent afterwards. Then his cards became fewer and further between; Anne Marie went off to college, and got married.

But finally she was here to do what he'd told her: to let Italy soak into her skin like the sun. She wanted to see it all, the canals in Venice, the Coliseum in Rome, Michelangelo's statue of David in Florence. But first she had a date to meet him. After harmlessly fantasizing about him off and on for some twenty years, it was time to put the dreams to rest and get on with her life. But if by chance dreams did come true . . . well, it couldn't happen at a better time.

As they approached San Gervase, she craned her neck to the right for a quick look out the window. It was everything she'd imagined: a picture-perfect town squashed into a ravine with shops and white-washed villas perched on the cliffs. Scarlet bougainvillea tumbled over balconies and climbed walls, and wild poppies covered the ground. There was a small sand beach below, and best of all there was the sea, sparkling in the sun, cool and inviting, impossibly blue.

Anne Marie stumbled off the bus, grateful to be on firm ground at last. She rolled her suitcase behind her down narrow, winding streets, inhaling the scent of jasmine and mint and lemons, of lemon candy and lemon granita.

On her way down the street, she accepted a free sample of limoncello in a small paper cup, the local lemon liqueur that was so strong it burned her throat. Her stomach was doing flip flops at the thought of meeting Giovanni.

What if he didn't recognize her after all this time? What if she didn't recognize him? Maybe they'd just have coffee and she'd give him the high school year-book he'd left behind when he returned to Italy and that would be it. Surely she wasn't naive enough to think he'd throw his arms around her and confess he'd always been in love with her; that he'd never forgotten her and had been waiting for her all these years.

But if he did that and said that, they'd go up to her hotel room overlooking the Mediterranean, and with the air filled with wild herbs and flowering vines from the hillside below and the sea breeze blowing in the window, cooling their over-heated bodies, he'd tell her that he'd never forgotten her. He'd never been able to love anyone else.

He was so strong, he'd literally sweep her off her feet. They'd take their clothes off. She'd blush when he told her for a forty-one-year-old woman she looked good, no . . . great. He'd fondle her breasts that were still firm, caress her still flat stomach, admire her hips that were wide but not too wide. And he . . . he'd look like the statue of David on the post card he'd given her long ago. Her skin tingled just thinking about it.

Her skin tingled, and the perspiration trickled annoyingly between her breasts. Her long hair lay heavy on the back of her neck. She had to get it cut. Right now, even if she was late for their meeting. She was beginning to adopt an Italian attitude. If she was late, he'd wait for her.

Miraculously she came to a cool dark shop with a sign on the door—Salone de Bellezza. The smell of shampoo and hair spray hung in the air. A woman in a blue apron motioned for her to take a seat. Anne Marie nodded and, while she was waiting, thumbed through a fashion magazine with a picture of a Sophia Loren look-alike. The model's hair was reddish brown, cut in layers that brushed her high cheekbones.

"Like that," she told the stylist, surrendering herself into the woman's hands.

And what hands they were! Anne Marie rested her head against the edge of the sink while those hands rubbed, massaged, sprayed hot water, then rinsed with cool water. She gave a shiver of pleasure as the hands worked in shampoo and conditioner and something else that exuded the essence of lavender and mint.

She forgot her worries about losing her husband and finding Giovanni. She forgot she was on a schedule and just let herself float away on a cloud of fragrance and sensual pleasure. She'd never known how sensitive her head was until this woman took charge with her magic hands and her potions. Every bone is her body had turned to jello; every remnant of tension had melted away. Anne Marie closed her eyes while the woman cut and shaped and blew her hair dry and then sprayed it.

"*Prego, signora.*" The stylist lifted the smock off, and Anne Marie opened her eyes at last.

She blinked at her reflection in the mirror. What had they done? Her hair was no longer dull brown with streaks of gray. It was the color of the hair in the magazine. They'd misunderstood—she'd only wanted it cut! It brushed against her cheekbones, making them look higher, giving her an exotic look she'd never had before.

The entire staff of three women appeared behind her, beaming at her reflection with pride. They murmured things like "bella," and "grazioso." What could she say? She forced herself to smile and thank them.

She paid a ridiculously small amount for such a total transformation and walked into the afternoon sunlight, feeling its heat on her bare neck. She felt naked; she'd had long hair forever.

If only Evie could see her now! "You have the perfect excuse for skipping Dan's wedding," Evie had said. "You're no longer the pathetic ex-wife, you are a woman on a romantic tryst to meet her lover in Italy. Out of all the girls in our class who were in love with him, he chose you. He heard about the divorce. Now he wants you. He even sent you a ticket. First class."

"Who's going to believe that?" Anne Marie scoffed, shaking her head.

"Okay," Evie conceded. "Business class."

So she'd borrowed the money, packed her bags, and left. She would have gone steerage class on the first boat. She would have mortgaged the house. Anything to escape the wedding of the year, when Dan married his dental hygienist with the perfect teeth and the perfect size-four figure. Since the divorce was so "amicable," the whole town expected good old Anne Marie to show up with a smile on her face and a gift under her arm. Hah!

Instead, she was on her way to a rendezvous.

But what if Giovanni had changed? What if he weighed three-hundred pounds? What if he brought a wife and five children to meet her? What if he was single and wanted to marry her so he could get a green card? What if he wore his shirt unbuttoned to the navel and had four gold chains around his neck?

She'd find out very soon; it was almost two-thirty.

She found a taxi on the main street across from the small sandy beach with bright blue and white beach umbrellas. As the well-aged Fiat with an equally well-aged driver made its way up into the hills above the town, her ears popped and she felt dizzy.

Finally they pulled into the circular driveway of the four-star Hotel Athena on the edge of the cliff. When she got out of the taxi, her knees buckled. Nerves? Altitude? The driver set her bag at the hotel's open glass doors. She held out a handful of euros and he carefully picked out what she hoped was the right amount.

For a long moment after the taxi pulled away, she stood in the quiet tiled driveway, taking slow, deep breaths until she felt almost normal.

There were no cars parked in the driveway. Through the open doors she peered into the cool, elegant lobby. There was no one there. No dashing Italian with a sexy grin. She reminded herself he was Italian and he'd be late.

Suddenly she was aware she was not alone. The sensitive skin on the back of her neck felt as if some-one brushed it with a feather; she felt someone's eyes on her. She whirled around.

There he was, leaning against the brick wall that separated the street from the driveway. Tall, lean, and muscular, he was wearing wrap-around sun-glasses, black jeans and a blue shirt. It was not unbuttoned to the navel. He wore no gold chains. He was taller than she remembered. Harder, older. Well, what did she expect? She hadn't seen him in over twenty years.

She didn't realize she was holding her breath until she exhaled. Her mouth was so dry she could barely speak.

"Giovanni?" she said walking slowly toward him.

He took off his sunglasses. There was a long silence. "No," he said.

His gaze locked with hers. Her bare arms were covered with goose bumps. She couldn't seem to catch her breath. Of course it wasn't Giovanni. His eyes were not black, they were a light brown or . . . or . . . green or something. She couldn't tell without getting closer, and there was no reason to get any closer. His face was all angles, with enough character lines to be interesting and squint marks at the corners of his eyes that showed how much time he'd spent in the Mediterranean sun. She stood rooted to the spot.

She had to say something, or move, or walk away. Anything to break the spell he'd cast on her. What must he think of her, standing there staring? An American woman desperately looking for an Italian lover to make her vacation dreams come true? How could he know how she'd been looking forward to this moment for the past twenty-three years, but that he wasn't the one she'd been waiting for?

Too bad, a little voice inside her said.

"Welcome to San Gervase," he said in Italian-accented English that made every word sound like a caress.

"Thank you," she managed. "Are you . . . ?" He must be somebody, something . . . "Chamber of Commerce? Bureau of Tourism?"

"No," he said again.

Okay, it was time to stop staring. She gave him a brief smile, turned around and crossed the driveway—and tripped on a crack in the tile. She wasn't nervous or excited just because a sexy Italian man had looked at her with interest and spoken to her. She'd been in this country for only a day and already knew Italian men were like that. It didn't mean anything.

She picked up her suitcase and looked over her shoulder before she carried it inside. Just one more look, to make sure he wasn't a figment of her overactive imagination. The man was still standing there, leaning against the stone wall as if he were part of the scenery. Like an extra in an Italian movie, the quintessential Italian stud, hired to give the place ambiance or give tourists a photo opportunity.

Inside the lobby, Anne Marie filled out the registration forms, handed over her passport, and asked the clerk if anyone had asked for her. He shook his head and summoned a boy to carry her bag up to her room for her. Before she followed, she took one more peek out the front door. He was still there. She turned quickly, her heart was racing.

Oh, yes, he was still there—and he'd been staring at her.